THE ZION
COVENANT
BOOK 3

Munich Signature

THE ZION
COVENANT
BOOK 3

BODIE & BROCK THOENE

TYNDALE HOUSE PUBLISHERS, INC. • WHEATON, ILLINOIS

Visit Tyndale's exciting Web site at www.tyndale.com

TYNDALE is a registered trademark of Tyndale House Publishers, Inc.

Tyndale's quill logo is a trademark of Tyndale House Publishers, Inc.

Edited by Ramona Cramer Tucker

Designed by Julie Chen

Published in 1990 as *Munich Signature* by Bethany House Publishers under ISBN 1-55661-079-3.

First printing by Tyndale House Publishers, Inc. in 2005.

Scripture quotations are taken from the *Holy Bible*, King James Version or the *Holy Bible*, New International Version® NIV® Copyright © 1973, 1978, 1984 by International Bible Society. Used by permission of Zondervan Publishing House. All rights reserved.

This novel is a work of fiction. Names, characters, places, and incidents either are the product of the authors' imaginations or are used fictitiously. Any resemblance to actual events, locales, organizations, or persons, living or dead, is entirely coincidental and beyond the intent of either the authors or publisher.

Library of Congress Cataloging-in-Publication Data

Thoene, Bodie, date.
  Munich signature / Bodie & Brock Thoene.
    p. cm. — (The Zion covenant ; bk. 3)
    ISBN 1-4143-0109-X (sc)
    1. Lindheim, Elisa (Fictitious character)—Fiction. 2. Holocaust, Jewish (1939-1945)—Fiction. 3. Refugees, Jewish—Fiction. 4. Jews—Austria—Fiction. 5. Boys—Fiction. I. Thoene, Brock, date. II. Title.
PS3570.H46M8 2005
813'.54—dc22
                                    2004019087

Printed in the United States of America

11   10   09   08   07   06   05
7   6   5   4   3   2   1

Acknowledgments

August 8, 1989, marked the remembrance of Tishrei B'Av, the day the temple was destroyed in Jerusalem. It also marked the Yahrzeit of our own bubbe, Naomi Samuels. Her life and work and wonderful personality are much missed in this world. With hearts full of hope we look forward to the certain day when we will all break bread together in the courts of the temple that will stand into eternity!

Until that day, our work continues. With much love, we thank Joseph Samuels, who continues Naomi's research with such dedication! Our gratitude also to Linda Gerber, who has made the typing of volumes of research a labor of love.

GERMANY

POLAND

•Prague

CZECHOSLOVAKIA

SUDETENLAND

(ONCE AUSTRIA)

HUNGARY

FINLAND

SWEDEN

NORWAY

ESTONIA

NORTH
SEA

DENMARK

BALTIC
SEA

LATVIA

LITHUANIA

GREAT
BRITAIN

London

NETHERLANDS

•Hamburg

BELGIUM

•Paris

GERMANY

•Berlin

Warsaw

POLAND

SOVIET UNION

Prague

CZECHOSLOVAKIA
(before Munich Agreement)

Munich

Vienna •

FRANCE

SWITZERLAND

(ONCE AUSTRIA)

HUNGARY

RUMANIA

SPAIN

YUGOSLAVIA

ITALY

BULGARIA

CORSICA

•Rome

ADRIATIC
SEA

ALBANIA

SARDINIA

MEDITERRANEAN
SEA

GREECE

Tikki Thurston crossed her arms and glared angrily at the bright cherry red BMW parked in the garage of Embarcadero Motors. The hood of the automobile, propped open like a giant mouth, swallowed the mechanic as he leaned in over the engine and muttered, "Uh-oh. Hmm. Hmm. Too bad."

Mark had often told her that this was the best BMW mechanic in San Francisco. That fact alone made words like *uh-oh* seem even more ominous. She felt as if she had gone to the dentist for a checkup and found out that every tooth needed a root canal and a crown. Mark had always taken care of details concerning auto repair and maintenance. Tikki had never even spoken to the mechanic before today. When the tow truck had arrived she had simply repeated the only name she had ever heard in connection with car repair. "Embarcadero Motors, please." That was where Mark would have had the little BMW towed—if Mark had been there.

But Mark was *not* around. He had left her five months ago for a young woman who worked as a paralegal assistant in his law firm. He did not like being married to a musician, he had said. He needed intellectual stimulation in his life. A thinking woman. He wanted to talk about politics and court cases and issues that really mattered. Bach and Mozart put him to sleep, not to mention Tikki and her drivel about concerts and auditions and matters in the orchestra. In the end, he claimed, it had destroyed whatever interest he might have had in her.

She glanced at her watch. It was already a quarter past six. Past closing time. She stared at the mechanic's back and wondered if he would charge her overtime, double time, or time and a half. She could tell this was going to be expensive, whatever was wrong.

"Uh-oh," the mechanic said again. He clucked his tongue like a doctor studying the X rays of a terminal patient.

"It's bad, then?" Tikki asked timidly.

"Bad." He eased himself out from under the hood, pulled a rag from his back pocket, and wiped his hands.

He sniffed. "This car is twelve years old. Even a BMW has to throw in the towel eventually." He shrugged.

"*That* bad?" Tikki wanted to cry. She did not need this now. Not tonight. She remembered the letter in her purse. *That man* was coming to the concert tonight! She might need her car for a fast getaway!

"How many miles have you put on the old girl?" The mechanic leaned in the window and peered at the odometer. He gave a low whistle. "A hundred seventy-two thousand. An honorable life."

Tikki did not tell him that the odometer had broken eight months before. "Isn't there some way to fix it?"

"Sure. Rebuild the engine. Why don't you tell that rich husband of yours that you need a new car? Better yet, *I'll* tell him!"

The mechanic didn't know. Of course, there was no reason for him to know. He was not in their circle of friends. "Mark and I are . . . not together anymore," she answered.

The mechanic did not seem surprised. Hardly anyone stayed married anymore. It was unlikely that Tikki would get a new car out of the divorce settlement. After all, Mark Thurston was an attorney. He had figured out all the angles long ago. "Mark took the new Porsche and left you with a twelve-year-old BMW?" The mechanic looked amused. She did not see the humor of it.

"How much will it cost to fix the engine?" she asked wearily as she opened the trunk and pulled out her cello.

"Several thousand. You might want to consider buying a new car."

"Traitor," Tikki muttered to the little auto as she slammed the trunk down hard. "I'll need to know *exactly* what it will cost," she replied curtly to the mechanic.

"Sure, I can give you an estimate." His face still registered amusement.

An estimate. It could not possibly cost more than a new BMW, and right now she was in no position to buy anything. Tears stung her eyes as she fished the plastic bag containing her long black concert dress out of the backseat. This mess with the car was just one more thing. Insult to injury. A hundred times she had considered quitting her job and going back to her family in Israel. She had called Jerusalem twice at a cost of seventeen dollars for three minutes of homesick conversation with Rachel and Moshe Sachar. There were no positions at all in either of the major orchestras in Israel. There were no prospects of openings in the foreseeable future. As tough as things might seem for her in San Francisco right now, life in Jerusalem would be impossible—except for the fact that Tikvah would be home again, surrounded by the love of her mother and father.

In that instant she thought about the letter in her handbag. *I knew your mother*, the man had written, *a long time ago in Austria*. The stranger did not mean that he knew Rachel. He was speaking of Tikvah's real mother, the mother she had never known. He wrote about Leah Feldstein, the great cellist who had once enthralled all Vienna with her music. Occasionally over the years Tikki had run across people who still remembered the genius of Leah Feldstein. In Jerusalem Tikki had grown up in the shadow of that great talent. She had studied and practiced and played with the knowledge that she would never match the level of talent her biological mother had possessed. Tikvah would never be the principal cellist with the orchestra, and long ago she had given up the dream of performing as a soloist. Yet tonight, once again, as third chair cellist in the section, she would perform for an old fan of Leah Feldstein's. *I knew your mother a long time ago in Austria.* . . .

The old ones who came brought their memories of Leah, hoping to hear some fragment of that talent that had been lost forever at the birth of Tikvah. They were looking for Leah. Instead they found only Tikvah. Third-chair cellist with the San Francisco Symphony Orchestra. Failed wife. Migrant musician forced to live far from her home and family because of job availability. Tikvah Feldstein Sachar Thurston, who now did not even have a car of her own in which she could flee from the probing questions and wistful memories of her mother's old admirers.

Tonight this old man—recently widowed, he wrote—would come searching for his youth, for a part of Vienna that had died when Hitler had marched in. He would look at Tikvah and comment that she was very much like her mother except for the blue eyes. Leah's eyes had been brown, warm and rich like chocolate. They all remembered that. Brown bobbed hair. Bright smile. Slight build. Strong hands. The similarity stopped there. Leah had been everything her daughter Tikvah was not. No doubt Leah would have been able to captivate a man like Mark. Mark would never have left a woman as confident and brilliant as Leah.

Tonight, no doubt, Tikvah would again be weighed in the balance of an old man's memory and be found wanting. With that thought clanging in her ears like the bell of a trolley car, Tikvah hailed a taxi to take her to the concert hall. The taxi driver was Iranian—a fact which almost amused Tikvah, considering the terrible news blaring over his radio of Iran's latest threats against Israel. Only in America would an Israeli cellist place her life and her instrument in the backseat of a cab driven by an Iranian. Even without knowing her origins, the man drove as though he wanted to kill her. He swooped over the San Francisco hills and darted among the fleet of other taxis, honking his horn and swearing loudly at the foreign infidels who had taken to the roads. Tikvah determined that from now on she would ride the rapid transit system until her car was fixed. Better to brave a possible mugging in the Bay Area subway system than to be locked in a four-wheeled Roman candle with an Iranian driver.

She paid the fare and tipped the man extra in a subconscious attempt to placate his madness. It was still an hour and a half before the concert, but Tikki hurried toward the light that emanated from the glass door of the musicians' entrance of the concert hall. She felt pursued somehow, and the auditorium seemed like a beacon of safety to her. Awkwardly wielding the cello and the dress, she slipped in from the cold of the San Francisco evening. Up a short flight of a dozen steps the security guard sat reading the *Chronicle* at his desk. He glanced up as she hefted her instrument up the stairway. His normally pleasant black face reflected some concern, and he lifted a hand as if to stop her. She paused two steps from the top of the landing.

"Hi, Freddy," she said, puzzled by his gesture.

"You're early," Freddy replied, looking down the hall beyond her vision. "I told him you wouldn't be here till nearly eight. I told him he oughta wait till *after* the performance."

"Who?"

At her question, a tall, powerfully built man stepped out of the corridor. He was about six foot two, his sandy hair sprinkled with gray. He was dressed in a three-piece pin-striped suit. *Looks like an attorney*, Tikvah thought. *Mark had an entire closet full of suits like that.* The man's shoes were impeccably shined in spite of the rainy weather, and he carried a trench coat over one arm and held a cup of coffee in his other hand. His face was rugged, etched rather handsomely with lines of concern. He had a thick mustache that concealed his upper lip. His nose had evidently been broken in the past, but the slight bend added to the air of masculinity.

"I told him you weren't goin' t'be here till later," Freddy said irritably as he glared at the man.

"I wanted to wait," the man explained, setting his coffee cup on the desk and extending his hand to Tikvah.

She did not move from the step. Cello in one hand, dress in the other, she could not accept his handshake. She was not sure she wanted to. She was in no frame of mind to talk to a lawyer. No doubt Mark had sent him over here for some detail in the divorce settlement.

"If you're here on behalf of Mark . . . " She stepped past him, avoiding his hand.

"Mark?" the unknown man asked, inclining his head slightly. He let his eyes slide from her face to the cello case. "You didn't get my letter?" His expression was clear, but his voice was slightly slurred.

"Your letter?"

"Yes. I wrote you." He let his eyes flit from her face to the cello, then back again eagerly. "You are Tikvah?"

Tikvah looked toward Freddy, who rolled his eyes.

"Yes."

"And you have brought Vitorio along with you?" Now the man stepped toward her.

"Vitorio?" How could this stranger know the name of her instrument, the name Leah had given the old Pedronelli cello?

"You look so much like Leah!" He was almost bubbling with excitement. "I would have known that you were her daughter even if I had only seen you passing in the street." He reached out and touched the cello case with a familiarity that made Tikki step back. It was as if he had touched *her*!

"But—" She tried to clear her mind of all the concerns she had lugged into the hall with her. "Are you . . . ?" She could not remember the name of the man who had written her. In any case, the fellow blocking the hall appeared far too young to have known her mother in Austria.

"Yes." He nodded and crossed his arms almost shyly. Gentle emotion softened his eyes as they searched Tikvah's face. "So much alike," he whispered. "Only her eyes were brown."

Yes, this was the man who had written the letter. This was the doctor from UCLA who had traced the daughter of Leah Feldstein through the Israeli government and had come to San Francisco to hear her play. "Yes. My mother had brown eyes, I am told. I never saw them myself." There was resentment in her voice. This man had come here on some sort of pilgrimage. There was nothing to pay homage to. He would leave disappointed.

"I remember her eyes. Brown eyes. Warm, and full of love." He ignored the stiff comment of Tikvah. "And old Vitorio . . . " He touched the case again. "He was a friend. He sang to me. Do you mind?" He was eager again. "May I have a look?"

Tikki let her breath out in slow resignation. She would let him see the instrument. Then he would go away and she could get back to her life. What was it with these people? these old friends of Leah Feldstein? "Doctor—" She could not remember the man's name.

At this moment Freddy, the security guard, rose to his full height of six foot four. "You want me t' throw this fella out, Miz Thurston?" His hands were open and his arms poised for the grab. "If you don't want t', you don't have t' show him nuthin'," he growled.

The stranger's expression changed to one of hurt astonishment. His smile faded, and he looked quickly at Tikvah to see if her level of hostility matched that of the enormous black man. "I assure you—," he stammered, as if suddenly aware of the quiet misery in Tikvah's eyes— "I didn't mean to—"

Freddy lowered his chin in an officially threatening glare. "If you want t' see the instr'ments, that's what we got the ticket office for. You can buy a ticket like anybody." Then Freddy muttered in Tikvah's direction, "Jus' say the word, Miz Thurston, and this guy is on the pavement!"

"No, no, Freddy." Tikki put a hand on the massive arm. "It's all right."

"If I'd a know'd you didn't know this dude, I wouldn'a let him in here!" Freddy seemed disappointed that he would not be permitted to thrash the man in the three-piece suit. There had not been much opportunity for him to display his prowess in a place haunted by these classical musician types. Not like the rock concerts down at Moscone Center where he had regularly been called upon to bash the heads of groupies and drug addicts.

"No, really," she said in a soothing, almost worried voice as the stranger straightened his tie and ran his finger over his mustache nervously. "He's all right. An old friend of my mother's." She wished she could remember the signature on the letter. *Doctor . . . something.*

"I'm sorry, really. I shouldn't have bothered you before." The stranger started to reach into his coat pocket, but when Freddy stepped forward, he hesitated and held his hands up briefly. "I am just reaching for my ticket. You see, I already bought a ticket." With thumb and index finger, he gingerly pulled out an envelope emblazoned with the logo of the symphony hall. The words *KRONENBERGER* and *WILL CALL* were scrawled across it.

Kronenberger! That was the name!

"It's okay, Freddy." Tikvah smiled now. "Doctor Kronenberger wrote me beforehand. I just wasn't expecting him before the concert. And I was expecting someone quite . . . *different.*" She didn't say that she had been expecting someone quite old. An old widower. Retired-type doctor.

Freddy's mouth was a perfect upside-down *U* of suspicion and disapproval. He sat down slowly and reluctantly. He was just doing his job.

The tall Dr. Kronenberger laughed with relief now and waved the envelope slightly. "As a matter of fact, I purchased several tickets. I'll be here for a week, you see. Interviewing for a position in the pediatrics department at the University Medical Center, and I . . . well, I bought tickets for several performances. I was hoping—" he was bubbling again— "hoping I might . . ."

"I am not Leah Feldstein," Tikvah replied softly, almost apologetically. "She was a virtuoso. Like Yo-Yo Ma."

The doctor shook his head. "Better than Yo-Yo Ma, I think."

"You must have been very young when you heard my mother play."

"Very young. But I have managed to acquire a few of her early recordings, and I assure you—"

Tikvah blinked at him in astonishment. "But you . . . you must have been—a child!" She herself had only heard two recordings of the pre-war Vienna Philharmonic Orchestra. How had a man this young managed to collect—? "You have recordings?"

"Two dozen. She was remarkable." His eyes shone with gentleness again as he studied Tikvah. "And you seem so much as I remember her. I was only five. Six. It was such a time then. And there she was in the center of the whirlwind. I remember it all very clearly. Quite clearly."

Tikvah's own eyes filled with tears and her throat constricted. "I never knew my mother."

Dr. Kronenberger reached out to take the cello from her hand. "I thought perhaps that was the case. When they told me your mother had died in 1948 and that she had a daughter born the same year, well, I felt somehow that I needed to talk to you. To tell you what she was like from the perspective of a child. I thought perhaps I could share with you what I remembered, give you my memories, and—"

Tikvah was unable to speak for a moment. She stood gazing in a puzzled way at the man who now held Vitorio. She had heard so much about Leah in Jerusalem from Yacov and Rachel and Moshe. She had heard of the music of the virtuoso of Vienna. But here was so much she had never known. "Why?" she asked the doctor.

He touched her elbow as if to lead her down the hallway to a practice room. "Because," he replied quietly, "we are a generation of children who grew up never having the chance to know our parents. I met your mother at the Musikverein in Vienna in the same hour that my father was killed."

Tikvah followed him down the hall as though he was now her guide.

"She hid my brother Louis and me in a practice room beneath the stage while Hitler himself prowled above our heads," he continued. "And later, she blocked the door and took our Vitorio—" he hefted the cello case—"yes! This *very* instrument!" Pausing mid-stride, he gazed into Tikvah's eyes.

She was smiling, making his memories her own.

"And she played the Bach Suites for us," he concluded.

"The Bach Suites!" Tikvah breathed. "That was what I played for my first recital." She was trembling like a little five-year-old, thinking of a young boy wandering deep within the bowels of the Musikverein of Vienna.

"Yes!" The doctor saw the excitement in her expression. "I thought you would want to know. I *knew* you would." He opened the door of a dark and empty practice room, then stepped aside. "And I came here to tell you more than that . . . there is *so much* more." Switching on the light of the little cubicle, he whispered, "My name is Charles. Would you . . . play the Bach Suites for me on Vitorio?"

It was a simple request. Tikvah granted it with a nod. Tenderly she unsheathed her bow and took the venerable old instrument from its velvet nest.

Charles Kronenberger sat across from her on a piano bench and let the tears stream as she played the bright and uncomplicated tunes in their easy key signatures one after another, in the same order Leah had played them.

When Tikvah finished, she lowered the bow and sat silently across from the man who seemed no longer to be a stranger. "Like that?" she asked after a long pause.

Charles nodded. "Just so. I was not able to speak then." He touched his hand to his mustache as if that explained it all. "I could not tell her . . . how . . . *beautiful!*"

"Only the Bach Suites," Tikvah began.

He raised a hand to stop her words. "Vitorio is the same. The songs are the same. But what I wanted to tell her . . . something different than the *sound* of the music. Something *more* beautiful. It was in her face when she played." He closed his eyes as if the memory was fresh before him. "I couldn't tell her then. Couldn't speak. But I can tell you now. I saw that same beauty in *your* face, Tikvah." He smiled. "Do you know you are beautiful, Tikvah? *Beautiful!* Like she was. I saw it in her. I was not expecting this . . . not in you."

Tikvah blushed and lowered her eyes. She had not thought herself capable of blushing anymore. "Please," she protested, not sure she wanted to hear this. "Please, I–I . . ."

"I'm sorry," he agreed quickly, as if he knew he was saying too much too soon. "I . . . I'll be here a few days." He was gazing strangely at the cello now. "Do you like . . . Chinese food?"

"Are you asking me to dinner?"

"There's a place just off Washington. The Far East Café. It's the real thing. Peking duck and . . . after the performance we could take a taxi—"

"No taxis." Tikvah laughed. "How do you feel about lugging Vitorio along on a cable car?"

1

Living Windows

Throughout this terrible night, the soft glow of the moon illuminated the stained-glass windows that ringed the cupola of the Great Synagogue of Nuremberg. Windows crafted four hundred years earlier told the story of the seven days of creation, of the fall of man, the great flood and the waters that carried the ark of Noah. Bright panels of color and light wound around the gilded dome, wordlessly displaying the history of the Torah. Generations of children had memorized the stories by sight as they sat beside their swaying fathers in the sanctuary below. Little boys craned their necks backward to ponder the image of father Abraham offering his son to God on the altar of Moriah while the ram God had provided struggled in the thicket.

Would Abraham really have plunged the knife into Isaac?

The vision of faith made sons tremble beside their fathers.

Would Papa plunge the knife into me?

Sibling squabbles took on new meaning as children contemplated the glass panel depicting Joseph in his coat of many colors being sold into slavery by his brothers.

Ah, how his father Jacob grieved when the brothers returned with the torn coat!

From this point, half the curve of the dome was dedicated to the slavery of Israel and the life of Moses. Ten plagues upon Egypt. The pillar of fire. The crossing of the Red Sea. Moses receiving the tablets of law on Mount Sinai while the ungrateful Hebrews reveled in sin at the foot of the mountain. Was there anything more frightening than the face of Moses as he smashed the tablets in anger and pronounced judgment against the instigator of the rebellion? Here was a picture of God's wrath against the sinners who had forgotten their deliverance.

Until this night, those little boys who had grown to manhood beneath this vivid tableau could not imagine anything more fierce than the wrath of God. But this was Nuremberg. This was the German city where the Nazi laws against Jews had first been passed three years earlier.

This was also the great gathering place of the Nazis each year in September. By the thousands, the Hitler Youth came to march and drill with their burnished shovels. Searchlights lit the skies of Nuremberg. Rallies were held and speeches were made by all the great party leaders. Year after year the ranks of the faithful had swelled until thousands were now hundreds of thousands. There was no field large enough to hold them all, these children of the Aryan race.

Hitler himself had pondered the problems. He had studied the map of Nuremberg with his architect, Albert Speer. His eyes had traced the boundary of the Jewish Quarter of the city, and with a sweep of his hand he had condemned that section to destruction. By the expression of his will, the Great Synagogue of Nuremberg was to be demolished.

Tonight the fierce hatred of the Führer of Germany seemed stronger than the prayers of the generations who had gathered beneath this cupola. Once again no stone would be left upon another. Instead of prayers to the God of Abraham, praise would be lifted up to Hitler in ten thousand mighty Heils!

Two hundred brave Jewish men had gathered beneath the dome tonight. Silk prayer shawls covered their heads as they intoned the last prayers that would be prayed in this place. And God mourned for them as Jacob had mourned for his son Joseph when the patriarch saw the torn coat. The light from the moon streamed through the stained-glass windows and fell in brightly colored patches on the white prayer shawls. Tonight every man, like Joseph, wore a coat of many colors. They took on the hues and the substance of the stories portrayed above them. They became one with the suffering of the ages. Suddenly the grief of their fathers had fallen upon them, and they became living windows that wept and prayed as the shadow of destruction moved nearer with the morning light.

"Again we are destined to wander in the wilderness," whispered the ancient rabbi of Nuremberg. Tears streamed down the lined cheeks and dampened the soft white beard. "Unless we have a miracle."

"Ascribe unto the Eternal glory and might."

The groaning of the steel tracks of the demolition equipment could be faintly heard.

"Ascribe unto the Eternal the honor due unto His name."

Next came the low rumble of engines—the bulldozer, the crane with its wrecking ball.

"Bow ye down unto the Lord in the adornment of sanctity."

Voices shouted, "Juden!"

"The voice of the Eternal resounds above the waters."

"Jews out! Jews out! Jewish vermin out of Germany!"

"The voice of the Eternal thunders above the mighty waters. The voice of the Eternal in strength."

"Destroy the Jews! Bring it down on their heads! Down! Down with the temple!"

"The voice of the Eternal doth shatter the cedars of Lebanon!"

A bullet through the head of Moses on Sinai burst the window into a thousand fragments, which showered down on the congregation. Raucous voices called, "Blow them up!"

Within the dome the prayers continued. "The voice of the Eternal flasheth with a flaming fire: the voice of the Eternal causeth the oaks to tremble, and maketh the forests bare; and in his temple everything bespeaks his glory."

One after another the stained-glass windows shattered, and the slivers rained upon the heads of the mourners until they were forced to take cover beneath the long wooden benches.

As the report of gunfire died away, a voice boomed over a bullhorn: "In the name of the people of the Reich—in the name of the Führer, Adolf Hitler, you are ordered to leave this building or it will be brought down on you!"

Again the chanting of young Nazi voices began. A full minute passed, and then the bullhorn bellowed over those voices: "We give you just one minute! Evacuate the building, or you will be destroyed with it!"

No color was left in the Great Synagogue of Nuremberg. The aged rabbi gathered up the ark and raised his gnarled hands to bless the last of the congregation as each man picked up a shard of glass and filed out to face the angry mob. "Direct us toward thee, O Eternal, that we may return indeed."

As the old rabbi stepped from the synagogue, the wrecker's ball swung hard against the cupola, crushing the Star of David. The ark was snatched from the old man's arms, and the scroll was trampled beneath the feet of the crowd. Prayers shawls were ripped to shreds. Faces of the Jews were spat upon and bloodied.

Some from among the congregation were hauled off to concentration camps for their act of prayerful defiance. Others were put to work in the public parks of the city clearing the grass with their teeth. The rabbi of Nuremberg was shackled hand and foot and loaded onto a truck

bound for Hamburg. There a ship waited; by the personal order of Adolf
Hitler the old rabbi was to be put aboard to head a congregation of
doomed men and women. There was an irony in such an ending, which
pleased the Führer very much.

◈

Persistent sunlight had been seeping in around the window shades for
nearly two hours, but Elisa ignored it. She lay quietly beside Murphy and
watched his broad, muscular back rise and fall in the even cadence of deep
sleep. She wished he would wake up and take her in his arms again, but he
did not, so she contented herself with studying the topography of shoulders and admiring the smooth, olive-colored skin stretched tight over his
ribs. She traced the boundaries of faint tan lines that remained from last
year's short-sleeved shirts and swim trunks. On the left shoulder blade
was a small, strawberry-colored birthmark. She decided she would kiss
it—but later, when he was awake. Like an explorer in a new land, she
claimed John Murphy for her own and happily memorized the landmarks of his body.

It was their first morning together. Strange how quickly the horrors
of last night receded in her mind; thoughts of their fearful flight from Vienna and the battle at the National Theatre did not come to her this
morning. She heard the rattle of pots in the kitchen and the voice of Dr.
Litov when he came to check little Charles, but those sounds seemed like
part of a distant dream. While Murphy slept, she wanted only to lie beside him. So many mornings had been wasted without him. She would
not let go of this one easily.

She stretched out her left hand and held it just an inch above his
head. The blue lapis wedding ring on her finger meant something now.
More than little leaves of gold against a blue stone backdrop, it was a
pledge: *"This is my beloved, and this is my friend."* She whispered the words
of Song of Songs 5:16 entwined in Hebrew letters with the leaves.

As if in response, Murphy sighed but did not turn to face her. "You
awake?" he asked drowsily.

"Um-hmm. Hours."

He reached back to take her arm and wrap it around his middle.

She moved closer until she was curled tightly against him.

"How come you didn't wake me?"

"I wanted to watch you." She kissed the birthmark on his shoulder blade.

"Did I drool?" he asked jokingly as he raised her fingers to his lips.

"I don't know. You were facing away from me."

"It's a good thing, too. If my face looks as bad as it feels after last
night—" He rolled over and grinned.

Elisa winced. His left eye was swollen nearly shut and his cheek was red from the flame of Albert Sporer's gun.

"Oh, Murphy!" Elisa looked pained.

"Just tell me you didn't marry me for my looks."

She giggled, then caught herself. "I didn't marry you for your looks," she repeated, then dissolved into laughter again at the sight of his lopsided face.

"Or for my money?" He pulled her closer.

"No. That is why *you* married *me*, remember?"

"After last night I think I'll give you a refund." He kissed her.

"Disappointed?" She ran her fingers through his hair as he pushed her gently back on the pillow and then raised up on one elbow to gaze at her appreciatively. Her golden hair fanned out on the pillow, and her blue eyes sparkled with amusement as she gazed back at him.

"What a way to wake up," Murphy murmured as he pressed his mouth against hers. There was no reluctance in her kiss.

She held him tightly as a rush of warmth surged through her. "Murphy," she whispered.

He smothered her words with another kiss. "I can tell," he said breathlessly, "that you're going to be like Chinese food."

She pushed him away, startled by the strange remark. "What?"

He smiled and traced the line of her throat with his finger. "I thought I was full, and an hour later I'm hungry for you again."

At that, she reached out for him. "When I think of what I've been missing!"

"That's all . . . I . . . have . . . been . . . thinking."

☙

The room was exactly as Elisa Murphy had described it. Leah Feldstein felt lost in the middle of the massive feather bed. She pulled the crisp, clean sheets up under her chin and lay staring up at heavy wood rafters stained dark by centuries. Here at the Wattenbarger farmhouse there was a sense of safety beneath these stout timbers, just as Elisa had told her. For the first time in months Leah had slept the night through, waking only to hear Otto's tearful farewell.

Strange man. Brave man, to return to Vienna when he might have stayed here.

Someday perhaps she would be able to thank him properly. Then in a stab of painful memory it came to her that he was returning to Vienna with the name of Shimon Feldstein seared in his mind. Would he find Shimon? Would he be able to help him?

Such thoughts and questions robbed Leah of the peace she had felt only moments before. She sat up and frowned toward the shuttered window. Outside she could hear the sound of horses stamping impatiently at a rail. The jangle of bits and bridles mingled with urgent voices.

"We can take them as far as Gustav Stroh's hut on horseback."

"Small groups—two, maybe three at a time. Gustav can guide them over the Zillertal, and young Henri can take them to Father Prato in Italy."

"Otto says we must hurry. We have days at best before they are back in force." Leah recognized the voice of Frau Marta. There was no hint of dread or grief in the farmwife's voice. This morning she seemed fully in charge of her emotions as though she had not been forced to bid her eldest son farewell.

Leah wrapped a quilt around her shoulders and stepped onto the cold floor. She tiptoed close to the window and held her breath as she listened to them discussing the escape of their fugitive guests.

"And the woman Otto brought last night?" a male voice said.

Leah peeked through a crack in the shutter. This strong, red-bearded young man was Franz, the one who had fallen in love with Elisa when she had stayed at the farmhouse with her family.

"Poor dear," Marta said. "I put her in the garret room. Let her sleep through breakfast. She is a dear friend of our Elisa, Franz."

Franz placed a saddle squarely on the back of a mare whose red hide matched his beard. "That may be, Mama, but I think we should take each group out in the order they came to us. *Ja*, Papa?"

"Leah is her name. She looks as if she could use the rest. Pale as a glacier. No sunlight for weeks. All shut up in a little flat in Vienna, Otto told us."

Leah stared up at the timbers. She was not at all unhappy about being last on the list to leave this place. Perhaps Otto would somehow find Shimon while they waited here. Then they could leave Austria together over the Zillertal. They would be together in Italy and in Switzerland and then, perhaps, Jerusalem? This would be the best place, the closest place to wait for Shimon to join her. She exhaled loudly; in her excitement she had lost the flow of the conversation taking place beneath her window.

Three children stood tearfully in a half circle around Frau Marta. The oldest was a boy of eleven or twelve who raised his chin manfully and bit his lip to control his tears. Two little girls wept openly as Frau Marta daubed their tears with her apron and smoothed their long braids.

"There, now, no need for tears. When this is all over, as it surely must be soon, you will come back and stay for as long as you like and help Papa Karl milk Gerta and Zillie."

"We will miss you," sniffled the smaller of the two girls. "Who will sing to us and pray with us at night?"

Marta pulled the child close. "Everywhere there are those who love to sing with children and pray with them, too. In Italy you will be with a priest for a while; such prayers you will hear!"

"Can he bake good roggenbrot?"

"You have become an admirer of Tyrolean rye bread, eh?" Marta paused dramatically. "No one bakes it as I do." She clucked her tongue. "But I have sent fresh loaves in your packs."

"Mama"—Franz held the horses by their reins—"we have to go. Come, children. We have a long journey. Come, we must hurry."

Wrapped in her quilt, Leah watched the sad children mount their horses and follow Franz into the woods. Their heads were turned to stare back longingly at the farmhouse until they could no longer see it.

When they were out of sight, Leah heard the soft voice of Frau Marta as she stood gazing after them. "*Grüss Gott!* May our Lord go with you, little lambs!"

After a long time, Marta wiped her eyes and turned to look up at the crucifix that hung above the door of the house. She made the sign of the cross and entered. There were others still to care for. The rest was in God's hands.

2

Fire and Water

The expression on the face of Ernst vom Rath was grim and worried. He did not act the part of a young, carefree German diplomat out to see the sights of Paris. A strong spring wind whistled through the steel skeleton of the Eiffel Tower as he followed Thomas von Kleistmann up the steep metal steps of the structure.

Thomas glanced over his shoulder as if to encourage Ernst in the arduous climb. Ernst held up the small box camera in response as the tower elevator whirred quickly by them. The lift was crammed with tourists peeking out through the iron grid. As the eyes of strangers peered down on Ernst and Thomas, the two men paused on a landing. Ernst snapped a picture of Thomas with Paris in the background. Then Thomas took the camera from him and vom Rath posed, but he did not smile. He had not smiled since Le Morthomme, known as the Dead Man, had been shot dead in the bookstall. An absolute silence had fallen. No word of instruction from Berlin. No attempt at contact from agents of Britain or even of the French government.

Thomas leaned against the rail and gazed pensively over the city. "Well, what do you suggest we do now, Ernst?" The wind tugged at his overcoat and mussed his thick black hair.

Ernst looked through the viewfinder and snapped another photo. "The consummate tourists, eh?" he said solemnly. "Followed by the Gestapo, we wander through Paris. Visit the cabarets and cafés and hope for some encouraging word."

"And if we are contacted?" Thomas looked at the empty steps above and below as if he were examining the structure. Satisfied that they had not been followed this time, he sighed with relief. "How can we know that the contact is not one of Himmler's men? Gestapo in sheep's clothing?"

The frown on vom Rath's brow deepened. "Just so. How can we know?" He met von Kleistmann's gaze. "What have we gotten ourselves into?"

"Much too late to wonder that now." Thomas changed the topic with a wave of his hand. "They say the Führer is furious at the accusation that he might have had an eye on invading Czechoslovakia." He smiled. "Goebbels is very adept at propaganda, is he not? Creating the image of innocent Hitler, slandered and indignant before the world?"

"That is what worries me." Ernst buttoned his coat against the wind. "Perhaps the British do not believe—"

"And if they do not believe?"

"They will not attempt to reestablish a link with the German High Command."

Thomas clapped him on the back. "If that is the case, then we will no longer be conspirators against the Reich."

"Then there will be war."

"That may be so anyway. We have done what we could to stop it."

Ernst looked angry. "You sound relieved that it might be over."

"I am only saying that there is nothing we can do."

"You might return to speak with Churchill," Ernst argued.

"What is there left to tell him?" Thomas said logically. "What? He announced our rearmament figures in Parliament. 'Yes, quite. The Reich is jolly well working toward building an air force that can decimate Europe?' This is not news. The American flyer, Charles Lindbergh, has already told the world that the German Luftwaffe is unbeatable."

Thomas gazed up through the metal at a crisp blue sky as though he could already see German airplanes there. "I am afraid, Ernst, that all the facts and figures we have passed along at risk to our lives have only caused the English government to cower in fear and beg for peace. Perhaps they have come to doubt that my warnings are truly from the German High Command. Perhaps they believe that I am being sent with this information at the bidding of the Führer. Surely it is no longer any secret that he wishes the whole world to fear him."

Vom Rath almost smiled at the irony of the British response to their information. "Warned about plans for Czech invasion . . . " He faltered, then began with a new bitterness in his voice, "And they buried their heads deeper in the sand. Now the Führer screams against the lies that accuse him of plotting such an invasion, and Chamberlain seems quite sympathetic and sorry for all the fuss."

Silence fell as the footsteps of a man and a woman sounded on the stairs above them. Ernst pretended to fuss with the camera as a young couple passed them. When they were out of earshot, Ernst spoke. "Again I ask, Thomas, what are we to do?"

The most sensible conclusion, it seemed to Thomas, was to do nothing. He was convinced that Hitler's grand plan for the Greater Reich could not have been altered in spite of the ravings over the radio. "I am due for a leave. Berlin."

"You will speak with Admiral Canaris then."

Thomas did not reply. The mention of Canaris' name made him suddenly nervous. He stared angrily at Ernst. To speak that name was to somehow risk that the wind would hear and carry it to the ears of a thousand enemies. Thomas himself had been forbidden to mention Canaris in connection with this operation. How did Ernst know that the chief of the Abwehr had anything to do with this?

"No, Ernst," he replied at last, "I am simply going home. No matter what it may have become, Germany is still my home. There is nothing left for us to do, you see? I think the English gentlemen are quite full of information about the state of German military readiness. And as for the Czechoslovakian question, it seems obvious that the British have no real interest as long as England and France are not affected."

He gripped Ernst's arm. "I am telling you that there is no one on that side of the Channel who cares what Germany does or who is at the helm. You see, Ernst? We are quite alone. I feel homesick for what my life once was." Thomas inhaled and continued to look out over the gardens and rooftops of Paris. He thought of Elisa and of her family. He thought of his own betrayal, and of this failed attempt to somehow make it right again.

"Yes, alone," Ernst replied glumly.

"To tell you the truth, I think I would not have minded so much if the fellow had shot me instead of Le Morthomme. If there is another war, I will not want to spend my tour of duty in the Abwehr. No, I will go to the front. I will look for an honorable way to end what has turned out to be a life of dishonor. There will surely be someone with a rifle on the other side who will rejoice to kill a German officer; don't you think so, Ernst?"

"Perhaps it will not come to that."

Thomas laughed, denying vom Rath's hope for peace. "There is nothing left for us here, Ernst. No doubt the Führer is drawing up his plans for eliminating the Czechs right now. I am going home. To Berlin. I will request transfer to the regular army. The Czechs are good fellows, I hear. I want to be in the front of the unit when the Wehrmacht crosses the border."

An unseasonably cold wind blasted in from the North Sea and swept upriver sixty-three miles to the teeming port of Hamburg. Some citizens raised their eyes to the leaden sky and proclaimed that they had seen such a wind bring snow. Tiny gray flakes, soiled by the smoke from the steel plant, swirled earthward and dissolved into sooty puddles the instant they touched the cobbled streets. No one seemed surprised or alarmed by the occurrence. Some even joked that now that the Führer had the steel plants working at full capacity, their heat would warm all of Hamburg—perhaps all of Germany—until the snow would never stick again.

Inside the Thyssen Steel Works, the furnaces of the Reich fumed and hissed with the heat of molten metal and white-hot fires that seared away all thought of the cold wind outside. These fires, which created steel for tanks and ships and guns, were fueled by the flesh of men. Furnace doors radiated an unearthly light, illuminating the shining bodies of convicts chosen from the living dead at Dachau for their strength and size. Weary arms lifted heaping shovels of coal to the thrumming rhythm of machines and the *clank* of metal against metal as the production of armor plate for the battleship *Bismarck* continued relentlessly.

Like cymbals and kettledrums, the factory boomed out a symphony to hell, devouring the bodies and souls of those who fed the inferno for the Reich.

Shimon Feldstein had worked his shift for sixteen hours, taking the place of a man who had collapsed and died in front of the open mouth of the furnace. His sense of his own pain had long been dimmed as he dug his shovel into the black heap and tossed coal back to the insatiable fires.

Boom! Dig. Crash! Swing. Boom! Dig . . .

Sometime his shift must end. Sometime. If it did not, then he would die like the man who had fallen and convulsed at his feet. Then the heat would stop. The thirst would be quenched. Someone else would take his shift. There was an unending supply of labor for Hitler's Four-Year Plan. Shimon would not be missed. Not be mourned except by Leah.

The thought of her helped him lift his arms once again as it had a thousand times over the months. The image of her face stirred his heart with a will to survive.

Overhead, the giant kettle of molten steel swung from the fire toward the machine that would hammer it into plate metal for the pride of the Reich—the battleships being built in Hamburg's shipyards.

Sparks flew up from the glowing yellow liquid as the kettle rocked a bit in its ominous transit above their heads. At this point the sweating

Nazi foreman on the catwalk above them always stepped back behind the shelter of his glass cage. Eyes protected by dark goggles, he would watch with pleasure as yet another stream of refined steel spilled from the lip of the receptacle to be counted in the day's twenty-four-hour quota.

The plant never shut down. The fires never ceased to burn. The steady cadence of his convicts was seldom broken. The foreman had trained his workers that even in the event of heatstroke or death the movement of the kettle above them was what they lived for. Interruptions would not be tolerated. A delay in production meant beatings, extra shifts, less food. His methods had worked well thus far. Tonight Shimon remained for an additional twelve hours as an example of a worker who mistakenly stopped to look for a fallen comrade. The big sweating Jew had knelt and called for help and begged water to touch the lips of a convict already dead. Others in the unit would think twice before they broke the momentum again.

The boom arm holding the hissing steel trembled and groaned as it supported its burden. No one looked up at the noise. The foreman had shot workers for less. The roar of the blasting furnaces was numbing. There was never silence here. The moaning of a hook or the quavering of the container was not a matter for contemplation.

It was not the deafening roar that caused the men below the molten river to look up for an instant to see their own death pouring from the beams above them. It was the light—blinding, brilliant, beautiful in its horror. Screams were lost in the din, and oxygen was sucked from seared lungs as the flesh was consumed from brawny backs.

Explosions followed as the liquid metal touched the heaps of coal and ignited them instantly. In a fraction of a heartbeat, Shimon caught sight of the limp body of the foreman as he tumbled from his catwalk cage and fell headfirst into the leading edge of a second fierce explosion.

Raging agony clawed Shimon's back as he was lifted off his feet and hurled spinning into the air. The artillery of careless haste turned the mighty steel factory into a crematorium within seconds after the first flowing metal touched the coal. There had been no chance to run. Few of the workers who died in those brief moments even knew what force consumed their lives.

The lights from cars and fire trucks and ambulances seemed dim as they remained a block from the searing heat of the blaze. Sirens were drowned out by the noise of the roaring inferno and the groaning of twisted metal as the factory fell in on itself.

Reich industry officials shouted their replies to questions from dozens of reporters who gathered at the scene. "Causes will be thoroughly investigated . . . widows and orphans compensated. . . . No doubt the work of Jews and foreign saboteurs. . . . Steel production will be delayed only a short time. A matter of days."

It was common opinion that no one could have survived the blast. Besides the handful of loyal Nazi foremen who were lost, the rest had only been common criminals anyway. The Reich had been fortunate in that way. "Survivors? The devil himself could not live through that hell! Heil Hitler!"

⚭

Shimon clung to the piling of the dock a hundred yards from where the demolished factory burned. The fires lit the dark night like daylight. Fragments of the building, blown with him into the river, now burned on top of the water.

The pain that raced up and down Shimon's neck and back caused him to scream again and again, but his voice went unheard or unheeded. He longed for death. Such agony was too great for him to consider the miracle of survival. He did not ponder how he had come to fall in the water as the world all around him had disintegrated. Had he been blown free of the building? Had he crawled to the pier and thrown himself in the cool water? Had some gracious hand lifted him up and shielded him?

It did not matter. Yet another explosion shook the night. Shimon ducked his head as a shower of metal fell into the water around him. The air itself was charged with heat and fumes that almost choked him. Death would be merciful.

The air was torn by a series of blasts. With his last strength Shimon slipped beneath the water and held his breath as another shower of debris crashed into the waters. Only his hands remained exposed as he gripped a rusty iron spike protruding from the splintered wood. To let go of that spike would be to let go of life, to slip away forever and inhale the cold waters of the Elbe River into his tortured lungs. And yet, Shimon could not let go. Again and again his thirst for air thrust him to the heated surface where he gasped and shouted Leah's name before he submerged himself beneath the waters once more. "Leah! Leah! Dear God—"

All through the terrible night he gripped the spike until at last the fires blended into the daylight and died away. As dawn broke he heard the exclamations and curses of his Nazi masters as they prowled the boards on the dock above him.

"The work of Jews and saboteurs. Two hundred dead inmates, more or less. A small factory—not much loss to the Reich, after all."

The skies above Hamburg were still black with the smoke of last night's explosion. The sidewalk was covered with soot. But the old woman did not seem to notice the mess.

In spite of her seventy-eight years, Frau Trudence Rosenfelt carried herself with a certain dignity and determination that made the crowds in front of the Hamburg Office of Immigration part when she approached. Perhaps it was the cane that made the people step back for her and the little entourage that followed after her. She held the cane high and in front of her face, like a drum major leading a band in a Fourth of July parade back home in New York. Her diminutive form was dwarfed by heads and shoulders all around, but there was the cane, clearly visible even to the smallest of the seven Holbein family members who followed quick-march behind the grandmother they called Bubbe.

Frau Rosenfelt's granddaughter, Maria, was seven months pregnant and waddled after Trudence like a duck. Maria's five daughters followed like stair-step ducklings, kept in line by their father, Klaus, who protected the rear of the procession. Tall and gangly, Klaus could easily spot Bubbe's cane as they snaked through the throngs of frightened Jews who had gathered outside the Reich office in hopes of obtaining precious exit visas.

"Stay close, children!" Bubbe Rosenfelt called in a high-pitched voice. "Link hands!" she ordered in English. Often she spoke to her family in a muddled combination of English and Yiddish, the mother tongue of her old New York neighborhood. In more recent times, however, she had taken to weeding out the Yiddish from her vocabulary and concentrating strictly on proper English sentence structure.

Since Hitler had passed the Nuremberg Laws against Jews, and the family porcelain factory had been confiscated by the Nazi state, the old woman refused to converse in German. "So teach the children to speak good American, Maria," she often admonished her granddaughter, named for an old Italian-Catholic friend who still wrote from the Bronx. "To speak German? That language they need like a *Loch in Kopf*! Like a hole in the head, *nu*? I'm telling you, we are going home to New York!"

To speak the language of a maniac like Hitler, according to the old woman, a piece of *narrishkeit*! Foolishness. Hitler had not only cursed the Jews with that *paskudne* mouth of his, he had cursed all of Germany! It was time for every Jew with brains to get out. To leave for the *goldeneh medina*, America, where the streets were paved with gold. And so what if the streets were not really gold? At least there were no Nazi thugs there. No Nuremberg Laws. No Nazi People's Courts. No Gestapo or concentration camps. In America, Hitler was a character in the funny papers. That alone, to Bubbe, was worth more than gold.

This old woman, who led her little brood up the steps of the imposing Nazi edifice, had become an object of admiration and envy among the Jews of her Hamburg neighborhood. Frau Trudence Rosenfelt was an American, after all. She might have married Herbert Rosenfelt, may he rest in peace; she might have been fifty years in Germany, but she had never given up her citizenship in the Golden Land! Everyone knew she was go-ing back. Every *shmo*, every *shmendrick*, every *shmegegge* on the block could see that. And no doubt she would manage to take her granddaughter and that tall noodle-of-a-husband Klaus, along with the children, too!

What only a few Jews in Germany could accomplish with a hundred trips to the Reich Office of Immigration, Frau Rosenfelt had managed to accomplish with a mere handful of visits to the stern Nazi officers who were in charge of granting or denying exit visas. Today the old woman had come to fetch the promised visas for her and her family. The pre-cious Ausweis papers would be ready today at two in the afternoon. The grim-faced German officer with the thinning hair and the wire-rimmed spectacles had told her as much.

It was five minutes before two when Frau Trudence held out her American passport to one of the two tall Nazi sentries on duty at the door. The handsome young man stared hard at the faded photograph on the passport; then he stared hard at the wrinkled old woman who stood defiantly in front of him.

"Tell him in German that I am an American," Frau Trudence in-structed her granddaughter in English. "Tell him I may be an old woman now, but my passport is current, and I am an *American*!" She held her prominent nose aloft at those words. Her every mannerism dared the young man to attempt to stop her.

Quietly Maria repeated the words that Bubbe had proclaimed loudly in English. Mrs. Rosenfelt could have spoken in German, but she would not profane her lips with *that* language!

Now the sentry asked why Maria and Klaus and five little girls had also come to the office.

Mrs. Rosenfelt understood him and answered in English. "Tell this *shmo*—" she inclined her head slightly at the sentry as she instructed Maria—"that you are *my* family. Americans by right."

Dutifully Maria repeated the words.

The sentry nodded curtly and stepped aside for the old woman and her entourage. They passed beneath the glare of the German eagle that perched on the swastika above the glass doors of the lobby like an iron vulture choosing which Jews to devour. Mrs. Rosenfelt had determined long ago that the Nazi appetite for violence would not be satisfied with the flesh of her family.

The children bunched up tightly around the legs of their mother and their aged great-grandmother. Klaus placed his long, thin hands on the shoulders of his two oldest children, Trudy and Katrina. Mrs. Rosenfelt was the only one who did not seem at all intimidated by the myriad Blackshirt SS men who emerged from the lobby elevator.

Other small cliques of hopeful Jews turned their eyes away from the tramp of Nazi jackboots on the marble floor. Mrs. Rosenfelt, however, followed the swaggering brutes with her eyes as they moved toward the doors and saluted the sentries with a chorus of "Heil Hitler!"

"*Nebech!*" the old woman muttered under her breath in a tone of derisive dismissal. So this was what she thought of those members of the master race.

Klaus raised his eyes in amused surprise. Then, as if capturing some fragment of her courage, he allowed himself to look at the Blackshirts as they pushed brutally through the crowd outside the building. A stream of additional epithets ran through his mind, but he would not utter them until they were all safely away from this cursed land. Klaus glanced back at the old woman who was also dressed completely in black. He had never seen Bubbe in any other color; Maria had told him that since Herbert Rosenfelt had died twenty-six years before, the dressmakers of Hamburg had been instructed to bring only black fabric for the fittings of Frau Rosenfelt.

From her black high-buttoned shoes to the tall black lace collar of her dress, Bubbe Rosenfelt was a visual anachronism. She did not seem to fit in this century, let alone in this terrible decade of flourishing anti-Semitism. She carried a reticule—a black velvet drawstring bag—around her neck. Inside the bag was a small coin purse, a compact with powder, a mirror, and a handful of peppermint candies that she would present to her five great-grandchildren as rewards for appropriate behavior.

A pair of pince-nez glasses dangled from a silken cord attached to the third button of her blouse. If a child misbehaved, the old woman would simply raise those glasses to her nose and balance them there to cast a glare of disapproval toward the offender. Squabbles, tantrums, or sloppy table manners were stopped and corrected instantly with one narrowing of those faded blue eyes. Then the old woman would arch her right eyebrow slightly and let the pince-nez fall to the end of its cord. It bounced and swung from her bosom like a miniature hanged criminal. The effect was quite successful.

Confronted by these arrogant Nazi officials, Mrs. Rosenfelt had used the same tactics on them. It took a brave man to stare down the outrage in the old woman's eyes. So far, not one Nazi bureaucrat had managed to do it.

At first Klaus had assumed that it was because of the way Bubbe Rosenfelt dropped the word *American* like a bomb. After all, Hitler still had hopes of appeasing the Americans. As their struggle to obtain exit visas had progressed, however, Klaus had begun to realize that the old woman's citizenship had little to do with her power to intimidate. She simply treated the whole German master race with the utter disdain they deserved so completely. She was too old, she said one evening over coffee, to let these Aryan bullies *shtup* her. There was only one concern left in her life since they had stolen her beloved porcelain factory to make commemorative swastika plates—she was going to take her family *home*!

Bubbe was fearless because, at seventy-eight, she was unafraid for herself. Yet fear for her family had made her stand toe to toe with every Nazi official in the immigration office. "Go ahead! Throw an old woman in Dachau, why don't you! And an old American woman, at that! Just see what the American press will have to say about you then!"

For three months the Nazis had hoped she would simply die. When she had not obliged them, they granted the papers. What every Jew in Germany needed now, Klaus and Maria decided, was a grandmother like Trudence Rosenfelt!

At precisely 2:00 PM, Frau Rosenfelt stood before the desk of Colonel Hans Beich. Klaus, Maria, and the children stood behind her in an expectant semicircle.

"We have come for our papers." Bubbe Rosenfelt fingered the pince-nez as she peered down on the balding head of the colonel.

The colonel spoke a heavily accented English laced with German idioms. "Frau Rosenfelt." He appeared nervous. His voice was higher than usual. "You are quite punctual." Rubbing his hand through his thin hair, he smiled slightly. "However, I regret . . . your papers are not here."

"Not here?" she uttered with disdain. "Then you are telling me that the German Reich is not punctual?" This was a high insult to the Prussian sense of precision.

The colonel drew himself up. "There is some problem. The husband of your granddaughter—" he looked at Klaus for effect—"he taught chemistry at the University of Hamburg, no?"

Klaus felt himself grow hot beneath the gaze of the officer. Of course he had taught at the university. If Hitler had not created laws banning Jews from teaching positions, no doubt Klaus would still be there.

Frau Rosenfelt stepped between the colonel and Klaus. She held her cane in one hand and the pince-nez in the other. "What has that got to do with anything at all?"

The colonel cleared his throat. He would have liked to continue to stare at Klaus as if he were an offender, but the old woman blocked his view. "The . . . authorities . . . felt that perhaps since his position was in chemistry . . . there was research going on at the university, and there was some concern that perhaps . . . Klaus Holbein might have some information that would be best kept within the borders of the Reich."

This was utter and complete nonsense, Klaus knew. He was simply a professor. A teacher of chemistry. What could he know that might harm the Reich in any way? He started to speak, but the old woman inclined her cane slightly, a signal for silence in the ranks. The pince-nez was raised dramatically to the nose, and she glared at the colonel with a look that made all the children cling to their mother.

There was a long and terrible silence. The colonel began to sweat. He squirmed a bit. Then Bubbe Rosenfelt spoke. "So. First the Reich and the Führer deprive my grandson of his livelihood because he is a Jew. Then they say he cannot go elsewhere to find a life because he is a Jew. I will tell you what state secrets Klaus knows about the Reich, Herr Colonel. Klaus knows precisely which members of the Aryan master race were unable to pass the course in chemistry at Hamburg University. A frightening thing to think of, that perhaps an Aryan might not pass a course taught by a Jew."

"Frau Rosenfelt, I assure you, the authorities are checking—" The colonel could not tear his eyes away from the pince-nez. The old woman had him.

"Good! And while the authorities are checking, I shall wire my nephew, Franklin D. Rosenfelt, who will certainly wire the Führer when it is learned how badly we are being treated here!"

Klaus and Maria exchanged looks. The great-nephew Bubbe had mentioned was less than two years old. He lived in a place called Brooklyn and had acquired his unusual name when he was born on the same night Franklin Roosevelt won his second presidency. Of course, Roosevelt and Rosenfelt sounded quite similar to the German ear, and the Nazis did indeed suspect the president of being Jewish, but perhaps this was taking family connections a bit too far.

But beads of perspiration formed on the brow of the Nazi officer. "Franklin D. Rosenfelt? You mean—?"

The old woman rose up on her toes. The pince-nez stayed perched on her nose. There was power here. "Exactly!" spat Frau Rosenfelt. "My great-nephew. He will be quite interested to hear the trouble we have been put to over a few small documents. He will certainly relay such information to Hitler. The embarrassment of holding his relatives in Germany when they wish only to go home—" Now the old woman let the pince-nez drop to the end of its cord. It jerked and bobbed. The lynching was quite effective. The colonel put his hand to his own throat as he stared at the pince-nez.

He smiled nervously. "One moment, Frau Rosenfelt." He said the name with an astonishing respect. He rose from his desk and clicked his heels before he hurried from the office.

One hour later Bubbe sipped tea in her parlor with Maria and Klaus. The five girls were presented with peppermints and sent off to the bedroom to concoct a play.

"I told Sadie that naming that child Franklin Delano Rosenfelt would come in quite handy as the years progressed. *Oy!* But I did not think it would be so useful so soon!"

Along with the peppermints, she had pulled out a handful of travel documents and exit visas from the black velvet handbag. She fanned them out neatly on the tea table and counted them again.

3

Barriers

Bubbe Rosenfelt had accomplished much through sheer bluff and bravado at the Hamburg Office of Immigration. All of that meant nothing, however, as she stood at the high counter of the American Consulate and peered through her notorious pince-nez at the stubborn American clerk.

"I'm sorry, Mrs. Rosenfelt." The clerk shrugged in bureaucratic helplessness.

"But surely you can see that the papers granted by the Nazis are valid for only two weeks! You don't have eyes, young man? If my grandchildren are not out of here within two weeks—" she drew a finger across her throat in an unmistakable gesture—"like a chicken at the butcher's!"

The "young man" behind the counter was actually more than fifty years old. His gray hair was parted in the center, and he wore a high celluloid collar that had been an American fashion when he left the country years before. Years of experience had taught him now to turn away even the most persistent individuals. This old woman was no match for his expertise.

"Look, Mrs. Rosenfelt, there are laws now restricting the number of immigrants we let into America. Remember? Fifteen years ago there would have been no problem."

"*Oy!* Fifteen years ago Hitler was hanging wallpaper, not Jews!" She let the pince-nez fall. "Fifteen years ago Germany was a cultured, civilized country!"

"That may be so, but the fact remains that all quotas for immigration have been filled. For months the quotas of Germans have been filled.

Every Jew, every Democrat, every Socialist in the Reich wants out of here. What are we supposed to do about it?"

"Give them a place to go, maybe? Save a few lives?"

"America is already packed with a lot of hungry people. Men out of work. Looking for jobs. Trying to feed their kids, see? Sorry, Mrs. Rosenfelt. There just isn't any room on the list for your granddaughter and her husband and five more children. My hands are tied. The quota is filled."

"How many a month is my country letting in now?" she asked bitterly.

"A thousand."

"Only eight hundred," the old woman corrected. "And such a big place, too."

"And what kind of life do you think anyone is going to have if we throw away the quotas and let every undesirable—"

Mrs. Rosenfelt slammed her cane on the counter to silence this discussion.

The head of the clerk snapped back in startled indignation.

"Enough talk, already!" Her faded blue eyes blazed angrily. "The Nazis have not made it half as hard to leave as you make it to go. How long is this waiting list of yours?"

"A year." He continued to stare at the cane. Perhaps this mad old woman would decide to use it on him.

Mrs. Rosenfelt's eyes narrowed. She smiled shyly and reached out to touch the clerk's threadbare suit. "You look like a fellow who could use a new suit of clothes. Perhaps shoes, also? Or an automobile?"

His eyes widened and he drew back from her. "Bribes won't do you any good. It's been tried. I'm telling you, the list is the list. That's the only way."

"Then you are a fool." She leaned forward. "Two weeks we have before the papers expire."

"You can go back to America anytime."

"*Oy!* So now you think I would leave them?"

"Work on this back in the States. Send for them."

"Two weeks the Nazis have given. No more. They will not renew their travel documents." Her gnarled hand was clenched in a fist. "Your kind I have seen a thousand times. Money is a language you understand. This is a language I can speak, *nu*? List or no list, we must leave Germany within fourteen days. We will leave, and you will be a rich man for having helped us."

The clerk stared sullenly at the stubborn old woman in front of him. She was making it impossible. Yes, the lists were full, but perhaps there was another way. There was the freighter. But there was a waiting list for that as well. A share for him and a share for Captain Burton. No one needed a visa to get on a freighter like the SS *Darien*.

"Maybe there is a way."

"I thought so. Nothing but a lot of *shtuss* you are giving me. Always there is a way."

"There is a ship leaving Hamburg Tuesday morning. Maybe I can get your family a place on it."

"I thought you could. And where is this boat going?"

Now the clerk smiled. "Away from Germany, Mrs. Rosenfelt."

"That's it? Away? So, away *to where?*"

"Just *away*. For you that should be good enough. You can go ahead to the States and work on their papers in the meantime. Day after tomorrow the ship leaves, and they are safe."

How could it be that a ship could leave Germany without a destination? The old woman nodded once and frowned with the realization that the quota of every nation was filled to capacity with the names of hopeful, desperate Jews. And so such a ship would become its own nation, an island of refuge until a port could be found.

Slowly Bubbe Rosenfelt raised her pince-nez to her nose. This was not what she had bargained for, yet it was better than nothing at all. "And how much will this cruise around the world cost? I am listening. How much to save the lives of my family?"

⨕

The doctor was Czech, Charles knew, but now the kind man spoke to him in heavily accented German. "Never was there a little boy so lucky as you, Charles." The broad face hovered over him like a bright full moon. The doctor looked like the man in the moon, Charles thought, but he could not tell him that. Charles could not communicate well at all since Louis had gone. Now that he was feeling better, Charles thought how very much he would like to see his brother and share his secret that the man in the moon had swooped down to help him through this latest illness.

The doctor squinted as he took Charles's pulse. "Strong. Yes, yes. You are feeling better now?"

Charles nodded. He was much better now than he had been that first dreadful night they had arrived in Prague. His ears had become infected, and for days he had endured searing pain. There were, in fact, days that were only a blur in his memory. Images of Elisa and the tall American, John Murphy, floated through his mind. Charles liked the American who was always telling him tales about America and children who lived there. He liked Herr Theo, who also had been ill; and he liked Anna, who sat and read to him by the hour and stroked his hair as his mother had once done. Yes, Charles was feeling better, but the one ache that had not receded was his longing to see Louis again. Louis. Father. And in the darkest nights when the pain awakened him, he cried for Mommy, although he knew she was gone to heaven.

Murphy stepped through the door of the bedroom. He was all dressed up in a black coat and a crooked bow tie and shiny shoes so that he looked like a waiter in a restaurant. "How ya doin', Champ?" Murphy asked brightly in American. Murphy often spoke American to Charles and then translated the meaning. Someday, Murphy promised, maybe Charles and Louis could go to America, and it would be important to understand the strange language even though the boy's cleft palate made it impossible for him to utter even one word.

Charles pulled his frail hand out from under the blue down quilt and gave Murphy the thumbs-up signal. Another way to say "Okay," Murphy had told him.

At the sight of the thumb, Murphy roared with laughter and returned the sign. "Okay, kiddo! Swell!"

These were other ways Americans expressed approval. Charles had decided that there were far too many ways for him to learn them all, but he liked that Murphy was teaching him all the same.

The doctor wiggled a finger in his own ear as if to clear away the strange jumble of sounds emanating from Herr Murphy. "Do you understand what this crazy American is saying, Charles?" The doctor laughed.

Charles nodded and raised his thumb again.

"When he's well enough to travel," Murphy said in Czech, "Elisa and I will take him back to America. To New York, where you say that doctor can repair his mouth. He will need to understand a little English."

The doctor nodded as he replaced his stethoscope in the big black bag. "That sounds quite unlike any English my poor ears have ever heard."

"Believe me—" Murphy winked at Charles, who could not understand any of the conversation now—"what I am teaching him is a great deal easier to speak than Czech! He would have to have a palate as strong as a nutcracker to say hello in your language!"

"That may be so." The doctor smiled in agreement. "But Czech is a beautiful language, a language of poets. And we shall hope that Herr Doktor Sohnheim in America shall perform his miracle for the child." Now the doctor closed his bag and clucked his tongue in disapproval. "Unbelievable that the Nazis should refuse this child surgery to repair his deformity. And then also to remove Herr Doktor Sohnheim from his position at the university hospital in Berlin."

"What the Nazis have lost, America gains. What they did not tend to for little Charles will be taken care of. The same doctor who might have mended him in Berlin will now have the opportunity to do so in New York."

Once again, the doctor spoke German to Charles. "You see, my boy? You are *very* lucky, indeed!"

Charles nodded, although he had understood nothing but his own name and the mention of another doctor and a place called New York. Murphy had mentioned the place before. Charles would like it, Murphy had promised. Charles dreamed about seeing this place with Louis. Moving pictures. The game called baseball. Parks to play in without fear of the Gestapo. And sausage called hot dog, which Charles would eat when his mouth was well. Such dreams were almost too wonderful! When Charles thought about it all, sometimes he would cry out with the joy of it, which made poor Frau Anna come running to the bedroom to check on him. She always seemed frightened, and now, Charles resisted the urge to cry out when he was happy. He saved his utterance for his most lonely moments, when he thought his heart would break with the need to see Louis. Father. Mommy. And then when he cried, Anna would call Elisa, who sat on the edge of the bed and played dear old Vitorio for him as Leah had done. Elisa did not play nearly so well as Leah, but she made Vitorio sing for him all the same. The Bach Suites were his favorite. Little happy dances. And always after hearing them, he was cheered.

"It just must be the cello for you, eh?" Elisa often teased. "You will not content yourself with a violin, which I can play fairly well?"

Each time Charles shook his head from side to side. No. The violin would not do. Somehow the old cello had become a voice for him. A prayer. A hope. He was never quite so lonely after she played. He could close his eyes and think of Louis sitting next to him in that little room beneath the stage in Vienna. He could remember Leah's strong, gentle fingers as she worked to teach him the simple melodies. When he was well enough to sit up, Charles determined he would try to play Vitorio himself. Then Elisa could play along with him on the violin.

Elisa's clear, bright voice preceded her into the room. "How is our boy?" She swept in, shining and beautiful in a long white gown. She looked like an angel, Charles thought. *Very pretty.* Even a boy almost six could see that.

"Better!" Murphy exclaimed. "Almost well, says the doctor."

Elisa smiled at Charles and bent to kiss his forehead and smooth his tousled hair back. Charles wanted to ask her where she was going all dressed up. Murphy might look like a waiter, but she looked like a countess or a queen in a picture book. He wished she would tell him where they were going.

"My strong, brave Charles," she whispered. "Such a good patient."

She was so beautiful that Charles decided he would marry her when he grew up. Herr Murphy would not mind, he reasoned. He and Murphy got along very well together.

Elisa spoke in Czech to the doctor. They always did that when they did not want Charles to understand, and he hated the exclusion. The doctor smiled and waved a farewell, and Elisa turned her attention to Murphy's crooked bow tie.

"Darling," she said, kissing Murphy on the chin, "you look as if you tried to hang yourself."

"I did it this way on purpose." Murphy kissed her lips and pulled her close to him. "So I could get you like this." He laughed at her playful disapproval. They had forgotten Charles for a moment. Charles liked it when they forgot he was watching. He did not like it when they remembered and stepped out of the room to continue their grown-up play.

"Murphy!" Elisa scolded. "Not in front—"

"Oh." The self-conscious smile appeared. "Right." Murphy let her go and said good night to Charles, tousling his blond hair and adding how happy he was that his little friend felt so much better.

One last kiss from Elisa on his forehead and then they stepped out of the room, leaving Charles alone to wonder what it was all about.

✆

As the last rays of sunlight reflected on the tall spires of Hradcany Castle, forty servants completed the monumental task of lighting six thousand candles on the crystal chandeliers of the great reception room.

On the cobbles of the square below, pedestrians looked up toward the shining windows and commented as the bulbs of dozens of news cameras popped, sending small explosions of light into the darkness. Musicians entered the vast building through a side entrance lined with burly, grim-faced security guards. The guards had been recently chosen from the finest and strongest officers in the Czech Army. They towered over the tiny president and were prepared to offer their own lives so that what had happened at the National Theatre would not be repeated. President Beneš now walked and talked and slept and ate and worked behind a human wall that protected him against the menace of Nazi and Sudetenland Germans who wished him dead and plotted his end.

Tonight the president of the most enlightened democracy in Europe held a celebration honoring the man and woman who had risked their lives to save his. But even on this joyous occasion, the specter of fear huddled behind every door and made itself felt as handbags and instrument cases and overcoats were searched for weapons. The near assassination at the National Theatre had proven how very close death was for President Beneš.

And if Death walked like a shadow behind the tiny form of this man, then it loomed up like mountains around the nation itself. The Death's-Head units of the SS cast longing, hungry looks across the borders into Czechoslovakia. Even as the music played within Hradcany and the crystal chandeliers illuminated the gold-leaf splendor of the great palace in Prague, another scene was taking place in Germany. Fury and hatred simmered up, blackening the hearts of those who listened to the ravings of the beloved Führer:

> *"Czechoslovakia must be wiped off the map! It will be wiped off the map! It is my unshakable will that we accomplish this! Listen! We will not back down from those subhuman pygmies again! October first we will hold Czechoslovakia in our hand! And the fingers of the Reich will slowly close and clench until there is no life left there but the life we bring!"*

❧

Admiral Canaris was unmoving as he scanned the request of Thomas von Kleistmann. He raised his piercing blue eyes to stare angrily at the handsome young officer across from him. "What good do you think this will do?" he asked.

"What way is left for any German officer with honor?" Thomas replied.

"Self-centered prattle!" Canaris snapped. "Do you think I do not see through your intentions, von Kleistmann? Ultimately you intend to lay down your life for the sake of the Fatherland."

"Why not? What else should I hope for?"

"There is no Fatherland left. No truer patriotism than to live and serve honor as a traitor to Hitler and his Reich. *Live*, and serve truth!" Canaris slammed his hand down on his desk.

"How can I do that in Paris? Without a contact?" Thomas challenged.

"Patience," Canaris replied, tearing the transfer request in half and dropping it into the garbage can.

"How can I know if I am approached that the courier will not be an agent for the Gestapo? How can we know anything anymore?"

"You are afraid of the Gestapo? You, who want to be first across the

line when Hitler storms the Czechs? You, who long for death from the rifle of an enemy? I tell you this—if you die from a Czech bullet, you have
been killed by a man defending his nation! If you die at the hands of the
Nazi Gestapo, you die at the hands of traitors who will destroy all that is
good about the German people! Turn your eyes to the truth, Thomas, as
your father would have done! You may die, as I may certainly die, but we
must not view death as simply an end to our suffering! If it is to be, then
we must give death purpose! We must fight against the evil that has
taken hold of our people and our country!"

"The English will not lift a finger. The Führer is right."

A slight smile crept across the lips of Canaris. "What have the English
to do with this? This is our battle first." He leaned forward and whispered with a frightening intensity, "Has the Führer made you believe
that he is invincible also? Have you listened to the lie?"

"I have wished only to die now, as my father did."

"Months ago I told you to put away hope for your life. I did not mean
that you should abandon all hope." Canaris seemed disappointed. "This
is not the way any of us would have chosen to serve. But it is the only
way left to us." The little man stood slowly and turned to look at a wall
decorated with yellowed photographs of battleships and submarines
with rows of young sailors standing at attention. "Tonight Hitler will review the troops as they march before the Chancellery. I want you to
come with me. To remind yourself why you must stay where you are."

Thomas had been given an order. He saluted in acknowledgment,
then lowered his eyes. There was an eagerness in the voice of Canaris
that had not existed when they had met in Vienna. Could it be that the
chief of German military intelligence had some new hope? Thomas did
not question Canaris further. "These are the soldiers who were on the
Czech border two weeks ago."

Canaris put a finger to his lips and smiled. "No one is supposed to
know that. Not the British. Not the French, not even the Führer." He
sniffed slightly and shrugged. "The question of the hour is, why are they
back from the border? And how might we keep them from returning
there?" He looked up at Thomas, who was a full twelve inches taller. "Instead of crossing into the Sudetenland to die with them, Thomas, you
might consider how you can help to keep them right here on German
soil, eh?"

4

Celebration in the Shadow of Darkness

Elisa's gown was shimmering white silk adorned with tiny, hand-sewn sequin leaves flowing from her shoulder and her waist. Tonight as she held tightly to her husband's arm and ascended the grand staircase to the ballroom, heads turned to watch her and eyes glanced in envy at the handsome American newsman who held her hand and leaned close to her. There was not a man in the vast hall who would not have willingly changed places with John Murphy tonight.

To have such a woman at your side!

Murphy grinned slyly at Elisa and whispered, "That does it. Next time we go out I'm going to make you wear coveralls and an overcoat."

"You don't like my dress, Murphy?" She was smiling, aware that he was crazy about the dress. He had asked her to put it on and take it off again at least a half dozen times before tonight.

"Yeah. And I like what's *in* it, too!" He grinned. "So does every other guy in the place." He squeezed her hand when a Czech nobleman, complete with monocle and a chestful of meaningless ribbons, clicked his heels and bowed deeply as she passed.

Elisa nodded politely, then said softly to Murphy, "At least they aren't tackling me and throwing me on the ground tonight."

"Don't think they wouldn't like to." Murphy drew her a little closer as they reached the top of the stairs.

A man in a powdered wig and a bright red uniform announced them to the crowd in the main ballroom: "Madame Eliiiissssaaaa Murphy and Monsieur Johhhhn Murphy!"

Heads turned in unison, and a polite patter of applause broke out in the room. Murphy smiled and rocked on his toes nervously. He had covered these swank events a million times, it seemed, but he had never been the guy at the top of the stairs.

Elisa leaned in and said through her smile, "I'm not accustomed to this. Usually I'm just part of the band, you know."

Murphy laughed out loud, relieved that she was feeling as out of place as he was. When President Beneš showed up, Murphy would be able to practice his craft a bit—ask a few questions and maybe scoop the rest of the guys. But for now, this crowd was just a bit too hoity-toity. Of course their upper-strata social standing did not keep the old geezers from clicking their heels and twirling their mustaches and gaping at Elisa like a bunch of love-struck teenagers.

"Let me know if any of these guys makes a pass," he said in English. "You've got a husband who loves you, you know, and I've got a pretty good right cross." He wagged his fist.

Elisa stood tiptoe and kissed him playfully on the chin. "You already proved as much when you captured Albert Sporer, darling. I don't think any of these gentlemen would dare to try to get past you."

Her words made Murphy feel like he had as a kid walking the picket fence in front of his girlfriend's house. He was nuts about Elisa. She was Myrna Loy and he was William Powell. Gable and Lombard. Romeo and Juliet! He was convinced that nobody had ever been in love before them. Nobody had ever felt this terrific or been this happy! Elisa and Murphy had *invented* marriage, and woe to all those poor single swells who thought bachelorhood was something to hold on to. Of course, Murphy conceded, there was only *one* Elisa in the whole world, and it might be different being married if it wasn't to her.

"They're drooling." Murphy laughed as he escorted Elisa to the dance floor. He wanted to thump his chest like Tarzan and yell, *She's mine, fellas! You can all go home now!*

"Murphy, behave," Elisa said demurely as he took her in his arms and they swirled off to the melody of a Strauss waltz.

"You're a good dancer," Murphy commented over the music.

She accepted the compliment with a smug nod. "I have played this melody enough. It's a treat to dance to it."

"When we get to the States I'm going to take you to Radio City or the Algonquin to hear Benny Goodman. Maybe Glenn Miller. I'll teach you to boogie-woogie!"

As she laughed at his strange comment, someone tapped him on the shoulder, cutting in. Murphy had not expected that. He reluctantly yielded his partner to a tall, bespectacled man dressed in the uniform of a colonel. Murphy's delirious cloud of joy evaporated as the suave young officer swept Elisa off into the crowd on the dance floor. Murphy looked impatiently at his wristwatch and wondered if thirty seconds was long enough to wait before he cut in again. He hesitated several seconds longer and then followed in the direction Elisa had disappeared. Thirty seconds was too long to wait.

The music stopped and the glittering crowd applauded and filtered from the dance floor to the sidelines. Murphy barely noticed the smiles of young ladies and matrons as he passed. He was too busy scanning the assembly for some sight of Elisa. Briefly he hoped that he would not spend the rest of his life so miserable out of her presence. They could still officially be considered newlyweds, however, so he allowed himself the luxury of missing her even after a few moments. *Especially with her in that dress.* Every other dame in the room was dressed in an old horse blanket compared to Elisa! As a matter of fact, every other woman in the room *looked* like an old nag compared to her.

Murphy still could not quite believe that Elisa was actually his wife. The thought of it made him grin all over again. He spotted her at a table next to a giant swan ice sculpture and noted the gaggle of gentlemen swarming around.

Sorry, boys; she's taken. He walked toward her nonchalantly as she raised her eyes to meet his. Some eager young buck was talking to her, but she was looking at Murphy. Smiling at Murphy. Drawing Murphy to her with a look that whispered that there was nobody in all the world for her but him. He winked at her and she winked back, a gesture that silenced the chatter of the man beside her. The man bowed slightly and backed away as Murphy approached.

"Missed you," she said in English. "Nobody here has ever heard of boogie-woogie." She raised her eyebrow slightly. "The lack of real culture here is astonishing, Mr. Murphy."

He laughed loudly enough to receive a number of disapproving glances. "What do you say we blow this joint after the main course?"

Elisa exhaled in frustration. Murphy was constantly tossing out American phrases that were beyond her comprehension. "Blow this joint?" she asked.

"Scram. Skedaddle."

"Oh. That explains everything." She took his arm. "If my husband were here he would . . . *belt you* . . . for talking to me that way."

"Very good, Elisa." Murphy nodded and kissed her hand. "You're a quick learner."

"I have an excellent tutor."

At that moment the trumpets erupted in a fanfare and the orchestra played the Czech national anthem. The slight form of President Beneš appeared at the top of the stairs. Bodyguards stood at a discreet but watchful distance. Beneš walked from handshake to handshake as the men surrounding him vigilantly scanned the outstretched hands and faces of the guests.

Murphy tugged Elisa forward to meet the president. The diminutive man's eyes met his. Behind Beneš was the officer who had been wounded in the arm by the first shots that night at the theater. The dark shadow of memory was still on the face of Beneš as he reached for Murphy's hand in firm greeting and then bowed to kiss Elisa's hand.

The music began again as Beneš straightened and gestured toward the guests. "Are you enjoying the celebration?" he asked kindly. "Our way of saying thank you. Also our way of letting the Nazis know we are still very much alive, yes?"

"They must be quite certain of that after finding the Czech Army waiting at the border, Mr. President," Murphy said in grim acknowledgment of the recent crisis. "You are the one nation in Europe that has faced down Herr Hitler and won."

"I regret that our military action on the frontier forced us to delay this party for so long." Beneš turned and addressed Elisa. "If I had been aware that you were so *very* beautiful, we would have abandoned everything else to offer you our hospitality."

Elisa smiled in thanks. "Hitler has declared that he never intended to invade the Czech frontier," she said quietly. "But my brother Wilhelm is a pilot. He saw the German divisions. You must be quite proud that you have faced the Dragon and he has backed down."

Beneš did not seem to hear her words. His face clouded for a moment. "The Dragon is still a dragon, Mrs. Murphy," he replied with a frown as the orchestra played the "Blue Danube Waltz." Then, catching himself, he extended his hand to her. "Would you honor me with this dance?"

Murphy stepped back as Elisa danced away with the president of Czechoslovakia. This was one dance Murphy would not attempt to cut in on.

"A beautiful woman, your wife." The wounded officer, arm in a sling, smiled admiringly toward Elisa and the president. Elisa stood several inches taller than the diminutive Beneš, and this disparity in height made her stand out all the more. "He dances with his savior," said the officer.

"How is your arm?" Murphy was not really interested in talking to the man, but felt cornered.

"A slight wound. Grazed the bone. Only my arm, and not our lives." Now the officer clicked his heels and bowed slightly. "I would shake your hand in gratitude for that, but as you can see—"

Murphy cleared his throat self-consciously. "Sporer was only one man. Your army stood up to the Reich, and Hitler backed down. That is quite an accomplishment."

The officer gave a short, bitter laugh and slid the fingers of his good hand beneath the red sash of his uniform in a pose that made him look like Napoleon. "Not such an accomplishment, John Murphy. Hitler still has his eye on our frontier in the mountains of the Sudetenland. He will not attempt to cross our border if we let him know we will fight for our line of defense." He shook his head. "No. Herr Hitler will attempt to win our Sudetenland by using men like Albert Sporer. By stirring up riots with the aid of his Nazi stooges. Then, with the performance of such fellows for the whole world to see, he will claim that the Sudetenland people have wanted to belong to the Reich all along. Only when he has convinced the world of that will he dare to march."

"No one will buy that," Murphy said, but he did not believe his own assertion.

"Oh? Did the world not believe it about Austria? How many Austrians voted for the Anschluss according to Hitler? Ninety-nine percent, they say. Of course there was only one name on the ballot. Only one choice, and that was 'ja'!"

"Most intelligent people know the truth."

"The problem is not in knowing the truth. It is in acting on it, Herr Murphy." He grinned. "At least we have one Nazi criminal where he belongs. Albert Sporer is imprisoned below us, you know."

Murphy looked at his feet and the polished parquet dance floor. "Just like the devil."

"Chained in the dungeon of Hradcany Castle. Beneath the lights and the music of the very men he might have murdered. Fitting, I think."

With that, the officer snapped his fingers and summoned a waiter. With a sweep of his hand, he motioned toward a round table, tiered like a cake and laden with pastries. "I would like you to carry an eclair down to the dungeon," he told the startled waiter. "Yes. To the lowest level."

"The dungeon, Colonel?" The waiter squeaked and then glanced at Murphy to see if the colonel had gone mad. Murphy shrugged his amusement at the strange order.

"Take it to the guard with my instructions that it is to be given to Albert Sporer. Sporer is to be told of the celebration we have here tonight in honor of the defeat of the Führer's plan. The president of the Czech democracy is dancing at this moment with the woman who stopped the assassin."

"Yes, Colonel." The waiter scurried away to find a particularly large and tasty eclair.

Murphy nodded in appreciation as the music stopped. "A fine sort of mental torture, Colonel," he complimented. "Of course, if you were in a dungeon in Berlin, I can assure you that the Nazis would send you something besides an eclair."

"When one has a devil in the dungeon, it seems appropriate to remind him that there are still free men walking about. Do you not agree? A taste of democracy for the tyrants and assassins."

Murphy laughed out loud. "I would like to quote that for my paper, Colonel, but there are a lot of hungry readers out there who would be happy to give up their freedom for an eclair."

"Ah, yes. Difficult times. Difficult."

President Beneš, pleasantly flushed and out of breath, escorted Elisa back to where Murphy and the colonel stood. Beneš kissed her hand and then peered up at Murphy. "All this beauty and she can also outrun the opera-house guards, too! All she talks about, however, is her husband, Herr Murphy. She says you are quite a journalist. And that for weeks you have tried to get a—a *scoop*?" He looked at Elisa questioningly. "That is the correct word?"

She nodded. "An American news term."

"Ah, yes." Beneš said thoughtfully. "I have made her promise not to talk about it next time we dance and in return, Herr Murphy, you shall have your *scoop*. Shall we adjourn to my office? We can talk while the colonel keeps your lovely wife company. He can dance with only one arm. Indeed, she will be much safer with a one-armed man."

Murphy smiled his thanks to Elisa and followed the president and his covey of bodyguards out of the ballroom.

⋐ঌ

Another kind of music was being played in Berlin. As the candles of Hradcany flickered hopefully, the Hitler Youth lit their torches and followed rank upon rank of SS Blackshirts in an endless march to honor the pagan German gods. From the balcony of the Chancellery, Hitler stood with arm outstretched above them in blessing. As the fires of the torches illuminated him, a million voices joined in this song of praise:

"Adolf Hitler is our savior, our hero.
He is the noblest being in all the world.
For Hitler we live!
For Hitler we die!
Our Hitler is our lord
Who rules a brave new world!"

If such adoration pleased the Führer, his pleasure was not reflected in his face. Grim, unmoving, he watched them. These were his people, and he was their god. The seven hundred thousand youths he had torn from the church only four years earlier now became the fulfillment of his prophecy. *"I will see again in the eyes of youth the gleam of beasts of prey!"*

Tonight, those young eyes shone the flame of hatred. They reflected the face of their Führer. Their lord.

If parents grieved for their lost children, no one listened—not even God, it seemed. There was a new god in Germany now, a new order.

Hour after hour the procession continued. When other members of his Nazi entourage tired of the sameness of the spectacle and moved restlessly from the balcony, the Führer did not notice.

The thump of drums permeated even the thick walls of the Chancellery, where Admiral Canaris had retired for a few minutes' respite from the racket.

Colonel Oster sipped a cup of cold coffee and leaned in to ask Canaris, "How does our Führer keep his arm up like that all the night?" There was a twinkle in his eyes, and Canaris shut him off with a look of warning. Hermann Göring stood gorging himself at the buffet table not ten feet away. He stuffed his belly with food and filled his ears with gossip. Any critical word would find its way back to Hitler.

Canaris raised his eyes to Thomas von Kleistmann, who chatted amiably with Göring. Göring had flown with the young man's father over France in the Great War. He had been present when von Kleistmann's father had been killed. This fact had boosted the career of Thomas in spite of his unfortunate entanglement with the daughter of a Jew.

Ah well, such youthful foolishness could be forgiven. Hermann Göring bore the young officer no ill will. Together they would forget the past mistakes and march forward for the Fatherland.

The conversation between Thomas and Göring pleased Admiral Canaris. Such attention brought von Kleistmann that much closer to Hitler's inner circle. Such nearness might yield an unexpected item of information to help their cause. To stop the inevitable. To stop the god of war from overtaking them all.

Colonel Oster raised an eyebrow in astonishment. "Our Thomas is doing well," he said as he tasted a sandwich. "It was a good idea to call him back from Paris for the holiday."

"Göring was fond of his father. Wilhelm von Kleistmann was a hero for the Fatherland. It cannot hurt us if Göring and Himmler bring him close to the Führer." His words were barely audible. He kept his eyes fixed on a beautiful young woman who was talking to yet another member of Hitler's inner circle. Anyone watching Canaris would have suspected that he had an interest in her, that his whispered words were some obscene appreciation of the woman provided for the pleasure of the officers at the review.

Oster nodded and smiled as the young woman noticed them. "That fat, overstuffed hog has spent the whole evening at the buffet table. Von Kleistmann will have to learn to eat like a pig if he is to keep up with him."

Canaris turned toward the heaping table. "And what do you suppose they are talking about?" Just then Göring threw his head back in a burst of laughter.

"Certainly not Czechoslovakia," Oster retorted dryly.

"Nor Jews." Canaris walked the brief distance to the buffet and took a plate as if he wanted to eat. Göring spotted Canaris and good-naturedly slapped him on the back.

"A good fellow you have here, Canaris! I have just been getting reacquainted with the son of Willie von Kleistmann!"

"I thought perhaps it was only fair for Thomas to share in the celebration remembering the fallen—"

"Ah, yes! The fallen! Just what we were talking about, eh, Thomas?" Göring nudged Thomas in the ribs and laughed again. "Yes, yes! The fallen! We were discussing the difference between the whores in Paris and the whores in Berlin! There is no difference, eh, Thomas?"

As if in agreement, Thomas shrugged. It was plain to see that Hermann Göring was drunk. Not out of control, but certainly drunk.

With half a smile Oster added, "I would have thought you would be talking about the difference between French art and German art." Oster knew that Göring had amassed a fortune in collecting the art of arrested Jews. The jibe went right past Göring.

"Whores! Art! What's the difference? Culture is culture, *ja*?" Göring stuffed a slice of ham in his mouth and continued to talk. "And we agree that German culture is the purest . . . the most *spiritual.*"

Thomas cleared his throat. "Perhaps more spiritualist than spiritual." He raised his eyes toward the doors that led to the balcony and the torchlight procession. There was indeed an eerie spiritual quality to it. Göring did not notice the look of understanding that passed among the men around him.

"German culture," he roared again. "Haven't you read Rosenberg's papers? The most unfortunate thing that happened to our tribe was the advent of Christianity. This religion of weaklings . . ." Now Göring was on the offensive. He was well aware that Canaris was a Catholic. He bowed in mock apology. "In most cases, not all."

Canaris did not comment. This was the language that begged for confrontation, and any confrontation in the matter of the church was dangerous. "So—" Canaris attempted a smile—"you have decided that the ladies of Paris cannot be compared with those of the Fatherland—"

"Yes!" Göring interrupted. "But I still have only half convinced him about German art. Perhaps—" he patted his wide belly as though he had finally had enough—"perhaps I can show you something to convince you about that also, *ja*?" He took Thomas by the arm and motioned for Canaris and Oster to follow.

"The parade—" Thomas tried to protest as Göring dragged him out into an enormous marble corridor and then walked toward the elevator.

"There will be hours more of this yet." Göring would not be dissuaded. "The Führer will not come in until the last little Nazi has goose-stepped past him. Come, come. I'll show you."

Drawn by a morbid curiosity, Thomas, Canaris, and Oster boarded the elevator with their intoxicated guide. Göring ran the elevator himself. His cheeks were flushed with excitement, and his eyes were bright like a child playing hooky from school. He laughed as he moved the lever and the elevator lurched downward with a loud whine. Göring prattled on about the virtues of German artists and the fact that Hitler himself was an artist and a man of great spiritual superiority. Did not the Führer possess the genius and the sensitivity to move the very soul of the German people as the gods of old had done?

Canaris and Oster exchanged glances. Yes. Hitler was an artist. A failed artist. How much better for them all if he had been accepted into the Vienna Institute of Art and was painting pictures instead of rearranging maps.

The elevator plunged downward. Deep beneath the ground level, a catacomb of rooms and reinforced concrete had been built for the Führer and his staff in the event of war. Göring had laughed and told Hitler that if any enemy bombers ever broke through to drop even one bomb on German soil, Göring would change his name to Meyers and wear a yellow star. For now, the rooms held a wealth of confiscated art.

"You are lucky I bring you here." Göring smiled, showing yellow teeth, as the elevator doors slid open. Beyond were utter blackness and silence, a heavy contrast to the cheering jubilation and tramp of boots on the streets far above them.

The three guests exchanged glances as Göring stepped out into the dark hall and waited for them to follow.

Canaris was first. "Darkness," he quipped in a humorless tone. "So this is the German art and culture you have brought us halfway to hell to see?"

Göring laughed, unaware of the bitterness that was thick in the voice of the speaker. "God creates light and beauty out of darkness, Herr Admiral." Göring clicked his heels and bowed slightly as he reached out to touch a light switch.

A string of bare bulbs illuminated gray concrete block walls. The German swastika emblem, topped by an eagle, was the only adornment in this drab corridor.

Göring marched ahead of the silent trio. The air was thick and the weight of the earth seemed to press in on them. Only Göring did not notice.

"In there, we keep the Raphael." He gestured toward one door after another. "There Rubens. A da Vinci or two in there . . . " Göring seemed immensely pleased but did not open the doors of those rooms or offer to let them see the stolen treasures. "The Führer is planning a huge museum in his hometown, you know. Speer is designing it now. It shall be the greatest and the largest in Europe." Now he paused in front of a drab metal door that looked just like any other. "And there will be a special room for the work in here. You will see. Proof. It is absolute proof."

"Proof?" Oster sounded amused. "Of what?"

In reply, Göring threw open the door and switched on the light. Before them, taking up nearly an entire wall, was a painting so frightening and fearful that Thomas backed up a step and stood holding tightly to the doorknob.

Demons and transparent human spirits writhed in torment across the dark canvas. Above it all, astride a powerful horse, Adolf Hitler peered from a whirling mass of smoke and bloody vapor. His eyes peered at them from beneath the dark shock of hair. Lips were tight beneath the small mustache. There was indeed a power in this morbid likeness that sent a chill up the spine of the little audience.

Tears filled Göring's eyes and at last he spoke with a drunken slur. "What did I tell you? A perfect likeness, ja?"

Canaris spoke first. "Perfect. Hardly the sort of painting that will excite the masses to anything but fear."

Göring turned to him in wonder. "But don't you see? You don't recognize the artist, Herr Admiral?" There was a strange smile on his lips. "It is the work of Franz von Stuck."

"Franz von Stuck?" Oster stepped forward. "Impossible!"

Thomas moved forward to look at the signature at the bottom of the painting. *Franz von Stuck. My first oil painting. 1889.*

Göring gave the explanation. "The year Adolf Hitler was *born*. You *see*? And Franz von Stuck painted this—the birth of the German god Wotan."

"God of Creation. God of Destruction. God of Opposites." Oster's usual flippant tone faded off with a shudder.

"Proof! Hitler *is* our god, you see. Can't you see? Von Stuck was *given* this vision! This prophecy! *It is the Führer!*" Göring's voice was an awed whisper. He continued to gaze at the evil face that stared out from the center of the whirling mist. It *was* Hitler! There was no mistaking the features.

Thomas backed from the room. He felt suffocated beneath the weight of the earth and the dark force of the eyes that gleamed from the painting like those of a ravenous beast. It was this gleam the Führer desired in the eyes of his followers. Thomas heard his own heart drumming like the snare drums of the procession.

Nothing but a painting, the year of his birth!

Adolf Hitler! God of Destruction! How could a handful of mere men fight against—

Suddenly the eyes of the painting bored into Thomas' soul, searching out his hidden plans and hopes. Some said Hitler could read minds. Everyone knew that he called upon mediums to read the future. Could he see them now, this evil god? Did he inwardly count the men who did not stand beside him on the balcony with outstretched arms? The thought made Thomas want to run. But where could he hide from such eyes?

5

The Face of Evil

Albert Sporer had been placed in solitary confinement, yet he shared his cell with many others. He sat on the straw pallet and drew his knees up to his chest as three large rats scurried to fight to the death for a small piece of eclair. These creatures were the true inheritors of Hradcany, he thought. They owned the foundations of Prague, as had their fathers and generations of vermin before them.

Tonight Sporer leaned against the damp wall of his tiny cubicle and watched as the rats attacked and bit and tumbled across the slimy stones in mortal combat. *To die for an eclair!* The miniature drama amused Sporer. He touched his tongue to the custard and then bit off another tiny fragment and spit it into the fight. Four more rats rushed from a crack between the stones and joined the battle. Another morsel. The rage was renewed. The vicious attacks became more violent.

There was much that man could learn from rats. Indeed, a morsel of promise, a half-truth tossed into the road, could cause men to kill one another. Was this not the plan the Führer had for the Czechs in the Sudetenland? Toss the German citizens some promise of supremacy over their Czech neighbors, and they would riot and kill in order to join the Reich. Such a plan would work—of that Sporer was certain. Unlike his furry cell mates, he would walk out of this place soon enough.

Sporer raised his eyes to the low stone roof of the cell. He took another bite of the eclair and smiled. They would not dare execute him. They did not have the courage for that. They would leave him here as a bargaining chip, to be tossed onto the table when the time came. And it would come. President Beneš would be forced to sit across from the

German-Czechs like Henlein and Frank, and he would ask them what they wanted in exchange for peace within the borders of Czechoslovakia. Sporer would be one of the items they would request.

Sporer would be free, and he would retrace the steps that had brought him here into the dark dungeon of Hradcany. Here in the midst of the stench that permeated these stone walls, Sporer could see everything quite clearly: the woman in Otto Wattenbarger's office, the way Otto protected her. Had she not crossed the border from Austria to Czechoslovakia the first night of the Anschluss? Ah, yes. And that same woman had arrived at the National Theatre in time to stop the murder of Beneš. Elisa was her name. Otto's woman. And now, at this moment, directly above his head, that woman was dancing. Is that not what the guard had said? The woman who had thwarted him was dancing with President Beneš!

The conclusions had come to Sporer the instant he had seen Elisa framed in the doorway of the presidential box. He had known then who had betrayed him, who even now was in Vienna betraying the cause of one Volk, one Reich, one Führer! Sporer would go free, and he would settle with Otto. He would make the beautiful face of the woman look somewhat different in her mirror, and then he would display her for all to see. The penalty for traitors to the Reich is not merely a cell filled with rats or an eclair sent with a mocking message! Yes, when the Gestapo crossed the frontiers of Czechoslovakia, Albert Sporer would march with them. And on the points of two lances he would carry the heads of those who had mocked him and his Führer.

◗◖

Thomas recognized the two leaders of the Czech-Nazi Party immediately from among the General Staff officers who crowded the room. Karl Hermann Frank and Konrad Henlein looked out of place in their ill-fitting brown uniforms. Whenever the Führer mentioned the problem of racial Germans living in Czech territories, they moved slightly in their chairs as though the very reason they had come to see Hitler had somehow been altered.

As Hitler paced across the front of the conference room and back again, Thomas watched only the two Czech-Nazis. Hitler spoke of the need for the German Army to cross the border. The two men exchanged unhappy looks. Perhaps they had only wanted financial aid from their German counterparts. Was it possible they did not welcome the thought of a German invasion of the Sudetenland just as the now-bewildered Austrians regretted the German invasion of their homeland?

The face of the Führer reddened as his declarations escalated. "So, a man like Sporer means nothing to us!"

No one dared to interrupt.

"He has failed us. Beneš still stalks around the Prague castle making speeches about the Czech determination to fight." Hitler raised his fist to the heavens and shook it. "Sporer failed in his effort and so has failed the German race. He has failed his Führer! And if they kill him? What difference will that make to us? You imbeciles fail to see that every political disadvantage can be turned for our benefit! They will try him. *Ja!* He will be found guilty and executed."

Again Henlein frowned and glanced at Frank.

"And what can be done to stop it, mein Führer?" Henlein asked in a croaking voice.

"Stop it? We welcome it! Such an event is exactly what we need if you are doing your job with the people in the Sudetenland. Riots—that is what is called for. And with those riots will be inevitable clashes of the Czech military against the civilian population! People will die!" Hitler shrieked those words and slammed his fist on the table. "People *must* die! If they do not, then what reason have we to intervene? You and you—" he pointed first at Henlein and then at Frank— "you must make certain of this. And always you must demand more of that pitiful Czech president than he will give you."

"But . . . we have a price on our heads! He will not negotiate with either of us!"

The Führer's eyes blazed. "He will! He will beg you to come to the table! Beg you to stop the bloodshed! And when he asks what you want? You ask for more and more and more until he cannot give you what you want." Hitler looked pleased. He swept a hand toward his military staff. "Then we will enter. It will come. October first."

Hitler was finished. Exhaustion showed in his eyes. He turned to look at the door as though he were too weary to walk to it. Without so much as a good night, he left the room. Henlein and Frank looked pleased but confused.

General Franz Halder stood and nodded slightly. "So you have your assignments," he addressed the two men. "And so now we continue our staff meeting. You will excuse us. Heil Hitler." With that he dismissed the two, and they fumbled clumsily to gather up notes for questions they had not been allowed to ask.

The bile of disdain rose in Thomas' throat as Henlein and Frank left the conference room and shut the door quietly behind them. These were the stuff great treasons were made of. Between the two of them all of Czechoslovakia had been condemned and would certainly fall, unless—

Canaris stood and addressed the group. "I propose we adjourn to a more comfortable place." No man would dare speak openly in this room. No doubt it was filled with hidden listening devices.

"A brilliant plan," said one for the sake of the microphones.

"He has never been wrong yet."

"Such a Führer we have!"

"I only regret he does not allow a drop of schnapps in the entire Chancellery."

"It would make our conversations much more civil."

The lack of alcohol on the premises was, in fact, a positive aspect of Hitler's personal preferences. It gave these men good reason to leave the grounds. No doubt the Führer would hear such words and would be pleased that he had made grown men scurry off like truant schoolboys for a little taste of schnapps. Such small displays of power over the personal lives of his officers gave him great enjoyment.

Thomas left the Chancellery with Canaris. He stared at the huge columns of stone and the carved eagles at the top of each floodlit pillar. The cobbles were littered with trash from the night's orgy of power. The square was quiet. Empty. Thomas looked up toward the balcony where Hitler had stood for hours with his arm outstretched.

Thomas gasped as he saw the form of Hitler standing there again. Canaris followed the gaze of Thomas, and in a final gesture he raised his hand as if to salute. Hitler remained unmoving. Brooding. His face was illuminated from below by the lights. His face was the very image of the German god Wotan, who had stared out from the canvas of the painting tonight.

Was such a likeness cultivated by Hitler? Had he planned the makeup and the lighting and the setting? Had he made certain that Canaris and Oster and Thomas were taken to view the occult masterpiece? Or was Adolf Hitler truly this dark pagan god of German creation and German destruction? The thought made Thomas shudder. The skin on the back of his neck tightened as Hitler stepped back into the curtains. The shadow of Evil moved across the square, touching each man who walked there.

↬⟨♥⟩

There was a brooding silence among the General Staff after the meeting with the Führer. Thomas sat to the rear of the room, just behind Admiral Canaris, as the German staff officers and commanders paced and smoked and mentally plotted their course of action before they uttered a word.

For Thomas, the fear he had felt crossing the Chancellery Square had entirely vanished. He was exultant and hopeful as he inwardly recited the names of the great German patriots who were gathered here. Generals Franz Halder, Ludwig Beck, Georg Karl Heinrich von Stuelpnagel, and Erwin von Witzleben, commander of the Berlin garrison. General Georg Thomas, controller of armament. General Erich von Brockdorff-Ahlefeld, commander of the Potsdam garrison. General Count Wolf von Helldorf, in charge of the Berlin police.

General Halder stood facing the window that looked down on the dark, empty Berlin street. "General Walther von Brauchitsch, commander in chief of the army, has been informed of our gathering and has given his approval," Halder said quietly.

His words vanquished whatever doubts might have remained in the minds of the military leaders. Halder turned toward Canaris and, looking past him, focused his stern gaze on Thomas.

"You have spoken to the leaders of Britain." He stepped nearer, and his eyes seemed to bore through Thomas as if the general could search the intentions of those leaders through this junior officer of the Abwehr.

"I have met with Anthony Eden," Thomas offered.

"Former foreign secretary to the Chamberlain administration." Canaris tossed a file folder onto the table. "His opposition to Italy—indeed, his opposition to Chamberlain's offered friendship with the Führer—led to his downfall."

Halder frowned and flipped open the cover, revealing the handsome young British politician who had fallen victim to German pressure in his own country. "Yes. A pity. He would have been useful to us. Sympathetic, at least." He glanced up sharply. "But you have also had discussions with Winston Churchill; is this correct?"

Thomas nodded. "He alone seems to see the situation clearly."

"He is without any real power." Canaris sighed, tossing yet another file full of clippings from British newspapers that criticized Churchill's pessimism. "He is called by the London *Times* 'The Jeremiah of our age.'"

"Is this supposed to be a criticism of Churchill?" General Beck seemed surprised. "Do they not know that the prophet Jeremiah was accurate in his cry of doom?"

"Read for yourself, General," Canaris commented dryly. "They mean to offer no compliment to Churchill."

Von Helldorf smiled cynically and snuffed out his cigarette in the overflowing ashtray. "Can it be that the English press is as taken by our dear Adolf as the German press seems to be?"

"What German press?" von Brockdorff growled. "We have no German press left. All journalists with any sense have fled or been beheaded. Like Walter Kronenberger." Von Brockdorff was well-known for his disapproval of forced sterilization and abortion. He had followed the Kronenberger case to its bloody end in Vienna. "All we have left to us is Doktor Joseph Goebbels and his Ministry of Propaganda. Have we forgotten? That club-footed little fiend! The question of the hour is why such a monster has not been pronounced racially unfit by the Reich and sterilized."

"He must be among the first to fall into our net." General von Stuelpnagel narrowed his eyes and shifted in his chair at the vision of Goebbels behind bars.

General Halder patted the dagger he wore on his belt. "And then perhaps we of the General Staff may demonstrate our opinion of who in Germany is worthy to be sterilized, eh?"

A low chuckle of angry agreement filled the room. "Our Führer must be included in that. And Hermann Göring, of course!" Canaris added to the amusement.

"Have we left out Himmler? Sadistic little schoolmaster of the SS?" Halder finished the roster of Nazi leaders.

General von Witzleben cleared his throat loudly and tapped his fingers impatiently on the tabletop. "Such conversation is amusing among angry schoolboys. But it will take much more than a small dagger to emasculate the most powerful and evil men in our nation. We must have a plan."

"The Führer has marked October first as his date for the invasion of Czechoslovakia. That gives us time to make our plans and to carry them out," Halder replied coolly.

The others leaned forward. It was time to get down to business. "We have the summer to plan the coup," Beck added.

Halder's gaze moved again to Thomas. "You must maintain contact with the British leaders."

"Churchill is not a leader," Canaris interrupted impatiently. "He is now without political power in England. Those men who hold the reins of government in England have been warned by the British ambassador here in Berlin to receive no unauthorized visits from anyone claiming to represent the German Reich."

"Ah, yes. That little English pipsqueak Neville Henderson. Totally enraptured by Hermann Göring, I hear. Göring took him stag hunting at Karinhall and the two are fast friends. Even dear Adolf is on fine terms with Henderson." Von Helldorf's voice was filled with contempt for the British ambassador who seemed so vastly provincial and ignorant in affairs of state that everyone wondered how he had come to hold such a prominent position in the foreign service. Even Hermann Göring, who pretended friendship with the little man, snickered behind his back.

General von Witzleben grimaced distastefully at the thought of

Henderson. "So he has given the advice of Göring and Hitler to the English leadership. They will not deal with anyone not sent as an official representative of the Führer." He threw his hands up in frustration. "What are we to do then?"

Again the room was silent. Thomas furrowed his brow in thought. Perhaps there was more power in the voice of Winston Churchill than the generals thought. Perhaps . . .

Canaris spoke quietly, choosing his words with care. Already every man in this room was a target for execution if their plans were even suspected. "Perhaps it is just as well we cannot make contact with Chamberlain and his weak cabinet. Could we be safe if we took them into our confidence?"

"No," responded a quiet chorus of voices.

"Well, then," Canaris said, "we must simply maintain contact with Churchill. Inform him of our hopes, even if we do not reveal all our plans. Thomas here has the man's confidence. Perhaps we may gain some understanding of the mood in the British parliament. And we may be able to present some facts to Churchill that will awaken the English to their own peril as well as the peril of Czechoslovakia."

Canaris gazed around the room, meeting each man's questions with his piercing blue eyes. "Churchill is a man of honor, as we in this room are men of honor. The British press may be rife with fools, but it is still a free press. The American press may also be crying for peace and the policy of appeasement, but there are some who are not afraid to speak openly." He exhaled loudly and sat back. "Hitler believes himself to be the German god of Creation and of Destruction. As sane Christian officers, we have no duty but to stop this madness. It is indeed madness, gentlemen."

☙

President Beneš sat opposite Murphy in a large overstuffed chair that made the tiny man seem even smaller. He crossed his legs and leaned back as two brandy snifters were placed on the table between them.

Murphy was mentally filing away the details of the president's office. Broad, burled walnut desk, so big it might easily serve as a bed. Dark oak-paneled walls that glowed with a reddish tint in the light of the chandelier. Floor-to-ceiling bookshelves filled with books by Americans about American democracy. Next to the bookshelf, a montage of American presidents—Washington, Jefferson, Lincoln. In the center of that, a black-and-white photograph taken at the construction site of the Lincoln Memorial, the young Beneš standing before the statue of Lincoln.

As if reading Murphy's thoughts, Beneš sipped his brandy thoughtfully and then remarked, "President Lincoln. A hero of mine. I went to school in America, you see. Learned everything one might learn about the history of your people. Fascinating. Something a young democracy like ours hopes to emulate." He raised his eyebrows and looked back at the photograph. "Your President Lincoln was a brave man. Civil war is a tragic thing. And yet he was able to save your country."

So this is it, Murphy thought. *He brings up the issues tearing his own country apart by bringing up our Civil War. He is giving the American journalist the angle on the story.* It was a good angle, and Murphy let himself be led by Beneš.

"You came very near to imitating President Lincoln in the theatre," Murphy commented.

"The comparisons have been drawn in the American press and elsewhere." Beneš studied his brandy, swirled it once, and inhaled the aroma casually. "You submitted the story, did you not?"

Murphy shrugged slightly. "It seemed to fit."

"It fits very well. Your American readership will see this?"

Even a blind man would see that the Czechs tottered on the brink of civil war. The racial Germans bordering Germany in the west shrieked for autonomy. Their leader Henlein was in direct contact with Hitler. The attempt of Albert Sporer to kill Beneš was simply one more incident in a long list that continued to grow daily. "America is well aware of what is happening here."

"Aware, yes. The question is whether they care what happens in our faraway little democracy."

Murphy could not answer that question. After all, his story about the assassination attempt did not make the headlines. The strikes at the Goodyear tire plant in Akron dominated the front page. Matters of domestic importance generally took the highest place on the publishers' list of priorities. Even in Trump Publications, European issues were far down the line.

"What are your plans, Mr. President?" Murphy avoided expressing his opinion on the last question.

"Plans? We plan to stand firmly united as one nation, of course. The same plan your President Lincoln had for the United States." He smiled.

This was no scoop. Merely platitudes. "More specifically, it is well-known now that the Henleinists in the Sudetenland are being given instructions from Berlin. The Nazi Party is alive and well and growing within your borders—"

"As it is in the borders of your own nation," Beneš replied without a trace of emotion.

The comment threw Murphy off a bit. "Yes, well—"

"We were deep in negotiations with Henlein when we heard that the German Army was poised at our doorstep ready to strike. Even though we had met nearly every demand of Henlein's Nazi Party—virtual autonomy for the Sudetenland, independent elections of racially German officials, and so on." He waved his hand. "Even though we offered him what he wanted, he broke off the talks. You must ask yourself why, Mr. Murphy. And then you must answer the question for your readers so they might understand what is happening here."

He paused and sipped his brandy again. Then he continued slowly and deliberately, as though he were explaining the matter to a child. "Henlein and his cronies have been ordered by Berlin to ask for more than we could ever give them. And yet we are prepared to give them anything they ask for. We do not wish a civil war in Czechoslovakia, you see. Still, they have broken off talks. They want the flag of the Reich to fly from the spires of Hradcany. They wish to give Herr Hitler any excuse to march against us. If Hitler takes the fortifications in our Sudetenland, it is only a matter of time before he is here. In Prague. In this office."

Again Murphy repeated the question, "What are your plans?"

President Beneš leaned forward, his eyes fierce with determination. "To fight them, of course. Britain and France will stand by their treaty with us. They must, or the war they so dread will begin here!" His fist was clenched as he spoke. Here was a man with his back against a very high stone wall, and he had no choice but to fight. Murphy stored every look on the face of Beneš, memorized every nuance in his words.

"Do you believe it will come to that?"

Beneš smiled slightly as he considered his own doubts. "Honestly? No. The Germans cannot desire war. They seek to take our country without firing a shot. The Great Powers and the League of Nations will not allow this to happen. They are not so foolish. Certainly they are not."

"Hitler says he never intended to invade two weeks ago—"

"Hmmm. Yes. He did say that." Beneš raised his eyebrow in a way that expressed his amusement at the story. "I read it in the papers also."

"Would you Czechs fight Germany alone?"

"Yes." The answer was unequivocal. "We would have no choice. But surely we have shown our determination already."

"And your ultimate plan for the Sudetenland?"

"We will continue to negotiate with those of our citizens who have racial grievances. Let me put it to you this way: Suppose in your own tragic Civil War that the North and the South had managed to come to full agreement? Suppose the president accepted the demands of the Southern states? Yet even with those demands met, the British had supplied the South with arms and men, and had stirred up small segments of society to riot against the government. What would be the motives of the British to have done such a thing?"

Murphy searched his mind for the details of history that might have encouraged such policy from the English. "Forty years before they had lost the War of 1812 to us. Before that they lost the Colonies. Perhaps . . . they might have wished to regain their hold in the South?" Murphy enjoyed such games. Again he was being led by Beneš, who was playing *what if* in order to demonstrate his own precarious position.

"Yes. And so it is with the government of Hitler. Henlein's followers believe they are negotiating for more independence in our Sudeten territory. They are accepting funds from the Führer, who will chew them up and spit them out." Beneš sighed. "Hitler cares nothing for the Germans who live in Czechoslovakia." He shook his head. "They will be devoured like the rest of us. Hitler wishes to take our land. Has he not written it? Why do they not read what he has written on the matter? From here he will progress to the east—if he has his way. But he will not, Mr. Murphy." The old confidence returned. "We will master this problem, and it will stop here."

Murphy believed the little man. It was easy to understand why he held the respect and confidence of his people. It was also simple to see why Hitler so desperately wanted Beneš dead. "These are things I will relay to the States," Murphy promised as he ran through a dozen more questions he wanted to ask. "And now, would you—"

Beneš silenced him with an upraised finger. "And now, Mr. Murphy, we must talk about you for a moment before we end our little chat, yes?" The eyes showed a gentle concern that flattered Murphy in spite of the fact that he wanted to continue the political discussion.

"Me?"

"A little information we have picked up." Beneš raised his hand to the silent assistant who stood a few paces away. The man laid a file folder in the hand of the president and then with a bow, stepped back. "Here is your *scoop* . . . did you call it?"

Murphy sat forward in his chair. He was quite satisfied with the information he was being given. What could be more of a scoop than a personal interview with the president of the beleaguered little nation? "I appreciate—"

Again, the wave of a hand silenced him. Now the eyes of the president became troubled as he silently skimmed the file. Several minutes passed. At last, Beneš looked up. "You speak several languages quite well. Do you read our language also, Mr. Murphy?"

"Not fluently," he answered apologetically.

"Then I shall interpret this for you, my friend." Another long, searching look. "We have it on good authority that your lives are in great danger here in Prague."

"Our lives?"

"You and your wife. Beautiful woman," he added. "But beauty is of little value to the Gestapo and the SS. Both of you will be killed if you stay in Prague. Our agents send a warning that you must not return to Germany or Austria for any reason."

"We had not intended to do that."

"Wise. The Gestapo has an order that you are to be arrested as spies and executed summarily. I would imagine that the execution would include elements of torture in order to make you tell where you got your information about the attempt on my life."

Murphy frowned and nodded slowly. So it was official in the German circles. American citizenship made little difference in such a matter. Men and women, regardless of nationality, had simply disappeared without a trace in the Reich. Someone would certainly raise a stink about it, but that would not do them a bit of good after the deed was accomplished. "Okay." Murphy swallowed hard as he momentarily reverted to speaking English. "We expected this."

"Perhaps you have not expected that even here the order stands."

"Here in Prague?" Murphy repeated.

"If the president of a country is not safe, then what protection do you imagine you might have here? There are agents of the Gestapo and Hitler's SS in every capital in Europe now. Mr. Murphy, I would recommend that you take your lovely wife and leave Europe—soon."

"We had been planning to go back to the States. Eventually."

"Soon." Beneš repeated the word with urgency. He tapped the file. "And once your wife is safe, her family as well. You must arrange for their immigration as soon as possible. Have you not heard of the German law of the blood? When one family member transgresses against the will of the Führer, then all members of the family are held responsible."

"Theo and Anna." Murphy said their names absently.

"Yes. And their sons."

"You know about them as well?"

"Dear Mr. Murphy, there is little we do not know. And I assure you, although it is difficult to admit, our intelligence service is not even half as thorough as the Nazi Gestapo. Himmler has done an excellent and ruthless job in his gathering of information. Some areas of information are incomplete. There are still men working for us who are in the midst of their operation, but the bottom line is this—you risked your lives to save mine. Your lives are still at risk. The risk to you grows more extreme

each hour you remain here in Prague. The Nazi regime is built on ruthless terror and . . . vengeance. You and Elisa are targets now."

"You are certain? We are in danger now?" Murphy had been so happy
that even the slightest thought of danger had not entered his mind. Now
these words made him want to hurry down the hallway and wrap his arm
protectively around Elisa's waist. The thought of losing her . . .

"Do not doubt what I tell you. We have stationed guards around the
Lindheim home. You will not see them, but be assured they are watching carefully. Two men have been arrested near the place in the last
week."

"Arrested? But why?"

"We are handling the matter quietly. But it is well you remain vigi-
lant in the time you remain here—which must not be much longer, I
pray, for your sake."

Murphy absorbed the blows like a punch-drunk prizefighter. "I will
contact my publisher."

"We have taken the liberty of doing that for you."

"What?"

"One of our American agents has spoken face-to-face with Mr.
Trump on the matter."

"Well . . ." Murphy was speechless. Should he thank President Beneš
for such dreadful news? "I don't know quite what to say."

"Good-bye seems to be the most sensible thing to say, Mr. Murphy. I
cannot say that it has been pleasant meeting you; however, it has, I trust,
been most enlightening to both of us."

Murphy hesitated. "Most enlightening. But I . . . I don't want Elisa to
know about . . . about the fact that we might be . . . some sort of target."

The president pressed his lips together. "I had assumed as much.
That is why I met with you alone."

"Her family . . . her father . . . well, you obviously know the details."

Beneš nodded as Murphy continued. "They have been through
enough already. Getting Elisa into the country is no problem since we're
married. And we have already made contact with the State Department
about the Kronenberger child. A temporary visa for medical aid will be
issued. But they have not been encouraging about Theo and Anna and
their boys. The quotas, you know. Filled. And not just the U.S. quotas."

Beneš sadly shook his head. "We have not turned the refugees from
our doors here in Prague. They come here even knowing the fact that we
are Hitler's next target. Have you seen the thousands that crowd outside
the embassies to beg for visas? The press of desperate human beings has
closed Embassy Avenue to traffic. And they continue to come again and
again."

Beneš extended his hand. Murphy bowed slightly in the custom of Europe. He was saying farewell to far more than one man. "Perhaps one day I will be able to tell my wife and her family of your help this evening. Until then, I alone must offer you my thanks, and my prayers, that it will go well for you and your country."

A smile played on the lips of Beneš. "Then farewell, John Murphy. A safe journey for you."

6

Flight from Terror

"You are awfully quiet." Elisa leaned her head against Murphy's arm as they walked slowly onto the Charles Bridge.

Murphy did not answer, but turned to gaze back toward Hradcany Castle, where he knew the light in President Beneš' office still burned. Murphy sighed, then looked past the row of stone saints that lined the bridge to where St. Nepomuk stood before an audience of flickering votive candles.

"Are you cold?" he asked Elisa as the damp mists of the river enfolded them. A chill much colder than the river mists penetrated Murphy's heart. He had been subdued and preoccupied since he had emerged from the office of the president.

"I'm fine." Elisa hugged his arm tighter, aware that something deeply troubled Murphy.

They walked on in silence for a few more steps until Murphy paused beside the statue of St. Nepomuk. He and Elisa had walked all over the city of Prague for weeks. He had stopped to kiss her a thousand times— in front of the library, on the steps of Tyn Church, outside the butcher shop, on the curb where the trolley car made its stop. Her kisses and her smile had nourished him. He had given no thought that any other soul on earth might be watching them.

Tonight she tilted her face up toward his. Her lips were parted in an expectant smile. Was there ever a more romantic place than here on the Charles Bridge? In the flickering candlelight with the rush of the river against the ancient pilings below them, the air was sweet, mingling with the scent of her skin.

And yet . . . suddenly the night had become full of unseen watchers. In the dark shadows enemies nudged one another and whispered, "*He will kiss her again here. Now is our chance. One little shove and they are drowned in the Moldau.*" The windows of crooked houses now seemed like dark eyes concealing the evil that pursued them.

"Murphy?" Elisa whispered. "What . . . ?"

He stood very still, looking past her to the gatehouse where their taxi had dropped them several minutes before. There was movement in the shadows. The substance of his fears took the shape of reality. Human forms watched them from beneath the arches.

Murphy took Elisa by the arm and pulled her back from the railing. They were sitting ducks out here on the bridge! Any crank with a rifle could pick them off easily. "Come on," he said roughly.

"Murphy?" She peered back toward the gatehouse where Murphy's gaze returned again and again. He quickened his pace until she was almost running to keep up with him. The chill of old fears swept over her, and she did not need to ask any more questions. The sickening feeling she had known in Vienna and Germany overtook her with a violence that shattered the delight she had carried with her from the party.

Home was just across the square, around a corner on the narrow lane. Breathlessly she clung to Murphy as their shoes echoed against the cobblestones. Steep gables appeared to lean toward them. In every shadow now lurked some unknown danger that Murphy felt, yet could not speak of.

Elisa's eyes brimmed with tears as they rounded the corner and came within sight of the brightly lit windows of the little Prague house. Warmth and safety were there. She broke free of Murphy's grasp and ran up the steps. Almost desperately she clanged the heavy iron door knocker as Murphy rushed up behind her and stood between her and the street with his eyes scanning every rooftop above them.

Anna opened the door with a smile, but the smile quickly faded as the two pushed in past her and Murphy slammed the door and bolted it.

"Children!" Anna cried. "What is it?"

Elisa exhaled loudly with relief, then turned in confusion toward Murphy. "What *was* it Murphy?"

How could he explain? Their circumstance had not changed at all except that now he *knew*. "Nothing." he shook his head. "I . . . I guess we just got a little spooked. I did, I mean. Like a couple of kids in the dark." He feigned an embarrassed laugh, and Elisa eyed him irritably.

"I was simply following Murphy, Mother," she said haughtily. "I was not spooked."

"Right. That's why you ran up the steps ahead of me."

"Well . . . " Anna looked from one to the other. "Theo has gone on to bed. He bids you good night. I will make you tea if you like, and then there is something important in the parlor."

⟳

Two telegrams waited on the glistening walnut piano. Anna had propped them up against a candlestick, and Murphy guessed that she had probably stared at them anxiously all night.

"Perhaps it is word from Leah." Anna smoothed her hair back from where it had fallen across her forehead. "Both of the wires came by the same courier not ten minutes after you had gone."

"Leah," Elisa said hopefully as she held the envelopes and closed her eyes in a hope that was almost unbearable. "Murphy, quick—" She shoved them into his hands.

He held the same hope. If Leah had escaped from Austria, she would certainly let them know where she was and what her plans were. Every day had been marred with the absence of that news. "You open them." He thought it would be best if Elisa read the words herself.

She shook her head and stamped her foot impatiently. The telegrams were addressed to him, the gesture said. Why was he wasting time?

Anna discreetly remained a few steps away as Murphy tore open the envelopes and began to read. Elisa pressed herself against his arm and had read through the first message before he finished.

"America!" she exclaimed. "So soon?"

Anna stepped nearer and stood tiptoe as she tried to see the message over Murphy's shoulder. "From Trump, my publisher in the States," he explained, then read aloud:

"Murphy Stop Most urgent you return States at once Stop You and wife booked with Kronenberger boy leaving Southampton the 15th on *Queen Mary* Stop Will meet you at dock in New York Stop Trump"

Anna sat down slowly on the piano bench. "The fifteenth? But that is only a few days. Oh dear! Leaving Prague so suddenly?"

Elisa seemed not to hear. She shook Murphy's arm impatiently. "The other one, Murphy," she urged. "Maybe it's from Leah." The thought of a trip to America had not yet penetrated her excitement.

Murphy grimaced as he read aloud the second wire. It was from Timmons and Johnson in Paris. Elisa groaned in disappointment at the signature.

"CALL PARIS INS OFFICE SUNDAY 2 PM PARIS TIME STOP
NEWS OF KIDS' FAMILY STOP TIMMONS AND JOHNSON"

The kids referred to in the wire were Charles and Louis. Timmons
and Johnson had obviously come across some important news about
the Kronenberger family.

Elisa could not muster any enthusiasm for that possibility. She
turned away from Murphy and stood with her hand on her forehead.
She was swaying slightly. Murphy laid the yellow telegrams back on the
piano and put his hands on her shoulders. Tomorrow was time enough
to consider a trip to the States and a phone call to Paris. For now, however, the weight of worry and uncertainty about Leah and Louis was almost crushing.

"No word." She sighed. "Still no word."

"They are all right," Anna answered softly. "Karl and Marta
Wattenbarger are capable people. Good people. If Otto reached the
farmhouse with them—"

"Oh, Mama!" Elisa cried as she turned to embrace Murphy. "We
don't even know that much! Don't even know if Otto got them out of Vienna. And if he didn't, we won't know . . . not ever . . . what has become
of them! There is no way to get through to the Wattenbargers."

Murphy stroked her hair. The white dress shimmered in the soft
lamplight. This was not the way he had hoped to end the evening. "You
can't let yourself worry about it anymore," he said gently.

"Not worry?" She drew back from him as though the words had
burned her. "How can I not worry? Haven't we been through enough agony when Papa was arrested? When will they leave us alone?" She pulled
loose and sank down next to Anna on the piano bench. She began to cry
softly as Anna put an arm around her.

Anna looked at her new son-in-law apologetically. For twenty-four
years she had been comforting Elisa. It was a hard habit to break. "Your
husband is right, Elisa," Anna chided, but not unkindly. "There is a hope
that heals and also a hope that can destroy you if you hold too tightly to
it. Hope first in the same hand that delivered your father. God knows
where Leah is, Elisa. Have you forgotten that?"

"Oh, Mama!" Elisa wept even harder now. Murphy looked helpless
and unhappy. He picked up the telegrams and put them down again.
Maybe it was better to let the women sort these things out.

"Anna," he began, "Elisa—I'm going on to bed now." He tugged at
his tie as if to make that point. "You two talk it over. I . . . wish the wires
had been what we were waiting for."

Elisa simply nodded. Anna gave him a reassuring wink. It would be all right. Elisa would pull herself together. Maybe tomorrow they could talk about something else. About a trip to America. About news of the Kronenberger family in Paris. *But for tonight*, Anna seemed to say in a look, *Elisa needs time to cry*. There had not been one tear shed since the night they had returned to Prague together. Perhaps loving Murphy had left no time for sadness and doubt about the fate of Leah.

"A good cry," Murphy muttered uncomfortably in English. "My mother used to say every woman needs one sometimes." He half smiled as Anna nodded. Then he gazed miserably at Elisa. He wished there were something he could say or do to cheer her up. When he made no move to leave, she looked up at him. Her eyes were bright with tears. *How can a woman look beautiful even when she cries?* he wondered. It made his heart squeeze.

"I'll be along later," she croaked.

He was being dismissed. There were things he just could not take care of for her. "Yes. Then . . . *Grüss Gott*, Elisa."

☙

Elisa closed her eyes and listened as Murphy's footsteps retreated down the hall. All the simmering worries about Leah and little Louis had surfaced with paralyzing intensity. She did not try to speak of it, nor did she need to. It was enough that Anna understood the silent grief of *not knowing*! Was there anything worse than this gnawing uncertainty? Why had she not heard from Leah? Obviously Leah had not yet been able to make her way to freedom. But was she safe? Had she been captured? Would there come a time when Elisa would be forced to tell Charles that his brother was dead as well?

Terrible images filled Elisa's mind like the plot of a tragic play. She imagined Nazi SS and Gestapo agents pursuing Leah through the mountain passes. The victims in the Vienna Gestapo headquarters suddenly had Leah's voice and Leah's face! Louis whimpered in a dark corner; then he shouted as he had that last horrible night in the apartment in Vienna, "I cannot go anywhere without him. I want Father! I want my mother!"

Tonight the reasons they had not left Vienna together were forgotten. Guilt hovered above Elisa. She was safe, and Leah was not! Why had she consented to their separation? It had made sense that night. Now it made no sense at all.

"You will be together again," Leah had promised Louis. She had not offered that comfort to Elisa. Leah had not said, "*We* will be together again." No. The two friends had said their farewells. Both, perhaps, had sensed that it was forever. At least for this lifetime. Still, Elisa could not accept the finality of that parting—not tonight, when reality crowded out the carefree joy she had felt with Murphy.

"Oh, Mama," she whispered to Anna, "tonight Murphy was afraid. I felt it in his hand. Saw it in his eyes, and suddenly I was terrified again."

Anna chose her words carefully. There was so much to fear. So many things that played upon the mind and called out from nightmares. "I feel it, too. A hundred times a day it all comes to me—what we may be facing, what many are facing now."

"How do we keep going?" Elisa shook her head in helpless frustration. "All around it is so dark."

Anna nodded. There was no sense in making such feelings sound trivial. To deny such fear was to lie. It was real. The darkness was real and the fears were justified. "When I am most afraid I remember what my mother used to say: 'Put on your hundred-year glasses, Anna, so you can see yourself a hundred years from now.' Where will you be in a hundred years? Where will I be? And Papa? And Wilhelm and Dieter? And your Murphy? And Leah?" Anna had listed the most important people in Elisa's life. In a hundred years they would all be together—somewhere besides Prague.

"A hundred years is a very long time to wait." Elisa managed a smile.

"It will pass much more quickly than you can imagine. And be certain, Elisa, it will pass."

"But in the meantime?"

"In the meantime you must finish your tea and wash your face and say your prayers."

"And go to America?" Elisa asked painfully.

"For the sake of Charles. Yes. There is much the boy still must go through, and we must be strong for the sake of the children, Elisa. We must teach them to live now, but also to see their lives through those hundred-year glasses." Anna frowned. "Such a point of view somehow makes each moment, each action, each prayer seem much more important, I think. Especially in such dark times as these."

Just for a moment Elisa slipped into the dark room where Charles slept. The cello case was open in the corner. The child opened it each night before he went to sleep. Its dignified presence seemed to comfort him with the promise that he would indeed see his brother Louis and dear Leah once again.

Elisa let her eyes linger on the instrument. She pictured Leah sitting in the shadows behind it. If she listened carefully, she could hear music. Elisa smiled. A hundred years from now the old cello would probably still be around. Another generation of musicians would play the music of Bach and Schubert and Mendelssohn, just as others had played the songs before Leah and Elisa were born. The thought warmed away the chill of fear that had gripped her heart. She gazed tenderly down on Charles. His head was turned on the pillow as if he had been listening to music. His fingers curved as if he touched the strings.

Elisa stroked his forehead, smoothing back a lock of soft blond hair. He sighed with contentment and his cheek moved as if he would smile. *Very soon you will smile, Charles. And very soon you will speak and sing like other children,* she thought. What would this small, frail boy say? What gentle words must live in such a heart!

Charles opened his eyes and gazed up at Elisa in drowsy contentment. Those blue eyes smiled and spoke clearly to her. He reached up and slipped his fingers into her hand as if to say, *"It will be all right. Do not worry, Elisa. You will see. We will be together again, all of us. And even a hundred years will not seem like a long time."*

⚭

It was an event that called for celebration in the city of Hamburg. Since early morning, busloads of Hitler Youth had been arriving on the docks to wave their Nazi flags and to shout obscenities as the Jews passed through the gauntlet of SS soldiers and Gestapo guards on their way to the freighter.

Most of the Jews were children, not older than those who cursed and spat on them from the sidelines. Some of the Jews were women, ringed by frightened little ones who clung to their skirts and trembled before the angry mob. A few, very few, were men who had managed to avoid arrest as enemies of the Reich. They all had one thing in common—they were the lucky Jews in Germany, the ones who had by some miracle managed to buy their way out of the country. They were eight hundred souls who were fortunate enough to be granted exit visas. They were leaving Germany with nothing but the clothes they wore on their backs. But they were alive, at least. They were indeed lucky.

"Filthy swine Jews!"

"Get out! Jews out! Jews out!"

"May you drown like rats!"

"Stinking . . ."

"Christ-killing filth! Good riddance!"

Plank by plank the eight hundred climbed the ramp and crowded onto the deck of an ancient, rusted hulk that had never been built to carry human cargo. There was not room for even one hundred on the freighter, but eight hundred gladly crammed together in the cargo hold, the narrow corridors, on the steps, and in the galley. Small groups claimed a place beside a coil of rope or beneath a rust-streaked porthole.

The Gestapo still prowled among them, stepping over bodies, checking papers for the thousandth time. Here and there shrieks of grief and terror rose up as the state police chose one more victim to sacrifice, one more enemy of the Reich to tear from his family! And the numbers dwindled from eight hundred to seven hundred and eighty-four. Eighty-three. Eighty. Seventy-nine. Seventy-six.

Below on the quay the Hitler Youth shouted for blood as Jewish criminals with ashen faces were led back down the ramp. "Kill the Jewish filth! Wipe them off your boots! Don't bring them back into Hamburg alive!"

Truncheons and hobnailed boots motivated those who tried to cling to the rails of the ship. "So you thought you were safe! You thought you would get away!"

It was the living example of the child's board game played happily by the Aryan schoolchildren of Hitler's Reich—roll the dice and land on the proper square, and you chase the Jews out! It was an event of such joyous celebration that the brigades of Hitler Youth would remember the sight for a lifetime. They would someday tell their grandchildren: "I was on the docks cheering when we shoved the last stinking Jew into the water!"

Of course, these were certainly not the last Jews in Hamburg. But they were the last who would leave the country legally with an exit visa. No doubt the government had other things in mind for the Jews who remained behind.

As wives wept and watched their arrested husbands being dragged toward the waiting police vans, the mooring lines were cast loose even before the ramp was raised.

Applause and still more curses rose up to drown out a last farewell.

"Philip!"

"Daddy! Daddy!"

"Johann! Liebchen! Johann!"

A hail of rocks and bottles and spit flew upward onto the decks to christen the creaking hull with Aryan contempt and hatred. Seven hundred and seventy-six lucky Jews were leaving the German port of Hamburg that morning. The free press would cover that departure. News and photographs would grace the back pages of several European newspapers as proof that Jews . . . some Jews . . . were indeed allowed passage out of Germany. The Führer *encouraged* Jews to leave, as a matter of fact. Had he not sent the legions of his youthful disciples to cheer the departure?

Yes. Jews could leave Germany if they so wished. If they paid their taxes and fines. If they took no more than twelve marks out of the country. If they were not considered potential enemies to the Reich. If they signed a release extolling the kindness and fair treatment of the German government. If they . . .

Slowly, slowly, the listing, rusty hulk of the SS *Darien* rumbled out of the port of the Elbe River toward the safety of the open sea. The *Darien* had charted no course for the journey. The captain of the ship, the crew, the passengers still did not know their destination. They had no distant harbor to look for, no future home. No nation on the face of the earth had yet granted the *Darien* permission to anchor. No government had offered haven to these homeless ones who crowded sun-cracked decks and searched the jagged skyline of the nation that had once been home.

The ocean swells were a more solid place to stand than the soil of Germany now. Those whom they had left behind were condemned to drown in a storm more violent than the North Sea could ever devise.

The SS *Darien*. Destination: unknown. Cargo: seven hundred and seventy-six lucky Jews.

7

Training Ground

The terrorist training grounds of the Nazi SS were tucked into the hills a few miles beyond Munich. The barracks housed men from many different countries whose leaders had formed a common bond with the Third Reich.

More than languages separated the units. Racial barriers were a common problem in the training of these men. Those of Aryan blood from Czechoslovakia despised the Arabs who had come for training from Palestine. The Aryans from France likewise hated the Spanish terrorists who had been sent by Franco.

Stronger bonds united them, however. Each unit shared the goals of the triumph of Fascism, the hatred of Jews, and the destruction of the Western democracies. Even in Germany, these things transcended the issues of race and German culture. Hitler himself was a leader who said that the issue of race was simply used to unify the masses toward one goal.

Thirteen Arabs had come for training at the request of Haj Amin el Husseini. The annihilation of the Zionists was his goal, and it bonded him strongly to Hitler. Today those dark-skinned Arabs stood in a semicircle among a group of twenty-two Germans from the Sudetenland of Czechoslovakia.

At the center of this group was an aging Mercedes with an open hood. Beside its right front fender stood Georg Wand, a man small of stature but great in his accomplishments for the Reich.

An observer looking over the tall stone wall of the compound might have mistaken this gathering for a lecture on auto repair. In fact, it was a demonstration of the ease with which an automobile and its occupants might be blown to pieces.

Georg held up the length of copper pipe for all the group to see. It was the most ordinary sort of pipe used in all modern plumbing, he explained through an interpreter. Sealed on one end, the pipe was then packed with explosives, and a spark plug was placed in the other end. To the spark plug a wire was attached.

Raising his voice as he pointed beneath the hood, he smiled benignly. "This is the distributor. You see these wires lead from the distributor to the spark plugs of the engine! So! It is a simple matter of unplugging one wire from the spark plug and attaching it to our little bomb. When the victim starts the car, the electric charge runs through the wire, and the spark plug ignites the explosives."

He attached the device in seconds as a murmur of approval passed through the students. It was so very easy. One could do it by feel in the dark!

"And now, shall we demonstrate what happens?" The group followed him meekly into a concrete bunker. Dark glasses were handed to them as they took their places to peer out at the Mercedes. Georg Wand counted to three and turned the remote switch that started the car. In that instant a scorching blast tore through the metal of the machine and a cloud of fire consumed the interior, devouring the dummies that had been placed there for effect. The hood was shredded and sent flying fifty feet in the air, along with bits of glowing metal that would mow down anyone in the immediate area. Well-placed, a car bomb could be a device that might kill and maim hundreds!

The students applauded as the last chunks of metal fell to the ground around the burning skeleton of the automobile.

Georg Wand posed the question: "How might you use such a device in Jerusalem?"

Hands went up. He chose a young, rather Aryan-looking Arab to answer. "In the Jewish shopping district. Or perhaps at the motor pool of the British headquarters."

"And what will be the effect of such devastation?"

"Terror!"

"To what end?"

"To frighten the government into accepting our demands."

"Which are?"

"The immediate closure of Jewish land purchases and Jewish immigration."

Georg Wand smiled approval. His gold tooth glinted. "Good. *Very* good! And now . . . in the Czech Sudetenland? What are your goals?"

The answer of the Sudeten-German trainee was stopped short by the emergence of a tall black-shirted SS officer. He strode through the students and bent to whisper a summons in the ear of Georg Wand. Teaching terrorist tactics to men from beyond the borders of the Reich was a duty that fell outside of Georg's usual assignments as a Gestapo agent. It was a hobby, really, which satisfied his wish to see military action. Now Heinrich Himmler had something more important for him to test his mental powers on.

"Sergeant Richter will now take over the class," Wand announced without ceremony. "I am called to Berlin. I wish you all the best of success. Heil Hitler."

A smattering of applause followed him from the bunker and across the field where the Mercedes burned. Wand was an excellent teacher. In times past he had made an excellent terrorist as well. But he would never belong to the SS, and this fact was the one disappointment in his life.

⏝

Every bridge across the Elbe River was crammed with noisy throngs of Hitler Youth. Rocks and bottles, spittle, rotten vegetables, and bags of human excrement rained down on the decks of the freighter. These were Germany's farewell gifts to the *Darien* Jews. This was the way the superior Aryan master race said good-bye to the subhumans of the Jewish race.

Mrs. Rosenfelt remained across the street from the horrendous scene as the freighter moved slowly past. In her hand she held a rose, the first hopeful rose of spring to bloom. She had plucked it from her garden this morning and had planned to toss it from the bridge to Maria. A foolish gesture, impossible with the hysterical mob shouting on the riverbanks. An old woman could not hope to swim against that tide of human debris to toss one small rose in the midst of the hail of filth. Bubbe Rosenfelt held tightly to the rose as she gazed sadly at the backs of the screaming Hitler Youth. She could only hope that Maria and Klaus had somehow managed to get the children safely belowdecks, away from the violence of the demonstration. The decks would be cleaned up easily enough, but the young minds of the little ones might hold such a terrible memory forever.

The old woman turned away. Cane in one hand, rose in the other, she marched quickly toward the Gothic arches of the huge Catholic cathedral that served the sailors of a thousand ports. From the building's high bell tower, perhaps she could catch one last glimpse of Maria and the children.

The jeering voices rose to a fevered pitch behind her. She quickened her pace until the hard cobbles jarred her bones. Breathlessly she climbed the worn stone steps and pushed hard against the iron doors. Heavy as they were, they swung in easily on well-oiled hinges.

Her own breath echoed hollowly in the vast, deserted sanctuary. Straight ahead the marble floor stretched at least one hundred yards to an altar that once had been adorned with a crucified and bleeding Christ. Mrs. Rosenfelt remembered that Christ. Years ago the craftsmen of her factory had worked to repair the figure after it had fallen with the cross above the altar. She drew her breath in sharply as her eyes moved downward from where the cross had been. The swastika emblem and portrait of Hitler now filled the most prominent position in the nave. Scenes from the Old Testament had been removed from stained-glass windows. *There must be nothing Jewish here, no contamination in the Reich church!* The porcelain figure of Mary and the Christ child had been removed from behind the altar. *So this is what Frau Haefner had wept so loudly about!* Bubbe remembered the grief her beloved housekeeper endured when her church was desecrated by Hitler's godlessness. Nazi banners hung from every arch, above each entrance to every alcove.

Mrs. Rosenfelt saw it all within a matter of seconds and then turned away and hurried toward the narrow steps to her right that led up into the cathedral spire. From there she would see the freighter, the ark of her hopes. From there she would hear only the wind and the flutter of bird wings as she said her own good-byes. High above the youth of Germany who had grown rabid with hatred, she would lay down her rose.

Each step of the long climb became increasingly difficult as she realized the effect of years. There were times when she forgot that she was old. These steep stairs reminded her. Her lungs burned, and twice she stopped to lean heavily against the cold stone wall of the spiral staircase, trying to catch her breath. Always in her mind was the thought that the freighter was slowly moving away from her, that it carried in its rusting hull everything she loved. *One look, one last glimpse of them! Only a little look, God!*

The last twenty steps reared up before her. The great iron bells were plainly visible. So near! Sunlight streamed in through the open arches. Mrs. Rosenfelt forced her legs to move. One distant good-bye. She recited their beloved names now as she struggled toward the window. "Maria . . . Klaus . . . Trudy . . . Katrina . . . Louise . . . Gretchen . . . Ada-Marie . . ."

As she reached the light and leaned against the stone railing, she remembered the baby, the one whom only God knew. "And may you be born in a free land, little Holbein!" She wept as she caught sight of the rust-streaked ship. Small dots of color and movement marked the passengers on the deck. *Among them, my family*, Bubbe Rosenfelt thought. *Keep them safe, dear God!*

She looked past the Brownshirts and upraised fists of the Aryan youth who still hounded the passengers from the shoreline. Her old heart pounded in her ears as she laid the rose on the stone ledge and stood watching until the freighter passed out of sight.

The crowds below began to disperse, but Mrs. Rosenfelt remained in the church spire for a long time as the empty gray river flowed on toward the North Sea. She clutched her black velvet reticule in her hand and suddenly remembered it was still filled with peppermints she had meant to give to the children.

With a slow sigh, she shook her head and brushed away a tear that had trickled down her lined cheek. "Be good, my little ones," she whispered. *"Sehr gut, Kinderlach!"*

☙

Murphy awoke early with his head full of lead paragraphs and bits of conversation from last night's interview with President Beneš. Sleep would be impossible until the story was written. Strong coffee, a pen, and paper seemed more important than the rest.

Elisa was still sleeping when Murphy slipped out of the bedroom and padded quietly down the hall toward the kitchen. He passed the room that Elisa's brother Dieter now shared with Charles, and then he tiptoed past Theo and Anna's door.

He need not have bothered being so quiet. Theo and Dieter sat pensively across from one another at the kitchen table. Little Charles had carefully erected a wall of dominoes on the floor near the large gas stove, where Anna stood poised with a coffeepot in her hand. The old-fashioned American-made radio in the corner softly carried an urgent and troubled voice into the room. Murphy stood motionless in the doorway. He recognized the voice as that of President Beneš.

Anna looked up, shook her head, and then motioned for Murphy to sit down.

"Accordingly"—Beneš was arriving at some momentous issue, Murphy realized—"since our government is challenged from without on every border, it is the decision of the government that every man between the ages of sixteen and sixty will be called up and registered to serve in the defense of our nation."

"Good!" Young Dieter slapped his hand triumphantly on the table. "I am sixteen! I can fight! Wilhelm is off flying his airplanes, and I am as tall as he is."

Anna appeared pained. She had already let her oldest son join the Czech Air Corps. Must she also offer Dieter to the cause?

Theo cleared his throat. He nodded at Dieter. "The age limit includes me as well. We will register together."

Anna set the coffeepot down with a clang, drowning out half of Beneš' last sentence. "No!" she said angrily. "I will not allow it. That I will not allow, Theo! You are barely recovered from a year in Dachau, and I—"

"But I *am* recovered, woman!" Theo shot back with uncharacteristic brusqueness. "I was an officer in one of the greatest air corps in the world during the last war, and I can—"

"And now the very air corps you fought with will drop bombs on our heads!" Anna's eyes blazed. One son was enough. Now Dieter *and* Theo? It was too much!

"All the more reason I should offer my experience to the Czech military! And that I will do! I am far younger than the upper-age limit."

"Prison aged you ten years!" Anna was near tears.

Murphy started to rise. He was not comfortable in the midst of a family argument. Little Charles gaped wide-eyed at Anna and Theo. He followed their conversation like a spectator at a tennis match.

"Come on, Charles," Murphy said grimly to the child.

"No!" Anna put her hand on Murphy's arm. "Please do not go! Tell Theo—tell him we can go to America too."

Murphy sat down slowly. Beneš still droned on in the background, but now no one was listening to him. "To get a visa to the States is a difficult process these days," Murphy answered quietly. He and Elisa had discussed it several times, and he was certain that she must have talked to Anna about it. "But it will not be impossible once Elisa is there."

"A kind thought, Murphy," Theo answered politely, although his cheeks were still flushed with anger. "But I cannot see how we can think of leaving now when the Czechs are threatened."

"How can we *not* think of it?" Anna cried.

Dieter drew himself up very tall and affected a stance that made him look like a young version of his father. "I am old enough to fight, Mother." Dieter lifted his chin defiantly.

"And old enough to be killed." Miserable and desperate, Anna clutched her blue dressing gown over her heart. "But too young to die! Theo!" She turned on her husband. "Can you not see where this foolish loyalty will lead us? Theo—"

Theo hesitated, as if he was suddenly unwilling to cause Anna any further pain. Then his voice became a gentle coaxing to reason. "How can we leave here, Anna dear? Have you forgotten our son? Have you forgotten that Wilhelm now serves with the Czech Air Corps? His term of service is five years. *Five.* We cannot leave him to fight alone."

Tears spilled from Anna's eyes. All the men looked embarrassed as she sat down facing away from them. Murphy was the first to speak after a long silence punctuated by her sniffles. "Perhaps it will not come to that," he said hoarsely. "Maybe there will not be a fight against the Nazis. The measures Beneš is taking—thirty divisions called up, and now registration of civilians. These sorts of things seem to cause Hitler to waver. He was stopped at the border in May, even without the help of the French and British."

"There, you see, Anna?" Theo soothed. "Just for safety."

Murphy saw his chance. "Yes. Yes . . . for safety, Theo. Maybe it is a good idea for safety if we at least begin the process of acquiring visas to America for you all. Just in case. It is not a reflection on your courage, no more than it was for you to flee Germany."

"Listen to him," Anna begged. "Here is a little sense!"

Theo frowned, then looked at Murphy and spread his hands in a gesture that said, *I am listening.*

Even Charles studied Murphy now. This was important. Murphy chose his words carefully. "That night you took the plane in Berlin, I thought there never was a man as brave as you, Theo." Murphy meant what he said. Theo must not see himself as a coward, but rather as a target for the SS and the Gestapo if Hitler should invade Czechoslovakia. "If things should come to the worst for this place, in spite of what brave men may do to stop it, you can see that you would be among the first targets of the Nazis. You are not only a Jew, Theo; you are among those men Hitler considers traitors to the Reich. Your son is in the Czech—"

Theo drew back angrily, even though the word *traitor* was not Murphy's label, but that of the Reich for those who had fled. "Traitor! I a traitor? *They* have tarnished my Iron Cross! *I* fought for the Fatherland! *I—*"

"It is Hitler who is the traitor," Murphy interrupted. "He has destroyed the very constitution of the republic he vowed to uphold. We know that, Theo, but you see, that is the point. The Weimar Republic of Germany no longer exists. Wrong has become right, and the world is turned upside down! If that horrible law—which is not law at all but evil and madness—if it should come here, then there is nothing a good man can do but leave—or die. And this time Anna and Wilhelm and Dieter would die with you. I do not doubt that."

It was evident by the look on Theo's face that he could not doubt it, either. Anna's eyes pleaded with him as he thought for a moment, then sighed and rendered his decision. "Now we live within the protection of the democracy of the Czechs. We are bound to obey their law. Between sixteen and sixty—every man. That is what the president has declared."

"But, Theo!" Anna began to protest.

Theo silenced her with a look and an upraised hand. "Let me finish," he said calmly. "I must out of good conscience offer my experience as an air corps officer to this government. They have a fine force. Better even than the French, I think, after talking with Wilhelm. I might be of assistance in training flyers. I can be of great service here."

He hesitated, and Anna did not interrupt this time. There was something else he was thinking; she could hear it in his tone.

"But I think in the interest of *safety* and good sense, it is reasonable—even important—that we do everything possible to obtain visas to America."

Anna slumped with relief. Murphy nodded, suddenly aware that President Beneš had stopped speaking and military music was being played. "A wise decision," Murphy said. "I will pick up Charles' medical visa this morning at the American Embassy. I will bring back the applications. There is no sense in taking chances, Theo."

"We have no chances left to take, do we, Murphy?" The matter was settled. "So, Anna. Breakfast for your men, eh? We will talk with Murphy. Dieter and I can register for defense at the downtown police station while Murphy visits the American Embassy. And perhaps lunch at the beer cellar near the Rathaus?"

Murphy was disappointed. He could not join Theo and Dieter, and this had been his first real opportunity to spend time with his father-in-law. "Not today. Sorry. I have a story to write and send on to London. My interview with Beneš. And then—" he looked toward Charles, even though he had not meant to—"I have another important call to make to Paris."

"Another time, then," Theo said, knowing that they were nearly out of time to spend together as a family. Very soon Murphy would take Elisa back to his country, and who could know how long it would be until they were all in the same room again?

The coffee had only begun to percolate when Elisa appeared at the door of the kitchen, sleepy and a bit disheveled. "Oh, you let me sleep too long," she chided Murphy, then moved to kiss Theo, Murphy, Dieter, and Charles in turn. "What have I missed so far this morning?" She hugged Anna briefly.

"Nothing at all." Anna nudged her toward a chair. "I have not even made the eggs yet."

8

Message in a Bottle

This morning Prague was a city of crowds and lines. Quiet cliques of desperate, worried men spoke in low voices and cast anxious looks over their shoulders as if they could see the fear that stalked them.

Murphy parted company with Theo and Dieter at the barricade that sealed Embassy Row off from motor traffic. Beyond the barricade thousands of refugees were camped in the street and on the sidewalks. Murphy could not guess at the numbers who had come here to this street from Germany and Austria in hopes of getting a visa to . . . to where? As he picked his way carefully through the weary crowds, he stood out among them. He was clean, well fed, and his suit was pressed and spotless. Haunted eyes followed his progress toward the American Embassy. He was obviously not one of them. Not on the run. Not threatened with deportation. He was not hungry or homeless. They stood back and let him pass. He had someplace to go.

The tall iron bars of the American Embassy had become a prison that kept these desperate multitudes out. Daily Hitler raged about the thousands who had fled his tyranny. They were traitors and dangerous criminals who must be deported back to the justice of the Reich for punishment. Many nations had turned the refugees back at their borders. The French had bowed to pressure from the Nazis and were now shipping those without visas back to Germany. But the Czechs had not closed the doors. Jewish relief organizations had joined forces with Catholic groups to provide some meager meals of soup and bread to those who jammed the public parks and packed the rail stations.

A crowd fifty men deep stood in a widening circle outside the American Embassy. From sidewalk to sidewalk they waited in a silent, expectant vigil for some sign of hope from the representatives of the *goldeneh medina*, the golden land across the ocean that could never be threatened by men like Hitler and his Nazis. No hope was offered. The crowds had grown since Austria had fallen in March. Each day more were added to the numbers, but still there was no word of hope. Madam Liberty, it seemed, had closed her eyes. Just as it was the night a poor Jew named Joseph arrived at Bethlehem with his exhausted wife, Mary. There was no room for the homeless. And so the huddled masses remained huddled here, where the American flag waved above this one small building.

Murphy lowered his eyes. He could not force himself to meet the questioning stares of these people. Their heartbreak and disappointment tore at him. *No room? Can't we move over a little and find room for them? What are people back home thinking of? These thousands could be absorbed and lost in one square mile of New York!*

All around he heard the cries of children, but other than those wails of small discomfort, there was no complaint from the masses. There was only silence.

"Excuse me—" He let his American accent creep into the German words he spoke. "I am American. *Bitte. Bitte.*" He moved easily toward the massive gates. He let his eyes follow the black bars upward to the deadly spikes at the top of the fence and then to the flag that waved above the compound.

Men stepped back to let him through. He sensed their envious eyes on him and was somehow ashamed that it was so easy for him to approach the flag. *Was it this easy for my grandparents?* he wondered. *Had they simply paid their fare from the old country and stepped into the light of Liberty's upraised flame?*

The marine on duty in the guardhouse focused on him. It was easy to tell Murphy was American. He did not look afraid or hopeless or hopeful.

"You got business inside?" The marine was already unlocking the gate.

For a moment Murphy imagined the crowd storming the gate. They did not. "Yes." Murphy flashed his American passport as a dozen ragged men stood craning just for a glimpse of it.

Murphy slipped through the narrow opening in the gate. It clanged shut behind him. *An authoritative clang,* Murphy thought as he hurried up the stone steps of the old mansion. *The kind of noise that means no monkey business.* Keys jangled. The gate was secured again.

The consul in charge of the visa process was not only harried and offi-
cious but rude. He glared at the requests presented by Murphy as if they
were obscene messages scribbled to annoy him. Thick glasses made the
man's pale blue eyes seem large and bulging. Maybe he had been reading through too many applications, Murphy reasoned. The guy's eye-
balls were about to drop out onto his desk.

"Your applications will be considered in turn—"

"But my wife and I are leaving for the States, and since you will need
verification that my father-in-law can indeed support himself before you
grant the visas—"

"All in turn!" The little fellow moved a stack of applications from
one side of his desk to the other. "There are thirty-five thousand Jewish
and Austrian refugees wandering around out there. Every one of them
wants to go to America! Every last one of them."

"I know all about that." Murphy smiled sympathetically, although
he would have preferred shouting back at the man. There was something
unsettling about the fact that the fate of thousands rested in a pile of papers on the blotter of a fellow who seemed near a nervous breakdown.
"This is really rough on you, isn't it?"

The clerk sat back with a loud sigh. "You can't imagine. There are at
least six hundred thousand people still in Austria who fall into the category of subhuman. Did you hear? Did you? Two hundred suicides a day
in Vienna alone. They are rolling carts through the street to gather the
Jewish dead. Like a plague. Save Hitler the trouble. And now we consuls
have orders to screen every applicant—every one—for the *possibility* that
they might come to the States and become dependent on public aid. Not
only *that*—" he mopped his brow—"they practically have to be inde-
pendently wealthy because they cannot come in here and tell us they
have a job lined up in America. The law states that they *can't* work, because that would be taking American jobs."

Murphy slipped a folded fifty-dollar bill across the consul's desk. He
lifted a finger to reveal the denomination. "My father-in-law can verify
all of it. A hefty bank account. No plans to take American jobs. Two sons
of school age." Murphy smiled conspiratorially as the man caught sight
of the bill.

The bulging eyes extended farther from their sockets. "Good heavens, no! Put that away!" he hissed. "That could cost me my job. A fellow
was just sacked in Vienna for the same thing!" Again he mopped his
brow and shifted the applications. "The matter will be resolved in time."
He raised his voice so that any bystanders would hear his official tone.

"President Roosevelt has called for a major conference of thirty-three nations to discuss the issue of the refugees. Such matters will be settled in Evian. A great humanitarian, our President Roosevelt! All these . . . people . . . will be discussed in Evian! Until then you will just have to take your turn like everyone else, Mr. Murphy. That is only fair!"

Murphy had not expected a political speech. He sniffed and put the fifty back in his pocket. It was important to remain calm in spite of the fact he wanted to grab this guy by his collar and shake his teeth out. "Things are heating up here, friend," Murphy tried to reason. "Theo Linder has already escaped from Germany, then Austria. What happens if Prague caves in?"

"I suppose he will have to go elsewhere, and then it will no longer be my problem, will it?" Snippy. Effeminate.

Murphy swallowed hard. He took a deep, calming breath. He would take this up with normal people in New York. He placed the papers on the top of the stack. The man quickly moved them to the bottom.

"A conference about refugees, huh?" Murphy strained to be polite. "In Evian? A good idea. Probably take a load off your mind." Murphy stood abruptly and towered over the little man's thinning hair. "You know," he added, "maybe you ought to take a little vacation. Rest your eyes. A man could go bald with this kind of pressure."

The clerk looked as if he might cry. "Oh dear me, yes," he panted. "So many decisions. Thank God for President Roosevelt. Thirty-three countries! The Evian Conference—that should relieve a little pressure on us Americans, I should say." He patted his hair protectively and then raised his head to call, "Next? Who's next?"

⟨৩⟩

It was Timmons on the line from Paris. The connection was tenuous at best and Murphy covered one ear with his hand as he strained to hear.

"Talk louder Timmons. Timmons? Can you speak up?" Murphy was shouting into the receiver but was still uncertain if Timmons could hear him.

"Murphy? Hey, Murph, did you—"

"Louder!" Murphy shouted, but increased volume did not seem to make the conversation any more coherent.

"Murph, when you asked me and Johnson to investigate the possibility that the Kronenberger boys had relatives somewhere, we ended up here in Paris. Rumor has it that the boys have a great-aunt." There was definite excitement in Timmons' voice, and Murphy hoped their efforts had paid off for the children.

"I said—" Suddenly the dreadful crackle on the line disappeared and

Timmons was shouting quite distinctly into Murphy's ear. "I said, the old lady is dead! Died last month of influenza."

"You mean the aunt?" Murphy was still shouting.

"Yeah. Gee, Murph, you don't have to yell. Yeah, the aunt. The aunt of Kronenberger's wife. The old dame croaked. From the sound of the French authorities she didn't have two sous to rub together, either. No relatives besides her and the kids. 'Course the Frogs don't know about the boys, or they'd be after them to pay the old lady's debts."

"That's it, then," Murphy said quietly as the weight of disappointment flooded him.

"And that ain't all. They're selling her stuff at an auction to pay for medical bills and burial. Johnson managed to buy an old photo album off one of the gendarmes at the warehouse. There's plenty of news clippings from Germany. All the scoop on the whole Kronenberger affair. You think the kid might want it?"

"Someday . . . maybe."

"You want us to send it? Or what?"

"Sure." Murphy decided at once that he would not mention the death of the old woman to Charles. It would serve no useful purpose; the child had been through enough loss already. "Send it to the London INS office. I'll get it there."

"Yeah." Timmons sounded thoughtful, even subdued for Timmons. "So what now, Murphy? What are you gonna do with the kid?"

"Get him to the States. There's a doctor there who can put him back together." He laughed bitterly. "And get this. The doc is Jewish. From Germany. He could have fixed the kid all along, except that the Nazis didn't want Jewish doctors in Germany to work on a kid they decided was unworthy. Nuts. Senseless, you know, Timmons?"

The telephone faded in and out again, obscuring Timmons' response. "I should have stayed a sportswriter . . . " was all Murphy could make of his reply; then the line crackled and hummed and went dead.

Sixty-eight miles from the mocking, jeering crowds on the docks of Hamburg, the Elbe River emptied the listing freighter into the North Sea. Flocks of seagulls circled overhead; their cries seemed to echo the curses of the Hitler Youth: "Die! Die! Die!"

The thrumming ship's engine beat like a defiant heart long after the last reluctant gull wheeled around to ride a tail wind back to the shores of Germany.

Steady swells took up the rhythm, catching the bow of the freighter like a cold fist and throwing it back onto the water with an impact that made every pilgrim long for the land he had just left. *What could they do to us that would be worse than this?* The euphoria of leaving and the grief for those left behind combined with an unrelenting nausea to which every passenger yielded. Those on the decks were thought to be lucky. Groups who had fought for some dim interior shelter now regretted that they had not settled for the cold wind and salt mist and a rusty rail to retch over. Rusted portholes were pried open in hopes of catching some breath of fresh air belowdecks. The pounding engines were answered with groans.

Only three hours from the shores of Nazi Germany, the cloud of despair deepened. *Can dying be any more terrible than this?* No one among the passengers was spared. The plague of seasickness had come upon the House of Israel, and even the most resolute and energetic were stricken. These were a people unaccustomed to the sea, after all. These were teachers and bank clerks and shopkeepers and housewives and grocers. Most had never been on the water aside from a Saturday ride in a rowboat on the Aussen-Alster. This was no ship, it seemed, but a rolling, lurching, never-ending carnival ride! *What could Hitler do to us that would be worse?*

Perhaps nothing. Perhaps that was why they had been allowed to sail—to save the Nazis the trouble of disposing of the remains. Were the oceans not already dotted with a thousand ships like this one? Legal and illegal, refugee ships bobbed out across the waters from the Reich in search of a homeland. "Coffin ships," the newspapers called them. Dozens had sunk, simply disappeared with their unfortunate cargo. "The drowning of unwanted cats," Himmler was heard to remark. "Into a sack, and toss them to the fishes. Quick and easy, if you ask me."

∽◯∾

Like the cone of an enormous bullhorn, the ventilation shaft extended up through the pipe like a barricade, and within that circle Maria and Klaus Holbein huddled with their five children.

Klaus, a tall, Lincolnesque figure of a man, had stumbled from the tiny compound to the rail numerous times. His stomach was quite empty by now, but the sound of his own sickness seemed to trigger an epidemic of retching among the children.

Maria, so pale beneath her dark complexion that she looked green, sat with her back against the cool, vibrating vent shaft. Three small tousled heads lay in her lap. The faces of her children were ashen; mouths gulped the salt air and dark eyes stared dully at the bow of the ship as it rose and fell on the seas.

"How much longer, Mama?" young Trudy moaned. Trudy was

nearly eight. She had already asked the question a dozen times, and her entreaties sparked a babble from the three children who lay next to her.

Some spark of impatience found its way to Maria's mind. She had told Trudy. "We have only just left. It could be days!" She drew her breath in with difficulty as she tried to find an answer that would satisfy her. "I . . . told . . . you—" She could say no more. The anger subsided and she let her head fall back with a *clunk* against the metal.

Five children moaned in unison and then fell silent. Maria's hand rested on Gretchen's head. Katrina leaned against her mother's arm. Maria felt as though she could not move even if she wanted to. She let her gaze drift dizzily to where Klaus leaned over the rail and inhaled deeply. There were twenty other travelers between him and the vent pipe. He would have trouble getting back to their space without stepping on them.

"Mama? How long?"

Maria did not try to answer. She did not really know the answer. *How long will we be sick? How long will the ship rock like this? How long until we get off? How long to our destination?* Maria herself had asked those questions a thousand times. No one had any answers.

"We are . . . safe now," she managed. "Away from Germany."

If they had not been so terribly ill, that thought would have sent up a cheer from the company. Instead it brought more moans. Klaus straightened himself and exhaled, letting his cheeks puff out with some relief. He swayed with the freighter as he looked back over the minefield of passengers and belongings between him and his family. With a slight, almost imperceptible shrug, he turned back toward the rail and ran a long, bony hand over his face. Maria understood the gesture. It was difficult enough to contemplate walking a few paces, let alone to think beyond this moment. One more question rose up: *Did we make a mistake to leave?* To that question Maria silently moved her lips. *Nein!*

The hair on Klaus' head stood up in dark, wiry strands. His large ears protruded from his head, and for an instant Maria imagined the stiff breeze would snag the ears of her beloved and blow him off the deck.

The image made her anxious. There were no life jackets to toss into the dark seas. Only half a dozen lifeboats. If he was swept away, how would she manage the children?

"Klaus?" she called feebly. He did not hear her. "Klaus?" she called again, wanting to pull him into the security of their little compound beneath the ventilation shaft.

"I'll get him, Mama." Trudy raised her head and struggled to sit up.

Trudy was a good girl, a helpful child, even if she did ask too many questions.

Maria put her hand on Trudy's forehead and pressed her back. "No. No. Let it be. Your father has many things to think about. He needs a little peace." *He needs to be alone.* She did not say the last words out loud because there certainly was no way for anyone to be alone on this vessel.

Klaus turned again. His deep brown eyes met Maria's weary gaze. He almost smiled, and she read his thoughts as he shrugged sheepishly. *So, here we are! This is what we spent so many months longing for and praying for! Look, Maria! The sea voyage we always wanted!*

Maria raised an eyebrow and answered with a half smile. Klaus looked down at his feet and began his slow, precarious walk back through the prostrate bodies to his family. Maria saw the humor in this as well. Klaus liked her sense of humor. Even in the most dreadful circumstances, Maria had always managed that smile.

"Pardon me. *Bitte. Bitte.* Ah, pardon, Frau . . ." Klaus stepped over his suitcase into the circle of safety. There was still no place to put his feet without stepping on a sprawled child. In invitation, Maria tugged the limp figure of little Katrina into her arms.

"They seem to have settled a bit." She patted the empty square of deck and Klaus awkwardly folded his body downward to sit beside her.

"This will pass," he said with a nod.

"Of course it will," Maria answered. "Everything in our stomachs has passed already. What is left? Besides the baby—"

Klaus exhaled with the same sigh that puffed out his cheeks—a nervous habit, one he adopted when he was not quite certain. "This is the worst of it. You'll see. By tomorrow the children will not even notice the swells."

"At least no one is thinking of food now, eh, Klaus?"

He patted her cheek. "Or anything else, my beauty." He winked, then tucked a wisp of Maria's brown hair back beneath the navy blue shawl she wore. "All appetites have grown pale, I fear."

She smiled weakly into the gentle face of her husband. Ten years of marriage had produced five bright, happy children. Neighbors commented on the regularity with which Maria Holbein had delivered baby girls. It had become a joke among the other professors at the University of Hamburg, where Klaus had taught chemistry until 1935: "Klaus Holbein and Maria—what chemistry between them, *ja*?"

Somewhere along the line Jewish babies had ceased to be a laughing matter. Jewish chemistry professors had become something to despise. One thing had led to another, and finally to this tiny fragment of iron tossing about on the North Sea. Klaus was thirty-seven, Maria just thirty-five.

"The appetite will return—" Maria touched his cheek—"when we have found a harbor."

Klaus raised his chin slightly and looked away as if to sniff the air for land. "A port. Yes." He gazed down at his now sleeping children. "Stuffed into this leaking bottle, we have become God's message to the conscience of the world, Maria. Floating, bobbing along. And will they stoop to pluck us from the waves, I wonder?" The amusement faded from his eyes and deep sadness settled in.

Maria did not answer him. A little hand reached up and tugged on the sleeve of his tweed overcoat. It was Katrina, looking up from Maria's lap. Her eyes were clearer now, but still pained by a tummy that would not be still. Klaus leaned down to kiss his daughter on the forehead. "What is it, Katrina?"

"Papa?" the child asked, her brown eyes eager, "will you tell us again about Noah? about Noah and his family in the ark?"

Now other eyes opened and looked toward the lean, gangly man who was father, protector, provider, and storyteller.

"Yes, Papa."

"Tell us, please, again!"

Maria cleared her throat and raised her eyebrow again. Amused. The gesture that Klaus loved. "Yes, Husband," Maria added her voice. "Noah and the ark. All the animals at sea. What a mess that must have been! But leave out the same details God has left out of the story, will you? There is much, I now realize, that God did not tell about."

9

Aboard the Ark

It was hours after nightfall before the ocean swells finally collapsed beneath a curtain of thick fog. Klaus and Maria sat with their backs against the vent shaft as the five children used their parents' laps and legs for pillows.

The steady drone of the aged engines still pulsed from the foghorn. "Like the mating call of Noah's elephant," Klaus whispered with a weary smile.

Earlier Klaus had draped a large blanket over the shaft to make a sort of shelter for them. The cold ocean mist penetrated the makeshift tent easily, causing the family to huddle against one another for warmth.

There seemed to be no hint of sorrow now about leaving Germany. They had lost everything, given up everything for a place beneath the vent shaft. Life had been stripped bare of all illusions of what was important. Divested of all superficial worries, Klaus and Maria had found everything that really mattered—their family. To sit with each other and the five children beneath a vent shaft in the fog was the entire focus of all joy and thankfulness. They were alive. They were together.

Had there ever been a time when they had worried about bills? This moment drove that memory from their minds. Had Klaus ever longed for a radio for their apartment? He could not remember the longing. Was it true that Maria had once sat at the table and wept because all five children needed shoes at the same time? That all seemed so long ago. Another lifetime before this, perhaps.

Now silent tears streamed down Maria's face and blended with the mist. Here was joy. Five tousled heads. Five sets of little feet. A husband beside her. No one missing. None had been lost. Soon they would be with Bubbe in America. Boiled down to raw essentials, Maria and Klaus discovered that the only thing essential now was life itself. Neither of them tried to speculate on where they would spend the rest of their lives after they left the place beneath the vent shaft. Perhaps there would be a warm stove and a kitchen table and steaming cups of tea in their future, but they did not imagine that any place on earth would ever seem as wonderful as this place.

On the ship's bridge, someone clanged the hour on a little bell. It was eleven o'clock. Nearly the end of The Day they left Nazi Germany. Despite seasickness and overcrowding and uncertainty, it had been a perfect day for them.

Here and there across the crowded deck there was soft weeping and muffled moans of grief from those who had not been so lucky as Klaus and Maria. There were those among the refugees who had first lost everything, and then had lost someone. *To lose someone,* Maria thought as she listened to the sobs of a woman beside the rope coil, *that is to lose everything!*

Maria rested her cheek against the arm of Klaus and closed her eyes as shadowed figures moved to comfort the woman whose husband had been arrested by the Gestapo that morning.

"Go to sleep, my Maria," Klaus whispered. "We are together." His words were a benediction that ended months of worry about travel papers and Gestapo raids. "All of us. Safe."

Earlier Klaus had explained to the children that Noah had not known where the ark would finally come to rest. The important thing was to get on the boat, to escape the flood and destruction that would surely come. God would find a harbor for them. Somewhere there was a nation that would hold out the olive branch. Somewhere there was a Mount Ararat where this ark would rest.

◎

Maria was not certain how long she had been asleep, or if, even now, she was not still asleep. The constant vibration of the ship had lulled her into dreams that stayed with her even after she opened her eyes. In counterpoint to each dull pulse of the giant pistons, she thought she had heard yet another faint thump and the voice of a man crying weakly for help: "Help me! For the love of God . . ."

Maria sat up beside the slumped form of Klaus. She wiped her eyes with the back of her hand and leaned close to him to see if perhaps he was crying in his sleep. His lips did not move. His breath was steady and even, matching the cadence of the ship's internal rhythm.

A dream. You have been dreaming, Maria, unless the ship itself calls out. The thought made her shudder. She listened hard, scanning the sleeping shapes that littered the deck like discarded sacks. Had someone called? Was someone having the nightmare they had all lived through these last months?

"Help . . . *bitte* . . . help me!"

There it was again. Faint, but clear. Far away, as though it came from the bowels of the ship itself. "*Bitte* . . . help . . ."

Ghost ship. Coffin ship. So they had named the little freighter with its cargo of hated Jews. Did the souls of these now cry out as one to the night?

A cold chill of dread coursed through Maria. All the pleasant thoughts of a few hours ago disappeared. Each thump of the engine was answered by a sharp *clang, thump! Clang, thump!* "Help . . . *thump* . . . me!"

This was no dream. The voice did not come from anyone on deck. Indeed, it echoed hollowly from the broad cone of the ventilation shaft— from inside the freighter!

Maria's mouth was dry. She tried to swallow and then reached out to nudge Klaus awake. Deep in sleep, he moaned a protest and tried to brush her hand away.

"*Bitte* . . . for God's sake . . . *hilf mir bitte*!" The words were followed by a groan.

"Klaus!" Maria hissed, pounding on her husband's arm.

Irritated, Klaus sat up reluctantly, and three children protested the motion of their human pillow. "What is it, Maria?" His voice was sharp. "You want me to run downstairs for a cup of tea?"

"Shhhhh!" she insisted, putting her hand on his shoulder and raising her nose as if to sniff the air.

Thump. Clang. Thump. Clang.

"Just the engine."

"No! *Listen!*"

Clang. Thump!

"It is the engine. You woke me to listen to—"

"Help, please," the voice cried out again.

Now the eyes of Klaus widened.

"There, you see?" Maria was exultant. Yes! Klaus had heard the voice.

Klaus leaned forward, repeating the steps she had taken to determine where the plea was coming from. *Not the deck.* The voice called out again, and Klaus placed his ear against the metal ventilation shaft. He gasped as the clanging sound rang out again.

"Here!" he cried, jumping to his feet. Children tumbled unhappily onto the planks, and the blanket shelter came loose and fell down over them.

"What's going on?" shouted an angry voice from a few feet away.

"We are trying to sleep here!" protested a woman, struggling to sit up.

Klaus stood on his toes and peered down the curved horn of the giant shaft. "Is someone in there?" he cried.

Faintly the voice replied, "Please! Help . . . me!"

Maria struggled to her feet and stood at the elbow of Klaus. Others among the passengers stumbled to the shaft.

"There is someone down there!"

"You're all dreaming!"

"No, I tell you—*there*! Did you hear that? A voice!"

As if strengthened by the presence of humans, the voice cried an urgent explanation. "Please! A rope, or I shall fall! The grid broke beneath my feet. . . ."

Klaus shouted to the woman by the rope coil, "Bring some rope!"

Two frail old men tottered to fetch the end of the thick braid.

"Please!" begged the voice in the shaft. "I cannot—"

"It's a sixty-foot drop if he falls through the shaft," someone muttered.

"What is he doing in there, anyway?"

"What are we *all* doing on this ship?"

His five excited children clinging to his legs, Klaus fed the rope down the shaft. "It is coming! Hold on! Tell us when you have it!"

"So dark . . . black down here." The voice echoed. "Hurry."

"It is coming!" Klaus reassured the man, trying to imagine how anyone might survive in the shaft that dropped straight down. Was the prisoner bracing himself with hands and feet? If so, how would he grasp the rope? Might it slide right down past him?

"Here! I . . . hold on to your end—"

A dozen passengers and two dozen excited children grasped the rope to brace it against the weight of the voice. Like a giant fish on a line, the voice became the weight of flesh and bone suspended in the middle of the vertical shaft.

"Pull him up!" Klaus grimaced at the weight and leaned against it as the group moved inch by inch across the deck in a tug-of-war. "More men!" Klaus groaned as the weight slipped back several inches.

Fortified by the addition of several scrawny adolescents who answered the call, the rope began to move up more quickly.

"I see light!" the voice called loudly. "Thank God! Thank—" And then the voice emerged from the horn of the shaft. The face was blackened with soot. The face had no beard or hair. Large hands were caked with blood and dirt. The voice belonged to a huge man who had been stripped of every excess pound and who now was simply an enormous blackened skeletal frame. This strange apparition slid from the shaft and then, still clinging to the rope, shot out of the cone and crumpled down onto the place Klaus and Maria had chosen for their quarters.

A spotlight shone down from the bridge, showing that the man was completely naked and blackened not from soot alone but from burns that ran in a curved line from the back of his neck to the sole of his right foot. The festering wounds reeked. Their catch from the ventilation shaft was unconscious. Possibly they had rescued him only so he could die in the open air.

Children clung to Maria. "Mama! He is lying on our bed!"

"We need a doctor here!" Klaus knelt beside the injured man but was afraid to touch him.

"He is burned."

"From being in the shaft?"

"No. This is a shaft for fresh air. Something else—"

"I am a doctor!"

"Let him through. Let the doctor through, please."

"You think he escaped from the Gestapo?"

"What else? We have all escaped from the Gestapo, *nu*?"

After a few minutes of speculation and examination, the injured man was carefully moved belowdecks. He would probably not live, the doctor had muttered. How could such a battered creature survive?

Barely twenty minutes had passed since Maria had first heard the feeble call, and the excitement was over. The family had lost two precious blankets to the man from the shaft. On any other occasion she might have fretted over their loss. But not tonight.

ᑎᕼ

Charles could not think why Anna and Elisa seemed so sad. As for himself, he was ecstatic at the thought of his first airplane ride. Theo, who now wore the uniform of an officer in the Czech Air Corps, had told him all about the way the wind would pass beneath the wings to hold the aircraft up. He had told him stories of daring pilots from Germany in the last great war. Charles had sat all evening on his knee and listened as he spoke about the young men he now trained to fly at the airfield just beyond Prague. Dieter was there now. He slept in a large barracks with fifty other cadets who were part of the program Theo worked in.

"Before you leave tomorrow," Theo said, looking very brave in his uniform, "I will take you for a tour, Charles. Maybe Dieter can show you his bunk, and if there is time, perhaps, how would you like to go up for a ride in a training craft?"

Charles nodded enthusiastically. This was more than he had dreamed. Better than Leah's promise of running through green grass or climbing a tree! When he saw his brother again, he would draw a picture to show him how Theo had taken him up in the sky. Much higher than climbing a tree!

Theo laughed and mussed Charles' hair, then lifted him back onto the floor. "There's a good boy, Charles! You will like flying, and I will take you up and have you back before Anna can say a word."

Charles simply gazed at Theo. Always before, Charles had thought that Theo was an old man, but now, in his dark green uniform with the insignia of an officer on his arm, he seemed not to be old at all. No, Charles decided, Theo was really a young man with silver hair and bright blue eyes that sparkled in a craggy face. His shoulders were broad and his posture as straight as any officer Charles had ever seen.

As for the limp Theo walked with, it was just another sign of what a great pilot he had been. Theo had let him touch the jagged scar of his war wound as he told the story of what had happened in France. He spoke about the Red Baron and another pilot named Wilhelm von Kleistmann, who was killed in a crash. Also he talked about Hermann Göring, who had flown with his squadron. Göring had liked Theo very much; they had been friends once.

"Theo!" Anna scolded from the doorway. "What tales are you telling the child? Hermann Göring, indeed!"

"He likes my stories; don't you, Charles?" Theo defended as Charles nodded his enthusiasm. "Besides, Anna, it doesn't hurt the boy to know that even good men can go bad."

"Hermann Göring was never a good man!" she said severely. "A greedy buffoon. Hungry for food. For women. And now for power. I never liked him."

"You always were a better judge of character than I." Theo reached for her playfully. "Now tell me what you are really angry about."

"You. In that uniform. A volunteer, you said."

"And so I am. Just a volunteer. But don't you feel safer seeing me in a uniform again?"

"Last time I saw you in a uniform, we lost the war!" Anna pulled away and left the room.

Theo sighed. "Women. Beyond understanding, Charles. You know, she married me because I was so handsome in my uniform." Then Theo told Charles of Anna and his first meeting. How he had gone back again and again to hear Anna play the piano concerto by Schubert. How he had waited outside the stage door because he had fallen in love with her so completely. "And she also fell in love with me," Theo finished. "And she still loves me, or she would not be so angry. Do you understand, child?"

Charles shook his head in a solemn no. He wished Theo would get back to the war stories.

"Ah, well, I shouldn't expect you to understand. You have to be Murphy's age before it becomes important." Theo gazed thoughtfully at his spit-shined boots. "Perhaps I should have a fatherly talk with Murphy before they leave tomorrow. No use letting the women in this family hold all the cards."

෨෮

After dinner Anna and Elisa cleared the table, washed and dried the dishes, and put them away, while the men talked in the music room.

Their faces were serious when the women entered. They had spent the hour discussing details of business and the possibilities of political events that might threaten them.

"The nation that controls the skies will also control the world—" Theo stopped short as Anna and Elisa entered.

Serious discussion was put away. Anna sat at the piano and Elisa produced her violin. Charles, sensing that such a gathering might also need a cello, grabbed Murphy by the hand and dragged him off to fetch Vitorio from the corner of his room.

Murphy marveled at the little boy's sensitivity as he propped up the case and opened it, then pulled back the silk scarf that covered the gleaming wood.

The boy crossed his arms and gazed at the instrument with satisfaction. *"There,"* he seemed to say. *"Now we have a trio!"*

For a moment Anna considered the instrument, then absently said, "If you like, Elisa, we can keep Leah's cello here for her. It would save you the trouble of—"

The pain on the face of little Charles stopped her. He groaned and shook his head wildly.

No, the cello must not stay here. He would not go without Vitorio! That was his only promise that he would see Leah again. And if he saw Leah, then he would also be reunited with his brother, Louis. Vitorio must go with them to America!

"No, Mama." Elisa gazed sadly at Charles. "Do you hear me, Charles?" she asked, reaching out to touch his arm. "We will take Vitorio with us."

"Along with your violins?" Anna seemed surprised. "You will look like a traveling orchestra."

"The gangsters will think we are carrying very large guns." Murphy winked at Charles now, which made him smile in spite of the scar. "Fellows like Al Capone carry their machine guns inside violin cases, see?"

"Well, we cannot leave Leah's cello in Prague, Mama," Elisa said. "Leah told Charles it is a magic carpet."

"Yes," Theo added. "Enough magic to keep the plane up even without wings. No doubt Leah will reach America before we do—"

Anna looked up at him sharply. He ducked slightly and concentrated on the floor.

"Yes." Elisa appeared as if she might cry. Who could say how long it might be before they were together again? "When Leah writes, you must tell her how to contact us."

"If nothing else, we can give her the name of your bank." Theo was serious. A small fortune was being transferred from their Swiss account to Chase-Manhattan on Elisa's behalf. Until they were settled in, any urgent messages would also be passed through the bank in New York. More than simply a personal margin of financial security for Elisa, such a vast amount might have other uses, Theo had explained to Murphy. The uses were unspecified, but Murphy had no doubt that Theo was speaking of the black-market trade for American visas and passports. If there was difficulty obtaining those precious documents through the legal channels in the States, then Murphy would find a way to purchase them—just in case the situation in Czechoslovakia deteriorated.

Murphy also understood quite clearly that the personal fortune of Theo and Anna Lindheim was still actively purchasing the lives of prisoners attempting to flee Germany and Austria. Here in the relative safety and comfort of the house on Mala Strana, a very quiet, personal battle was still taking place between Theo and the Nazis who had thrown him into Dachau.

Twice, in the delirium of his fever, Theo had mentioned the covenant. A priest. A cantor. A man named Stern. The strange reference of the Herrgottseck of Dachau. No one had asked him to explain these dark and frightening words. It was enough that he had been to hell and had survived. Could they ask him to speak of it? So much was simply accepted in silence that an explanation seemed somehow an invitation to destruction. The walls had listened in Germany. The walls had heard that Theo Lindheim gave funds to the dreaded Zionists. Here in Prague might the walls also hear and whisper tales of the covenant to those who walked in darkness beyond the Charles Bridge? And might not those enemies come here to the house on Mala Strana to quietly slit the throat of such a man?

Theo understood all of this quite clearly. The American bank account might serve many purposes. He would leave it to his son-in-law to choose the best purposes if things went badly in Prague.

Murphy was grateful that Anna and Elisa seemed oblivious to the shadow of danger that he felt deeply through Theo tonight. The two played beautifully together—something Mozart had written for piano and violin. Murphy could not recall the name of it. Little Charles sat beside Vitorio and occasionally cast a comradely look toward the instrument. It was as though he could sense Leah and Louis very near to him, Murphy thought. There was deep contentment in the boy's eyes as he absorbed the music like a tonic.

Much too soon it was over. The two women sat together on the piano bench and hugged and wept a farewell to their last evening together for what must be a long time.

Murphy and Theo exchanged a firm handshake. There was so much Theo had left unspoken. Murphy hoped the day would never come when he regretted not asking.

10

Reduced to Prayer

First it was fierce thirst that pierced Shimon's awareness; then he heard the angry voices arguing above him.

"Medical supplies onboard this ship . . . inadequate . . . criminal lack of supplies, Captain." Angry words aroused Shimon to foggy consciousness as he lay facedown on the narrow cot. He was aware that his feet stuck over the end of the bed and his right arm hung limply down off the side. There were voices humming around him. Two men argued above the chorus of crying children and distraught women.

"Look, I am just the captain. Paid by your own people in Palestine. They equipped the ship for five hundred, and now we have nearly eight hundred onboard."

"A proper infirmary was specified. Proper medical supplies are crucial in such conditions. This man may very well die tonight if—"

"His name isn't on the passenger list. A stowaway. If he dies, it will save us the trouble of handing him back to the Germans, now won't it?"

Shimon moaned softly. He barely had the strength to take another breath, let alone strength enough to run.

"It is your own pocket that has benefited by the overcrowding of this ship. Everyone with funds enough has purchased a place. I demand to know if we have food enough."

"If you are careful, there's enough. I accepted additional refugees out of the kindness of my heart. You should thank me."

The engines of the ship drowned out the doctor's response as Shimon drifted into the twilight of awareness. He tried to remember how he had come to be here. How many days had he been hiding? Fire and explosions. Screams of the dying. His own screams. What did it all mean? Where was Leah? Had everyone in the orchestra been killed? A train wreck?

The pieces of the puzzle escaped his grasp. He opened his eyes and stared at the gray steel wall of the tiny infirmary. Flakes of paint and rust clung to the rivets and traced the welded seams. Shimon blinked and closed his eyes again. What had the captain said? *If he dies, it will save us the trouble of—*

The voice of the doctor rose in anger. "There's not enough morphine to get this man through the night."

"Then you'd better save it, Herr Doktor. I counted a dozen pregnant women on the deck this afternoon. If this man is going to die anyway, you'd better save what you have for the living."

Again Shimon opened his eyes. He tried to turn his head but he could not. Something had happened. The pain was not gone, but it was dulled. Morphine. The doctor had given him morphine. *Not enough to get this man . . .* Shimon moved the fingers of his right arm. They were bandaged. His back and right leg were also bandaged. When had this happened? Shimon could not remember. He opened his mouth and tried to speak. A searing thirst choked his words to a hoarse whisper. "Thirsty."

The arguing men fell silent.

Shimon was vaguely aware that one man, the captain, left the room. Gentle hands guided a spoonful of cool liquid through his parched lips. Most of it ran back out onto the thin mattress.

"There now, fellow," the doctor crooned. "Yes. Thirsty. A little water for you. Take it slowly." Another spoonful touched Shimon's mouth. The metal bowl of the spoon tapped against his teeth. He clamped his lips tightly around it to capture the water. His throat had forgotten how to swallow. How long had it been since he had tasted water? "More!" he gasped as the cool liquid slipped down his throat.

"Yes. But very slowly, friend." The doctor offered him another spoonful. A gentle hand rested on his forehead. "You have been through much."

Shimon began to cry—pitiful little sobs, tearless whimpers. His body did not have enough fluid left to spare for tears. How could this kind man know what he had been through? How? Shimon wanted to ask him, "*Were you there? Do you know? Do you remember? Tell me, please!*" But Shimon simply wept and sipped the water and tried to remember how he had come to be here.

"There, there now, friend," the doctor crooned. "Drink first and then sleep. Yes. That's it. Close your eyes and let your body rest."

☙

The small brass bell above the glass door jangled noisily as Bubbe
Rosenfelt entered the offices of the Thomas Cook Travel Agency on the
promenade just across from the Binnen-Alster Lake.

Behind the counter sat a bookish little clerk with thick round glasses
and a powder of dandruff on his navy blue suit. He looked up and immediately greeted her in a crisp British accent.

"Mrs. Rosenfelt! How very good to see you! Very good to see you
again, *indeed*!"

She had difficulty returning his enthusiasm. It had been impossible
to sleep through the night, and her hands trembled with the strain of the
last few weeks.

"Good morning, Mr. Hart." She did not attempt to conceal her concern. "You have my tickets?"

"You are early," he chided.

"It is eight o'clock. You open at eight." This was not a question.

"Yes, of course. But even so I was not expecting you until after tea."

"So, today you can have tea a little early, Mr. Hart. Today you can
have it at eight in the morning instead of four in the afternoon. I'm here
now. Do you have my tickets?"

He noticed the old woman's shaking hands. Her voice cracked. He
could see the stress in her eyes. The sight instantly sobered him. For
twenty years he had been an agent with Thomas Cook. He had sold Mrs.
Rosenfelt a ticket to America a month after Germany had lost the war in
1918. She had lost her two sons in that war, and not since that time had
he seen her in such a state.

"For twenty years you have been purchasing tickets from Cook, my
dear Mrs. Rosenfelt. I learned long ago to have your tickets ready at
least a day early." He hoped this reminder of their long-standing association would cheer the old woman. It did not. She stared at him
strangely as if in this one moment she could remember each detail of
those twenty years. Every small business trip to Paris or Brussels or
London had been arranged through this agency. Often they had chatted about special arrangements to be made for shipping the porcelain
with her. He had come to know little bits and pieces of business about
Rosenfelt Porcelain Company. Now, of course, the Rosenfelt factory
was owned by the Reich. The old woman had not had much reason to
travel since then.

"Thank you, Mr. Hart." She raised her chin slightly as if to cut off her
own memories. "A fast ship to New York, I hope."

"The *Cristobel* from Hamburg to England. Then passage on the *Queen*

Mary from Southampton to New York. There is not a faster ship on the seas. Although the French think they have one in the *Normandie*."

"A new ship?"

"You will be pleased, I think. First class, of course. And on this crossing, the *Queen* will attempt to break the speed record of the *Normandie*. Fast she is, indeed, Mrs. Rosenfelt. You shall see New York within the week."

Bubbe Rosenfelt nodded curtly. She had expected him to perform his task well. It did not seem to occur to her that the booking on the *Queen* at such short notice was a small miracle. The great liners were filled to capacity these days with Americans leaving Europe.

"My trunks . . ." She fumbled in her black velvet handbag for the folded check. "Will you arrange for a porter to pick them up at my flat tonight?"

He frowned. Always before, the trunks of Mrs. Rosenfelt had been picked up at the gate of the large Rosenfelt estate on the Aussen-Alster. That, too, had been confiscated by the Nazis when the factory had been Aryanized. Now the old woman lived in a small flat a few blocks from here. It had been difficult to arrange for a porter to fetch her trunks. Germans were forbidden to act as servants to Jews. No German porter would go near her place. Finally Mr. Hart had arranged for an English porter from the *Cristobel* to retrieve her belongings.

"Tonight at seven?" he answered. Then, more out of curiosity than need for an answer, he asked, "And will you want me to book a return voyage for you, Mrs. Rosenfelt?"

A slight smile curved the corner of the old woman's mouth. "At my age, Mr. Hart, it is foolish to make long-range plans, *nu*?"

"I am sure you will outlive us all, Mrs. Rosenfelt." He sounded appalled.

"I may well outlive any Jew who is *meshugge* enough to book a return voyage to Germany." The smile disappeared and her eyes widened at the truth in her words. "And I will certainly outlive any Jew who stays here."

The little clerk cleared his throat uncomfortably. "Terrible times," he muttered. "Terrible . . . terrible."

She leveled her gaze on him. The old dignity returned. "I hope you have your travel arrangements in order, Mr. Hart. Things are not looking so good for the courtship of England and Germany either, *nu*? A few more weeks, and the Führer might pull the trigger—and every Englishman still in Germany is a bug beneath the jackboots."

The little clerk sniffed uneasily and rummaged through his neat file for the old woman's tickets. This was not a subject he wanted to linger on. "We all have confidence that Prime Minister Chamberlain will come to some agreement with the Führer. He has pledged himself and Britain to peace, you know."

"So!" She frowned and reddened a bit. Her chin lifted higher as she slowly raised the pince-nez to her eyes. "So, it is peace Chamberlain wants, eh? He should have thought of that when he let the Wehrmacht march into the Rhineland! And then into Vienna."

These were dangerous words. Mr. Hart hoped no German pedestrian would come into the office before she left. "Not our affair. No indeed, Mrs. Rosenfelt."

She would not be silenced. "When you're all running around London looking like a bunch of flies wearing gas masks, write me in New York, Mr. Hart! Tell me then it is not your affair!" The old woman was angry now. He had never seen her angry except for one occasion when her baggage had been lost.

The clerk smiled mechanically as he pulled her tickets from the file. "Ah! Here we are. Everything in order." He pretended not to feel the old woman's fierce eye on him as he scanned the documents. "All in ship-shape order, Mrs. Rosenfelt!" Too cheerful. Strained. Unpleasant. He wanted her to leave. He slipped the tickets into a brown manila envelope emblazoned with the logo: *Thomas Cook—See the World, Land, and Sea!* He slid the envelope across the counter to her. For a moment he wondered about the old woman's family. The granddaughter, Maria. He would not ask. Would not prolong the encounter.

It seemed a very long time before the old woman picked up the envelope. Her hands were no longer trembling. She was cool and aloof. "I will expect the porter at precisely seven this evening then." She let the pince-nez drop to the end of the cord in a gesture that said, *Or else.*

"Of course, Mrs. Rosenfelt." She was leaving and the clerk was relieved. Two SS soldiers strolled by the office window outside. The old woman turned on her heel and marched out behind them. "Have a pleasant journey," called Mr. Hart, but she seemed not to hear him as the bell above the door rang angrily.

ᖇᖀ

Each year on the anniversary of the death of Herbert Rosenfelt, Mrs. Rosenfelt made a trip to the Jewish cemetery to commemorate his Yahrzeit. Before this Nazi nonsense had begun, she had always imagined herself someday resting peacefully beside her husband beneath the white carrara marble headstone: *Trudence, wife of Herbert.* Then it would have been the duty of Maria and the great-grandchildren to make the annual pilgrimage, place a pebble on the headstone, and say the required prayers.

No Jew in Hamburg, or all of Germany for that matter, had foreseen

that politics would interrupt not only the traditions of life but those of
death as well.

For the last time, Bubbe Rosenfelt pushed open the squeaking
wrought-iron gate of the cemetery. Glancing over her shoulder, she spotted two Brownshirt Nazi youths strolling outside the high walls two
blocks away. They did not seem to notice her as she slipped inside the
grounds and closed the gate behind her. She sighed with relief. Everyone
knew the stories of these young Aryans who lay in wait outside the syna-
gogues and cemeteries to beat Jews who came to visit such places.

She looked over the vast field of crowded headstones. Here were old
friends, members of the inner circle of her life with Herbert in the old
days. Here were weddings and births and proud parents at a son's bar
mitzvah. Here were parties and quiet chats over lunch, an evening at the
opera, bright songs at Hanukkah, and the mellow chant of prayers during the Days of Awe. One by one old friends and relatives had come to
join the generations in this quiet field. Linden trees budded each spring
and shed in the fall to blanket old residents and new arrivals with leaves.
Those who had once wept here beside a loved one were, soon enough,
the cause of new tears. This was the only place in Hamburg Mrs.
Rosenfelt regretted leaving. For a Jew, the cemetery was the last neighborhood that was safe in Germany. Unfortunately, one had to be dead
in order to experience that safety. Hitler raved that the only good Jew
was a dead Jew. Mrs. Rosenfelt often replied to the maniac on the radio
that the only *safe* Jew was a dead Jew!

She stooped and picked up a pebble beside the headstone of Emma
Goldfarb. Emma had always been a bit of a yenta. One could not share a
luncheon with her without hearing every last detail of who was doing
what to whom, or who had a son or daughter running off with one of
them. Now just about everyone Emma had gossiped about was dead
also. In retrospect, it made such idle conversation quite absurd.

"Well, Emma," Mrs. Rosenfelt said wryly, "here's something to gossip about. Trudence Rosenfelt is *finally* leaving Hamburg! You said for
years I was an American at heart. Criticized me for not giving up my
American citizenship. So. I'm telling you that you were right all along.
Nu? My grandchildren I have sent off like merchandise on a freighter.
And I am not staying around to have my headstone shot up by the SS for
target practice, either!"

Mrs. Rosenfelt had never much approved of Emma Goldfarb. She
had been quite overweight and had dreadful table manners. In spite of
the seriousness of the woman's death, Mrs. Rosenfelt had giggled when
Herbert commented on the strained look of the pallbearers as they had
carried the coffin through the iron gate.

Ah, but there were others here! Others who had slipped away unexpectedly. Friends who had been cut off too young, and whose faces the old woman now remembered as more youthful than her own granddaughter's! How had they stayed so young in her mind, when *she* had become so very old?

She walked slowly among these old acquaintances until she came at last to the three headstones that anchored her heart to this small patch of earth.

Herbert Rosenfelt
Beloved Husband of Trudence
Beloved Father of Michael and Daniel

On either side of this stone were the markers of Michael and Daniel. Although neither of the boys had been buried here, Bubbe had needed the stones as a shrine to their memory. Sweet Michael had left little Maria as a reminder of his life. Daniel had never married. Now, only Mrs. Rosenfelt remembered the curly haired baby who had grown twenty years to manhood only to be cut down in one moment of war.

The old woman stood quietly beside the graves and mourned again. *So young, so young! So very young!*

"Michael," she whispered, "your little Maria is thirty-five now. Already she has lived to be older than you were. You would be a grandfather, you know! *Oy!* You were so very young. And now, look at your old mother, will you?" Tears streamed freely down her cheeks. "I have come to promise you I will not let them perish! And so I must leave this place. I will not visit again. No. My sons. My husband. Sweet Herbert, I cannot come again on your Yahrzeit. . . . " With that, she reached out and touched each stone as though she were touching the faces of her loved ones. She placed the pebble on top of Herbert's stone in a long row of pebbles that counted the visits she had made. Softly she rehearsed the ancient prayers and prayed new prayers for Maria and Klaus and the children.

Birds chirped insistently in the branches of the stately linden trees overhead. Time passed too quickly in this timeless place. Time had stopped for the husband of her youth, and she had grown old without him. In fifty years, she thought, perhaps some young Jews would stumble on this site and would notice that Trudence, wife of Herbert Rosenfelt, was not resting here beside her husband as she had planned. They would now know the reason. In fifty years even the Hitler Youth would be old men. Many would be dust beneath the linden trees of some other cemetery. And then, who would remember that even here the long arm of Hitler reached out to deny the final goal of an old woman?

"And so, *shalom*, my dear hearts," she murmured. "*Shalom*. For Maria. For Klaus. For the children. I must live until they have no need of me! If God is willing," she whispered as she closed the iron gate, "*they* will live to remember why I am not beside you, Herbert."

⟨ഔ⟩

The North Sea was called the German Ocean by some. The name seemed quite appropriate now. Klaus helped Maria walk the length of the warped deck in hopes of helping her work out the stiffness in her muscles from their cold night onboard the *Darien*.

Two great battleships flying the flag of the Reich cut across the path of the little freighter. Their wakes exploded like giant surf against the bow of the ship. An old rabbi stared after their retreating hulks and patted Klaus on the arm as he steadied Maria against the rocking.

"*Oy!*" exclaimed the old man, thoughtfully stroking his beard. "You think this means we have frightened them away, maybe?"

"We are much closer to the shores of England than Germany now," Klaus said angrily. "They have followed us here to let us know—"

"Let us know? *Vas?* Let us know?" The rabbi nodded and considered.

"To let us know they could sink us," chimed in a young man of about eighteen named Aaron.

"*Nein, kinder!* Then God has told them the truth, *nu?*" The rabbi shook his finger in Aaron's face. "Nobody sinks us unless God, blessed be He, gives His permission!"

A small group of wary passengers laughed more from relief than from true amusement.

"So, Rebbe?" Maria held her hand to the small of her aching back and straightened. "Have you got a way to make sure God does not give them permission later?"

Voices chimed in: "A blessing! Give us a blessing, Rebbe! A prayer we can pray, maybe! A battleship prayer!"

The old man looked around approvingly. "Such a congregation here!" He nodded. "Yes. We have a minyan and more. Then we will make a battleship blessing, *nu?*" He rested his bearded chin in his hand and stood for a long moment of deep thought that no one dared to interrupt. He raised his gnarled hand like an ancient tree branch conducting the winds of the great German Ocean. He began: "May the Eternal, blessed be He, bless and keep the Nazi ships—"

A groan of disapproval rose from the ragged ranks of the minyan.

Has the rabbi lost his mind in the wind, you think? So old, he has forgotten which side God is supposed to be on!

"Wait a minute! Wait a minute! I am not finished yet!" The rabbi protested the interruption of his blessing. "May the Eternal," he began again, "blessed be He, bless and keep the Nazi ships . . . an ocean away from us!"

A pattering of pleased applause rose up with the blessing of the aged, exiled rabbi from Nuremberg. The smokestacks of the battleships slipped below the horizon as if they had fallen off the edge of the earth. Everyone hoped that was the case, anyway. This blessing was repeated up the steps and down the steps above decks and below. It added flavor to the tasteless breakfast of porridge. It quelled appetites of hatred and turned fear and anger into happy laughter. *To bless the enemy with such a blessing! May the Eternal, blessed be He—hear that one, eh, Chaim?*

When the rabbi donned his tallith, which billowed like a banner in the harsh ocean breeze, many men who had not attended services or stopped by shul for years found themselves drawn to this flag of prayer. *What else is there for us to do now, eh? We are reduced to praying. Not such a bad place for hopeless men to be.*

〜∞〜

After morning prayers were prayed and the Eternal was thanked for holding the leaking freighter up from the bottom of the North Sea, the old rabbi organized a Torah school for the children. "Who knows how long we will be on this floating island, *nu*? Should the brains of our kinderlach be turned to unkosher seafood in the meantime?"

By special dispensation, little girls were also permitted to join in the holy study of Torah. This met with the approval of almost everyone onboard the vessel, since most were not at all religious and had not clung to the old ways. It was decided that the rabbi of Nuremberg was quite progressive, even though he looked like something from a Polish ghetto and most German Jews wanted to shed that old-fashioned image. "What will it hurt, a little Torah? And he lets the girls study, too! Progressive, that's what! If we land in America, this will be looked well upon!"

There were a few hard-core Orthodox who did not approve. They considered themselves the only Jews, the only true Jews, on the entire ship. Because of their holiness, the Eternal, blessed be He, might save the rest. But there was also the possibility that because of the unholiness of all the others, the Eternal, blessed be He, might send along a big storm, and *whoosh*! There goes the whole ship. That small, unhappy clique of thirty-seven huddled forlornly in a bleak corner of the cargo hold. "Did you hear he's letting the girls study Torah with the boys? *Oy!* Now we shall certainly sink!"

The sun came out and the waters nearing the shores of England were calm. Some considered it a good sign. Because the rabbi had not actually cursed the battleships, God was sending back the blessing to the fragile human cargo on the *Darien*.

Whatever it was, Maria was thankful for the warmth of the sun and grateful to the rabbi for rounding up the little ones and putting their minds on something other than their misery. Klaus rested against the ventilation shaft and Maria sat comfortably in the crook of his arm. The baby moved within her, and she laid her husband's hand on her bulging stomach and waited expectantly for another kick. The baby was obliging.

Klaus opened one eye and smiled at Maria. "This one must be a son, I think," he said drowsily.

"You have said that every time, and every time I have another girl!" Maria chided.

"So? I won't mind being so outnumbered as long as all my girls are as smart and pretty as you."

Maria cast a long look at their five daughters who sat in a row at the Torah school. The sunlight shone on their braided hair. Each child had hair color in varying shades of golden brown. Trudy, the oldest, had the darkest hair, and then, in order, Katrina, Louise, Gretchen, and little Ada-Marie, who seemed to be enjoying the excitement of the story of the Red Sea more than anyone! Here was blessing. Maria felt it all over again as she looked at their children. They were not unhappy. They did not seem to notice that they had no home. Or that they slept on the deck of a ship. There had been a slight murmur about the porridge, but they were hungry enough that it had disappeared all the same.

At lunchtime, bread was blessed and served with a very thin potato soup. They were close to England now. Seabirds flew behind them and raced before them. Captain Burton found the music of the BBC radio and turned it on over the loudspeakers for everyone to hear. A buzz of excitement swept through the congregation. *So this is England! They are playing Mendelssohn! How long is it since we have heard Mendelssohn?*

Very few among them understood the crackling British voices that began their urgent recital over the air. It was news. Maria was grateful that the majority did not understand. She was sorry when others, who knew she was fluent in English, gathered around her for an interpretation.

> *"Riots have rocked the British mandate of Palestine for a month without letup. Last night several British police were murdered execution-style by an Arab mob protesting further influx of Jewish refugees from*

Europe. As the general strike called by the Mufti increases in violence, Prime Minister Chamberlain has promised to take another look at the question of immigration. Meanwhile, in response to the state of emergency, all illegal immigration of Jews to Palestine will be stopped. Those arriving without proper visas will be summarily returned to their ports of origin. In other news today—"

The loudspeaker abruptly fell silent. Captain Burton stepped from behind the grimy windows of the bridge and emerged from his place at the helm for the first time. Maria had never seen him before. In the last twenty-four hours he had been a shadow moving behind the glass. Now he leaned against the rusty rail and stared down, searching the faces of these strange people he had agreed to carry away from Germany. He wore a blue cable-knit sweater that was torn at the seam beneath his arm. His trousers were grubby khaki. His features were shielded by the cracked brim of his captain's hat and a full reddish beard streaked with gray. Maria could not tell if he was an old man, or young. He hardly looked like a man with the dignity one would expect of a captain. But then, this ship was only barely a ship.

He chewed his lip thoughtfully, then spoke in a loud voice. His words were relayed down the steps belowdecks. "I heard the news this morning. I thought you should hear it as well." His German was passable. Easy to tell he was American. "So the English have closed off Palestine to us. I had thought that was the most reasonable destination. This changes things."

Hardly anyone on the ship knew there was a destination. Most had dreamed of America. "So where are we going, Captain?" an old woman called up.

"Southampton first. England. We are in need of supplies. Medical and otherwise. Then we'll head for New York."

"But quotas are full in America!" someone else shouted. This information alarmed Maria. Surely full quotas would not affect them once Bubbe Rosenfelt got to New York to work for their visas.

"Every quota is filled," said the captain. He was blunt. A realist. But then, why had he taken on this human cargo? "But we have to go somewhere. Unless you want to go back to Hamburg?"

A resounding "NO!" filled the North Sea air. Did they hear it in Hamburg? With their rocks and bottles and spit? Did they hear it in Palestine? With their doors shut and locked?

"Then Southampton it is. And then New York, if you please." He turned on his heel and returned to his dingy throne room.

11

Our Enemies Rejoice

Elisa clutched the edge of her seat as the little Pan Am passenger plane rumbled over the southwest face of the mountains that bordered Czech-Sudetenland and Germany. *Everything looks so beautiful from the high perspective of a bird,* she thought. *Beautiful and peaceful.*

She did not need the commentary of a guide to point out the landmarks of what had been her native country. A hundred times as a child, her father had taken her flying over the bucolic German countryside. Yes, Elisa knew it well, and she understood how the most beautiful music on earth had been created within these borders.

Neither she nor Murphy mentioned the fact to Charles that their aircraft was just above the heads of the leaders of the New Germany who would be quite pleased if these passengers died in a flaming air crash. The child seemed unaware that men like Hitler or Himmler or Göring could look up from their balconies and see the plane easily as it soared through German airspace. Charles was fascinated with tiny toy cars creeping along the highways and little boats that floated on the silver ribbons of rivers and canals below.

Two Luftwaffe fighter planes buzzed the passenger aircraft. When Elisa visibly paled at the sight of their swastika emblems, Murphy reached out to take her hand in his. With a reassuring look, he wordlessly told her she must not worry. Then the fighters banked and retreated with amazing speed back toward Frankfurt. The incident lasted only seconds, and yet Elisa remained rigid with fear even after their plane reached the flat farmlands of Holland.

Charles sat with his forehead plastered against the round window throughout the journey. If the military aircraft had frightened him, he gave no sign of it. His eyes grew wide as their plane finally began its slow descent toward the grassy airfield outside Amsterdam. He laughed with such a total absence of fear that at last Elisa sat back and relaxed enough to pat him on the back and point through the window at the old buildings and canals of Amsterdam.

"Instead of roads, you see . . . lots of little canals all over the city. And people ride in boats here and there."

Charles pointed through the afternoon haze at the docks of Amsterdam. Like ducks on a pond, ocean steamers lay moored in the harbor.

"Tonight we board a little steamer that will carry us across the Channel to London," Elisa explained. "Two days in London, and then—" she looked happily at Murphy—"then we go to America."

Charles nodded enthusiastically and clapped his hands. Then he winked knowingly at Murphy and held up his hand to make a circle with thumb and index finger that said *okay*!

"Nothing to it, eh, kid?" Murphy said, but his face was clouded with a concern that made Elisa's smile dim.

"What is it?" she asked quietly.

"Nothing to it," Murphy repeated the words in a tone that was heavy with foreboding. "From Prague to the Netherlands in less time than it takes for a little nap." He frowned and looked questioningly at Elisa. Did she hear the reason for his apprehension? "Your father is right, you know. The country that rules the skies will rule the world."

Charles looked eagerly back out the window as the runway rose up to meet their wheels. Elisa simply stared in blank horror at Murphy. Everything was *so close* on the Continent! Even this plodding little passenger plane had cut a swath across three countries within a matter of hours. She considered the lightning speed of the German fighter planes that had roared across their path.

Her voice faltered as she asked the first question that entered her mind. "How long—" she cleared her throat to begin again—"How quickly could one of *them* fly from here to . . . England?"

Murphy understood her perfectly. "Less than twenty minutes." He looked away, not wanting her to see in his eyes his deepest fears.

"To London?" She did not notice the jolt of the landing. Charles clapped his hands in delight again and tugged at Elisa's sleeve. She did not acknowledge him. "Do the English have such aircraft?" she asked.

The hum of the engines sputtered and died. "No," Murphy answered grimly as he gathered up his belongings and squinted into the bright light of the opening hatch.

◈

Their passage was booked on a steamship that would carry them to London within a matter of hours.

The little trio stood near the bow of the ship and let the salt air sting their cheeks and blow their hair. Murphy had one hand on the shoulder of Charles and the other wrapped around Elisa's waist.

Somehow this slow, old-fashioned method of travel helped to calm Elisa. The Channel had separated and protected England from the Continent for centuries. Great armadas had sailed against her and been broken in pieces on her shores. Surely, Elisa reasoned, the water could not be crossed by the Nazis without great sacrifice, even if the fleets came in airplanes rather than in ships. Surely the Channel must still afford the British the protection of isolation.

She would ask Murphy to explain it all later. She wanted to know everything he knew. She wanted to know the name of that fear she had seen in his eyes. When Charles was out of hearing, she would ask Murphy what it all meant.

◈

"Frau Trudence Rosenfelt?" The iron-jawed matron stared at the old woman with contempt. "So. You are going back to America at last. After the Rosenfelt family has stolen from the good Aryan people of the Reich."

Mrs. Rosenfelt drew herself up in indignation. The matron sneered and adjusted the Nazi armband on her brown uniform. She looked very much like a bulldog, Mrs. Rosenfelt thought. All bully and swagger and bluff. "Yes. I am going home. Only it is the Aryan people who have stolen from my family. I am not the thief here."

The sneer turned to instant rage. "Silence! Old Jewish pig!" The woman kicked the trunk the porter had hauled to the dock where the *Cristobel* was moored. Mrs. Rosenfelt was surprised that it had not been loaded already. She was startled that of all the passengers, she and two others had been detained on the quay and escorted under guard to the small, dark room in the back of the Port Authority's office.

"I am an American citizen, I remind you—"

"You are a Jew! You are a smuggler and a spy!"

"What are you doing with my trunk?" Mrs. Rosenfelt took a step toward her steamer trunk. The seal of the Gestapo had been stamped across it in several places.

"Your trunk! Old Jew! You tell us now what you are doing stealing art treasures from the Reich? Eh, old sow? It is enough to have you thrown into prison!" The Nazi matron enjoyed her work of intimidation.

Mrs. Rosenfelt did not give her the satisfaction of letting her see the fear that filled her. She had heard of this last-minute persecution. Indeed, she had seen it the morning Klaus and Maria had sailed on the *Darien*. The Reich officials had swarmed the decks beating and arresting anyone who opposed them. It was also common for small objects of art or foreign currency to be planted in the suitcase of someone whom they hoped might be able to pay additional money to escape the country.

"I cannot think what you are raving about." Mrs. Rosenfelt lifted her chin defiantly.

The matron swaggered toward her. The dark roots of her blond hair were plainly evident. "You deny that you were once the owner of Rosenfelt Porcelain?"

"Of course I do not deny that!"

"And your factory was Aryanized, was it not?"

"Yes. Speaking of thieves, your government took everything. My company. My home—"

"Shut up, old Jew! I am speaking!"

"Go right ahead, *nebech*! But what you say does not change truth."

"The truth!" The matron jerked her head up like a sleuth who has discovered a clue. She raised her thick finger and leveled it at the trunk. "The truth is that all porcelain formerly in the possession of—"

"*Oy!* I must not forget. The Reich *also* stole our collection of porcelain. *Oy!* That along with everything else."

"Art treasures! Confiscated by the Reich."

"Three hundred years of Rosenfelt craftsmanship!"

"At the expense of poorly paid German laborers."

"Young woman, my ship is leaving any minute—"

"Without you! Silence, until you answer the charges!"

"What charges?"

"Smuggling! Theft!"

Mrs. Rosenfelt was certain that something must have been placed in the trunk in order to detain her. She had no financial resources left with which she could buy her way out of this trouble. "Theft?" she scoffed. "I demand if you hold me, you must call the American consulate at once!"

"We will call no one except the police van to take you to Gestapo headquarters where other smugglers are sent!" The woman leaned confidently on the large steamer trunk.

"What is it that I am accused of?" Bubbe replied in weary resignation. There was no use denying anything. For some reason she had become a target of this monstrous game that demanded all Jews leave Germany, and yet made it nearly impossible to do so.

The matron smiled grimly. Her right front tooth was capped with gold, which added to the impression that she was a caricature of the tough, hard Nazi jailer. "I told you, Frau Rosenfelt—stealing."

"Tell me, please, what I have stolen."

The matron leaned back and reached into a packing crate. From a box of sawdust and newspapers, she pulled a porcelain figurine. She held it up triumphantly and placed it on the trunk beside her. Light from a grimy window shone on the delicate figure of Mary and the Christ child.

Mrs. Rosenfelt gasped. The figure of Mary and her little boy had, indeed, been one of her favorites. "But . . . where . . . I have not seen that piece in nearly three years!"

"You admit you are familiar—"

"Familiar!" Mrs. Rosenfelt scoffed. Mary, with clear skin, bright eyes, and long dark braid, timelessly captured in a smile of delight as her young son held up a small wooden boat he had made for her. Here was a holy moment between mother and child. Yes, Mrs. Rosenfelt knew the piece well.

"When the thousand figures of the Rosenfelt collection were absorbed by the Reich, this was not among them!"

The old woman's heart fell. Could this be the reason they had detained her? She had given the figurine to her housekeeper, Frau Haefner. "I gave it to a friend as a gift."

"It was not yours to give!" the matron roared. Her face reddened with fury.

"It was mine. More mine than you can know. You see, I posed for the figure of Mary. My little son Daniel was the child Jesus," Mrs. Rosenfelt said quietly. "Yes. Mine."

The matron nearly choked at the words of the old woman. "You are saying to us, to the Reich, that you posed for this—"

A smile flitted across the thin lips of Mrs. Rosenfelt. "I was much younger then, I admit. Even a beauty—"

Her words were cut short as the matron spit in her face. "Sacrilege! A Jewess and her spawn posing for a holy—"

Bubbe Rosenfelt felt silent as she wiped the spittle from her face. For a moment she thought she would be ill; then a new indignation took hold of her. "I thought that is why Herr Hitler had all images of Jesus removed from the churches. You did not know your Christ was a Jew, Frau Matron?"

The matron was speechless in her rage. She gaped at the tender figure of mother and child. "You . . . you . . . this art is stolen, and now you will pay for it!"

"How did you come by it?" Mrs. Rosenfelt raised her voice gruffly.

"Your Frau Haefner confessed."

"Did she confess that her employer had given her a personal gift? Her heart had been broken by the desecration of the church by Nazi symbols, and so I offered her—"

"This is enough! Now I will call my Oberführer and we will see how you feel in a Gestapo cell!" The matron spun on her heel and reached for the door.

"Before you do that," Mrs. Rosenfelt said coolly in a voice that carried some dark threat, "you would be wise to contact Colonel Beich at the Office of Immigration. He might have some word of advice for you. Something about the family connection of this old sow, as you have so named me."

The matron seemed not to hear. She slammed the door behind her as she left the room. Mrs. Rosenfelt heard the key turn in the latch. The silent, empty room was a welcome relief after nearly half an hour of threats and insults.

She moved toward the old trunk and pulled herself onto it until she sat beside the porcelain figurine that had caused her so much trouble this morning. Poor Frau Haefner must also be in some sort of terrible trouble. Why would she confess a crime that was no crime at all?

Mrs. Rosenfelt looked down at the image of herself and Daniel so many, many years ago. Gently she touched the smooth, happy face of the child with her own aged finger. She could remember when the face of Mary had been her own mirrored reflection. Of course, no one could possibly see the resemblance now, but how wonderfully obvious it had been once! She had told Frau Haefner the secret when she gave the piece to her on their farewell. *"Remember, it is a Jewish mother and her son. Can you remember that, Frau Haefner? Will you still be able to pray if you think of that? Or must all Germans remove their God from their hearts to worship Hitler?"*

Frau Haefner had wept bitterly that day. Not only was her mistress being robbed of all her belongings, but after thirty-seven years of service, Frau Haefner was no longer able to work for a Jew!

What happened to my devoted housekeeper? Mrs. Rosenfelt wondered. *And what is to become of me?* She glanced nervously at her watch. There was less than an hour left before the *Cristobel* was scheduled to sail. The Nazis would certainly not allow her to leave in time. The trip to the Gestapo headquarters would take up most of the hour.

She clutched the porcelain figurine to her as if she had found an old friend. "Well, then, you have got me into this. How will you get me out of it?" Then she chuckled softly at the irony.

She had barely spoken when the door flew back and a young red-haired officer in a black tunic stepped into the room. "Heil Hitler!" he cried.

When she did not reply he looked momentarily confused.

"So, you are keeping me off the boat over this?" Mrs. Rosenfelt slid off her trunk. "You Nazis have taken Christ out of every church, and now you will arrest me for giving this to my servant?"

The young officer did not reply. He clapped his hands and shouted at two dockhands who waited nervously behind him. At the signal, they moved awkwardly into the cramped space and hefted the trunk.

"How long will you detain me?" Mrs. Rosenfelt demanded, still clutching the figurine.

The officer jerked his black-gloved hand out in a gesture that demanded she give him the porcelain. She held it a moment longer and then extended her hand and the figurine. A fraction of a second before the officer grasped the statue, she opened her fingers. He shouted as it tumbled from his grasp and smashed into a thousand pieces on the hard concrete floor. Head and arms, smiles and eyes, flowing folds of cloth and the tiny sailboat became sharp splinters that sprayed over the spit-shined jackboots of the startled officer.

His mouth opened and closed as he stared at the shattered glass littering the concrete. At last he whispered in disbelief, "It was worth thousands—*why?*"

Mrs. Rosenfelt did not feel regret for the broken figurine. Yes, it had been one of the best among the thousand or so that had been in their priceless collection. The piece had been famous. There were a few more in the edition. No doubt the Nazis would steal one from some other collector. Of course, it would not be the first of the edition, but—

"A tragic blunder on your part, Herr Officer," Mrs. Rosenfelt replied coolly. "Your first error is my arrest." Again she glanced at her watch. The great whistle of the *Cristobel* bellowed from the dock. "The second error is detaining me."

"I came—" he could not take his eyes from the smashed treasure at his feet—"I was coming to tell you . . . a mistake. We thought . . . that is, Colonel Beich says you are the aunt of . . . an important American . . . and . . ." To finish his stammering and incoherent thought, he clicked his heels and shouted, "Heil Hitler!" Shards of porcelain crunched under his boots.

"You are telling me I am free to go?"

He bowed slightly in agreement and clicked his heels again. "And I am instructed to tell you that charges have been—"

"Dropped." Mrs. Rosenfelt inclined her head slightly and picked her way out carefully through the mess. "*Oy*, such a pity you broke this. Worth thousands, no doubt."

The clean, sleek hull of the *Cristobel* was still waiting at the dock when she emerged.

❧

As the gulls above the *Darien* increased in numbers, wheeling and crying the approach to England, the ships and small fishing vessels in the sea lanes became a common sight. Trudy and Gretchen made a game of calling out each new sighting and then guessing the flag under which the craft sailed.

"England!"

"No, the flag is American—at least I think so—like the one on our ship."

There was a certain pride when, indeed, one of this vast and varied armada displayed a flag that was identical to their own. Somehow, sitting beneath this American flag made them all feel a small part of the mysterious and wonderful country. The colors were the same as the British Union Jack, but everyone knew that this was because the Americans had fought the English kings and tyrants to make their own country. A brave bunch, those Americans.

Great steamers and liners and freight ships much sleeker and newer than the *Darien* carried this banner. The glory of those vessels was keenly felt by the ragged voyagers who watched them pass and waved as if they were old friends meeting on the street corner.

Young Aaron, who had spent the afternoon on the bottom step leading to the bridge, paid little attention to the squeals of the little girls and boys who pretended now to be pirates searching for a schooner to pillage. Aaron had other matters of grave importance on his mind. Balanced precariously on his lap was a worn red volume, Karl Baedeker's *Handbook for Travelers*. It was a 1901 version describing Great Britain and Wales in the German language. The folding maps inside the book were carefully unfolded and held from ripping in the wind. The travelers' guide had once belonged exclusively to the young man, and he guarded its contents jealously from the old men and women who flocked around him like a herd of tugboats nosing an ocean liner.

When a dozen passengers pointed toward a spur of land jutting into the sea and called that this must be the mouth of the Thames, Aaron shook his head in solemn disagreement and the crowd waited expectantly to hear what place this was on the Baedeker's map.

"Spurn Heat," Aaron announced like a professor of geography. This strange British name was pronounced and mispronounced around the deck until the point of land disappeared in a mist and Aaron raised his hand to point and say, "Here is Humber and there is Gremsby."

"Humber . . . Humber . . . *Humber?* There is a place called *Humber?* But where is the *Thames?* And where is *London*, boy?"

Little fishing boats peeled off into another enormous-looking bay. "Still not the Thames," Aaron proclaimed with authority. "It is called the Walsh." He raised his chin slightly with a gesture that pointed to some distant place that only he could see. "Over there is a harbor called Boston on a river called Witham, which leads to another city called Leeds."

This lesson from Baedeker's was far more interesting than Torah school had been.

"What is next, Aaron? What will come after this Walsh place? *Nu!* Tell us, Aaron."

Aaron became a sort of prophet. "We follow the steamship lanes." The assembly looked at the water as if there were a visible lane the freighter would follow. *Hmm*s and *ahh*s of understanding rippled through the impromptu class.

Aaron continued. "Then we round a part of England that looks like a mitten." He held up his hand to display four fingers as they would be tucked into a woolen mitten on a cold day. On the tips of each finger he placed a city: Wells, Cromer, and Great Yarmouth rounded the curve, and Dunwich, the Naze, Blackwater, and Foulness followed his index finger.

These names were tried on Yiddish tongues without much success. At last, Aaron pointed decisively to the curve in his hand where thumb met the index finger. "And here is the *Thames!*"

Everyone held up imaginary mittens on left hands. A sigh of content-ment rose up through the flock. "The Thames is *here*! And the great city of London is *there* . . . right in the crook of your thumb. This lesson is as plain as a hand in front of your eyes! *Oy!* Who said this congregation does not know where we are going?"

The terror of battleship wakes diminished as eager eyes studied phantom maps and repeated foreign-sounding cities over and over again. "Perhaps in England we will have a chance to walk a bit on dry land while the captain provisions the ship, *nu?*"

"Already two days. The earth will move beneath us when we walk, we are so used to the wobbles of the sea."

"Still . . . solid planks. A store where we can buy a pillow maybe? a blanket? You think these English docks sell deck chairs?"

"You have money, Chaim?"

"More than that—maybe they will take that poor creature to a hospital. How he must be suffering! *Oy!*"

This sentiment was shared by everyone on the ship. Captain Burton, it was rumored, had already radioed ahead to the English authorities for an ambulance and a stretcher to carry the poor stowaway to medical help. Yes, this was a good thing, this stopover in England. The British were kind and gentle people, Aaron told them. His father had told him so.

At last, the *Darien* labored down the index finger to the crook of the thumb and the mouth of the Thames. Was it possible that all of them, even the surly Orthodox Jews, were now on the deck? The passengers were packed like kosher herring from bow to stern. The rabbi of Nuremberg began to sing in a quavering voice, and the hymn of praise was caught by stronger voices. They had so much to be grateful for. Here in these waters there were no Nazi battleships. No stones would be hurled at them from the docks or bridges. Here men were civilized, and such a thing could not happen.

♋

It was Trudy who first raised her arm to point at the little naval vessel speeding across the water toward them. "Look!" the child cried. "Look, Mama, it is flying the English flag!"

The Union Jack posed stiffly in the wind as the little boat altered its course slightly to intersect that of the *Darien*. Klaus swallowed hard. The men in their British uniforms stood scowling up at them. Their commander raised a bullhorn and shouted up to Captain Burton: "In the name of His Majesty, you are denied anchorage in British waters! Again, I repeat . . ."

Maria and Klaus looked back at the dim glass of the bridge. The shadow of Captain Burton raised a fist in defiance, but the thrumming engines of the freighter groaned and dropped to an unsteady heartbeat as the ship stopped in the water. The passengers moaned as one suffering human soul together. So this was their welcome to civilization!

What radio communication had been taking place between Burton and the port authorities? Klaus suddenly wondered.

"SS *Darien*!" the commander of the naval vessel bellowed. "You are denied anchorage in British waters! You will change course or we shall be forced to take punitive action."

Worried refugees crowded around Maria for an interpretation of the ominous-sounding words of the Englishman. "What is he saying? What? They will not let us stop even awhile here? First Nazi battleships, and now the English! *Oy!* We look so dangerous?"

The door to the bridge burst open. Maria could see the first mate at the helm. Captain Burton stood grimly gripping the railing as the naval vessel came alongside. Burton's lips moved, silently cursing the arrogant sailors who now called up, demanding to come aboard.

A rope ladder was lowered by a crew member who obeyed the single nod of Burton's head. The old rabbi from Nuremberg stepped near to the rail and muttered a prayer for deliverance as the British commander boarded with five armed sailors. Captain Burton did not offer to come down from his perch. Nor did he invite the British sailors up. He simply stood with arms crossed until they dusted off their white trousers and shielded their eyes against the sun as they looked toward him.

The British commander stood in the center of a semicircle of his men. Rifles were unslung and the men turned to face the crowd of refugees.

"I want *you* to tell them!" Captain Burton shouted. "Go ahead! Tell them that we are denied anchorage even for a few hours for provisions!"

The British commander put a hand on his hips, his legs apart to brace himself in case some desperate character charged him. "Your ship carries unauthorized cargo," he called back. "Potentially dangerous to our country as the immigration quota now stands."

"Tell them how you won't let us get close to shore because you are afraid some might jump ship and swim to land. Go ahead! Explain why you are doing this, Commander, after two hours of radio negotiation!"

The refugees pushed nearer. They seemed unafraid of the weapons.

Trudy hugged Gretchen, who proclaimed loudly, "I won't jump into the water unless God parts it again!"

Ada-Marie added in a small voice, "Mama, I cannot swim!"

The commander did not look at all distressed by the crowd around him. Indeed he maintained such a superior stance that Maria could not help but think how much like a German officer he seemed.

"This is not a matter that I have within my power to change," the Englishman said. "I am following orders from higher authorities. We have been warned that a shipload of illegal immigrants sailed from Hamburg. We simply have no room for you. The quotas are full, and—"

Captain Burton interrupted angrily. "And I explained that this is a *temporary* stop. A few hours."

"We refuse to take that chance. You will not be allowed any closer to Southampton or London. You have been warned."

As if to emphasize this point, two more British ships—coastal cutters—sounded horns as they raced to reinforce the first vessel.

"Then for the sake of human decency," Burton called back, "will you provide medical attention for the injured seaman belowdecks?"

He was speaking of the battered man from the ventilation shaft.

Every passenger knew the fellow was not a seaman, but perhaps these Englishmen would take him to a hospital on the land.

"You have received the reply of the immigration authorities on that matter as well, Mr. Burton. You say the fellow lost his papers? Without proper papers we will not take responsibility for—"

"Medical supplies, then?" Burton roared the question like an accusation.

The British commander hesitated. He turned and called down to his ship's crew. "Send a first-aid kit up here!"

A silent minute passed until a small white metal box with a red cross was brought up the side and given to the commander. This was taken by the doctor, who flipped open the lid, rummaged through the meager contents, and shook his head in dismay. "Our fellow has been burned. He will be in a great deal of pain when he awakes from our last bit of morphine. He may well die."

"Then bury him at sea!" the commander snapped. He turned on his heel and with two strides was over the edge of the freighter. His seamen followed. Those men, at least, looked embarrassed and ashamed by the incident.

Three defiant British craft now idled in the path of the *Darien*.

"What shall we do, Captain?" Klaus called up.

The captain's eyes were still hidden beneath the brim of his hat. He peered over the crowded deck and over toward the English flags that fluttered on the stern of each craft. He let his eyes linger there a moment and then glared at the sailors who manned the small cannon on those vessels.

Could they mean that they would fire on the *Darien*? Here, at the mouth of the Thames? Only miles from London and Trafalgar and Parliament. Could they do such a thing? England raged so against fighting any sort of war—was this happening here? But this was not war. This was law. This was illegal human contraband. This was "full quotas."

The captain did not answer. He reentered the bridge and shut the door quietly behind him.

Would he ram through these English boats? Maria wondered. The chug of the British engines was countered by a loud rumble as the freighter began to move again. It swung to port, out to sea. The harbor patrol escorted it ahead and on either side.

Klaus stood beside the doctor, who still held the first-aid box in his perspiring hands. The man was weeping silently. Klaus had not noticed before.

"Our enemies rejoice at this moment." The doctor stared at the red cross. "Can you hear them laughing? Can you?"

Klaus did not reply as the doctor made his way unsteadily toward the hatch that led to the infirmary.

12

England

Charles stood at the rail of the observation deck and gazed at the myriad large and small ships sculling across the water. There was land plainly visible on each side of the ship now.

"England," Murphy told him. "This is it, Charles."

Elisa stood, unsmiling, beside a telescope with a coin slot. "Would you like to see close up?" she asked. There was a weariness in her words that did not match the excitement Charles was feeling at his first glimpse of the mouth of the Thames.

He nodded enthusiastically as she deposited a single tuppence into the slot and the telescope ticked to life. Charles peered through the lens and swept the instrument from one side to the other until he was dizzy with the way land and ships whooshed past his vision.

"Only look at one thing at a time," Murphy instructed, holding the instrument steady. "Close one eye and look with the other."

Charles obeyed. Holding his hand over his right eye, he looked with the left. Now he could see details: a fishing boat with men hauling in nets; a steamer like the one they were traveling on; garbage scows, hauling the trash of London and Southampton out to sea; and three little Navy ships bobbing in the water beside a much bigger ship. Here were sailors with cannons and many people on the decks of the big ship. There was a British officer in a white uniform with gold braid on his shoulder. There were all kinds of people on the big ship. Old and young. Mothers with hands on the shoulders of frightened-looking children. The English sailors looked afraid, too. A ragged man on the deck of the bridge looked as if he were shouting. It was all close up like a scene in a silent movie Charles had watched once.

Charles lifted his head and suddenly the ship and the people were far across the waters again. Murphy did not notice, but there was something familiar to Charles in such a sight. The boy pressed his eye back to the telescope. He saw men in long black coats and little round hats, with bearded faces. These were Jews, Charles knew. Maybe not everyone on the ship, but at least some of the people were Jews. Charles had seen such people in Germany. He knew that the Nazi Storm Troopers hated the Jews even more than they hated Charles and his cleft palate.

At the thought, he instinctively put his hand to where his muffler covered his mouth. It was important to hide such things as broken mouths and Jewishness. Perhaps even in England. After all, even here the English sailors had rifles ready to shoot the Jews! He shifted his focus to the small military craft hovering in the water beside the freighter: soldiers with helmets, cannons that pointed up toward the hull of the big ship.

Then Charles saw what the English soldiers were angry about. There was a faded yellow name on the nose of the big ship; the letters began *SS* and then there were more letters that Charles could not read. The *SS* designation was enough. This must be a ship filled with Jews and the *Nazi SS!* Those sailors would not want a ship with such initials in England!

The ticking of the observation telescope stopped and the scene went black, like a broken film in a motion picture theater.

"Well, what did you think of that?" Elisa asked brightly.

Charles wanted to answer. He nodded a thanks to her and then pointed far across the waters to where the little drama had been acted out.

"You could see all the way over there?" Murphy asked in mock amazement. Murphy could not see any of the details from this distance. Now Charles wished he had not used up all of the tuppence time himself. He wanted Murphy to see it, to explain it to him.

⟋⟍⟍

There was still a glimmer of daylight when Murphy and Elisa guided Charles toward the small water taxi that would carry them the rest of the way to London. The great Thames River was a nautical highway for these boatmen who ferried passengers from the great liners to their ultimate destinations.

Ten watermen gabbed together on the wharf like an exclusive club. There was some prearranged order that ordained who would take the next customer. Until each man's turn came up, he seemed not to notice the disembarking passengers. The watermen smoked their pipes and cigarettes with an air of nonchalance, like country squires after a partridge dinner. Conversation was split evenly between politics and the weather, both of which were equally changeable and gloomy lately. Leather-skinned faces often turned toward the sky above the Houses of Parliament.

"Did y' hear ol' Chamberlain speak over the wireless last night? The man ain't foolin' no one, I say. If things is really gonna get better, then why, I ask y', does Chamberlain carry that umbrella everywhere?"

"He's scared of them pigeons in Trafalgar Square, that's what!"

"Aye! The ol' man is scared one of them birds will think 'e is a bronze statue and dirty 's 'ead!"

"Naw! Chamberlain carries that umbrella in case Hitler decides t' drop bombs on England, that's all!"

Murphy cleared his throat to get their attention. "Personally I like the pigeon theory," he remarked.

The smiles of the boatmen faded. One of them had forgotten that his turn was up. Brims of caps tipped respectfully. Amusement disappeared from squinting eyes as the watermen appraised their unattended customers.

"It's your party, Darcy!" Hands shoved the boatman Darcy out of the circle.

Darcy was clad in soiled brown corduroy trousers and a jacket that matched. He wore a black eye patch over his left eye, and his embarrassed grin displayed a blank space where his front teeth should have been. He wore his boatman's badge fastened to his jacket. He flipped it with his thumb and sizing them up said, "Fares t' the Savoy is sixpence for each—you an' the lady an' the lad. Threepence for each trunk, sir. Tariff is fixed for us with the badge." He said this last so that Murphy would know he would not be cheated. He had already begun to hoist the trunk to his shoulder. Charles clung to the cello case. "An' y'll carry that yourself, lad?" He smiled toothlessly at Charles, who valiantly tried to lug the heavy case by himself. Finally Murphy reached down for the handle, and the two of them lifted it together.

A pleasant breeze drifted over the Thames as the water taxi carried them past the ancient sites that lined the river. The boatman kept a running monologue going on behalf of the trio. He pointed at each landmark and explained the history as if he had built the place with his own hands and then written the script for showing it to the tourists.

"First time in London, lad?" he asked Charles, but did not wait for an answer. "Well, then, that right there is the Tower of London! First it was a great fortress, see, but seein' as how the river is damp, they turned it into a prison for traitors where they waited till the axman chopped off their 'eads. 'Course, King 'enry the Eighth also chopped off the heads of several of 'is wives. Then Mary chopped off the 'eads of the Protestants, and Elizabeth chopped off the 'eads of the Catholics." He pointed first to Tower Bridge and then to London Bridge. "Why, I can't even count the number of fine English 'eads what 'ave grinned down from the spikes on me ancestors!" With hardly a breath drawn he squinted his good eye at Murphy and said, "And y're a Yank, ain't y'?"

"Yes, I—," Murphy began, but it did no good.

The boatman continued his monologue. He tapped his patch and described its origin with all the enthusiasm of the other landmarks. "I'm partial t' Yanks. Grew fond of 'em when we fought the Huns together in the Great War! Tha's where I lost me eye and picked up a bit of shrapnel in me leg as well. Bothers me a bit when it rains. Bothers me most always. Like now. As for losin' me choppers—" he grinned at Charles, who seemed fascinated with his mouth—"I just got up one mornin' and they come out like the stars. An' I tol' me missus she musta belted me in me sleep 'cause me teeth was just lyin' there in me bowl of porridge! What do y' think of that?"

Charles, understanding very little of the man's prattling, shrugged in response.

"A quiet one, ain't y'?" The boatman did not seem terribly disappointed that Charles was no competition for the airwaves. Ten minutes more he traversed the well-trod pathways of his memory for items that might be of interest to newcomers. "Why, everyone has 'eard the nursery rhyme 'London Bridge'! Y've 'eard it, lad! Sing it with ol' Darcy!" Then the boatman began a rousing solo rendition of "London Bridge." He stopped on the line "Take the keys an' lock her up . . . " The shadow of the great old bridge loomed above them. "See them pilings? Why, the old heathens used t' protect the bridge from harm! Bet y' didn't know that, eh?"

Just past London Bridge and round a bend of the Thames, the water taxi slipped into place along a row of boats at the dock below the Savoy Hotel. "Educational." Murphy fumbled for the tip and the fare as Elisa smiled and began her own conversation with the boatmen in the Czech language.

The smile of Darcy faded into a hurt look. "Didn't understand a word I said, did she?" he asked Murphy.

Elisa was now thanking him in French, then again in German; and then in Italian she briefly told him that he might apply for a position as a travel guide to Mussolini and Hitler together if they ever visited London. No doubt such tales would change their opinions about the gentle and civilized British.

"What's she saying?" the boatman whispered to Murphy.

"She says you would make a wonderful tour guide," Murphy replied.

Murphy tipped him enough so that he smiled happily. "Any time, gov'! Just ask for me by name. I got it all memorized, y' see." He bowed gallantly before Elisa. "When y' learn a bit of the King's English, miss, come back an' I'll tell it t' y' all again so y' know a bit about English culture and civilization, see?" Not waiting for a reply, Murphy took Elisa by the elbow and nudged her gently toward the steps that led up from the docks.

☙

The Dolphin Hotel on High Street in Southampton was not an elegant hotel, but it was clean and inexpensive which, for Bubbe Rosenfelt, was all that mattered. She and Herbert had stayed in the little establishment dozens of times. Herbert complained of the noise from the trains across from Radley's and the enormous Southwestern Railway Hotel, so staying at the Dolphin had become a habit that Bubbe had not altered even after Herbert had died.

Occasionally a new clerk would cock a suspicious eyebrow when he read the name Rosenfelt. Obviously Jewish. Why don't they go to Ramsgate for their holiday where there is a synagogue and a college for Jews?

Whenever clerks put on airs, Bubbe simply rang the bell again to call the manager. For thirty-eight years the management of the Dolphin had remained in the capable hands of Mr. Tyler, a stout, phlegmatic man with a wooden face unmoved by any trace of a smile—except when he saw "Missus Rosenfelt" had returned to his hotel.

This morning a young, haughty man with the precise accent of one who had attended public school received Mrs. Rosenfelt. He sniffed, and his mouth turned down at the corners when he read the old woman's signature. "So sorry, madame, we may be full tonight. The season, you know. Perhaps you would be wise to check elsewhere. Radley's, perhaps. Or the Southwestern Railway Hotel."

Without replying, Bubbe banged her hand against the bell on the desk. She waited a moment and then rang again.

"I am certain Radley's would have a place for you," the young man suggested again.

The cherrywood door behind him swung open and Mr. Tyler ambled out, looking as weary and uninterested as ever. Bubbe smiled as the man's fleshy lids opened with happy surprise at the sight of her.

"Why it's Missus Rosenfelt herself!" he cried.

The young clerk looked at him in amazement. He had never seen Mr. Tyler smile, let alone display excitement.

"So good to see you again." Bubbe extended her hand. It had been nearly three years since she had seen Mr. Tyler. He seemed a bit balder and a bit wider, but otherwise unchanged.

"I've thought of you often!" He was already out the swinging door to gather up her luggage. "Bless my soul! I thought you might have gotten ill or died without letting me know!"

"Would I do such a thing after thirty years?" She laughed.

"What room number are you in?"

"Why . . ." Bubbe looked momentarily confused. "Your clerk tells me there is no room for me here and suggested Radley's."

The smile on Tyler's face dissolved and turned to stone again. "What? No room?"

The clerk was now terrified. Work was so hard to get nowadays in England, even if one had a public school education. "Well, I thought—"

"You thought, you thought, you thought!" Mr. Tyler scowled. "Give me the key to number twelve."

"Twelve?" This was too much for the clerk. A suite with a sitting area and a private bath. Who was this old Jewish woman, anyway? Royalty? A member of Lord Montefiore's family? He snatched the key from its hook and handed it reverently to Mr. Tyler.

"Twelve indeed for our Missus Rosenfelt!" Mr. Tyler huffed and puffed toward the aged metal cage of the lift. "Have you been in America? Or still all the time in Hamburg?"

"Germany," she replied flatly. Her tone told him everything. It was happening again. She had predicted it before the Great War in 1914, and now there was more than a hint in her voice that war was coming. "And am I glad to be out of there, I can tell you, Mr. Tyler! *Oy!* Such a place! In Hamburg they are building battleships! And what battleships they are, too!"

"And your family?" he asked, struggling to stack the luggage in the lift and squeeze in after it. As he slid the grid shut, he turned back toward the wide-eyed clerk and said indignantly, "Radley's, indeed!"

Mr. Tyler refused her tip, as he had ever since she had become a widow. He loitered in the corridor and listened sympathetically as she spoke of Klaus and Maria and the children onboard the *Darien*. Had there been any word of a ship of refugees near Southampton?

Tyler considered the question and told her that he had not heard of anything unusual, and that certainly the arrival of a freighter full of German refugees would have caused a stir in Southampton.

"I am sailing on the *Queen Mary*," she said confidently. "And plan to have their papers in order by the time they arrive."

"They will land in New York, then?"

Bubbe Rosenfelt did not know how to answer. She was unsure where they would land. After all, travel arrangements had not been made by the offices of Thomas Cook. There was no itinerary. "My granddaughter and her family will be in New York, of course. That is where I will be. I began there and will end my days there."

"I have always had a hope you might settle here in Southampton." Mr. Tyler blushed a bit. Embarrassing for a man of seventy-three, but Bubbe Rosenfelt was still a handsome woman for her age. "Well, I'd best give that clerk a talking-to."

"Don't discharge him, Mr. Tyler," she said gently. "After all, the fellow thought he was doing his social duty for the sake of such a fine house."

The lower lip jutted thoughtfully forward. "Then I shall teach him the manners he should have properly learned in school, and I shall send him to the parson for a bit of a history lesson about the chap who said there was no room at the inn, eh?" He tipped an imaginary hat to Mrs. Rosenfelt, then moved with uncharacteristic determination toward the lift.

Bubbe stood at the door and listened to him mumble to himself all the way down, and she pitied the snobbish young clerk who had tried to send her away.

∽

Shimon opened his eyes at the sound of children whispering beside his cot. The faces of five well-scrubbed little girls blinked back at him as if he were a strange creature pulled from the sea.

The oldest girl held a green glass beer bottle filled with a bouquet of five white-paper lilies. The second oldest nudged her hard in the ribs and hissed, "Well, give it to him, *silly*!" The other girls joined in. "Give him the flowers, Trudy! Give him the flowers!"

"Hello," Shimon said in a hoarse voice that made them all fall silent as they gawked at him a moment longer.

At last the smallest of the girls moved forward a step. She put her chubby hands on the metal frame of the cot and leaned closer to study the bandages on Shimon's head. "Hello," she said in a small voice. "My name is Ada-Marie. Does it hurt very bad?"

Shimon cleared his throat. He was uncertain of his voice. It seemed like such a long time since he had spoken to a child that he was not sure his vocal cords would work for the occasion. "Ada-Marie is a very pretty name," he croaked. He did not reply to her question about the pain, which was still intense.

The other girls crowded forward. "And I am Gretchen."

"I am Katrina."

"My name is Louise, and she is Trudy." Louise jerked a thumb at Trudy. "Trudy is the oldest, which is why she gets to hold the flowers."

"But we all made one for you!" Gretchen said.

"Even me!" Little Ada-Marie touched a dilapidated flower with a pudgy finger.

"Mama helped Ada-Marie," Louise explained with an air of authority. "But Trudy thought of the idea."

At that, Trudy blushed and stepped forward with the rest to present the bouquet to the invalid stranger. "We hope you get better soon," she whispered, her blush growing deeper as he took the bottle in his massive hand and held it on the pillow.

"Yes!" Ada-Marie clapped her hands. "We are glad you did not die like the grown-ups said—"

A hard nudge from Gretchen silenced the little one. "Ada-Marie! Don't say such things!"

"Don't push, or I will tell Mama!"

From behind the little chorus the doctor chided, "That is enough, girls. We must let our patient rest."

Shimon looked pained. He did not want them to go. It had been so long . . . too long . . . since he heard small voices utter kind words to him. "Please," he gasped, "just a minute more. Stay." It was ridiculous, he knew, but there were tears in his eyes. He blinked them away and tried to smile. Flowers. Paper lilies made by children. Had he ever seen anything so beautiful before?

The doctor did not object to the request. The girls moved closer. The patient liked their gift. He liked them. It was very nice.

"What is your name?" Ada-Marie's braids shone in the light. Her eyes were blue like flowers blooming at Schönbrunn Palace. Bouquets of living flowers. Sweet-smelling skin. Pink cheeks. So very beautiful.

Shimon felt overcome by such beauty. He fought hard to control his emotions, recalling the harsh voices of guards shrieking out his identification number. *"You are not human; you are an animal, a number for the Reich, for the service of the Aryan!"*

"My name is Shimon," he answered. "My name is Shimon Feldstein. And I think these are the prettiest flowers I have ever . . ." His voice faltered. He closed his eyes.

Trudy whispered, "We will come back and visit you if you like."

Eyes still closed, Shimon nodded. The effort caused him to wince with pain.

"Maybe tomorrow, girls." The doctor's voice was kind.

Shimon heard shoes shuffle out of the infirmary. "Yes, please," he called weakly. Then he opened his eyes to stare at the bouquet of white flowers.

13

Jeremiah's Mantle

It was a short walk from where the Savoy Hotel overlooked the murky Thames to where Fleet Street sloped up Ludgate Hill toward the mighty St. Paul's Cathedral. A cloud of pigeons rose up from the tower as the bells rang the hour of nine that morning.

Murphy stopped and pointed upward, directing the attention of Charles to the birds. He put his arm around the boy's thin shoulders in a fatherly gesture that made Elisa marvel at the tenderness of the man she had married. She flushed with emotion and breathed a prayer of thanks for John Murphy.

"There was a terrible fire here in London right after the plague, you see," Murphy explained in German. "I think it was in 1666. And it burned so hot that the lead roof of St. Paul's melted and ran down the street." He pulled Charles close to the curb and searched the cobblestones until he spotted traces of that molten stream. "Look here, Charles!" he exclaimed with an excitement that made him seem like a boy himself. "The very stuff from the roof of St. Paul's!"

Charles shook his head in wonder, then looked from the leaded cobbles to where the cathedral now stood. He wanted Murphy to tell him more. Had he ever heard such stories or felt such enjoyment simply walking up a street? Never in his young life had he taken a walk without looking fearfully over his shoulder. Now he scanned up and down and everywhere to devour the sights and sounds of London.

Murphy needed no encouragement. "Just think of all the kings and carriages that have ridden over this street since then! And this is Fleet Street." He pointed up toward the building that housed the venerable

Times. "Even before the Great Fire, people were turning out books and pamphlets here. Publishing. Writing—"

Charles pointed at Murphy proudly.

"Yes, like me," Murphy laughed. "Booksellers still sell used books right up there in an open-air market." He pointed behind them to where the pigeons swirled back to their roosts in St. Paul's.

Elisa let her eyes linger on the place. She thought of her father's volume of *Faust* and wondered if the French bookseller Le Morthomme had a counterpart here in the London booksellers' market. Such a thought was an unpleasant interruption of the sense of peace she had felt a moment before. She shook her head as if to clear it from any questions that had slipped in. She was free from all that now. It had nothing to do with her life. Nothing to do with the reason they had come to Fleet Street.

"How much farther to the office?" she asked. Somehow even that was an intrusion. After all, they were going to the INS office to retrieve the scrapbook that had been kept by Charles' aunt. In the book was every gruesome reminder of what the child had been through.

Murphy looked pained. For a moment he had almost forgotten why they were here. "Not far," he said. "Not far enough." He raised an eyebrow and jerked his head toward the office displaying the INS logo. Then he added, "Maybe you and Charles should walk on up to St. Paul's, huh? Larry Strickland and the rest of the staff know all about this." He cleared his throat. He was not certain that it was wise to take Charles Kronenberger into a hive of journalists familiar with the whole story.

"We can feed the pigeons." Elisa smiled brightly, but Charles studied her with eyes that seemed to understand the situation in spite of the grown-up attempt to hide it. "Would you like that?" she asked.

Charles frowned slightly. He would have rather seen the inside of a Fleet Street office. Especially one where his hero, John Murphy, had worked. Hadn't the father of Louis and Charles Kronenberger been a journalist, too? There was something warming in the familiarity of this place. His father had also worked on a big newspaper in Hamburg. Charles remembered the busy clack of typewriters and telephones. He wanted to go with Murphy, but Elisa already grasped his hand and tugged him along after her. He peered back over his shoulder as Murphy waited and then jaywalked across Fleet Street to the office.

Charles pulled back against her hand and stalled to watch the tall, lanky American as he tugged the brim of his hat and strode into the office. A red omnibus zoomed by, and the wind from it ruffled the blue cotton scarf that concealed Charles' mouth. He put his hand up to it, then lowered his head. Tears stung his eyes at the thought that Murphy had not wanted him along. He had not wanted his friends to meet him.

Someday his mouth would be whole, and Murphy would not feel ashamed to take him into the office.

Somehow Elisa read his thoughts instantly in his eyes. She gathered him against her in a quick hug. "That is not it at all," she said in quiet German. "You are a celebrity, you see, Charles. A famous person because you got away from the bad men in Germany. Everyone will ask too many questions of you, and Murphy does not want you to feel bad. That is all."

His blue eyes brightened at her explanation. A single nod of acceptance answered her, and then he pulled her hand as if it were his idea to guide her up toward St. Paul's.

Piles of old books rested on makeshift tables in the stalls of a hundred booksellers. Tourists browsed and dickered over prices of rare volumes as Elisa and Charles wandered down row after row. Elisa paused at one table reserved exclusively for volumes of children's books. Thumbing through a book of nursery rhymes with Charles, she came upon the poem about London Bridge that the boatman had sung and explained so gruesomely. The book displayed nothing so grim as that in its pictures, so she purchased it and presented it to Charles with a slight bow. This was much more fun than feeding pigeons.

They passed slowly on to the next table. It was filled with books stacked behind a cardboard sign that read *Fine Rare Volumes*. Elisa considered the sign and searched the spines of old leather-bound books as she thought of her father's collection in Berlin. *What happened to those books?* she wondered. *Were they burned in the great bonfires that cremated human thought in Germany?*

She raised her head to look out over the bookstalls. Everywhere men and women flipped through pages, skimming the words of Shakespeare, Milton, Marlowe—writers who had walked here when Fleet Street had been young. She glanced back to the heap in front of them and spotted the gold lettering on a black leather spine. *Holy Bible*. She picked up the book with a sense of relief. So. It was still for sale in England. All Bibles had been burned in Germany.

"How much?" she asked the wizened old woman who ran the stall.

"Tuppence, dearie." She cackled her answer. "Cheap enough."

Elisa laid the copper coin on the table and took the precious book in her arms. She embraced it like one who embraces an old friend met in a faraway land. She smiled and said to Charles. "My first English Bible. A sensible thing to have since we are going to America." Aware that her countrymen in Germany were being sent to their deaths for possession of a Bible, she marveled at the ease with which she had purchased something so valuable. Suddenly she wanted to tell Murphy about it, wanted to show him and share her wonder at the event.

She turned in search of him. He was taller than almost everyone, and she was certain she would spot him easily among the crowd with bent heads and downcast eyes. Charles, clutching his book of rhymes, also searched the throngs of people. It had been nearly thirty minutes since they had left Murphy. Surely it was time for him to finish his business and join them again.

"Maybe we should go to the steps—" Elisa suddenly fell silent. Across the bowed heads of hundreds of browsers she saw a man staring unmistakably at her. He was three stalls away. His hand was on a book as though he were thumbing through it, but from beneath the brim of his hat he followed Elisa's every move. He smiled slightly, not minding that she noticed his interest.

Was he simply a man noticing a pretty woman in the book market? She felt the blood drain from her face. She looked past him, hoping for the arrival of Murphy. "Come on, Charles," she whispered.

Pulling Charles along, she moved quickly through the stalls as she made her way back toward the stone steps of the cathedral. The bell clanged out the half hour, and the pigeons rose like smoke again. Their shadow passed above them. Elisa looked behind her, expecting to see the man. Black fedora. Pin-striped suit. Eyes that followed her and questioned her.

Fear reflected on her face, and Charles clung tightly to her hand. She did not see the man who had watched her. He had not followed. She stopped and stood panting at the edge of the book market. Now her eyes searched the stalls for some sign of the man. He was gone—or perhaps he had moved to another bookstall.

Charles tugged impatiently on her arm and pointed up the steps to where Murphy stood with a bag of bread crumbs. When he smiled and waved, Elisa felt foolish. *It was nothing. Nothing at all. A curious look from a man. Nothing.*

"Out spending all my hard-earned money?" Murphy called. His hat was shoved back on his head, and he held a large paper-wrapped package beneath his arm. "Just like a woman. Out shopping when us fellas would rather be hunting birds, huh?"

⊘

It was easy for Charles to love the city of London. Much about it reminded him of Hamburg where he and Louis had been born. Was it the broad, murky Thames River filled with boats like the Elbe River had been? The London Savoy Hotel seemed much like the hotel where Mommy and Father had once taken Charles to meet the committee of pastors and laymen who discussed his case. The Atlantic Hotel in Hamburg had been a wondrous place, indeed. Father had carried him and Louis into the plush lobby, one boy in each strong arm. He had carried them past potted palms and high-backed, red velvet settees where later the boys had played hide-and-seek. Important matters had been discussed there at the Atlantic, and Father had left the place hopeful. Nothing came of that hope, but still Charles had happy memories of that magic day in Hamburg. Such memories made him ache for Louis and Mommy and Father once again. He stood between Elisa and Murphy in the lobby of the London Savoy and imagined that Louis was hiding somewhere behind a chair or a green fern or around the corner.

Elisa's voice carried disappointment as she spoke, and suddenly Charles listened to her again. "But Murphy, *must* you?"

"I won't be gone more than a few hours. A guy can't refuse to have tea with Winston Churchill, can he?"

"But today—our afternoon. What about the movies?"

Charles raised his eyebrows in alarm. Murphy had promised to take him to a real American double-feature movie. Two movies, Murphy had explained. Wonderful films called *The Thin Man* and something else that Charles could not remember. The film stars were very famous and the movie showed New York and San Francisco. Murphy had said the films would give them an idea of where they were going.

Charles tugged indignantly on Murphy's sleeve. "Huh?" Charles asked. This was an American word Murphy told him meant "I don't understand." Charles liked the word because he could say it perfectly, just like Murphy said it. "Huh?" Charles asked again.

"I have to go have a conversation with a very important fellow, you see." Murphy explained gently to Charles. "So I am counting on you to take Elisa to the movies." He pressed a bill into the child's hand, then whispered to Elisa, "I went to see the show twice just so I could think about you."

"Me?"

"You and Myrna Loy have so much in common."

"If you think flattery will make me feel less abandoned—"

"I'm not talking about your looks." He grinned. "I'm talking about your money!" He stepped back and held up the paperbound scrapbook as she playfully tapped his head with her handbag.

"Go on then," she said with mock aloofness. "And just for that, I won't tell you I'll miss you."

"Well, I'll miss *you*." He brushed his lips against her cheek and then kissed her lightly on the mouth. She was smiling and for a moment, Charles wondered if Murphy might change his mind and stay with them after all.

"Charles and I will have a . . . splendid time."

"A swell time," Murphy corrected with a wink. Then he placed the package in her hands. "I'll be back whether you want me or not." With that, he mussed Charles's hair and strode out of the lobby.

Charles felt disappointed. Elisa gazed after Murphy and sighed before she remembered that Charles was beside her. "A *swell* time," she repeated. "Well, Charles, shall we go see how the modern American woman keeps her husband nearby?" She touched his cheek and smiled at him. He thought he had never seen such blue eyes. He would marry her if Murphy decided to stay away. And he would take her to American movies every day.

"Uh-huh," Charles answered, taking the hand of his lady and leading her toward the revolving door at the far end of the lobby.

⟨ꟲ⟩

The trees and flowers of Winston Churchill's estate were in full bloom. The stately brick mansion of Chartwell seemed warm and homey amid the blossoming shrubs and the bright afternoon sunlight. Murphy felt none of the gloom he had experienced during his last wintertime visit to Churchill's home.

A plump, matronly housekeeper directed him from the patio down a meandering path to where the great man sat in front of a half-finished canvas. Dabbing paintbrush on his palette, Churchill glanced at Murphy, growled a greeting, and then put the finishing touches on his painting.

"Good afternoon, Mr. Murphy." He nodded toward the canvas. "Well, what do you think of my work?"

"Very nice." Murphy feigned admiration, even though the canvas was not even half complete. "So far, very nice."

Churchill squinted at the work and sat back with a disapproving grunt. "Not the full picture, however, eh, Mr. Murphy?" Now Churchill turned his gaze on Murphy. "Only half the story, as it were." He tossed the brush into a tin can filled with linseed oil and a dozen other brushes. Wiping his hands on a paint-spattered smock, Churchill then extended a hand to Murphy in greeting.

"Even unfinished it is quite nice." Murphy sat down on the stone bench beside Churchill.

"Rubbish!" Churchill snorted. "I have a studio full of them. They are too worthless to sell and too dear to part with. An addiction . . . that's what painting is. Steadies my nerves. Like a good cigar." As if to make the point, Churchill pulled two cigars from his smock pocket and offered one to Murphy, who declined with an amused shake of his head. Churchill shrugged and replaced the gift. "A dreadful habit." He struck a match on the sole of his Wellington and puffed on the stogie with satisfaction. "And a great pleasure. Somewhat annoying to my secretary, however. I have had to give up my smokes in the car. It makes her quite ill to take dictation and breathe cigar smoke while we career along the country roads. She turns the very color of green tobacco."

Murphy laughed at the story but was quite certain that he also would turn green in a closed automobile of such reeking smoke. "I tried smoking once. I was nine, and I set the haystack in the barn on fire. Nearly burned the place down, too. My dad says that the only good use of a cigar is to keep mosquitoes away in the outhouse."

Churchill chuckled. "We've had indoor plumbing for some time now, but I never got over my little habit all the same." He puffed in silence; the amusement faded from his eyes. He looked toward his painting again. "Not the full picture," he muttered. With a sigh he stood and paced a few steps to the edge of the pond before turning to face Murphy. "There is a good deal more to our picture than anyone is daring to show, Mr. Murphy. That is why I have asked you to come here on such short notice."

Suddenly they were no longer discussing paintings or cigars. "I was hoping we might talk before I left for the States."

"You are leaving tomorrow on the *Queen Mary*, I understand?"

"My wife and I and a small boy. A refugee from Germany. He requires medical attention in the States."

"The Kronenberger child." Churchill was already informed, and his knowledge surprised Murphy. "A few of us followed the affair in Germany. Dreadful thing. One must pause to wonder at a race of people who pour millions into the weapons of destruction and yet will not spend a penny to raise the quality of one child's life. The enormity of Nazi aggression often tends to mask the hideous offenses against individuals."

He lowered his voice. "But then, you have seen all that firsthand with your wife and her family. The rest of us may rage against the breaking of this treaty or that. We may fear the force of Nazi air power and discuss the plans of Hitler against the nations . . . and we forget what all that means to even one child like Charles Kronenberger."

Now Churchill looked out across the grounds. "One blade of grass is often lost to the big picture. Such are the affairs of politics and the lives of men." He walked slowly back to the bench and sat down. "And yet there are moments when the issues may well hinge on one another. The small story becomes the issue on which great matters are decided."

Murphy nodded, even though he was uncertain where the great man was heading with his thought. "I had planned to stay on in Prague for a while. My publisher arranged for the crossing. He intends to meet us in New York. From there I am not sure what issues I will be covering. I expect we'll be back in Europe within the month."

"Within the month," Churchill repeated vacantly, "Europe as we know it may no longer exist. That, my friend, is the big picture. Small details such as human life under the dominion of the Nazis seem to be of little concern to our mighty governments. That is the great tragedy of our time. Peace at any cost is not peace at all."

"President Beneš . . . the Czechs have managed to hold ground," Murphy began.

Churchill silenced him with a wave of his hand. "I would not want to be in the shoes of President Beneš. The ground he has held is quicksand, I'm afraid. Czechoslovakia is in the center of the storm. Germany on one side and Russia on the other." He pressed his palms together as if he were cracking a walnut between them. "Comrade Stalin has only just finished killing thousands of his best officers simply because he heard they might be friendly toward the Germans. By the time the purge in Russia is over, countless lives will be snuffed out."

"But Stalin has given no indication that he is interested in Czechoslovakia," Murphy protested. "The danger is from the West. From the Germans."

Churchill cleared his throat. "And what if our little friend Beneš should not only hold his ground against the Germans, but should find some way to sign a treaty with Herr Hitler? Suppose the Czechs should manage to solve this internal problem with the racial Germans in the Sudetenland? What then?"

"Then it would be settled. Things would quiet down, and . . ." Murphy's voice drifted off as he pictured the vise of Russia and Germany that held the Czech nation. Hitler raved against the Bolsheviks in Russia. Stalin declared that no one was safe with the threat of Nazi Germany in Europe. The government of Beneš was a democratic island in the midst of these two tyrannies. It was the thin line that kept two straining, snarling dogs from tearing each other apart. If that wall came down . . .

Churchill looked pleased. "I can tell the reality of the situation has penetrated your brain. And now, if only our own Prime Minister Chamberlain and the leader of France could see the situation as simply and clearly as we seem to." He sighed and slapped his thigh in frustration. "But they cannot seem to grasp its significance. If France and Britain do not stick by their treaty obligations to defend Czech soil from invasion, then most certainly we are looking into a dark future for Europe. Czechoslovakia is indeed an aircraft carrier in the heart of the Continent.

Either for Hitler or for Stalin—either choice is a dreadful prospect—or, if we stand firm for her, Czechoslovakia will be a stronghold for the democracies." Churchill puffed thoughtfully on his cigar as both men sat in silence.

It did seem like a simple matter, Murphy mused. Now the riots in Czech-Sudetenland made sense. The Nazi Party had gained a powerful political foothold in the mountainous region of Czechoslovakia. It was that very territory that served as a strategic military position for the Czech Army to keep Germany on its own side of the fence. If the Sudetenland was torn from the Prague government, then it would be only a matter of time before the Reich marched across the border. No doubt Russia would then advance from the north. The warring giants would crush the little nation—and with it, people like Anna and Theo would no doubt perish as well.

"Surely Britain and France will not let Beneš down," Murphy whispered.

Churchill chuckled grimly in reply. "Did you not hear what Chamberlain had remarked about the Czechs? 'Not top drawer,' he said. Not even out of the middle. Mr. Murphy, he has again stated his conviction that the Slavs are inferior, that we in England would be fools for considering going to war on their behalf. He is determined to give away the freedom of others to forestall the inevitable conflict that must come to our island in the end. Only six weeks ago he signed the Anglo-Italian pact with Mussolini that gives that dread government the right to pursue their aggression in Abyssinia and Spain. We British merely retain the right to stay out of it."

"I was in Spain for almost a year." Murphy's thoughts filled again with memories of bombed-out towns and dying women and children in the streets. "The Germans and Italians did not even bother to paint over their insignia on the wings of their planes. Target practice. That's what Spain and Abyssinia are. The Fascists are practicing for what they plan to do to England and any other country that gets in their way."

"Well, then. We see eye to eye on the matter, Mr. Murphy." Churchill clapped him on the back. "So what do you intend to do about it?"

Murphy laughed nervously. "Me?"

"You have a mighty pen and a willing publisher, I hear. These matters must be explained on your side of the Atlantic as well. A little pressure from President Roosevelt, and the American public might hold some sway over our umbrella-toting prime minister."

Murphy nodded. Again he imagined Anna and Theo, Elisa's family, in Prague. Indeed, in Germany they had been through enough for a lifetime. Now once again they faced the possibility of Nazi invasion. "First of all I'm going to transplant a few blades of grass—" he replied absently.

"Blades of . . . ?"

"My wife's family. Small details in the big picture. I have to make certain that we get them out of Prague."

"Not easy these days. They are Jewish, are they not?"

"Elisa's father is Jewish."

"The quotas of every nation are filled now. And the Mufti in Palestine has taken up the methods of his mentor, Herr Hitler. Daily the Arab population is rioting against the immigration of additional Jews into the Mandate. Of course, never mind that the majority of Arabs have come into British Palestine from other Arab countries. The Mufti simply will not have another Jew in Jerusalem, he says."

"Chamberlain isn't bowing to that kind of pressure, is he?" Murphy was astonished at this information. "He certainly won't revoke the British commitment to a Jewish homeland—not *now*, when there is nowhere else for the Jews of Europe to run."

Churchill did not answer for a long time. "It is common knowledge that the Arab Mufti Haj Amin and Adolf Hitler are on very good terms. Chamberlain seeks peace at any cost. *Any cost.* As long as it does not cost Britain." He cleared his throat again. "If I were you, Mr. Murphy, I would do my best to get your wife's family into America. Surely your publisher can assist you in obtaining visas for them. Within a matter of weeks the British government will close Palestine to all immigration. That is my prediction."

Raising his eyebrow slightly Churchill slowly shook his head. "I am afraid this Jeremiah has no vision of good things in the future. No. It does not bode well for any of us. We are being led, docile and meek, to the edge of an abyss. What voice will turn us around? Are we blind? Are we deaf?"

Churchill extended his hand in farewell. The interview was at an end. "You have a crossing to make, Mr. Murphy. I wish you luck. I have offered you no hope and have passed along the heavy cloak of Jeremiah. Perhaps we will meet again soon. Perhaps I am wrong, but I cannot even hope in my error any longer. Godspeed."

14

The *Queen Mary*

Two forged French passports for Louis Kronenberger and Leah were open on the table before them.

"But you see how very good the passports are!" Leah pleaded. "Can we not simply *drive* across the border?"

Marta and Karl Wattenbarger exchanged glances. "You tell her what you and Franz have seen, Karl," Marta prompted her husband.

The sad-eyed Tyrolean farmer spread his calloused hands in helpless frustration. "Everywhere there are photos now of you and Louis. Charles is also in the photograph. They have pieced something together. Identified you and Louis somehow. Your faces will condemn you. Here in Austria if you are captured, these passports Otto had made for you may well condemn him."

"The snows have melted," Franz said quietly. "We can take you out over the mountains."

Leah nodded bleakly. She had hoped that somehow Shimon would be freed and join her here for the journey. That was not to be. She cleared her throat in an effort to find words. "Then we have no choice."

"I am sorry," Karl said. "The choices are made for us in this."

The lines of Marta's kind face deepened with concern. "You must go to France from Italy. Hitler and Mussolini are cut from the same cloth, Leah dear. Soon Jews will no longer be safe in Italy, either. No matter how the Holy Father speaks out against such evil, the course there is set. *Do not delay in Italy!*"

"If we can reach Paris—" Leah closed her passport and pressed it in her hands—"I have friends there, two sisters who roomed with Elisa and me during our school days at the Mozarteum. They were luckier than we were." She smiled sadly at a memory. "Not luckier—they were smarter than we were. Elisa and I wanted to stay on in Austria to study and work at the Musikverein. They were ready to see the world. And so they took jobs in Paris."

"They will help you?"

"I soloed in Paris last year. Sonia and Magda begged me to stay in Paris with them, but by then, you know, Shimon and I were—" She sighed, full of questions about what might have been different if she had stayed. Perhaps Shimon would have joined her there. Perhaps . . .

As if reading her thoughts, Marta placed her hand on Leah's. "Do not begin to doubt God's guidance now, child. Do you think He could not see that two little lambs would need you to help them in Vienna? And so you are here now. We must not doubt . . . only *pray*."

✑

Anna found herself alone in the little house off Mala Strana Square in Prague. Theo, Wilhelm, and young Dieter remained on duty in the Sudetenland. Elisa and Murphy were gone.

In the morning Anna lay in bed too long—much longer than she had except when she was sick. There was no one to make tea for. She did not want breakfast. After a while the old house echoed with memories . . . happy memories, but they were echoes, all the same. She turned her face toward Theo's pillow. She had managed to live without him so long when he was in prison; would she now have to learn the language of loneliness again?

She was angry with him for running off to this duty. Had they not sacrificed enough time from their lives because of Germany and Hitler and his Nazis? Could they not just live now and forget about it?

She sighed and sat up. She was arguing with a shadow. Theo had given her his answer clearly enough. "*Shall I, who have suffered once, let myself forget the suffering that will come upon millions if the Sudetenland is lost? Anna, dear wife, I must serve my heavenly King by doing what I know is right. I made a covenant with dying men, a covenant with the Lord, that while I live I will follow the command of Psalm 37: 'Trust in the Lord, and do good!' I alone survived to fulfill that covenant. And so . . .*"

"And so he has gone," Anna whispered in quiet despair. She spoke to the empty pillow. "Again and again, Theo, you have taken up your cross, sometimes without telling me why or how or what you were up to. What about me? What am I supposed to do here in this empty house?"

☙

Trains from London emptied their passengers directly onto the docks of Southampton. Throngs of spectators had come just to see the enormous superliner, the pride of the Cunard Line. The sleek hull of the giant *Queen Mary* dwarfed every other ship in the harbor.

Elisa held tightly to her violin case and Charles shoved his hand in Murphy's pocket. Murphy pushed ahead through the crowds, using the cello case as a sort of shield before him. It was something Elisa had seen Leah do a hundred times over the years, and the gesture made her ache for her friend once again.

"Get your *Queen Mary* ashtrays right 'ere! Hey, gov'!" A vendor made the mistake of stepping into Murphy's path. "Buy the lad an ashtray, won't y'?"

The cello case smacked the wooden tray the man had slung around his neck, sending dozens of glass ashtrays crashing to the ground.

"Hey! What'sa idea? Hey you!" The red-faced vendor shouted at Murphy. "Look at me merchandise 'ere! Y've smashed everything!"

Murphy hesitated only a moment. "Sorry, fella," he called over the shrieking whistles of boats in the harbor and the clamor of a small brass band on the quay. "An accident—we've got a boat to catch!"

The furious vendor removed the wooden tray and blocked Murphy's path with it. "An' I got me a livin' t' make! Here, who y' think y' are? Twenty-four pounds of me merchandise in pieces an' y' gonna catch a boat an' not pay a brass farthing, I s'pose!"

The cello case pushed hard against the wooden tray. Murphy was nose to nose with the red-faced vendor. From the head of the gangplank the ship's officer called out over a bullhorn, "All ashore that's going ashore."

They had another hundred feet of crowd to push through to make it to the ship. A moment of panic seized Elisa. The glass of the ashtrays crunched beneath her feet. Of course this had not been even remotely Murphy's fault, but now the vendor was screaming for a constable.

The band began to play "I'm an Old Cowhand from the Rio Grande," the song that Murphy had sung for Charles. The boy was delighted. Elisa was amazed. She had not believed that Murphy's rendition had been a real song. It made her hope that the stories he had told her about Wild West shoot-outs were not about to be reenacted here on the docks of Southampton.

"Look! That American chap has smashed the poor fellow's things. And now he won't pay for the damage!" In a moment the rowdy crowd had turned its attention on the broken *Queen Mary* memorabilia underfoot.

"Murphy!" Elisa called in desperation as she was separated from him by a line of angry spectators. "Murphy! We will miss the sailing!"

Her words were drowned by the loud blast of the ship's horn, the final sign for boarding.

Their departure was turning into a nightmare. Charles's eyes filled with fear. Elisa saw him wrap his arms around Murphy's waist.

"Call a constable!"

"Why'd y' go an' smash the bloke's things, Yank?"

"Teach that Yank a lesson!"

"All the same . . ."

"Twenty-four pounds all in pieces!"

"The poor fella's entire living . . ."

All the while Elisa could hear Murphy angrily protesting that he was not responsible for the broken goods and that he would not pay twenty-four pounds for a lot of broken glass.

Again the ship's horn bellowed its warning. Passengers crowded the rails of the many decks. They waved and called to friends and relatives below as the indignation of the crowd on the dock continued to grow against the murderous, arrogant Yank who had mucked about, smashing a good bloke's wares!

Elisa could see only the top of Murphy's fedora. It was shoved back on his head. The cello case was still held high as a sort of protection. "Murphy!" Elisa called. "Murphy!"

"Get out of here!" he shouted back to her. "I'll meet you onboard!"

Then the cries of the spectators drowned out his words as more insistent cries for justice rose up.

Myriad bodies separated Elisa from Murphy and Charles. They were going to miss the boat, of that Elisa was certain. All their luggage was already onboard the great liner. Would the Cunard Lines refund Mr. Trump's money? she wondered. Would the Englishmen arrest Murphy and take him off to some terrible dark prison like in Germany?

Clutching the case of the Guarnerius to her, Elisa stood on tiptoe in an effort to catch a glimpse of Murphy and Charles. Murphy was still arguing angrily. The ship's horn bellowed again, and Elisa fought against the crowds to move toward the gangplank. If she could make it to the ship's officer, perhaps he could send someone to help. At least she could warn him that her husband and child were coming!

"Excuse me!" she cried. "Please, I am trying to get aboard ship!" The throngs parted at her words. She was making definite progress toward the enormous iron wall of the ship. Just ahead were the steps that led to the canopied ramp of the *Queen Mary*. "Please!" she shouted over the racket of the band. "Let me through!" With that, she pushed her way through the front lines of spectators who craned their necks upward and waved through the cloudburst of confetti that rained down on the docks. Sprinting toward the crew that manned the release of the ramp, she called. "Wait! There are more coming! Please wait!"

She climbed the steps and turned to scan the sea of heads. Finally she spotted Murphy and Charles. The child still clung ferociously to Murphy's back pocket. Elisa could see that Murphy had his wallet out. He was paying the vendor! She hurried up the ramp. The ship's officer, dressed in a white uniform with gold braid, stood at the head of the ramp studying a clipboard of names. He looked up and smiled hesitantly at the beautiful and disheveled woman who approached.

"Please!" Elisa cried. "You must delay just a moment longer! My husband and . . . our little boy! They are detained . . . in the crowd! Please . . . do not sail . . . without them!" She could scarcely breathe, and her words tumbled out in a series of breathless, choppy phrases.

"Your name, madame?" the ship's officer asked coolly.

"Elisa Murphy. My husband is John and the child Charles." She searched his list for their names.

She was so intent that she did not notice the two men who stepped up on either side of her until they touched her elbows. Their dark blue pin-striped suits and round derby hats seemed almost identical, like some sort of uniform.

"Mrs. Murphy," the man on her right said in a low voice, "you will come this way, please."

"But . . . my husband."

"Please, I assure you the ship will not sail without them." He pulled her away from the head of the gangplank.

"I would like to wait here for them—" Elisa attempted to pull free from their hands, but could not.

"They will not miss the sailing." The grim fellow was looking straight ahead as he spoke. He did not meet her questioning gaze.

Elisa found herself propelled into a narrow corridor within a few steps of where she had boarded. Crates of food were stacked everywhere. This could not be the way to her cabin, and these men were not members of the ship's company. The open hatch was closed behind them before Elisa could cry out her alarm.

"Where are you taking me?" She struggled and the grip on her arms tightened painfully. "Why are you—"

"This will do no good at all, Elisa." A third man stooped to emerge from a hatch a few feet in front of her captors. He was very tall, dressed in a fashion similar to the others except that he wore no hat and had a very thin mustache that followed the line of his upper lip. He was smiling. Pleased about something. He reached out to take the Guarnerius from

Elisa's aching arms. She opened her mouth to cry out, and a leather-gloved hand clamped over her face to muffle the scream.

The three men chatted for a moment as though there was nothing at all unusual happening.

"Frank managed to stop him all right?"

"Like a charm. He and the boy are still down there. Stuck in the middle of everything. It will be another five minutes before they reach the foot of the ramp."

"Then we should hurry," said the man holding Elisa's violin. "Mr. Tedrick is waiting at the Port Authority."

Elisa struggled to free herself. She fought, but the strong arms of her captors held her fast. The gloved hand simply moved slightly to cut off her air until she forgot about escape and struggled only to breathe. They lifted her bodily between them now and carried her through a maze of steep stairs that twisted down through a center corridor of the ship. They moved quickly, almost in a jog. There was no one else in the corridor, no one to question why they carried her down, why they held her.

Within moments they reached the galley deck of the great liner. Elisa could hear the clink of dishes and the carefree mingling of voices and laughter of the crew. Again the hand clamped tightly over her mouth. No chance to scream as the leadman twisted a lever on a watertight door and swung it back. A burst of daylight blinded Elisa for an instant. Then, blinking at the light, she saw a tugboat moored just outside. The faint sounds of the band and cheering voices drifted in. They were on the opposite side of the ship from where she had boarded. On this side of the liner there was no one to see what they did with her.

"Took you long enough!" called a fourth man in a suit from the deck of the tug. He was reaching up to grasp Elisa as they swung her out from the hull of the *Queen Mary* and dropped her down onto the deck. This maneuver took only a second; Elisa had a chance to gasp for breath and then attempt a scream before the fourth man covered her mouth with his hand. He jerked her arms back in a cruel hammerlock. Her eyes rolled back in pain as he shoved her into a cabin that reeked of fish and diesel fuel.

The two strong men jumped from the *Queen Mary* onto the tug, and then the third man tossed down the Guarnerius and closed the door to the hold of the ocean liner with a clang. No one noticed as the tug pushed off from the hull of the giant liner and chugged easily across the harbor toward a deserted dock.

◎৩

The ship's whistles were howling impatiently as Mrs. Rosenfelt showed her ticket to the officer at the top of the boarding ramp.

"Mrs. Rosenfelt." He tipped his hat. "First-class passage, right through those double doors to the purser's desk."

She nodded and, caught up in the press of the excited passengers, she was swept across the promenade deck and through the double doors marked Picadilly Circus. Stacks of steamer trunks were piled here and there in this main shipping square of the ship. Ladies in furs and the latest Paris fashions gawked in windows as stewards and porters scurried back and forth to make sure every passenger was in place in the proper room.

The walls and pillars of this main square were covered with a veneer of bird's-eye maple. Corridors branched off to dining rooms and smoking rooms and lounges in all directions. Broad stairs led down to the first-class rooms that stretched over one thousand feet from the bow to the stern of the great liner.

In the midst of such opulence, a dark shadow fell on Bubbe Rosenfelt. She turned a slow circle to fill her eyes with laughing, excited people. How different this was than the dreadful little ship where Maria and Klaus and the children now huddled! If only they could have come with her! Fare for passage on the *Queen* included all her meals and afternoon teas. Since the Reich had forbidden that she take any assets out of Germany, she had bought herself this first-class ticket. She would stay in a cabin that might easily have held her entire family. Instead, their fare to sail on the *Darien* had cost three times more for each than one ticket onboard the *Queen Mary*. What sort of food would they have on such a decrepit vessel? she wondered. Were they warm? Did they have good beds to sleep in? Such questions made her grief come fresh and sharp to her.

"May I help you, madame?" asked a steward in a crisp white uniform. He stepped from beside the purser's desk.

It took her a moment before she could answer. She struggled to pull the ticket from her reticule. "Room B-47." She made the words come, although her throat resisted. "My baggage was loaded last night."

"Down the main stairway and then follow the port-side corridor."

His explanation was interrupted by a tall young man with a small blond boy in tow. "I . . . I've lost my wife somewhere in all this." The man seemed flustered and unhappy.

"Probably in your room." The porter glanced at his ticket. "Ah, yes. You have a suite, I see. Have a look there first and then try the shops. Ladies and the shops, you know. Not the first lost wife we've had onboard."

"Could you page her?"

The steward swept his hand across the panorama of confusion. "Perhaps when we are under way."

Mrs. Rosenfelt stepped away from the unhappy man. He would no doubt find his wife. She, on the other hand, could only pray that Maria and her family were safe wherever they might be. It would have been such a simple matter to bring them along if it were not for the dreadful American visa restrictions. What an occasion of joy this Atlantic crossing might have been then!

She descended the grand staircase and stopped to glance back at the young husband and his boy. Something about the child seemed familiar . . . something. It did not matter. Perhaps she was simply looking at him because he was a child, like the great-grandchildren she had been forced to send on the *Darien*. The girls would have loved such a place! What fun they would have had together! Perhaps this boy would have been a playmate.

Bubbe Rosenfelt blinked back tears as she searched for her cabin along the corridor. Crowded with other passengers, the narrow hallway was nevertheless lonely. Three thousand people were aboard the liner, but all Bubbe could think about was the candy in the bottom of her reticule and the little girls who were not here to share it.

15
The Sacrifice

Murphy sat on the edge of the bed in their luxurious stateroom. Charles stood on a chair to look out the porthole as the last glimpse of England slid from view.

All the luggage had been promptly delivered to the room. Elisa's steamer trunk, a small brocade carryall, and two hat boxes were stacked neatly among the smaller bags belonging to Charles and Murphy. But where was Elisa?

Murphy and Charles had taken a turn around the promenade deck of the enormous vessel, hoping to find her. That deck was only one of several, however, and after forty-five minutes of wandering around, Murphy had decided that he could spend the entire voyage looking for her and she could quite easily be looking for him and they might never find each other. The great *Queen* was touted as a floating city. It was that, indeed. There was only one way to find Elisa—to return to their stateroom and wait for her to wander in like a lost pup.

They had waited here for an hour and fifteen minutes already and still Elisa had not showed up. Was she shopping? sipping coffee in one of the numerous cafés? sending a cable back to her parents in Prague?

Murphy stood suddenly and glared at the door. He was angry and worried. First more angry than worried, then more worried than angry. The ship's officer was quite certain she had checked in—quite. But then, he explained, he had seen hundreds of faces, after all.

"Charles, I'm going out again," Murphy said gruffly. "To the telegraph office. You wait here and when she comes in, don't let her go anywhere, will you?"

Charles gave him the okay sign, then turned back to the porthole as the fog enveloped the last point of land. Murphy donned his trench coat and slipped out into the cherrywood-paneled corridor. The stateroom was near the promenade deck, and the radio room was three decks below that and forward about half a city block.

He made his way to the lift, then changed his mind when he saw a dozen smiling couples standing in front of it. He took the stairs instead, clattering downward into the bowels of the ship.

Signs were placed at convenient intervals for any intrepid travelers who wished to explore the vast labyrinth of the *Queen*'s insides. Each landing displayed a map of that particular deck showing cabin placement and shops and restaurants. It was no wonder Murphy had not been able to locate his wayward wife, he thought as he scanned the map for the telegraph office.

The rumbling of the great *Queen* seemed much louder three flights down. Murphy pushed through the door into a corridor that was narrower than that of the upper-deck staterooms. Third-class cabins. No portholes. Murphy felt a bit more at home down here. Every Atlantic crossing he had made had been in third-class accommodations. Students and working stiffs and old ladies who liked shuffleboard—those were the standard fare down here.

He passed each of those types in turn; then the corridor branched off into a corridor lined with offices. *Ship's Steward. Head Chef.* And then, *Radio Room.*

Murphy leaned against the counter and pulled a blank tablet toward himself as the radio operator finished taking a message. It was a moment before the young man looked up. He was clear-eyed and apple-cheeked and somehow reminded Murphy of the nursery rhyme "Bobby Shafto's Gone to Sea."

"May I help you, sir?" He had the accent of English aristocracy, although he wore the simple uniform of a seaman.

"I'm looking for my wife." Murphy was suddenly embarrassed. Obviously Elisa was not here. "We got separated on the docks, and I thought maybe . . . she had come down here to send a wire."

"A wire, sir?" The young man eyed him strangely.

"Not to me—I'm *here*. But maybe she sent a wire to—"

"What's her name, sir?" He thumbed though a sheaf of yellow telegraph forms. "These are all the wires to go out."

"Elisa Murphy." Murphy craned his neck to see.

The young man straightened the stack and laid it aside somewhat self-consciously. He reached for the pad he had just been working on. "Then you will be John Murphy?" he asked.

"Yes." Murphy felt instant relief. So. She had sent a wire to her folks. There must have been quite a line holding her up.

The young man looked at him almost fearfully. "John Murphy?" He held up a single sheet by the corner.

"Yeah, that's me." Whatever relief Murphy felt vanished immediately as the scrawled message was laid before him.

"A wire for you, sir." Then he added, "I'm sorry, sir."

Murphy groaned.

FAINTED IN THE CROWD STOP MISSED SAILING STOP WILL CONTACT IN NEW YORK STOP LOVE ELISA

He held the note a moment, then crumpled it in his fist and shoved it into his pocket.

"So sorry, sir," the young man said as Murphy stormed from the office.

☙

The room was clean, at least. Stripped clean, except for an iron cot with a thin mattress covered by one sheet and a blanket. There were no toilet facilities. An empty tin bucket stood in one corner and a bucket filled with water in the other. Brick walls rose to a windowless height of fourteen feet, and near the ceiling one dingy transom window was ajar to give light and ventilation. This was better at least than a Gestapo prison. No one had cursed her or forced her to strip. But why . . . *why?*

Elisa had been left alone for three hours to wonder. Who were these men? Why had they kidnapped her? Had Murphy and Charles made it aboard ship, or were they also somewhere in Southampton? Again and again she ran through every scrap of conversation, every nuance of voice and appearance.

"Frank managed to stop him?"

"Like a charm."

"Mr. Tedrick . . . Port Authority."

She had been deliberately separated from Murphy. If her captors had thought that far, they had said only what they wanted her to hear. *Port Authority . . . Mr. Tedrick.* She assumed that this dreadful little room was somehow part of the port authority offices, but she had not seen this Mr. Tedrick whom they said was waiting.

There was only one thing she was sure of as the sunlight dimmed to twilight. She had missed the voyage. She was alone. Without answers, and without Murphy.

⌒

Anna climbed from bed and pulled the edge of the shade back to look out onto the cobblestone streets of Prague. Below her passed the endless stream of refugees who were pouring into the city from the Sudetenland. Czechs and Jews and Austrian Germans who had escaped the first on-slaught after the fall of Austria now congregated in penniless misery on the sidewalks and in the square beyond. She could see the ragged women with their children, making the best of it—at least they were still alive. Husbands worked to erect shelters from cardboard and packing crates and old tin. They had come here with some hope that the Nazi re-volt in their own territory would be stopped—stopped by men like Theo, Wilhelm, Dieter.

Anna let the shade fall back, covering the sight. She put a hand to her face in a moment of realization. She bowed her head. The words came clearly to her as if Christ Himself stood in the room: *"When he saw the multitudes, he was moved with compassion on them, because they fainted, and were scattered abroad, as sheep having no shepherd. Then saith he unto his dis-ciples, The harvest truly is plenteous, but the labourers are few; Pray ye there-fore the Lord of the harvest, that he will send forth labourers into his harvest."*

Anna gasped. She looked up, expecting to see the one who had just spoken. The room was still empty, yet now Anna hurried to dress. There were so many! She measured each room of the house with her eyes as she gauged how many could comfortably share the space. *One family in each room. Eight families. We will organize a staff for cooking right here and set up a soup kitchen for as many as we can.*

Within days, Anna had filled her house with grateful mothers and bevies of children. By the end of the week, two thousand from the square came twice a day for soup and bread, offered in the name of Jesus.

"The Lord bless you." Soup was ladled into cups.

"Jesus is with us." The bread was given.

"God has not forgotten." Milk to the children. Coffee for the adults.

Twice a week the grand piano was moved outside and Anna played joyfully for those who packed the street from one side to the other.

From this act of kindness, other Christians around Prague banded together until a dozen soup kitchens had sprung up and the multitudes were fed.

⌒

There was no one onboard the *Darien* who did not have a story to tell. Each had arrived at this desperate moment by a different route. Some had paid larger bribes and some smaller. Some had been among the first five hundred to purchase passage; others had come later through some miracle.

These different tales sparked a subtle resentment among the refugees. Those who had paid larger bribes resented those who had paid less. Those who had bought passage among the first five hundred resented those who had been squeezed in after the limit of five hundred had been passed.

"Why should we be sleeping on the deck? We were promised a cot!"

"Everything we owned to purchase passage, and they only paid . . ."

"We were the first, and now we are forced to give up our comfort so more can come!"

"Will the food hold out?"

"We were told . . ."

"There would have been enough for five hundred! But this!"

A Complaint Committee was formed.

"They might have allowed us to dock in London if there were not so many schleppers onboard."

"Do you know what I paid for this? I demand a cot!"

The rabbi of Nuremberg finally summed up the situation. "What did it cost us to get here? *Everything!* Once, some of us were rich. Once, some were not so rich, *nu*? Now we are all the same—poor. Early or late, we are all on the same ship. We are all passengers on the *Darien*. Neighbors. Family. Friends and enemies. Together now we are from *Darien*." He shrugged. "Only God knows who was rich and who was poor. And to Him it makes no difference. Such a sense of humor He has, *nu*?"

Captain Burton, however, finally settled the matter. Elusive and mysterious behind the grimy glass of the bridge, he issued orders that overruled the protests of the Complaint Committee. Belowdecks—from one end of the beam to the other—five hundred canvas hammocks had been hung. Women and children and the elderly would sleep in the hammocks. Young healthy males would sleep on the open deck. Tarps would be rigged to shield against the weather.

This was the law of the sea. This was tyranny.

"This is fair," declared the rabbi of Nuremberg. Every man on the Complaint Committee was assigned the task of helping women and children and the elderly to the hammocks below. After that, rich and poor, early and late, they worked together to rig the tarps that were to be their homes.

"I will see you in the morning." Klaus bent to kiss each of his girls good night. Two children to each hammock, they festooned the compartment like living bunting. Little Ada-Marie shared her mother's hammock. Trudy and Gretchen slept feet to feet, while Katrina and Louise swung in the hammock above them.

"When will we see you, Papa?" Gretchen looked worried and Ada-Marie lifted her chubby arms for one last embrace.

"When the breakfast bell rings we will eat our porridge together," Klaus promised. Gretchen made a face at the thought of the porridge served in the ship's galley. "Until then," Klaus continued, "I will think of my little caterpillars snug in their cocoons beneath the deck."

He turned to Maria and kissed her. A look passed between them. Klaus would have lain down beneath his wife's hammock if it had been permitted. But it was better this way. The rabbi of Nuremberg was right. It was fair for the men to camp beneath the stars while the women and children were snug belowdecks.

"At least we got in the stern," Maria said. "In the bow the hammocks swing every time we hit a swell. It is nice here." She felt tearful having to give up Klaus for all these suspended strangers. Many were seasick, and the hold smelled of vomit and sweat. It was not really so nice, but she would not form her own complaint committee.

"You will be warm here." Klaus bent very close to her face and touched her cheek with one hand and her swollen belly with the other. "Better for the children. Even this little one, eh?"

Maria put her hand on his as the baby kicked. "He says, 'Good night, Papa.'"

Klaus kissed her softly and then made his way past the three-tiered rows of hammocks to the steep steps.

"Good night, Papa!"

"Good night."

"Sleep tight!"

The voices of dozens of other children followed fathers and brothers up the metal ladder. Each with a different tale—some once rich, some not so rich—they were all one story now.

⌒☙

For the first time Shimon saw the face of the doctor. "Herr Doktor Freund," the captain called him. "See if you can get a little of this down him. Eighty proof. My own stock. Maybe it will help him sleep."

Dr. Freund leaned close to Shimon. He held a small glass of amber liquid in his hand. Sad brown eyes gazed hopefully through small round glasses. His head was bald except for a wreath of gray hair that circled from one ear to the other. "Drink this, my friend." He held the cup to Shimon's lips. "It will help some."

The scent of the whiskey was strong. Shimon battled the queasiness of his stomach as he sipped the liquid and coughed, then sipped again until it was gone. It burned his mouth and throat, searing a path to his stomach. Shimon tried to speak. He let his eyes wander from the face of Dr. Freund to the paper lilies that had been placed on the shelf opposite his narrow bed. He remembered the sweet concern on the faces of five little girls. "They were real," he managed to say.

The doctor caught his meaning. "Yes. They are real."

"I thought I had died . . . angels."

"No, you did not die. And they are little girls. They are the daughters of the woman who heard you in the vent shaft."

"The shaft . . . the fire . . . for a time I thought I was in hell. But this cannot be hell, can it? Not with children so sweet." Shimon gulped the air as a new fear assailed him. "Are you taking me back? *Back there?*"

"No. You are free, my friend. We are all free now!"

"Free." He said the word as though it were gold dust in his hand, as though his breath might blow it away.

"You are aboard the freighter *Darien*. A freedom ship to take us far from the Nazis."

"I am Shimon Feldstein." Shimon closed his eyes and repeated his own name.

"Shimon Feldstein." Dr. Freund straightened slowly. "You must set your mind on living. This is not heaven. It is not hell. It is the *Darien*."

✑

Murphy could not remember ever having been so miserable. This long night was worse than the loneliness he had felt when he thought Elisa had stood him up at the Musikverein in Vienna. It was worse than the months he had dreamed of her when there was no hope that she would love him. Now that she did love him, now that he knew firsthand what that meant, the agony of this senseless separation was almost more than he could bear.

Mechanically he had tucked Charles into his bed in the adjoining room. Somewhere from deep in his memories of childhood, he had remembered that kids need to pray before they go to sleep. His own mother had prayed with him, and both Elisa and Anna had spent a quiet moment at the bedside of Charles each night. So Murphy managed to mumble a self-conscious prayer; then when Charles had gazed soberly into his eyes, Murphy had prayed earnestly for Elisa: "*Hold her tight for me tonight, Lord, and bring us together again soon.*"

The prayer had been a concession to Charles, but it did somehow make Murphy feel better. Closer to her. Grateful that God was looking out for her. As Charles smiled at Murphy with his eyes, Murphy wondered which one of the two of them was more lonely. He propped the cello case open before he slipped out of the room. He wished that Elisa's violin were also in the stateroom. He would open it. He would touch the strings and think about her.

He opened her trunk instead, and the soft scent of her perfume wafted up and filled his senses. It was too much. He closed the trunk again, unable to bear such a vivid reminder of her. He looked at the still-made bed. This night should have been different. The thought made him ache. He slumped down in the chair and loosened his tie and hours later fell asleep out of sheer misery and exhaustion.

ↄↄ

Albert Sporer had not counted on the precise justice of the Prague government. His trial, while quietly conducted by the Czechs, was loudly denounced in Germany. Day after day the papers carried the horrendous reports that an "innocent" Sudeten Czech of German racial stock was being defamed and persecuted and tortured and now, finally, he was to be shot.

The verdict of the jury was unanimous. Albert Sporer was not only a Nazi and a traitor to the nation of Czechoslovakia, he was a proven murderer as well. His attempted assassination of President Beneš in May showed what sort of means and methods he would resort to for the sake of his dreams of Aryan superiority. Sworn witnesses who had fled Austria in terror the night of the Nazi invasion spotted his photograph in the newspaper. They came forward to testify that they had seen this man at the border, that he had not only brutally beaten a number of refugees but had summarily executed a man who tried to escape. The prosecution brought forth evidence that Sporer had been involved in a number of other crimes in Austria, all of which had been calculated for the ultimate fall of that nation.

As each member of the jury mouthed the word *Guilty*, three million Germans living in Czech-Sudetenland cried, "Innocent!" The failure of Sporer's attempt to murder Beneš had been a bit of a disappointment to Hitler. However, the tumultuous riots that were now rocking the Sudetenland because of Sporer's sentence of death caused him great joy privately and great anguish publicly.

Each day the Führer shouted his threat over the radio. Each day tension and violence between racial Germans and the Czechs increased. Here and there, men and women on both sides were killed. In Prague, President Beneš called for martial law in the Sudeten territory. Troops from the Czech Army patrolled the area. Their German countrymen bat-

tled them in Brno at a cost of nine Nazi lives. They formed their own Free
Corps to combat martial law. Swastikas were painted on the sides of
buildings and bridge abutments. *Heil Hitler! Free Sporer! Down with
Czech oppressors!* were painted on the boulders that lined the mountain
highways of Sudetenland.

Sporer was of more service to Hitler in his dying than he had been in
his living. He marched defiantly to the post at the back of the parade
ground. He handed a note to his Nazi attorney; smoked one last cigarette; declared loudly that his death and those of other Czech-Germans
would be avenged by his comrades across the border; and then, cursing
God and the priest and the Jews and the Czechs, he was shot.

Photographs of his body, riddled with holes and slumped at the post,
were published and widely circulated in Germany. What a triumph this
was for the Führer! Now the headlines raged:

> "Czech Sadism Rampant!"
> "Sudeten Germandom under the Knotted Whip of Prague Soldiery!"
> "Czech Militia Ravages Sudeten Germans!"
> "Organized Criminal Bands Attack Germans in Sudetenland!"

This was the hour of the Führer's greatest triumph in propaganda.

> "Czech Terror Becomes Unbearable!"

Carefully orchestrated by the Nazi propaganda machine, suddenly
President Beneš and the government of Prague became the villains and
the aggressors. It was almost forgotten that Albert Sporer had attempted
to assassinate the leader of Czechoslovakia, that he had been happily involved in the torture and murder of other innocent people. Suddenly
Sporer was a great hero of the Aryan race.

At the demand of the Nazi government, Sporer's body was shipped
to Berlin. There he was given a state funeral. In pagan ritual, his right arm
was cut off, and at the hour of midnight, it was offered up to the German
gods on a burning altar! Hitler strode onto a stage and addressed ten
thousand SS men who had assembled to pay homage. He raised his
head and sniffed the air: "What is that scent that hovers over us? It is the
smell of flesh—the flesh of a German, here sacrificed and offered up to
the glory of the Greater Reich. We shall not forget! We shall avenge!"

The roar of voices rose up with the smoke from Albert Sporer's right
arm. The god of Germany raised his hands. He was pleased with the offering, pleased with the praise. "Heil Hitler!"

16

My Fair Lady

Himmler had chosen subordinates for Gestapo work from among those who had exhibited the strongest loyalty for the ideals of the Aryan race. Not that these men themselves were ideal Aryans. Some were weak-eyed, as Himmler was. Many were narrow-chested, small of stature, swarthy in complexion. Not physically suited for the SS units, which required men of strength and Aryan looks, the Gestapo agents were picked for their mental devotion to the perfection of things German. They were ordinary. They had perhaps more to prove than those more perfect physical specimens. What they lacked in looks, they made up for in cruelty. Without flinching, they were capable of torturing a victim to the brink of death—but only to the brink, only enough to get the information they required. After this was accomplished, death was administered quickly with a bullet in the neck.

Such men had no fear of God or man or justice. They might as easily torture a priest or a nun as a common Jew. Nazi law was the only religion they cherished. Every man among them had proved his loyalty to the Führer from the first.

From among these ordinary Gestapo men, Himmler chose one to handle the matter of the failed assassination of Czech President Beneš.

Georg Wand at first glance had the appearance of a bank clerk or a shopkeeper from Unter den Linden. His face was thin, pockmarked from acne he had suffered as a youth. His eyes were brown, as was his thin hair. The eyebrows were too thick and met in the middle. He did not smile often, but when he did, a glint of gold from his capped right-front tooth was quite obvious. His body was also thin, his nose prominent; when Himmler had first seen him, he had commented that Wand had the look of an asthmatic, malnourished Jew.

Because of this ordinary, even homely, appearance, Georg Wand had much to prove. Of course his Aryan pedigree was impeccable back to 1800. Yet this search of his ancestors had not seemed like enough for Wand, so he had gone back another hundred years. Clean, clear, and perfect Aryan blood flowed through his veins. He was proud of this, but even such an exceptional lineage had not allowed him to be a part of the SS. Some said that Georg Wand carried his pedigree in his pocket next to his wallet and his Gestapo identification. If the prostitutes of the Berlin red-light district refused him for fear he was a Jew, he showed them his wallet, his pedigree, and his Gestapo identification before he finally had them shipped off to Dachau.

It was well known that Georg Wand did not like women. This made him especially useful in the prisons where women were interrogated. Where a man with less to prove than Wand might hesitate, this exceptional Gestapo agent proved his loyalty to the Fatherland time and again.

For all these reasons Himmler called him into his office following the ceremony for Albert Sporer. Had there been tears in the eyes of Wand as the smoke from Sporer's arm had risen? If Wand ever had a friend, Albert Sporer had been it. Sporer had brought him into the Gestapo. Wand had been with him in Vienna.

Himmler removed his gloves and tossed them onto the desk. He adjusted his round spectacles, preferring not to look at Wand's face. "Well, sit down, Georg. We have things to discuss."

Georg clicked his heels and obeyed. He did not reply, but sat in silence until Himmler passed him a copy of Sporer's last message. It had been decoded earlier, and Wand studied it with interest, even with some astonishment. In the letter two names had been deciphered. One name was that of Otto Wattenbarger. The other was that of Elisa Murphy. Of course the Gestapo had already marked Elisa Murphy as the one who had somehow discovered the plot and then warned Beneš. Her picture had been in newspapers on both sides of the Atlantic.

"Well, what do you think, Georg?" Himmler tapped his fingers on the desk blotter. "You know Otto Wattenbarger, don't you?"

"A good fellow." Wand scratched his head. "Hard to believe he is involved with anything." He scanned the message again. "You see here, not even Albert was certain if Otto was a traitor. This woman . . ." He picked up the newspaper from the file and studied her face. "Very beautiful. Involved with Otto?"

Himmler shook his head. "Otto is being watched, of course. If he is involved with anything, we shall know it soon enough. But the woman . . . there can be no doubt she was in the service of Prague." He picked up a pen and tapped the file with its point. "The woman we have no doubts about. Quite foolish of the Czechs to publicize her involvement. Of course we knew even before Sporer sent the message, but I think there is more to do than simply have her killed, don't you?"

"You want me to find out who was her contact? where the leak is?"

"It might have been Sporer himself. We cannot discount that possibility. He might have been attempting to blame Wattenbarger for his own indiscretion with her." Himmler strained to look at the photograph again. Shoulder-length blond hair, slim yet shapely, fine features. "You know Albert was weak-willed when it came to women of such Aryan beauty. He was always asking me to give him time with the young women in the Lebensborn program. In fact, he actually fathered at least two sons for the Führer. His life is not wasted."

Georg Wand had never been allowed to participate in the Aryan breeding program because of his stature and appearance. He resented the exclusion from such service, but he did not let Himmler see how the topic galled him.

"Was this woman a part of the Lebensborn, then?" Wand swept over the photo and imagined what perfect children such a specimen would bear.

"No. Never. She was a violinist in Vienna. We have asked around. Questioned the appropriate people. She left Vienna after her marriage to an American and was not seen there since. She left Prague with her husband and a child. Hans Erb followed her in London. Followed her and her husband to the docks of Cunard Lines in Southampton, where she boarded the *Queen Mary* for America."

"And?"

"Hans was delayed, as was Elisa's husband. She boarded the ship but somehow managed to get off it." Himmler passed yet another message to Wand. "As you see, Hans wired that the husband and the child are on the ship, but the woman is not."

"She is still in England?"

"That is something I wish you to find out."

"I will begin with the Cunard Lines. Hans is still following the husband?" Wand frowned. "Have Hans check for telegrams. A simple matter."

"He will stay with Herr Murphy in America in the event she shows up there. She is our point of contact, the strongest link we have in this chain."

"Why do we not simply *interrogate* Otto?"

"If we do not find her, then that is our alternative, of course. But what a pity to lose a loyal Nazi in Austria. She will, of course, tell you if Otto is involved. Then there will be time enough to deal with him." He chuckled. "We are certain of *her* treachery . . . and with that in mind I want you to use all your powers—your extraordinary powers with her as a woman, Georg."

Georg Wand looked again at the lovely woman in the news photograph. This was an assignment he would enjoy. He smiled, and Himmler saw the glint of the gold tooth.

◯◯

At first the face of the boatman in her dream looked like Darcy. He grinned toothlessly at her as he steered the little boat over the black water of the Thames River. Elisa heard the voices of a thousand children singing from somewhere in the fog: *"Take the keys and lock her up, lock her up, lock her up!"* Could they see through the darkness of the night? Were they on the banks of the river, watching as the boatman carried her away? *"Take the keys and lock her up, my fair lady!"*

She could hear the sound of oars dipping into the water. From somewhere the long, deep blast of a ship's horn called the last warning for passengers still not onboard. Elisa tried to cry out the name of Murphy but her lips would not move. She was too cold to speak. Her words froze on the air and were drowned out by the childish voices. *"Take the keys and lock her up!"*

The boatman grinned down at her. On both eyes now were black patches, and yet he was not blind. No. He seemed to see her as the grinning skull of Haydn saw her at the Musikverein. He spoke. Evil words that issued like smoke from his mouth. The flesh on his face dropped away, revealing white bone. "All the heads that grinned down from that tower. Can you see them?"

Elisa looked up from where she lay bound in the bottom of the boat. The White Tower was lined with the heads of innocents. Children. Each had a swastika etched into its pale forehead. Sightless eyes gaped at the river and the boatman and Elisa. *"Take the keys and lock her up, my fair lady!"*

The boatman spoke again, and still more flesh dropped away until he was only a skeleton within his clothing. "It is no different now. You will see. You will see. They who sacrificed the children to save the bridge . . . you will see . . . wall them up! Yes . . . we will wall up the children as an offering to the gods of war!"

Elisa formed the word *no!* She wanted to shout it, but it became a feeble whimper in her throat.

"Take the keys and lock her up, my fair lady!"

The stone arches of the bridge loomed above her. Moss formed at the base of the piers where the water rushed past. Now the voices came from the bridge itself. Elisa heard the jangle of keys as the boatman unclenched his jaws in a ghostly laugh and stood. He beckoned with his hand, pointing toward the stones of the bridge pier. A door appeared and opened to reveal a room. Suddenly she understood that *she* was to be sacrificed to some terrible ancient evil. *She* was to be walled up and forgotten for the sake of placating the darkness. The voices of the children turned to an insistent chant: *"Lock her up, lock her up, lock her up!"*

She tried to speak but could not. She tried to call upon the name of Christ for help. *"Lock her up, lock her up!"* the voices shrieked.

The boatman lifted her with his bony finger, and with a sweep of his hand moved her through the air toward the waiting cell. *"Lock her up!"* The chanting began to break into a thousand laughing voices now as Elisa fought to find her voice; to say the name of Jesus only once would tear down the walls, stop the mocking voices. But her lips could not move. Darkness pressed around her with a swirling weight that sucked her breath from her lungs. She fought, but the insistence of the voices was too strong, too loud.

"It is necessary to sacrifice the innocent," the boatman explained quietly. "Otherwise it might disturb things. You will see. You cannot save them. You cannot save yourself. And no one else cares." His skull began to disappear as the wall of her cell rose higher, brick by mortared brick. At last only his jaw was visible. His grinning jaw.

⌘

The jangle of keys and the slamming of the door were real.

The chill of the room penetrated Elisa's rough army-issue blanket. She curled tighter into a ball as she tried to warm herself. So cold . . .

She opened her eyes as the soft light of morning filtered through the high transom window. The steady bellow of a foghorn sounded at even intervals. Elisa counted eight beats as it echoed hollowly across the still water of the harbor. Metal buoys clanged as they rocked in the wake of some small fishing vessel returning home after a night in the Channel. There were no brass bands on the quay now. No ecstatic crowds or confetti. The *Queen Mary* was gone, and every minute took Murphy farther away from her.

Elisa was frightened. She lay shivering with a terror she had not known even in the prison cell of the Vienna Gestapo. There had been so little to live for then that maybe it had not mattered what became of her. Now there was John Murphy. "Murphy?" Tears stung her eyes as she twisted the wedding band on her finger. Had those beautiful moments together in the little room in Prague been a dream? Was she waking up to some terrible reality—had she never left that cell in Vienna? Was Leah still trapped in the apartment with two little boys? Every fear she had known over the last months of terror was now heaped together into one jumble in her mind. *So cold.*

Beside the steel door was her violin case. Beneath it was a stack of newspapers. They had not been there last night when the fat man had shut and locked the door. *This is not Vienna. I am still in Southampton. In England. And a prisoner!* Elisa sat up and wrapped the blanket tightly around herself. She could see her breath. Her teeth chattered with cold and fear. She tried to reconstruct those last moments on the quay before she had been kidnapped. The capture had been carefully planned, arranged so that Murphy could not intervene for days. How many days? she wondered. How long until he knew something had happened to her?

She walked stiffly toward the violin case and the newspapers. Just behind the stack of papers was a brown paper bag. She looked cautiously inside. It contained a pair of men's wool trousers and a dark blue cable-knit sweater. She slipped the sweater on over her blouse and then donned the baggy trousers, letting her skirt fall to the cement floor.

Draping the blanket around her shoulders, she looked into the bag again. There was a new toothbrush, tooth powder, and a hairbrush at the bottom. Somehow the sight of such basic requirements cheered her a bit. If these men meant to kill her, why would they give her a toothbrush? And why had they returned her violin?

She snapped open the case and frowned down at the precious instrument. It seemed untouched. She moved her fingers across the strings to prove that she was not still dreaming. *"Take the keys and lock her up, my fair lady!"*

Elisa shook her head violently, trying to rid her mind of the awful refrain. *Dear God*, she prayed silently, *help me. Only You can help me now.*

◯◑

Murphy was awakened by a soft tapping on his arm. He opened one eye to find Charles already dressed in the new woolen knickers Elisa had purchased for the trip. His tweed jacket was buttoned and his hair combed with a somewhat crooked part. A soft, gray silk scarf covered his collar, but Murphy figured that the kid had probably even tied his own tie.

Charles put his hand on his stomach. He was hungry. It was time for breakfast.

Murphy blinked at him in surprise. "You're as quiet as an Indian in a John Wayne movie." Murphy sighed and ran a hand over his sandpaper cheek. The dull ache of missing Elisa had not eased. He looked at the bed and then at the gray light that filtered through the porthole. Fog. He wondered if it would slow down the giant superliner as she raced toward New York. Murphy hoped not. Four days onboard the most luxurious ship in the Cunard Lines would be pure torture without Elisa. Today he would wire her in London. Maybe she could catch a plane and be in New York ahead of them.

Charles tapped on Murphy's arm again, breaking his reverie. Again he patted his stomach. It was time for breakfast, and Murphy needed to shave. The boy's eyes flashed impatiently. They had eaten in the state-room last night, and Charles wanted to go out now. Murphy was delaying the adventure.

"Five minutes to shower and shave." Murphy brightened at the thought that Elisa might find a way to make it to New York ahead of the *Queen*. It was possible.

He showered quickly in the tiny bathroom; as he opened the door to let the steam escape, Charles slipped in to watch him shave. Murphy lathered his own face and then, removing the scarf from Charles, he covered the child's jaw, carefully spreading shaving cream across the boy's upper lip. When he lifted Charles up to the mirror, the boy giggled with delight at the sight of his image next to Murphy's.

"Just you and me, huh, kid? A couple of bachelors."

"Uh-huh!" Charles giggled again as Murphy gave him his comb and showed him how to pretend to shave.

They shaved together, with Charles perched on the sink to imitate every stroke Murphy made. Elisa would want the boy to have a good time, Murphy reasoned past his own misery. She would expect Murphy to show him a little fun in spite of the fact she had missed the boat herself. Charles hesitated as Murphy shaved his upper lip. He seemed disappointed that the sudsy mustache had to come off. He had looked grown-up and very much like Louis with the mustache hiding his deformity.

Charles climbed down from the sink, away from the mirror, before he removed the soap. It was nice to have looked like other little boys even for a few minutes. It was nice to pretend.

Murphy was nearly dressed when the valet knocked and Charles opened the door to a slim, middle-aged man clad in an immaculate white uniform. Gray hair and dignified posture gave the man the air of a ship's officer or a Wall Street banker. He glanced at the bed, surprised that it was made. "You needn't make the bed, sir. Fresh linens every day."

"I fell asleep in the chair," Murphy explained as he tied his tie and fastened his suspenders.

Already the valet had gathered up Murphy's wrinkled suit. "A good pressing and I'll have it back to you this afternoon, sir." Then he paused and added, "And would you like your dinner jacket pressed for this evening?"

Murphy nodded. "Quite a roster of passengers onboard, I hear."

The valet recited names that were most familiar. "Quite. Everyone wants to be onboard the *Queen* when she breaks the speed record of the *Normandie*. Secretary of the Interior Harold Ickes and his new wife. The film star Eddie Cantor. And, of course, Henry Ford." The voice hardened at the mention of Henry Ford.

"Coming home after his visit with Hitler," Murphy remarked dryly. He was having trouble with his tie. He wished Elisa were here to help him. The valet took over the effort.

"Quite. They say it is the highest award offered by Nazi Germany. Did you see the photographs, sir? Award of the Grand Cross of the German Eagle." He tugged on Murphy's tie. "There you are, sir." He stepped back and studied the result.

"And you say Eddie Cantor is on the same boat with Ford?" Murphy frowned. "Should be interesting."

Now the valet smiled. "Quite."

"Dynamite."

"With short fuses, sir. One would not want to miss a meal. They have been seated at opposite tables, facing each other."

Such information made Murphy hurry his pace to the massive dining room. It was common knowledge that Henry Ford was among the men who had stirred the anti-Semitic feelings in the United States. He had published the pamphlet *Protocols of the Elders of Zion*, which Hitler himself claimed was a plan of the Jews to take over the world. Ford was also closely allied with Father Coughlin, the vitriolic Catholic priest in Detroit who raged against the Jews and against Roosevelt's New Deal, calling it the *Jew Deal*. On the payroll of Ford Motor Company was the head of the American Nazi Party, Fritz Kuhn, whose rallies were becoming more violently outspoken against the Jews in America and those who might wish to immigrate there. To Kuhn, Hitler was a hero. Maybe he was to Ford also.

Eddie Cantor, on the other hand, was not only Jewish, but definitely vocal in his hope that American immigration quotas would be changed. Both Father Coughlin and Henry Ford had verbally attacked Cantor. *Yes indeed*, Murphy thought as they entered the enormous dining room, *this will be an interesting voyage with those fellas onboard!*

Murphy had seen the photographs of Hitler and Henry Ford together. The sight had sickened and angered him, just as Charles

Lindbergh's visit with the Führer had done. What caused so many great Americans to make a pilgrimage into the presence of such an evil man? Was it their admiration of his political power? their mutual hatred of Jews and the claim that Jews were Communists? It was an interesting question, considering that Russia had also leveled its guns to the foreheads of the Russian Jewish population. It was a question Murphy hoped to ask these gentlemen of the American far right who pulled the wires until all immigration of the persecuted masses in Germany was stalled. Such questions awakened the reporter in Murphy as he and Charles entered the palatial splendor of the *Queen Mary's* dining room.

The aromas of bacon and sausage and eggs Benedict filled their senses. Crystal chandeliers illuminated the room. The ceiling, twenty feet high, had leaded-glass skylights. An enormous buffet table was topped by an ice sculpture of dolphins leaping from a sea of delicacies. At one end, a portly chef carved roast beef; on the other, a huge ham was being served. Waiters scurried across the rich, red floral carpet pouring champagne for some and coffee for others. All the while, a string quartet played the lyric melodies of Mozart from a corner stage.

Charles gripped Murphy's hand as the maitre d' led them to their table. Murphy's eyes scanned the crowd for some glimpse of Eddie Cantor or Henry Ford. White tablecloths. Red cloth napkins. Sterling silver tableware and china dishes edged with gold. Murphy wondered if Cantor and Ford would air their differences in a public explosion, or simply simmer like the food in the buffet steamers.

"You are seated here, sir." The head waiter bowed. Murphy barely heard him. He was still scanning the crowd.

"I hear Eddie Cantor is here," Murphy said quietly. "He's one of my favorite movie stars."

The head waiter smiled as he glimpsed the five-dollar tip Murphy slipped into his hand. In such a vast room, guests often needed help spotting the movie stars and celebrities who traveled on the *Queen*.

"Mr. Cantor is just there, sir." The head waiter nodded. "Table four. At the front near the string players."

Murphy spotted him easily now, dark-eyed and smoldering in his velvet chair. Apparently Mr. Cantor had not only seen Henry Ford in the flesh, he had also seen the photos of Ford and Hitler. From there it was easy to spot Ford. His table was just opposite Cantor's and filled with admiring yes-men and adoring women. Ford seemed to be enjoying himself. Ford had pretended not to see Cantor and was quite loudly making sure Cantor knew that the Ford magnate had no intention of seeing him, either.

The head waiter turned to go. Murphy stopped him with a question. "I understand Secretary of Interior Ickes is also onboard?"

"An interesting mix, eh, sir? Mr. Ickes is on his honeymoon, however, and will most likely come late to breakfast."

"Right." Murphy could certainly understand that. If Elisa had been here he would have skipped breakfast, too.

17

Fog

Aboard the *Darien*, First Mate Tucker was the eyes and ears of Captain Burton. Tucker, whose wind-weathered skin took on the appearance of tanned leather, was also the mouth of the captain. Orders from Captain Burton were, for the most part, relayed through this spindly, rubber-faced little man.

First Mate Tucker was from England—from Southampton, to be precise. He pronounced the name of his hometown with a thick cockney accent that sounded to Maria like "Sow'ampton." He called himself "Firs' Mite."

"Ah tol' the cap'n we ought naught put in at London. Now, at Sow'ampton they'd 'ave let us tike on s'plies!"

Maria, who in turn served as translator for the passengers, had to ask First Mate Tucker to restate each sentence several times before she caught the meaning. Even then she was unsure of his meaning except for those words borrowed from Yiddish.

"Nuthin' but shlemozzl . . ."

This meant confusion.

"Stumer an' gazzump, ah tell y'!"

Nothing but a complete loss and confusion, he was saying. Maria translated the first mate's anguish and embarrassment at having the *Darien* turn away from the port of London. She told the group clustered around her that the first mate believed they might have been allowed to dock in Southampton.

"Nae dou' 'bout it! They's all doolally in London!"

Maria considered this a moment longer. "The first mate says that there is no doubt about it. The officials in London are—"

Doolally? What is doolally?

Tucker had rolled his eyes and twirled his finger when he said the word. Such a sign could only mean . . . *crazy?* Confident in her interpretation, Maria reported that the London port authorities were *meshugge!* Everyone nodded in agreement.

This morning the wizened little man stood behind the table in the ship's tiny galley as the cook ladled out portions of porridge.

"We got no 'am n' h'eggs."

"No ham and eggs," Maria translated for those within earshot. Every Jew was grateful there was no ham.

"Ain't no bu'er."

"No butter."

"Ain't even got no ra'en toma'oes, neither."

"Not even rotten tomatoes, thank God."

"But y' can 'ave all the porridge y' can eats!"

"Lots of porridge to eat, however."

Lots of porridge was not what the children wanted. Trudy rolled her eyes and put a hand to her squeamish stomach. She thought of all those in the hold below who had not even bothered to get out of their hammocks for the breakfast call. She looked up at the gaunt face of her father. He looked windblown and cold after his night on the top deck.

"Why me an' me bruvver John was raised on such porridge, an' y' can see it ain't done me no 'arm." First Mate Tucker thumped his chest enthusiastically and grinned at a small, miserable little boy. "Auf wiff y', now, laddie!"

"Off with you," Maria mumbled in English, repeating the butchered phrase. Maria was next in line. She extended her tin plate to receive the ladle of sticky goo. "Thank you." She mustered a trace of enthusiasm, although her stomach rebelled at the gob on her plate.

"Got no 'am n' h'eggs." First Mate Tucker began his spiel again; then he noticed that it was Maria who stood before him. "Poor blighters don't speak a word of English, do they? Now, tha's awright! Y' can tells 'em fer ol' Tuck that we'll 'ave 'em talkin' like the king's own guard afore we reach port, eh?" He winked at Maria and dumped another helping of porridge onto her plate.

❦

As the waiter poured her coffee cup full, Bubbe Rosenfelt raised her glasses for a better look at the little blond boy holding so tightly to the tall, handsome man's hand. Something stirred her memory. Had she seen this child before? Bright blue eyes with long lashes. Straight blond hair poking out from a blue wool cap. Navy blue suit, cut in the fashion of an English schoolboy. The gray silk scarf. An aviator's scarf. All the little boys seemed to want to wear them since pilots and airplanes had come of age. Indeed, there was something familiar about this handsome child.

The boy looked up at the man at his side. The man seemed quite preoccupied, looking everywhere about the dining room. Bubbe studied the man's features now. If he seemed familiar, she reasoned, it was only because he slightly resembled the new American movie star, James Stewart. His face was a bit more angular, true, but he had a boyishness about him and a way of carrying himself that made him seem as if he might want to join a group of Brooklyn boys in a game of stickball.

The maitre d' led them directly to her table. They were to fill the two empty chairs on her right. Bubbe smiled pleasantly at the child. It would be good to spend the lonely mealtimes in conversation with a little boy. How she missed the children! She thought of the peppermint candy in her reticule. She would find some reason to present a piece to him.

Introductions were made of the five others who shared the table. "And this is Mrs. Rosenfelt. May I present Mr. John and Master Charles Murphy."

Bubbe Rosenfelt tried not to let her surprise show as Charles and Murphy took their seats. Of course. This boy's picture had been plastered on every newspaper in Hamburg two years ago. He and his brother. What was his brother's name? His father had published the newspaper. What was the child doing with this American fellow?

Charles sat at her right elbow. He searched the face of each adult around the table, finally letting his eyes examine the pince-nez glasses dangling from the button of Bubbe's black dress. She smiled down at him and then broke her own taboo about speaking in German. She slowly lifted the glasses and perched them on the bridge of her nose.

"I must wear these to read the menu, you see," she whispered to Charles in the precise accent of one who had lived in Hamburg for a long time.

His eyes warmed with the familiarity of that soft inflection. It had been a long time since he had heard words spoken with precisely that tone. It had been a long time since Louis had been gone, and longer still since Father had disappeared into the teeming masses of Vienna.

"Can you read the menu, Herr Charles?" she queried gently, now aware of why the boy wore his scarf even here. She did not wish to ask him anything that could not be answered with a nod or a shake of his head.

He answered with a negative shake of his head.

"Then shall I read for you?"

Charles nodded.

Murphy conversed lightly with the other passengers, keeping an eye on Charles and Mrs. Rosenfelt as he spoke. They had come too far to take any chances now.

Murphy watched as Bubbe read the choices from the menu card. Surely this dear old Jewish lady could be trusted with Charles! Surely here, on the *Queen Mary,* bound for America, Murphy could relax and not worry about being followed by Gestapo agents around every corner. Surely here, now, they were finally safe.

Bubbe held the menu card out at arm's length, and it caught the light. The menu was inscribed in gold on stiff linen parchment with the logo of the *Queen Mary* at the top. "You can have any of those choices that the waiter will bring you, or perhaps Mr. Murphy would not mind if you accompany me over to the buffet table, where we may choose anything we wish to eat?"

Charles nodded his head enthusiastically and tugged on Murphy's sleeve for permission. Murphy, bombarded by the opinions of a businessman from New Jersey about the differences between the French liner *Normandie* and the *Queen Mary,* had to ask Mrs. Rosenfelt to repeat her question.

"Would you mind, Herr Murphy, if I take your . . . ah, your *son* to the buffet table?"

At the word *son,* Murphy started. He studied the eyes that gazed deeply into his and saw compassion and understanding. "I am somewhat familiar with your *situation,* Herr Murphy," Mrs. Rosenfelt said with a tone that carried a profound significance. "I will be happy to accompany Charles to the buffet; he is quite safe with me, I assure you."

Murphy smiled. "Sure. There's nothing to worry about here." He turned to Charles. "You hungry, kid?"

Charles nodded. A muffled "uh-huh" ruffled the scarf.

He motioned toward the buffet table as Bubbe leaned toward Murphy. "I am from Hamburg," she said. "I thought perhaps Charles and I might become acquainted since we will be sharing the same table for the crossing."

"You're from Hamburg, too?" Murphy's face reflected a moment of apprehension.

"Originally from New York. I am leaving Hamburg for many of the same reasons as Charles, I imagine." Her words conveyed that she knew whatever there was to know about the Kronenberger affair in Nazi Germany. She, too, was acquainted with grief. "Would you mind if Charles helped me at the buffet table?" She displayed her cane, an indication that buffet tables were somewhat difficult. "To manage a walking stick, one's plate, and then to manage the serving spoon is somewhat complicated unless one has grandchildren nearby. My grandchildren are all en route to the States in a different way. Might I borrow Charles from you?" There was amusement in her eyes. Something about her made Murphy doubt that she needed a cane. Indeed, she hung the walking stick over her arm as she and Charles circled around the heaping table. Pointing at this tray or that tray, she held out her plate to Charles, who spooned the helpings for her. They admired the ice dolphins and then, together, they stopped to listen to the string quartet, paying special attention to the cellist.

Charles carried both heaping plates back to the table.

". . . and I have five lovely great-granddaughters. Trudy, who is named after me, almost eight years old. Then Katrina, who is very serious. Then Louise. Louise is almost six and very pretty. How old are you?"

Charles held up five fingers. He was also almost six.

"Gretchen is almost five. And then the baby is Ada-Marie who is four next month. *Oy!* Such a handful." Bubbe let a touch of Yiddish slip into her conversation. "Perhaps you will want to come and play with them when they come to New York. It would be nice to play with children from Hamburg, would it not, Charles?"

Charles frowned. He was not certain that he wanted to play with any children from Hamburg except for Louis. Every other playmate had been cruel. In the end he had not had any other friends but Louis, and only the company of his mother and brother. Then his father. Finally Leah and Elisa, and now . . .

"But then perhaps you would not wish to play with girls, *nu*? In Brooklyn where I come from, little boys play games called Kick the Can and stickball. You might enjoy that more. Still, there may come a time when you wish to meet some very pretty girls from Hamburg." She reached into her reticule and fished out a round, paper-wrapped peppermint. "My thanks for helping such an old lady. Now eat your breakfast, and afterward you can have the candy."

Eating in public was a difficult accomplishment for Charles. He bowed his head slightly and with his left hand he raised the scarf until it covered the bridge of his nose. He shielded his mouth with his hand as his mother had taught him, and then he chose very small bites. Soft things Bubbe Rosenfelt had said were good to eat.

Whenever any of the adults looked curiously at him, Bubbe Rosenfelt asked a question to distract them. Charles liked this old woman with her gray hair and her straight back and black dress and funny glasses and accent from Hamburg. She felt very much like someone from home. Comfortable. Like Louis and Father and . . . like Mommy. He wanted to ask her why her great-granddaughters were not on the boat with her. But then, none of his family was here either. Maybe it was just the way things were. Had they always been this way? he wondered. Some come to America on the *Queen Mary* and some on another ship while others cannot come at all.

In the corner the music reminded him of Vienna and Leah. Charles wanted to show Bubbe Rosenfelt Leah's cello. Then she would know that he really did know about cellos even if he did not know how to read the menu card.

◌◐

The sea of the gray Atlantic had risen again, and the swells that slapped the hull of the *Darien* were taking a toll on the passengers.

First Mate Tucker organized a battalion of adolescent boys headed by Aaron who swabbed the decks and washed the breakfast tins. Those passengers who could manage the climb had struggled up to the misty air of the top deck in order to breathe deeply and regain control of their churning stomachs.

For Tucker, so many passengers languishing on the deck meant an opportunity for an English lesson. Bandy-legged and rubber-faced, he strolled cheerfully among them asking in his cockney accent, "An' 'ow are y' tod'y?"

Broken English replied to his query, "Am I feelink fine, dank hue." Then another helping of porridge would be served over the rail to the fishes of the Atlantic.

Maria leaned heavily on the arm of Klaus as they staggered along the pitching deck. Trudy, Katrina, Louise, Gretchen, and Ada-Marie followed like ducklings in close order.

"Mama is sick," Gretchen explained to Ada-Marie. "See how white she looks."

"Papa also is white," Ada-Marie observed.

"It is the porridge," Louise said. "Like glue."

"I ate glue once." Ada-Marie put her hand on her stomach at the memory. "But I didn't get so white as Mama."

"That is because you did not eat it for breakfast," Katrina said. "If you eat glue for breakfast it makes you white."

Now Trudy, the eldest, spoke with authority. "It is not the porridge that makes everyone so sick. It is the waves. Lurching. Lurching. Lurching."

"Is that why we have no Torah school today? Is the rabbi from Nuremberg also sick?" Gretchen asked.

"Everyone is sick," Louise replied. "Except us. And I do not feel so good right now myself."

Ada-Marie spotted Tucker strolling toward their little procession. "He's not sick either."

Tucker waved broadly. He seemed not to notice that Maria was ill. "An' 'ow is Muvver Goose an' all the li'l geese tod'y?" he asked brightly.

They answered with one voice. "We are very fine, thank you, First Mite Tucker." Then Maria, Louise, and Trudy paused to lean over the rail. After a moment Klaus joined them to jettison his breakfast into the waters.

"Why don't you get sick, First Mite?" Ada-Marie asked.

"Because I lives 'ere. An' I'm used ter it, see? Y'll get used ter it, too," Tucker answered without sympathy.

"Please, God," Klaus gasped, "may we not be here that long!"

As if in ominous answer to that halfhearted prayer, the good ship *Darien* shuddered and died in the water. The thrumming of her engine stopped until only the splashing of waves against her hull was heard.

Tucker cursed, then scrambled toward the hold as the voice of Captain Burton shouted, "All hands!" over the loudspeaker.

Two other crew members sprinted for the hatch.

"What can it mean?" Maria whispered.

The ship drifted to port as a swell caught her. "We are not moving forward," Klaus said, still sick.

"Does this mean we will have to stay here a long time, Papa?" Gretchen looked miserable. She sank down to sit on the deck as other passengers clustered in small worried groups to speculate on what might be wrong.

Once again the stern voice of Captain Burton crackled over the speakers. "We have lost a steam line to the engine. A minor repair. We will be delayed an hour at most. Make the best of it."

⁂

One hour passed, then two. Still the engine of the little freighter did not spark to life. The heavy silence was augmented by the fog that closed in around the ship. Thoughts were lost in the lapping of water against the hull.

Shimon heard urgent whispering in the corridor.

"He can't be moved."

"Cap'n says ever'body up on deck. Even the sick feller 'ere."

"But he can't be moved. There is more danger to him up on deck. The dampness—"

"Look, Doc, all I can tells y' is tha' we're dead in the water in the middle of the shipping lanes. Smack in the center. We're pickin' up the radio of somethin' big."

"Then, can it not help us?"

"Help us? She can't even 'ear us! Somethin' 'as gone amiss with the transmitter, an' Cap'n says if she should ram us, we got more chance of survivors comin' out of the water if we're all up top."

"Some are so ill they cannot walk."

"Then we'll 'ave ter carry 'em. Includin' this big bloke, 'alf dead though 'e may be."

"Lifeboats. Life vests. Have we enough?"

"This ain' no cruise ship. She's a freighter, an' as such she's got enough of such items fer a freighter's crew."

There was a long silence as the meaning of the seaman's words penetrated Dr. Freund's stunned consciousness. A tiny, decrepit tramp steamer adrift in the shipping lanes of the North Atlantic. Radio transmitter too weak to send a distress signal but strong enough to hear messages of a large ship close by.

"Send me four strong fellows to carry the patient up," the doctor finally complied. "Although it will make no difference to him if we are rammed. He would be just as well off here below as in the icy water."

"Cap'n's orders," came the reply. "Ever'body on deck."

Shimon did not speak as four husky young men carried him up into the thick mist shrouding the open deck. At the instructions of Dr. Freund, they placed his stretcher beneath a tarp tent. All was silent except for the murmured prayers of the rabbi of Nuremberg. Family groups huddled together, clinging to one another as they stared out into the slate curtain that surrounded the *Darien*.

Shimon recognized the five little girls who had brought him the lilies. He could not remember their names. He tried to concentrate, tried to remember their names as he watched them cling to the skirt of their pregnant mother and lift hands up to their tall, gaunt father. Was there ever such pain on a man's face? The father of those children closed his eyes in tight-lipped agony at his own helplessness. He looked first at one child and then another. Whom to save? He could not save them all if the ship was rammed.

Shimon groaned with that man's agony. Five little girls. A wife. Shimon had only his own life to give up. What must it be like to wonder whom to save?

The rabbi now felt silent. The *Darien* moaned, metal creaking a protest as the water pushed her from one trough to the next. There was no human voice except that of the frantic, cursing seamen who worked below on the recalcitrant engine. Dull silence. Hearts racing. Breath that mingled with the fog.

Then one head raised as if to sniff the air. Another and another

turned to face the starboard side of the ship. In the distance the faint
rush of water could be heard, and behind that the low thrumming of an
engine.

Now everyone heard it. Straightaway to the starboard. Yes. They
could hear the engines of the great ship. *Rushhhh. Rushhhh.* So swift to
destruction. Right on course. Unheeding of the heartbeats, unaware of
the father who had decided they would all simply die together. He could
not choose. He *would* not choose among his precious little ones.

The rabbi began to pray again. Other voices joined him. Like the
sound of the wind through the trees, the great ship swept toward them
through the fog.

18

The Closed Curtain

Leah intertwined her fingers in the mane of the little Haflinger mare she rode. The trail loomed up the face of the mountain in a series of tortuous switchbacks. Hooves clattered and scrambled against the rocks, sending showers of pebbles and gravel sliding away from the narrow path to plummet down the thousand-foot wall.

"Stand in your stirrups," Franz Wattenbarger called back to her. "Put your weight over the mare's shoulders."

Leah obeyed immediately, as she had done whenever the handsome young Tyrolean man had issued some command throughout the long, arduous journey from the farmhouse. Now the house was a mere matchbox beneath them. In the last mile they had ridden above the tree line until the high valley where the farm nestled was a neat patchwork of newly cultivated field in the center of a carpet of green forest. One hundred yards beyond the trail, a waterfall gushed over the boulders and tumbled down into the abyss until it finally emerged as a thin ribbon of peaceful blue bordering the Wattenbarger farm. In the previous weeks, Leah had sat quietly beside that stream while young Louis had whooped and run in the wide fields.

Even though they were still within the boundaries of Austria, Leah had felt safe on the farm. Safe from the Nazis. Safe behind a tall green curtain of peace that surrounded the home of the Wattenbarger family. As the other refugees had been taken from the haven one by one, Leah had not felt an urgency to escape. She and Louis were the last of the little company to leave. If it had not been for the immense danger her presence brought to the kind family, she would have begged to stay. The words and prayers of dear Marta had brought her comfort and courage. She had found faith to trust that somehow God held Shimon firmly in His hand.

"I won't know how to pray without you to show me," she had whispered in her tearful farewell to Marta.

"Just talk to the Lord, child." Marta had embraced her and led her quickly to the side of the little horse. "And remember, it is written: 'Whither shall I flee from thy presence? If I ascend up into heaven, thou art there: if I make my bed in hell, behold, thou art there. If I take the wings of the morning, and dwell in the uttermost parts of the sea, even there shall thy hand lead me, and thy right hand shall hold me.'" Then Marta had pulled out a well-worn Bible from the pocket of her apron and tucked it into Leah's fleece-lined coat.

"But I cannot ride a horse," Leah had protested feebly.

At that, Marta had patted her cheek. "Sit quietly, Leah. She knows the path. She has traveled it a hundred times, and she will not slip."

As Leah glanced fearfully back toward the valley from the dizzying height, she clung to Marta's reassurances. She prayed. She had not been so frightened since the night Otto had taken them out of Vienna.

Five-year-old Louis, tied securely to a large, shaggy horse, was totally unafraid as Franz led him up the trail. Twice the child had nodded off to sleep, and Franz turned to Leah with the explanation. "It's the altitude. Lack of air makes the little ones sleepy. Every child I have guided out of here has dozed off. I learned early to tie them onto the saddle. Almost lost the first one. He fell off—lucky it was a wide spot in the trail!"

Leah was sore and exhausted, but not the least bit drowsy. She was not tied onto the saddle, and the thought of nodding off and tumbling from her mount kept her wide-awake. Inches from the hooves of the surefooted horse, the world disappeared. Leah kept her eyes plastered to the rump of the horse ahead of her. She imagined the Herrgottseck of the farmhouse. She could almost smell the fresh-baked roggenbrot on the cold alpine wind. She could feel the warmth of the fire and visualize Karl and Marta as they bowed their heads over supper and prayed for the safety of the travelers as they had done for each expedition that Franz had led to freedom over the weeks.

Leah could not help but wish she were back at the table with the old couple. How much longer would they have to ride before they reached the first hut and Franz would turn them over to the capable hands of yet another guide who would lead them farther toward the border?

"How much longer, Franz?" The question escaped Leah's lips the instant she thought it.

In reply, he pointed to a jagged outcropping two hundred feet above them where the sunlight struck the rock with a blinding light. The trail led up and around the rocky point and disappeared into a snow band. "The summit," Franz said with a jerk of his head. "There is a lake at the top where we will rest the horses and stretch. From there you can just see the hut. It is down a bit. Another mile."

The thought of a short rest beside an alpine lake caused Leah to want to kick the horse and urge her to hurry up the dangerous slope. As if reading her mind, the lead horse strained forward and quickened his pace as he clambered up the path. Leah's mount followed, crowding its nose against the rump of the gelding that carried Louis. The horses, too, seemed in a hurry to rest.

⌒⌒

A bank of clouds rolled through a mountain pass far below the little band of travelers. Leah looked downward at the small square of green in the valley that marked the peaceful farm. One last look. A final farewell. There had been so many of those farewells, and she could not help but wonder, as the clouds covered the valley floor, if she would ever again see her beloved Austria. It was as if God had closed a curtain, blocking that last nostalgic view from her. Now the world was the treeless, boulder-strewn mountain peaks above and tall, ever-changing pillars of clouds below. The rush of the wind blended with the roar of tumbling waters escaping from the cold grip of a glacier. Her breath and that of the horse drifted up on the cold air in a steamy vapor as they topped the rise and emerged at the summit.

There was no hint of green here, but a rocky shore led gently down to a small lake. Years of glaciers had deposited rocks and boulders everywhere. The horses picked their way carefully toward the water's edge.

At first glance, Leah noticed that the water was almost milky in color. The lake seemed to be a mere shallow depression on the stone slab. As they neared the water, however, she could see that her first impression had been wrong. The bottom of the lake dropped off to an unmeasurable depth, to burst out from the face of the mountain in gushing waterfalls and mere trickles that scarred the granite cliff.

Franz dismounted and then, as if to prove some unspoken theory, he picked up a stone and heaved it toward the center of the lake. It landed with a heavy *plop*, and Leah watched it descend until it finally disappeared into the black depths.

Franz smiled slightly. "Welcome to Funnel Lake. It has a dozen other names. A hundred other names over the centuries, but this is the name I call the place." He pointed across what would have been a valley, only the space was filled with an enormous glacier. "What the glacier does not want it pours into this funnel. Perhaps the entire mountain is a cone to hold the water." He shrugged. "Anyway, we can rest here a while. Not a very pretty place; but interesting."

"We are not here for the sights," Leah answered as she stiffly climbed from the back of her horse. She felt instantly shaky and short, as if she had lost inches in her height. She held to the stirrup as though she might fall down. "And may I never ride another horse," she muttered.

Franz laughed at her. "You will find your legs again," he quipped. "You will have to. Tomorrow you and the boy will be guided across that glacier." He jerked his head toward the white mass of ice again. "You will wish you had a horse to ride then, I am thinking."

Securing the reins beneath a stone, Franz moved to untie the sleeping child from his horse. At his touch, little Louis yawned sleepily and blinked in confusion at Franz. "Are we here yet?" he asked.

"We are here," Franz replied, embracing Louis and swinging him to the ground. "But we are not yet *there*."

As Franz and Leah shared the provisions Marta had sent, Louis entertained himself by tossing stones into the lake and watching them vanish.

"And how long will it be until we are *there*?" Leah asked, tearing a chunk of bread from the loaf.

"If we were eagles, the flight from the farm would be like that." Franz snapped his fingers. "Twenty-five miles across the sky into Italy. I myself have flown a glider from Innsbruk through the passes into Switzerland. But there is no hope of that now with the Nazis at every airfield, large and small. And so, since God has ordained that we will not mount up with wings as eagles, you must content yourself with being able to walk and not grow weary."

"I have not walked yet, and I am already weary." Leah leaned her head back and looked longingly into the darkening sky. "How long will we walk?"

"The best passes are closed by the Wehrmacht now. When they were all on the Czech border we took out seven through the Brenner Pass into Italy. Now I'm afraid it will be more complicated." He sighed and thoughtfully chewed a sausage. "There are ways. Tonight we will sleep in the hut of Gustav Stroh. He is the finest alpine guide in the South Tyrol. Tomorrow he will take you and the boy across the glacier, and then two or three days to the hut of another guide. From there it is a long hike until you come to a small village and the railway line. Then you may rest your weary feet and give thanks as you remember my little horses." He leaned back on the hard stone as though it were a feather bed. "By next month you will be happily in France and this will all be an adventure. A dream."

Leah was silent as she considered the long trek before them. Would

Louis make it? He would have to. Perhaps the time spent at the farm had strengthened his legs and his lungs. He would probably do better than she would, she thought with grim amusement. Then she remembered Shimon for the thousandth time. If Otto was somehow able to find him and help him escape, would Shimon be in any condition to hike out through these forbidding mountains?

"My husband," she said quietly. "If . . . will Otto bring him to the farm?"

A brief shadow of pain crossed the face of Franz when Otto's name was mentioned. After all, he had not seen Otto when he had come home that night. He had not had the chance to tell his brother anything. And now that he knew the truth and the reason for Otto's actions was explained, there was much Franz longed to say, but he could not.

"I hope Otto will bring your husband to us," Franz replied. He was not thinking of Shimon Feldstein, however. He simply hoped that Otto would return once more and that they might have a chance to speak, to embrace as brothers once again. "But I cannot say what Otto will do. He surprises me . . . always."

"If Otto brings Shimon to you, will you bring him out this way too? Over this same trail and to this lake and over the glacier?"

"There is no other way that is not ringed by the Nazis. No way out at all, unless you are an eagle."

The answer seemed to satisfy Leah. She looked at her surroundings with a new interest. *Shimon will be here soon.* She tried to imagine the big man sitting beside her, listening to the hushed whisper of the wind. *You see, Shimon, we will be safe soon. Together soon. These fellows know the way through the mountains. They know the way better than the Nazis, who do not know the way at all. They hate the Nazis, and so these Tyroleans will help us.*

For a moment that thought was comforting, and then as lightning flashed in the clouds below them, Leah shuddered again at the thought of walking out of these mountains. She raised her eyes to the spectacle that surrounded them.

∽

The very waves that pitched the tiny *Darien* unmercifully were hardly felt at all by those passengers onboard the *Queen Mary*. A giant floating island, a city encompassed by steel, the superliner cut through the water with an untroubled ease. It would take the *Queen* a mere four days to cross the Atlantic, while a ship like the *Darien* might cover the same distance in twelve days—unless a steam line ruptured.

Guests onboard the *Queen* could take a leisurely stroll through dozens of shops that were a showcase for the finest goods produced in

Europe. Barbers, hair stylists, shoeshine boys, and tailors—all made pa-
trons look their best for an evening at the movies or dancing in the ballroom, for listening to a classical pianist or playing poker in the gaming
room. For a while, it was said, men from many nations could sail beneath one flag in peace. At least that was how the advertising copy read.

The comment from the table of the automobile tycoon was loud
enough that Murphy could hear it. It was a woman's voice, shrill with
bitter amusement. "I hear they're playing an old Eddie Cantor film tonight. I'm sure I'm not interested in seeing a Jew put on a black face to
sing about his mammy!"

"No, Vera, *that's* Al Jolson!"

"Well, I declare! They all look alike to me!"

The comment was greeted by gales of laughter. A nervous silence fell
on the other diners. Eddie Cantor raised his eyebrows and smiled
slightly. A pronouncement was coming. "Can't tell Al Jolson from Eddie
Cantor, eh?" He stood and belted out a chorus of "I'd walk a million
miles for one of your smiles. My Mammy!" His voice rang throughout
the entire dining room and turned every head in his direction. A thun-
derous burst of applause followed as Cantor stood and bowed slightly.
Ford's table was silent and still.

Cantor saluted the lady who had made the acidic comment, then addressed her gallantly. "*That,* my dear lady, was Al Jolson's song!" Much
laughter. "Just wait until you hear Eddie Cantor sing!" More laughter
and applause. "But then, I can't blame you for not recognizing the difference. I certainly cannot tell one Ford automobile from another!"

The laughter was a bit strained as the Detroit magnate reddened and
glared at the boisterous woman who had begun the confrontation.
Eddie Cantor then dealt the final blow. "I, for one, simply would not
drive an automobile endorsed by the Führer of Germany."

Cantor bowed slightly and sat down again as fists thumped the table
in approval and chants of "Bravo! Well said!" echoed around the room.

Upstaged and put in her place, the humiliated woman fled the room,
while the automobile king remained rooted in his seat. After a moment,
the string quartet began to play a very tame piece by Chopin, and conversation returned to an excited murmur.

Murphy took out a notepad and scribbled the incident exactly as it
had happened. One quick wire sent from the ship to Trump Publications, and the story might even make the evening papers!

Murphy had just leaned over to ask Mrs. Rosenfelt if she would mind
if Charles sat with her for a few moments when a terrible bellow of the
ship's horn drowned out his voice!

Three short blasts and then a long blast sounded. Then total silence as the passengers stared at one another in concern. Once again the danger signal cracked the tranquillity of the morning. Three short and then one long.

Men and women rose from the tables to crowd the windows of the dining room. Charles grasped the hand of Mrs. Rosenfelt as the rush pushed them toward the port side.

The fog was thick, blending into the gray of the Atlantic. The horns bellowed again.

"There! Look there in the water!"

"It's a ship!"

"Have we rammed it?"

"What's happening?"

Dwarfed by the massive hull of the *Queen Mary*, the *Darien* bobbed like a toy boat in the wake of the great *Queen*. The rust-streaked coffin ship seemed like some ghostly apparition, barely visible twenty yards from where the liner now passed. Terror-stricken faces stared up from the jumble of tarpaulins and rope coils. Men and women clutched their pale children. So close. So near to disaster on this foggy morning on the North Atlantic. Black shawls, black eyes, and white faces were more distinct than the hull of the *Darien* itself.

The pale, frightened faces seemed to merge with the well-groomed reflections of those who gaped down at them from the *Queen Mary*. For only an instant, Murphy saw himself mirrored on the glass, and beside that image stood a tall, gaunt man with eyes full of anguish. That ragged misery pierced the elegance of the ship as someone muttered, "Refugees."

"Jews . . ."

"We might have rammed them."

"Wouldn't have even slowed the *Queen* down."

As the gray mist swirled around the *Darien*, finally concealing her from view, Murphy swallowed hard and stepped back from the window. Mrs. Rosenfelt remained with her forehead against the glass and her palm pressed against the pane. Tears streaked the old woman's face. She had dropped her cane. Charles stooped to retrieve it. She did not notice him standing at her elbow. She was whispering something quietly. Names. The names she had spoken to Charles. "Trudy. Katrina. Louise. Gretchen. Ada-Marie. Trudy. Katrina. Louise. Gretchen. Ada-Marie."

Murphy took her arm. Gently he spoke her name. "Mrs. Rosenfelt. Mrs. Rosenfelt, come away from the window. Come now."

❦

"I've got a story to write and file, kiddo," Murphy explained to Charles as they hurried toward the first-class playroom. "You don't want to hang around, do you?"

Charles did want to stay with Murphy, but he sensed the need of the newsman to work alone. The thought of meeting other children in the playroom filled him with apprehension. It had been a long time since he had played with any little boys and girls. Louis had been his only friend and companion. Any other children he had met had found some way to be cruel to him.

As Murphy led him past the gymnasium and the beauty salon, Charles felt his stomach turn over. He was trembling, but he did not attempt to protest to Murphy. He stopped only when they reached the door and the squeals of childish laughter drifted out. Charles could not even laugh like other children. What would he do if they expected him to speak?

His hand rose to the muffler as Murphy pulled the door back to reveal a room filled with a dozen children. A huge slide was built into one corner. Beneath it was a painted cave where two boys played Indians. Two little girls held a tea party with an assortment of stuffed animals.

"Look at me! Look at me!" cried an excited boy as he swept down the slide. His governess looked up from her knitting and nodded patiently.

A woman dressed all in white and looking like a nurse greeted Murphy with a smile and a clipboard with a white paper for him to fill out. Name. Room number. Where Murphy could be reached. Expected time of return.

Murphy patted Charles on the back. "A couple of hours or so and I'll be back."

Charles could not make his legs move forward. Not to the slide. Not to the building blocks. Not to the replica of the ship or the stuffed rabbits. He wanted to run after Murphy in panic, but the door had clicked shut behind him and Murphy was already gone.

The nurse studied the sheet, then leaned down and smiled into his face. She had gold-capped teeth and her face seemed very big. She tried to take his jacket. He held on to his lapels. The other children did not look at him; he was grateful for that. And then the nurse, in one swift movement, pulled the scarf from around Charles' mouth.

"It's awfully hot—" Then she saw his mouth and gasped.

Charles covered his mouth, but one of the little tea drinkers looked up and let out a cry. "Look at his mouth!"

Heads swiveled toward him. He whirled around, and with a groan he lunged for the door, surprised to find that it opened easily.

"Come back here! You! Come back!"

Charles felt the hand of the nurse brush his collar as he escaped; the stares of the children followed him down the wide corridor.

"Stop him! Oh, dear! This will cost me my job!"

Charles darted in and out among the adults who had come to swim in the pool or work out in the gym. He kept his left hand over his mouth, and with his right hand he pushed through any groups who barred his way.

A kitchen worker emerged from a narrow stairway. Charles ran past him and dashed up the metal steps in headlong flight. The worker muttered something about kids who played games in the back corridors of the ship when they had a playroom fit for a prince of England!

Charles did not stop. He was crying now. He was lost. He wanted only Murphy! He wanted the safety and the seclusion of their suite! But which way had they come? They had come down first. Which meant that their room was up—somewhere.

He burst through a swinging door and emerged into a corridor that seemed to stretch on forever. Rooms and rooms lined the hall. Of course it looked familiar. Everything looked the same. For a thousand feet two corridors ran along each side of the ship. Charles cried out at the immensity of it. How would he tell anyone who he was? Would they put him in a shopwindow where everyone would walk by and see him? *Lost little boy. Cannot speak. Very ugly. Please claim immediately.*

Other passengers swept by him, barely noticing him. He moved back in the shallow alcove of the service corridor. From this vantage point he searched passing faces. Where was Murphy? Would he be angry? Would he make him go back to the terrible playroom?

Stubbornly Charles wiped away the tears with the back of his hand. He was angry that the woman in white had taken the flyer's scarf Elisa had purchased for him.

Twice, Charles thought he saw Murphy. He leaned forward and squinted his eyes to see. But he was always disappointed. Surely Murphy must know that he had run away.

Charles was tired. He was scared. Closing his eyes, he slid down to sit against the wall. He hoped no one would take him until Murphy came.

19
Wall of Ice

From the vantage point of their summit perch, Leah could plainly see that the awesome mountain they had just ascended was nothing more than a mere foothill in the spine of the Kitzbühel Alps. To the north, the Kaisergebirge Alps loomed up. Beyond those serrated, forbidding peaks lay Germany. Like the jagged teeth of a hungry animal, the mountains to the north were a formidable sentry for the Third Reich and an obstacle to be feared by those who longed to leave that country. The thought made Leah shudder. Perhaps Shimon was locked behind that cold stone wall.

To the southeast loomed the equally forbidding Hohe Tauern, where the Grossglockner reared up twelve thousand feet above the valley floor. Its peak was always white and unchanged regardless of the season.

Franz followed Leah's gaze as they stood on a rocky outcropping. As if reading her fear at the thought of crossing such obstacles, he pointed to the southwest.

"You will leave through the Zillertal Alps." His voice was kind, even gentle.

"I cannot tell one from another," she whispered. "All are so vast."

"Do not look toward the most frightening of the mountains. Gustav will lead you safely through the Zillertal, just to the east of the Brenner Pass." He took her arm and turned her to face those peaks. Yes, they seemed much smaller than their brothers to the north and to the east. "Have you ever been to Italy through the Brenner Pass?" he asked.

She nodded. Hadn't every Austrian traveled that miracle road at least once? There were Nazi troops there now. They had returned a week ago like a sudden storm and the pass was closed again. "We cannot get through there. You said so yourself."

"Yes. True. But, you see, there are a hundred ways over the Zillertal if you have legs to carry you. There are secret, remote paths."

"Dangerous?" She could not help but ask the question.

"Without a guide? Of course. But you and the boy have a guide who will avoid every farmhouse and shepherd's hut. You needn't be frightened."

"I am only a cellist. He is only a boy."

"And the Germans who pursue you are only Germans. They do not know the way through these mountains." He smiled almost smugly through his thick beard. "They prefer the road through the Brenner Pass," he added disdainfully. "You will be a real Tyrolean before you are finished, Leah Feldstein! What an accomplishment you will have!"

She smiled doubtfully at his challenge. "I would prefer a warm compartment on a train."

"Dull. Too dull. Besides, several thousand who have tried to leave that way have found themselves locked in a cattle car instead and shipped . . . elsewhere."

Leah did not reply. Those were facts she knew all too well. As Franz busied himself with the horses again, she stood facing the Zillertal. True, these peaks were not so awesome as the bare stone fangs of the Kaisergebirge, or so high as Grossglockner, but they stretched on and on in endless layers like ranks of soldiers in line. The most distant mountains receded into pastel hues of mist until their details became obscured in the haze. They would meet those details soon enough, she imagined. And after her, Shimon would come.

She studied every aspect of the scenery and determined that as she waited for Shimon to join her, she would think of him coming here to Funnel Lake. She would leave her thoughts here for him to find as he hiked to safety. Every place her foot touched, she would imagine herself breaking a trail for her dear Shimon! Whatever lay ahead, that thought would make her journey easier. For the sake of Shimon perhaps she could walk and not grow weary. *Soon, Shimon, you will put your feet where I have walked, and our paths will lead us home.*

◯

The horses picked their way carefully down a narrow path that followed the outflow from the lake. High above them, the white ice of a glacier threatened to tumble down on them.

"Not a word from you," Franz had warned. "It will not take more than an echo to let this loose." He jerked his head toward the wall of ice. "Avalanche." He finished the warning with the dreaded word and then said nothing more. He did not need to say more.

The thought of such a cold and violent death made Leah want to muffle the sound of hard hooves against the stone path. She determined she would not look at the cap of ice at the top of the sheer stone wall. They surely had not come through so much to die in an avalanche. Nazis were a far more evil threat, and hadn't she and Louis survived them thus far?

Here and there among the cracks in the boulders that towered above them, flowers bloomed in fragile contrast to the mountain's stern immutability. Such fragments of color seemed out of place in the midst of hard granite. Yet they blossomed happily in the path of countless tons of rock and snow and ice.

On these small miracles Leah fixed her eyes as they moved through the gorge. Bits of red and blue and yellow bowed and bobbed on short stems protruding from the gray wall. There was not even enough soil for the horses to leave a track, and yet these flowers dared to bloom here. She determined to think of such things as they passed beneath the shadow of white death. She would think of what was just beyond this gorge—of the old guide named Gustav Stroh, of the young Austrian who would lead them across the border into Italy, and the priest who would help them into France from there.

Louis coughed, and the sound penetrated Leah's heart with a knife of renewed fear. Franz whirled in his saddle and glared at the child who looked fearfully upward. Could a noise as small as a child's cough bring the mountain down on them? Leah stared hard at a little blue flower. It would not take much to crush it.

She wanted to ask how much longer they would ride before they emerged from the gorge. Only a short ride to the hut of Gustav, Franz had told them. Until now he had not explained that this was the most dangerous part of the journey. To travel this pass in summer when the sun had warmed the glaciers was unheard of—until the German Army had closed all the passes into Italy except these death traps. Whatever ground could not be covered by the border guards of the Nazi forces, the Germans reasoned, would also be too dangerous for Jews and Socialists to escape over. Nature would eliminate the fools who dared attempt the crossing. And if a few stragglers happened to pass through nature's gauntlet, the men and dogs of the border patrol would snag them before they crossed to safety.

But some had made it. Leah and Louis were the last of the little band to leave the Wattenbarger farm, and all the others had made it, hadn't they? Franz and Gustav Stroh and the other guide and then the priest had led each group to safety. What had been done before would be done again—and then once again when Shimon came!

Leah comforted herself with those thoughts. She stared hard at the fragile little blossoms in the crevices and prayed silently that she might be as brave as they seemed to be. Even so, she thought that she had never heard any sound so loud as the hooves of the horses against the stones.

⟨∽⟩

Murphy inserted another sheet of clean white paper into the typewriter he had borrowed from the purser. The table was cluttered with open books from the ship's library. The floor was littered with wadded-up paper. In two hours, Murphy had managed to fill up four typed pages.

Perspiring with emotion, he told the story of the American grandmother forced to put her German family on a rusted refugee boat while she sailed alone to New York. As he described the near-ramming of the *Darien*, Murphy pressed his fingers against his throbbing temples in frustration. How could he relate in black-and-white print the agony etched on the face of the old woman? How could he relate endless months of red tape as the family had attempted to obtain visas to the United States?

The ship's library held an entire shelf of books dealing with immigration. Figures were easy to obtain. Immigration quotas were cut 80 percent in 1929. More than half the available spaces had been allocated to Great Britain and Ireland. The year 1933 brought only 1,798 Germans to the country. As Nazi persecution increased in 1934, only 4,716 Germans entered the United States. The number increased in 1935 to 5,117, but only one-third of the number accepted were of Jewish heritage.

But these were only numbers, not faces filled with grief and fear and longing for their families. Yes, the numbers told the brutal truth that the United States had slammed the door shut in the face of literally hundreds of thousands of persecuted Jews. But numbers were cold and unfeeling. Those onboard the *Darien* and a dozen other ships were real men and women who were crying for refuge and finding instead this wall known as The Quota. How many hundreds, maybe thousands, would perish because of this law?

Murphy thumbed through a thick, black-bound book entitled *The United States in World Affairs—1937*.

> *It was not because of unwillingness of the oppressed groups to immigrate that the United States quotas remained unfilled. Prospective immigrants were required to satisfy the American consular authorities that they would not become public charges in their new homes. The Nazi government made this impossible, since they restricted all removal of money or assets from Germany.*

In addition to this, the law states that immigrants must not take American jobs. Doctors, lawyers, teachers, men of all professions are left without assets by the Nazi government and thus are denied entrance to the United States in spite of the fact that they are qualified to work. American law forbids them to have a prior contract to work in the United States.

Murphy frowned as he read the passage. Such bizarre restriction made little sense, yet it was these very laws that now prevented the quotas from being filled by the desperate German Jews.

Such madness placed these people between the rock and the hard place, Murphy mused. "Between the devil and the deep blue Danube," he said aloud.

There was one additional requirement the United States placed on those who wanted to immigrate—a clean police record for the previous five years. The very thought of a Jew entering his local Gestapo office for a clean police record was absurd. But the consular authorities dealing with passports and visas were following the law to the letter.

Facts like these were only facts. Americans would no doubt read such statistics and then wrap the garbage in the newspaper and toss it away. But Murphy had more than facts now. He had names and faces of five little girls onboard that coffin ship: Trudy, Katrina, Louise, Gretchen, Ada-Marie.

CᎤᎤ

A fire blazed in the marble fireplace at the back of the enormous first-class lounge. Eddie Cantor sat alone in a blue overstuffed chair. Reading the newspaper, he was the picture of a man who did not wish to be disturbed. Murphy studied the gold-leaf mural of battling unicorns on the wall above the mantel as he tried to think of a gracious way to interrupt the bug-eyed comedian.

A heavyset matron in a fox coat beat Murphy to it. Tapping Cantor on the shoulder she giggled and cooed as she produced an autograph book and a pen. "I go to all your movie pictures. And I don't drive a Ford—I drive a Packard!"

"Good for you." Cantor was polite but obviously irritated when the woman sat down in the chair opposite him.

Stammering her name through a series of awed chuckles, she then proceeded to tell Cantor the story of her life, complete with the names of three former Wall-Street husbands, all of whom had left her well-off enough that she could cruise everywhere in spite of the Depression.

Cantor looked pained as he smiled and feigned interest. Murphy saw his chance. He straightened his tie and walked deliberately between the

two. He extended his hand to Cantor. "John Murphy, Trump Publications. Sorry I'm late for the interview, Mr. Cantor."

Behind him, Murphy could hear the woman sputtering. He winked
conspiratorially at Cantor, who joined instantly in the ruse.

"Fine, fine! Perfectly fine! Mrs. . . . the lady here was keeping me
company."

The woman's voice rose an octave with delight. "Keeping him company!"

"So sorry we have to rush off!" Cantor bowed gallantly and took
Murphy by the arm, escorting him quickly out to the promenade deck.
"Thanks, old man," Cantor said with a wide grin. "I owe you one. Care
for a drink? The old frumps rarely follow me into the smoking room.
What do you say?"

෴

Half an hour later Murphy had explained the plight of the Jewish refugees as he had heard it from Bubbe Rosenfelt. Cantor's wide brown eyes
brimmed with emotion at her story and that of Charles Kronenberger.
"I'm just a newsman." Murphy spread his hands at the frustration he felt.
"I report the news as it happens. These people—like Charles and Mrs.
Rosenfelt—they need something a little stronger. A voice, someone with
enough popularity to move public opinion to action."

"How can I help?" Cantor considered the dismal immigration laws
Murphy had explained to him.

"I don't know, but I've been in Europe. This is just the beginning.
There are millions more where they come from, and there is no place for
them to go. Not even the States. So many kids . . ."

Cantor exhaled loudly. "I've met a few senators in my time. Sung at
the White House a time or two. Franklin and Eleanor will hear about
this." He rested his chin in his hand. "If I do the talking, you'll make sure
it hits the papers?"

Murphy agreed. Here was a beginning. The only thing that moved
politicians was public opinion. A man like Cantor could influence the
public more quickly than the headlines of a hundred newspapers.

Cantor smiled as if reading Murphy's mind. "You know we already have
a politician or two on our side." Now Cantor looked over Murphy's left
shoulder toward the entrance of the lounge and waved. "For instance—"

Murphy turned to see the secretary of the interior return Cantor's
wave and walk right toward their table.

"Hullo, Eddie!" Harold Ickes pulled up a chair. "Mind if I join you?"
He was already sitting. He nodded his large head in Murphy's direction
and waited for an introduction.

Cantor sat back and crossed his arms. He looked pleased with himself, as if he had arranged the meeting. "We were just talking about you, Harold."

"Me?"

"Politicians in general. John Murphy here is a journalist. Interested in the refugee problem."

Harold Ickes' eyes lit up. Murphy was not expecting such an enthusiastic response. "Well, it would be nice if at least some of this made the papers!"

Cantor laughed. "You see, Mr. Murphy, there are one or two."

Ickes clasped his hands together almost as if in a prayer of thanks. "One or two, indeed. The State Department has an investigator in Germany right now to research the possibility that visas are being refused unfairly. The consuls are given the final authority, and they are simply turning applicants away out of hand."

Murphy smiled wryly. "Someone has finally figured that out, have they?" The sarcasm in his voice was unmistakable. "What will be done about it? Let's start with the people on the coffin ship we nearly rammed this morning."

At the mention of the *Darien* Ickes shook his head sadly. "Those people have left Germany without visas, no doubt. If they had the proper documents they would be onboard ship with us, wouldn't they? Their fate is in the hands of the State Department. Ultimately Secretary of State Cordell Hull."

"And we know how Hull feels about the refugee hoards," Murphy interjected. It was at the order of Hull that thousands of visas had been tangled in bureaucratic red tape and ultimately denied for questionable reasons.

Ickes nodded. "There is powerful opposition against accepting any more immigrants."

Cantor smiled grimly. "Especially Jewish immigrants."

Ickes could not deny that fact. "For nine years our own citizens have suffered hunger and unemployment in the worst depression of our history. The president—all of us—have an obligation to see to our own first. Things are improving at home. If we move carefully the climate will change."

"If we move too carefully," Cantor said quietly, "it will be impossible for anyone to leave Germany. The climate has intensified in the Reich, Harold. We may have run out of time."

"That is what I intend to say in my report." Ickes bit his lip. He leveled his gaze at Murphy. "You fellows are always looking for a scoop. Well, I'll give you one. I've combined business with pleasure on this trip. Looked into the caliber of people being turned away by our consuls in Europe. Doctors, lawyers. Professional men and women of every sort.

Great talents. Artists and musicians. Merchants. Every kind of person it would take to build a great community."

"Like a colony?" Murphy asked.

"Yes. In a way. We have an enormous area of largely unsettled land in Alaska. No one, it seems, wants to live there. Alaska happens to fall into my authority as secretary of the interior, and so—"

"You are considering settling refugees in Alaska?"

"It will all have to be approved by Congress, of course." Ickes frowned at the thought, then grinned. "The most vocal opposition we have are those biddies whose forefathers came over on the Mayflower. As far as they are concerned, settlement of the new world should have stopped with Plymouth Rock. Ellis Island and the Statue of Liberty should be blown up." He leaned forward. There was a twinkle in his eye. "But Alaska is the most enormous untapped wealth at our fingertips, and no one wants to live there."

"Except people with no place else to go." Cantor seemed pleased at the thought. The America-first crowd would certainly not be able to protest such a move.

"It is only a beginning, of course," Ickes was quick to explain. "We were considering that applicants would agree to stay and work in Alaska for five years before they would be able to reapply for settlement inside the United States." He spread his hands as if to invite opinion.

Cantor rolled his eyes and clapped Ickes on the back. "So this is how the secretary of the interior spends his honeymoon?"

Ickes shrugged off the jibe. He looked at Murphy, hoping for a positive response from this one member of the press.

"How long until such a plan could be in operation?" Murphy asked, the vision of the *Darien* fresh in his mind.

"It will have to go through Congress, Mr. Murphy. I am only one man." He hesitated. "A year. Possibly two. We cannot simply dump people in such a hostile land without some preparation." He sighed, wishing that there were more he could offer, some hope for those onboard the *Darien*. But there was nothing more. "Time—"

"Time is an enemy to these people, Mr. Ickes. They have run out of time."

"President Roosevelt senses that. I believe that is why he has called the Evian Conference. Out of representatives from thirty-three nations, we should find room for the refugees." Ickes raised his eyebrows in a gesture that seemed to express both hope and approval. "It is a beginning, at any rate. A place to hang our hat."

"Thirty-three countries," Cantor added. "Civilized men. Even the thought of such a humanitarian meeting must make Hitler tremble."

20

The Captor

Whenever he heard footsteps approaching, Charles looked up hopefully. When he saw that it was not Murphy coming for him, he ducked his head again and hid his mouth. He wished he had not run so far. If he had simply hidden on the same deck as the playroom, Murphy might have found him more easily. Now Charles was not even certain what deck he was on.

The thick-soled black shoes of an old woman approached. Charles looked away in disappointment as the hem of a black skirt passed by. Then the sound of footsteps hesitated and turned around.

"Charles? *Oy gevalt!* Is that you, Charles Kronenberger? Come out of the shadows so an old woman can see!"

Charles stood slowly and stepped out to face the old lady who had sat beside them at breakfast. Mrs. Rosenfelt. She looked much better than she had when she told Murphy all about her family. She was smiling now. A very kind smile as she unwound her black silk scarf and draped it around Charles' shoulders. "Terribly windy out today. Such a wind! Did it steal your scarf? Use mine." She stepped nearer. He did not look at her face now, only the strange little eyeglasses that dangled from a cord.

She gently lifted his chin and spoke in the familiar dialect of Hamburg. *So much like Father's words. And Mommy too, I think.*

"Well, Charles, did you eat your candy yet?"

Charles blinked at her. He reached his arms up to her and she held him in a quick hug. He let tears come. He was so glad she had come by. He wished he could tell her—

"This is such a very big boat," said Bubbe Rosenfelt. "I was quite lost, but now I know my way around. Our cabins are near to each other. Would you like to walk with me?"

⌒⊗⌒

Murphy had just finished the story when the door of the stateroom opened slowly.

When he saw Mrs. Rosenfelt standing in the doorway with Charles beside her, he jumped up, frowning. "Charles!"

"Mr. Murphy, you are busy I see. I just was seeing Charles home and I will not bother you."

"Come in." Murphy stood and offered her a chair. He looked at Charles. "I thought you were in the playroom. Are you okay, kid? I mean, you could have—" Murphy's shoulders sagged as he considered the horrible possibilities.

There was an awkward silence. Charles could not explain, and Mrs. Rosenfelt had not known how he became lost.

Just then the nurse appeared in the doorway behind Mrs. Rosenfelt. "Mr. Murphy!" she said breathlessly. "I've been looking everywhere! He just ran out, and it's such a big ship. I tried to find him, but—oh, Mr. Murphy," she finished in a rush, "I won't lose my job over this, will I? I mean, you won't tell—"

Murphy shook his head, still confused. "No, it's all right. No harm done, I guess."

Obviously relieved, the nurse disappeared as suddenly as she had appeared. Bubbe Rosenfelt looked down at Charles and put a hand gently on his shoulder.

"He did not like it so much there. *Oy!* Such a big boy should not be penned up in the playroom with little children!" She paused and studied him. In her soft Hamburg accent she asked him, "Would you like to spend some time with me, Charles? While Mr. Murphy works, I would very much like to play shuffleboard."

Charles nodded eagerly. He had found a friend.

Murphy looked up and saw Bubbe Rosenfelt smiling down at Charles. She, certainly, was harmless enough. And he did need to get his story in. "Would you like to go, Charles?"

They boy nodded vigorously.

"Well, I wouldn't want to impose—"

"Impose! You think I don't know a little something about boys? I raised two myself. I would enjoy the company of a young man from Hamburg!"

Murphy dashed off to file his story, and Charles joined Bubbe Rosenfelt on the shuffleboard court.

Two days passed and still Elisa had not seen anyone. Three times a day meals were slipped through a small metal slot at the bottom of the door while she shouted demands for an explanation. No one answered her except to ask for the empty tray of the previous meal. Apparently there was to be no explanation.

She had a sense that she was being watched. She rigged a curtain in the corner using her blanket and two loose springs she'd taken from her cot. With the heel of her shoe she hammered the springs into the crumbling mortar, then asked for another blanket, soap, and a towel. Those items were silently slipped into the room along with the next meal.

The newspapers that had been stacked beside the door that first long night now became a source of relief from the racking boredom of solitary confinement. The publications and periodicals were, without exception, American. They included issues of newspapers such as the Detroit *Daily Times* and the *Chicago Tribune*, as well as a sampling of minor publications from everywhere in the country.

Elisa read them at first hoping only to keep her sanity. Later as she scanned the pages fearfully, she saw that there was a similarity in each publication. They were American, and yet they were not from the same America that Murphy had told her about. They were American, and yet they spoke of the country in the same way Hitler had spoken about Germany! Names she had heard from Murphy were splashed across the front pages of the nation's major newspapers. Famous people she had heard of before were associated with groups called America First, German-American Bund, and Christian Front.

Beneath these banners Elisa read words that made her tremble.

> *America must join the trend toward Fascism as a member of world momentum. America may undergo a brief bath of violence, but it will be the same cleansing bath that awakened Italy, that awakened Spain, that awakened Germany. It will awaken thousands of Americans to a realization of menace. Let us understand that if civil war comes to this country it will not be a war to overthrow the American government, but to overthrow the Jewish usurpers who have seized the government and thought to make it a branch of Moscow!*
>
> *Now, if ever, the sons of Jacob must take a last desperate gamble and find out if they can actually seize the government of the country before the vigilante storm breaks and a major part of the seven million Yiddishers who have managed to get into this country are slated for deportation—or worse!*

Here were the writings of an American priest named Father Coughlin, who claimed that the Jews wanted war and profited from war. The government of the Czechs was castigated. The cause of isolationism was championed. The cry was sent out in dozens of American newspapers to close off all immigration to the dreaded Jews.

From early morning until the last rays of evening, Elisa pored over the newspapers. The latest showed a photo of the Detroit auto maker Henry Ford shaking hands with Adolf Hitler. Yet another showed a smiling, boyish Charles Lindbergh wearing his German medal and looking very pleased as he stood between Goebbels and Göring at an airfield.

One article in the *New York Times* compared the quotations of Father Coughlin and Goebbels about the Jews. The quotations were identical. Yet another showed members of the Christian Front parading in their brown shirts and carrying swastika banners.

Elisa shook with the cold of fear by the time she finished reading. These were the voices of hatred even in the beloved Promised Land Murphy had told her about. What difference would it make for a man like her father if they obtained visas to America? The hatred of Jews was just as strong there as anywhere.

She shuddered again as she read the pages of a newspaper published in Arlington, Virginia. Arlington? Hadn't Murphy told her that was across the river from the nation's capital?

> *Rich Jews have hired big buck niggers to attack white women. These Jews give the niggers plenty of money and tell them to go after the white women. Yes, these fellows down there are going to kill every Jew in their section of the South. Doesn't sound very nice, does it? Call it a pogrom if you want to, but it is the language the Jews understand. The Jews, you see, are guilty of sex crimes just like the niggers. I don't see any way out except a pogrom. We have got to kill the Jews!*

The floor of her cell was littered with the refuse of her dreams. She let this final scrap fall to the heap. Her food remained untouched beside the slot in the door. She stood slowly and gazed fiercely at the lock.

"What do you want with me?" she shouted. "What do you want? *What?*"

Her head throbbed from the force of the question. Sobbing, she sank back to the cot. For two days and nights the question had tormented her. "What do they want? Why have they brought me here?" she cried softly. *What use is all of this?* she asked herself as she stared miserably at the scattered papers. "All right!" she screamed again. "I understand! They are even there! They hate us even in the Promised Land! What has that to do with me? Tell me! Tell me, and I will listen!"

And so, she was broken. There was a message there that she could hear but not understand. It was a message of hatred and fear that spoke of civil war and the murder of Jews. She had grown to womanhood in the midst of such a message. It had almost destroyed her life. Had she not been on the very brink of better times? Must the message of hatred invade her soul again?

With this darkness fresh upon her mind, Elisa wept softly until at last she fell asleep.

～∽

The theft of copies of John Murphy's telegrams from the file of the *Queen Mary*'s radio room had been a simple matter for Hans Erb.

All the information that had passed between Murphy and his wayward wife was easily coded and relayed by wire back to Berlin. In the basement offices of the Gestapo, those pertinent facts had been decoded and passed immediately to Himmler, who relayed them to Georg Wand before he boarded the Lufthansa passenger plane bound for London.

FAINTING SPELL CAUSED BY INFLUENZA STOP RETURNED TO SAVOY HOTEL LONDON STOP DOCTOR SAYS POSSIBLY TWO WEEKS BED REST STOP WILL REBOOK ON *QUEEN* AND JOIN YOU IN NEW YORK STOP LOVE ELISA

PURE MISERY WITHOUT YOU STOP FILLING HOURS WITH WORK AND THOUGHTS OF YOU STOP I WILL BE WAITING ON DOCK STOP LOVE MURPHY

The handful of other transmissions were much the same. If, indeed, Elisa Murphy was at the Savoy Hotel and the wires were not some screen, then the matter of finding her would be simple.

Georg Wand arrived in London before the *Queen Mary* had come within view of the shores of America. Thus, he began an assignment that he anticipated enjoying very much.

Beyond the discovery of the whereabouts of Elisa Linder-Murphy, the activities of John Murphy had proved to be a gold mine of anti-Nazi actions. His conversation with the U.S. secretary of the interior in the first-class lounge was duly reported. The information was promptly relayed to Goebbels, then retransmitted back across the Atlantic to the American leader of the Nazi Party, Fritz Kuhn, and then through other channels to the great voice of American anti-Semitism and isolationism, Father Coughlin.

As head of the Gestapo and the most active promoter of purity in the

Aryan race, Himmler himself was fascinated by the very visible presence of the mutant Charles Kronenberger with John Murphy. What sort of propaganda would the Americans create with the little monster? he wondered. And would it still be to the advantage of the Reich to eliminate the child? Where was the twin brother, and why had he not also come to America? Had Louis remained in London with Elisa?

These unsettling matters were consigned to a file that would remain on the desk of Himmler until they were resolved on both sides of the Atlantic. He hesitated to present the matter to the Führer until then.

⚬⚬

The rattle of keys sounded outside the door. Elisa opened her eyes as a lightbulb flared to life above her. Her head still throbbed, and she shielded her eyes against the glare as the door swung open with a crash.

A very large man stood at the threshold and nudged the untouched meal tray with the toe of his shoe. The bulk of his body pulled at the seams and buttons of his pin-striped business suit. He was at least six foot three and could not have weighed less than three hundred pounds. He had heavy eyebrows and a thick mustache beneath a prominent nose. Crossing his arms, he simply stared at Elisa and waited for her to speak.

The springs of the cot groaned as Elisa stood to face the man. "How dare you!" she whispered hoarsely. Anger and indignation replaced all caution.

He cleared his throat, then addressed her as if he were the night clerk at the Savoy. "Your stay has not been unpleasant, I trust." A hint of arrogance and amusement crossed his face.

"In Germany one could expect such disregard of personal rights! But here!"

"You should know about that. You speak very good English for a citizen of the Reich." The fat man waved away her fury like an annoying insect. "Excellent English, Miss Linder."

"My married name is Elisa Murphy. I hold an American passport."

"Meaningless, I assure you." He smiled now, confident in his role of captor.

"Call the American consulate if you dare. Hoodlums! You cannot hold me."

"We have already contacted our American friends. This wedding ceremony you cling to so solidly was a sham. It seems the fellow who conducted it was simply not qualified. He has been reprimanded and demoted, of course. Shipped back to the States. But your passport is invalid."

"I do not believe you!" Elisa snapped. "And what does any of that have to do with this—" She swept her hand over the debris of the news-papers on the concrete. "Who are you and why—"

"Patience, Miss Linder." He nodded and she fell to a smoldering si-lence as he took a step nearer.

"I am no citizen of the Reich!" she spat.

"Oh?" He circled her once. "Ah, yes, you held a Czech passport. I re-member now."

"What do you want?" Her voice was shaking in spite of her attempt to control it. "Has this . . . is this something about my passport? Please, where is my husband?"

"You are not married, Miss Linder, as I explained to you. As for John Murphy, he should be in New York by tomorrow night. We have ex-plained your whereabouts to him and he is not unduly alarmed," the fat man whined in a patronizing voice.

"Please—" Elisa sat down on the cot. She could not think anymore. Could not find the strength to fight. "If you will contact John Murphy, he will explain everything."

"You mean about your need for an American passport in your work for the underground?" he probed.

Deny everything, Elisa! Deny everything that might be harmful! Had that not been the first rule? Elisa lifted her chin defiantly. "I do not know what you are talking about. If my husband and I were misled by a false clerk in the American Embassy, that is one thing. I can tell you nothing about any underground."

The fat man laughed heartily. "Very good! Very good, indeed! If that is the case, then you might explain how it is you knew about an impend-ing assassination attempt on the life of the Czech president?"

Elisa did not answer. She focused her eyes on the black-and-white newsprint of the *Chicago Tribune*.

The big man waited patiently. "A very interesting question, eh, Miss Linder?" he said at last. "You will have to think very hard before you come up with an adequate explanation for that."

"I owe you no explanation. It is you who must explain to *me*! Why have you detained me? Who are you? What right do you have—" She was shouting again. "This is England! Where is your warrant?"

"There are times even civilized men dispense with such bothers." He bowed slightly. "I assure you we have our reasons."

"My husband is a journalist. When he learns the truth of this—"

"He won't. It is quite a simple matter. We have taken care of it."

"You are Gestapo, are you not?" she asked in German.

The man roared, his huge frame shaking. "Gestapo? No, indeed. No, my dear!"

"You might as well be."

"I cannot believe you mean that. You cannot tell the difference in the way you have been treated? Good meals from the pub. Soap and towels and reading material."

"You are wasting your time with me." Her eyes blazed with rage. "Whoever you are, whatever you want from me, you are wasting your time."

He shrugged. "Would you be mollified if I were to explain that my name is Amos Tedrick and that I am an officer with His Majesty's Intelligence Service?"

"You lack intelligence if you think I will believe anything but that you are a hoodlum. A gangster who kidnaps women."

"Ah, well, as I thought." He frowned and clasped his hands behind his back, rising up on his toes. "We know all about the inner workings of the violin case, you know. You have smuggled a bit of this and that?"

"Musical scores. Jewish operettas. Items to infuriate the Nazi pigs." She let her look sweep over him in disdain.

He shrugged. "We have it all quite documented, you see. All your little travels. Berlin. Vienna. Paris. And in Paris, yes . . ." He pretended to think. "You visited our Le Morthomme, did you not? A fine fellow he was. Helpful. And you refused to help him with certain matters. A great disappointment to us."

"Le Morthomme. The Dead Man? A curious name." Elisa felt the blood drain from her face. Hadn't she been warned by Le Morthomme that the organization would make certain she would not live if she pulled out? Did she know too much? Had she seen too much of the inner workings of the underground network?

"Le Morthomme truly is a dead man now, you know." He rose up on his toes again. "Murdered."

Shock registered on her face—too late to call it back.

The fat man saw the expression and seized on it like a cat on a mouse. "You really would be insignificant to us if it had not been for Thomas von Kleistmann."

She did not answer as she suppressed her emotion even at the mention of Thomas.

"You know Thomas. We are certain of that." She was quiet and sullen, but he continued pacing the length of the room and back as he spoke. "There are other matters, but I suppose it will do us no good to discuss them here." He moved toward the door. "Get dressed," he ordered, slamming the door behind him.

For a moment Elisa did not move. She stared wearily at the powder blue skirt and blouse she had chosen to wear aboard the *Queen Mary*.

Both were stained with diesel fuel. She had folded them and put them at the foot of the cot. Mutely, she retreated behind her curtain and stripped off the warm sweater and wool trousers. She dressed hurriedly, feeling that somehow she was about to learn what this ordeal had been about. A muddle of thoughts assaulted her. *Not married! Invalid passport! Thomas involved again, and Le Morthomme murdered!* What did it have to do with her? Why had she been kept here if this man was really a British government official?

This time the man named Tedrick knocked before he entered. Elisa ran the brush through her hair, although she knew she was still a disheveled mess. He stepped aside and let her pass out of the cell into a larger dockside warehouse and then through the gloom to where a shiny black limousine waited outside. She was afraid as she stepped into the automobile, but she did not show her fears. The dark interior reeked of cigar smoke. After a moment Elisa's eyes adjusted. She gasped as Tedrick closed the door and a familiar face turned from the front seat to greet her.

"Elisaaa Murphy, isn't it?" Winston Churchill said in his characteristic drawl, extending his hand. "So sorry about the bother. I would have done it another way myself. All this cloak-and-dagger business. Amos thought you might be a bit reluctant to believe him, so he rang me up."

21

The Turtle and the Barking Dog

J ust behind the quay along the River Seine was the winding little street where Thomas spent much of his free time in Paris. The rue de la Huchette ran from the place St. Michel and ended at rue du Petit Pont. The street was only three hundred yards long, but it was long enough for the decrepit Hotel du Caveau, the Bureau de Police, and three of the most famous bordellos in Paris.

Eventually, every tourist managed to wander up the rue de la Huchette. The street had been made famous by the patronage of a host of American writers who had lived in Paris during the twenties. Just steps from the stalls of the open-market booksellers, it seemed to embody every cliché about the city. The police station existed in harmony with the maison de joie across the street, the house known as le Panier Fleuri, "The Basket of Blossoms." "Only in Paris!" the American tourists would exclaim loudly.

Often tourists from every nation would enter the Café d'Eiffel for strong espresso or a glass of chilled white wine. Thomas, dressed in street clothes, took his place among a group of regulars—writers, artists, Bohemians, and exiles. They gathered in that place each evening for no other reason but to talk and drink the night away. Students of the Sorbonne often joined the ranks of malcontents. Long-legged, dark-eyed girls smiled at Thomas with sensuous mouths. They tossed their long black hair like the manes of wild horses, beckoning him closer. Chianti splashed onto the tablecloth. Art. Music. Literature. Philosophy. The politics of the day. Everything was discussed in the fluid accent of the French language, a prelude that sometimes led to talk about love. It was empty talk, as short as a stroll up the rue de la Huchette, as meaningless as a visit to the Basket of Blossoms. Yet it filled the empty hours, even though it could not fill the emptiness inside Thomas.

Two trips to Berlin had etched the German Führer's madness more deeply into Thomas' mind. Torchlight processions to the accompaniment of slowly tolling church bells resembled the march of dead men toward the brink of a glowing inferno. In such dark ceremonies, Hitler administered the blood oath: "I vow to remain true to my Führer, Adolf Hitler. I bind myself to carry out all orders without reluctance. . . ." As the hour tolled midnight, men sold their souls to this vow. And the whole world, Thomas knew, was drawing near to midnight as well.

Each day he had hoped for some contact from the British, from Churchill. He did not trust the French, so when a dark-eyed beauty had claimed to be allied with those opposing Hitler, he had clicked his heels and bowed and left the little hotel room with a brisk "Heil Hitler!" He played the game well for the Gestapo agents he sensed were omnipresent in Paris. But he held out hope that at some point, as the riots in Czechoslovakia increased in intensity, the resolve of Britain and France to defend that nation would not crumble completely.

The tirades of the Führer were recorded and then shipped to various embassies around the world. In Paris, the broadcasts were played just after the evening meal, and members of the diplomatic corps cheered the vitriolic speeches as if they were boxing matches. A blow to the head of the Czechs! A crushing right to the jaw of the filthy Jewish swine! A left hook to the double-crossing French! Another blow to the Czech government of Beneš! And finally, a kidney punch to those soft-minded bleeding-heart Christians who defend the enemies of the Aryan race!

Thomas and Ernst vom Rath avoided looking at each other throughout these rebroadcasts. Both men smiled and commented on the mastery of Hitler's latest illuminating speech. Some said Hitler had become the messiah of the German nation. Others flatly declared that he was the long-awaited embodiment of the German god.

Thomas shuddered at such words. He remembered the painting deep within the bowels of the Chancellery in Berlin. Hitler believed himself to be god. "To total victory or destruction!" he shouted.

And the voices of thousands echoed, "Hail Victory! *Sieg Heil!*" The voices in the embassy joined in the chant: "*Sieg Heil! Sieg Heil! Sieg Heil!*"

Did the others see the fear locked in the eyes of Thomas? When the horrible charade sickened him to the point of madness, he forced himself to remember the generals of the High Command. *So near to the heart of this evil,* he thought, *how do they continue to hide their disgust?*

It was still weeks before they would attempt to arrest Hitler, Göring, Goebbels, and the dreaded commander of the SS, Heinrich Himmler. How could they conceal such a plan for so long while performing their duties under the watchful eye of this satanic madman? And if these chanting thousands turned on them in the end, supporting their new-found god, what hope would there be? Would they not be executed as others who had already tried to stop Hitler? Would they all end up twist-ing on the end of a piano wire, then be hung on meat hooks for display?

The weeks since the bookseller Le Morthomme had been murdered had been a jumble of fear and questions. Why Le Morthomme had been eliminated had been easy to understand. The man had been the main contact between the German Abwehr and the British for years. But who had killed him was a matter of concern for Canaris in Berlin. The British had not wanted him dead. The only reasonable conclusion was that he had been snuffed out by Himmler's Gestapo. If that was the case, how-ever, why hadn't Thomas been arrested? And why not Ernst vom Rath?

The elusive answer to this puzzle had left Thomas in a sort of purga-tory. Like a turtle facing a barking dog, he had pulled in his head and arms and legs for fear of having them lopped off by the Nazis. Incredi-bly, nothing had happened after the shooting. The bookseller had been given a proper Catholic burial. There had been no arrests in the matter. Indeed, the young assassin had melted into the back alleys of Paris and had not been seen since. Perhaps someone had paid him off for his act of treachery against the bookseller. Although Thomas held the belief that the bullet had been meant for him, he did not tell anyone. The en-tire matter had been dropped. The incident had been swept under the rug of French bureaucracy. Only now Thomas slept with a loaded gun under his pillow—just in case the matter surfaced again. Just in case one of the dark-eyed French girls who smiled at him from across the terrace at the Café d'Eiffel happened to carry a loaded gun in her handbag.

☙

It was a long drive back to London, but it was late and the highway was deserted except for the limousine.

Churchill held up the glowing stub of his cigar. "Mind if I smoke? Makes my secretary sick."

Elisa did not answer. Relief had been replaced by outrage. "You are supposed to be a friend of my husband!" she said accusingly.

"I had nothing at all to do with this," Churchill scowled. "Guilt is by association only, I assure you. And now, if Amos will kindly drop me at the mansion house at Chartwell, I shall settle with him later."

"We were quite uncertain of nearly everything about you," Tedrick said in defense. "Four days ago we discussed arresting you on a charge of espionage and murder."

"What?"

"Hear me out, if you please," Tedrick continued.

"Ridiculous!" Elisa sat forward angrily. "You deliberately held my husband back. Kidnapped me. Dragged me to the warehouse—"

"And if we had approached you with John Murphy at your side?" Tedrick asked. "What might he have done?"

"Every newspaper on Fleet Street would have had the story," Churchill muttered.

"They will have it soon enough!" Elisa snapped.

"That must not happen." Tedrick sounded thoughtful, almost apologetic. "That must never happen."

"One wire to Murphy and—," Elisa began.

"And a lot of people will die," Tedrick finished.

Churchill chuckled and eyed Tedrick. "No doubt John Murphy would start the massacre with you, Amos."

"There is some method to this madness." Tedrick sniffed and looked pained. "We might not have paid one whit of attention to you if it had not been for Herschel Grynspan."

Elisa gasped. "What does Herschel have to do with this? He is a child. A boy. His father was a tailor for my father in Berlin."

"Yes, yes. We know all that. A long-standing connection."

She did not attempt to hide her confusion. "But what has Herschel to do with anything? I have not seen him in nearly two years."

"We thought you might have seen him last month. In Paris."

"Herschel? In Paris?" Gradually it came back to her. The old tailor had sent his son to Paris. To an uncle or some relative. The boy had spoken of wanting to attend the university there, and then going on to Palestine.

"You do not deny that you have connections with him?"

"Well, no. I mean yes, I do not. I . . . I can't quite imagine Herschel mixed up in—"

"Yes. He is quite mixed up. Yes, Elisa, quite. We believe it was he who murdered Le Morthomme, you see. There is some speculation that he might have meant to kill another." He shrugged. "Regardless, surely you see the significance of such an event to us. Surely whomever he was working for understood how the death of such a man would cripple our communications with certain elements in Germany who are not, shall we say, favorably disposed to the Führer."

Elisa frowned and gestured helplessly. From the beginning she had guessed the significant role Le Morthomme must play as a contact between someone like Otto in Vienna and the British Intelligence Service. The strange little bookseller had been an important link for many government agencies in Europe; she did not doubt that. But how could a boy like Herschel have any connection with such matters? And how had she been tied to him? "I—" she paused—"until today I was not even aware that Le Morthomme had been killed."

"Indeed. By whom, we are uncertain."

"You said Herschel."

"Yes. We think he held the gun and pulled the trigger. But we had another meaning when we asked who was behind it."

"Ask Herschel."

"We have attempted to do that. We have been to the house of his uncle in Paris. The boy has simply vanished. But he left behind a sheaf of love letters to Elisa Lindheim, addressed to the Musikverein in Vienna. All returned to him unopened."

"Oh, Herschel!" Elisa felt ill. Maybe it was the reek of the cigar smoke. She leaned her head back on the seat and stared at the back of the chauffeur's head. "What have you done, Herschel?" she whispered. Then she eyed the now-sympathetic Tedrick. "I have nothing to do with this. You must believe—"

"We were hoping you might fill in a few missing pieces."

"In Austria I used the name Linder. Not a Jewish name. I have held a Czech passport since 1936. My father thought I would be safer that way. To a point he was right—of course, you know that too. Herschel was nothing more than a frightening annoyance. I never saw the letters he sent to me. A very wise and discreet friend returned them to Paris to discourage him from writing. I was Linder in Vienna, not Lindheim. I had Czech nationality until I married Murphy—which you now tell me was not a marriage at all."

Churchill turned to glower at Tedrick. "You could have left that detail out, at least, Amos!"

Tedrick shrugged off Churchill's disapproval. "There is one more piece of this puzzle, Elisa," he said almost gently.

"Please, tell me. I need to understand this."

"Thomas von Kleistmann."

"Thomas? Yes. He is in Paris."

"You know he has relayed some information to us through Le Morthomme."

"No. I did not know. But Thomas is no Nazi." She frowned. "How did you find out I knew him?"

"The Gestapo has a file on Thomas. The name Elisa Lindheim, Jewess, is quite prominent in their file. His file was photographed by one of our own agents when we were checking the authenticity of von Kleistmann's offer to help us."

"Then you know he is a good man. Suspected by the agents of Himmler, yet tolerated because of his father and the High Command."

"You are in love with him?"

"Once . . . I was." The question brought a flush of shame to her cheeks. She was grateful that the car was dark so they could not see. She could only guess at what had been in that file.

"He is quite important to us."

"Why are you telling me this?"

"He is as unsure about the reasons for Le Morthomme's death as we are. He is a frightened rabbit. Afraid of his own shadow."

"Then his shadow must be the Gestapo."

"We tried to make contact with him. He is not sure—"

"Which side you are on," Elisa finished for him.

"Quite right. Just as we have been unsure about you."

"And now that you are convinced I did not put Herschel up to the murder of Le Morthomme, will you let me go? To America?"

The car pulled up to the mansion house before Tedrick could answer. Churchill turned to Elisa and took her hand briefly. "A beastly business." He scowled. "I am sorry Tedrick here had to resort to such tactics. Good night." He touched the brim of his hat and slipped out without a word to Tedrick.

Tedrick resumed the conversation after they were under way again. "It is not so simple as all that." He snapped on a light and presented her with a thin folder from his briefcase.

Elisa opened it, surprised to see the American visa requests of her father, mother, and two brothers. Each was stamped *Denied*. She stared at them in disbelief. Why had they been refused? And now what were they to do? Was Murphy already aware that the applications had been turned down so soon?

"Mama," she whispered, "what are we to do now?"

Tedrick cleared his throat and switched off the light. "Rather stiff about allowing Jews to immigrate to America, you see. Officials there have invoked the immigration statute about foreigners becoming a public charge. Or taking the jobs of citizens already there. They leave very little room for anyone, you see."

Elisa held the folder in her sweating hands. She could barely speak. "Why . . . did you leave me those newspapers to read?"

"We thought you might be interested in the American sentiment. No use fooling ourselves, now, is there? It is as bad there as it was in Germany in the beginning. If you are set on running from the Nazis, America is not the place to run. John Murphy will not be able to pull the necessary strings to get your family through the immigration barriers, at any rate."

"What are you telling me?" Elisa asked wearily. All she wanted was straight answers. This man seemed incapable of that.

"We are quite prepared to offer you and your family British passports."

"And what do you want in return?"

"You need not deny that you have access to important information from the Reich. If you did not, President Beneš would be dead."

"All right, then—"

"We need you to help us reestablish our link from this side."

"In exchange for passports, safety for my family."

"That seems like a fair price."

"And for that, the payment?"

"A simple matter of crossing the Channel to Paris. Contacting von Kleistmann. Forging a vital link."

And so it comes full circle, Elisa thought as she replayed the events of the last few weeks. She was to meet Thomas once again, and now she would be bartering for visas for Theo and Anna, Dieter and Wilhelm.

"When will you let me have the passports?" she asked quietly.

"We must be certain now that Thomas von Kleistmann is not the one who arranged for Le Morthomme's murder. If that is the case, your duty is simply to report back here to me and to introduce him to his new contact in Paris—provided he is willing to continue on with us."

"What about Murphy?"

"He will have to console himself without you for a while, I'm afraid. We have sent him wires already. You have a touch of influenza and are unable to travel right away. We can keep the hound at bay for a few weeks if you will write him a little note. Tell him you miss him. You are anxious to see him."

Elisa pressed her fingers to her throbbing temples. She *did* miss him. Terribly. She *was* anxious to see him. "What about my own passport? Invalid, you said."

"We might arrange something. Of course, you will want to arrange for a proper wedding. Or perhaps you will not. Few people have opportunity of making that choice twice." He tried to be amusing, but his comment only drove Elisa to a sullen silence.

She had no choice at all. Not about anything. She had the strong feeling that her parents had been denied American visas for the sole purpose of giving Tedrick some control over her. She could understand why they had used the methods they had to separate her from Murphy. If he had gotten wind of any of it, it would have been plastered on the front page of every newspaper, and her photograph would have been sitting on the desks of Himmler and Goebbels in Berlin. She would never have been able to go to Thomas in Paris. Yes, she understood their game plan, but she could not forgive them for it.

"It seems that after checking on my qualifications—" she paused— "you have found me up to the job. Even if it is something I want no part of."

"You were part of it months ago." He tapped the violin case. "We cannot let such talent escape so easily."

"I am *forced* to agree with you. Except that—forgive me if I seem to have run out of trust—I want passports for my family *before* I leave for Paris."

"Agreed." Now Tedrick sat back against the plush seat. He sighed as though a great weight had been taken off his mind.

22

Shark Bait

Georg Wand carried the false passport of an Austrian Jew named Krepps and a forged British visa made out to the same name. Such identification placed him above suspicion as a Gestapo agent when he entered England.

A quick phone call from Heathrow verified his accommodations at the Savoy. Within the hour he sat in the posh lobby of the hotel and read a paper as a parade of humanity passed by. Assignments like this made his ordinary appearance an asset. He simply blended in.

Sooner or later, he reasoned, if Elisa Murphy was indeed at the Savoy, she would pass through this lobby. She would not notice him either. A woman of such great beauty looked at a man like Georg only in pity because he was alone and likely to remain that way. He had found that such emotions in women often worked to his advantage. How surprised those women had been when they found that Georg was so different than they had imagined! When their pity and revulsion turned to fear, he found his greatest sense of fulfillment.

He absently patted the coat pocket containing his passport. He would present himself to Elisa Murphy as a Jewish refugee. Her file indicated clearly that she had sympathy for the Jews. He would tell her that his wife had been detained. She would listen to his story and her heart would go out to him. *Such a fragile, innocuous man!* She would greet him each day in the lobby. She would tell him when she was due to leave, where she was going, when she would be back. They would be friends—and how surprised she would be when she discovered the truth!

The first glimpse of America was not the Statue of Liberty but a place called Sandy Hook Lighthouse. The waters around this beacon were filled with boats of all sizes that had sailed from New York Harbor to greet the *Queen Mary*.

The great whistles of the *Queen* bellowed a greeting that could be heard for ten miles. Charles put a hand to his chest as he felt the vibration from the sound. Instantly hundreds of other ships' whistles responded, creating an unending racket. Fishing boats, yachts, sailboats, and tugs tied their whistles open as the New York Harbor pilot boarded the *Queen* to navigate her into port.

From their place beside the rail at the bow, Murphy could see a flock of newsmen and photographers. A trip from Southampton to New York in four days was a feat to earn the *Queen Mary* a slot on the front page. She had beat the best time of the *Normandie*, the French liner, by more than two hours . . . in spite of the North Atlantic fog.

As the Statue of Liberty came into full view, many of the passengers raised their arms to mimic hers. Murphy, the wind stinging his eyes, stood silent. A thousand times he had imagined this moment, imagined Elisa at his side. He had wanted her first view of the Lady to be with him. Lost in self-pity, he then glimpsed the face of Bubbe Rosenfelt. Tears streamed down her cheeks. Suddenly, as he recalled the insistence of Secretary Ickes that any plan to settle Jewish refugees would take time, the smallness of his own disappointment became quite clear. If the *Darien* did indeed come to New York Harbor, Murphy had little doubt that it would be turned away. At least when Elisa arrived, there would be no question that she could stay.

Did the old woman have any sense of the tidal wave of laws and red tape in which the refugees aboard the *Darien* might drown? Murphy touched her lightly on the shoulder. She stubbornly brushed away her tears and raised her chin. "My family will be here soon!" she shouted above the din. "They will come there—" she pointed to Ellis Island to show Charles—"where my family first came to America. Thousands every day streamed from the little ships. No money. Nothing but their hands and their backs, Charles. But see how they have made America blossom!" She swept her hand across the panorama of giant skyscrapers. The buildings of Manhattan sprouted up like giant rows of corn. All this had flourished from the seeds of dreams, from the visions of children who had come with the huddled masses to create something from the poverty of their lives.

"There is still room," Murphy muttered. He could not even hear his own voice in the wailing of the whistles. It did not matter. He knew that refugees from a hundred freighters like the *Darien* could be absorbed into American cities and hardly anyone would notice. *Oy! Another man is coming to shul for prayers every morning! His wife and children seem like nice people. She bought pickles from Izzy yesterday!*

Holding tightly to Charles' hand, Bubbe Rosenfelt stared at the upraised torch of Liberty and then began to point out landmarks and buildings from among the craggy peaks of Manhattan. All the while she wept unashamedly with joy and hope that very soon she would be pointing out the same sights to her family.

Crowded pleasure steamers were crammed with sightseers who snapped pictures of the *Queen* and waved handkerchiefs as the great liner passed by. The *Darien* would take at least another week to reach New York. One week would give Murphy time enough to write a few stories, publish a few facts that might turn public opinion in the right direction.

๛

The docks of Cunard Lines, Pier 90, were crammed with reporters from every major newspaper chain. The tall chain-link fence separated arriving passengers from friends and relatives until baggage had been searched and duties declared. Murphy did not suspect that a reception committee was there to greet him and Charles, organized by Trump Publications.

Inside the customs house, a battalion of officers pawed through thousands of suitcases and steamer trunks and handbags while the impatient journalists clamored for Murphy and "the kid" outside.

Eddie Cantor, Harold Ickes, even Henry Ford with his Nazi medal, held little interest compared to the little boy who had lost his parents and had escaped from beneath the noses of the Nazis who had killed his father. The Gestapo had made a big mistake rubbing out Walter Kronenberger in the offices of the International News Service. The arrival of the dead man's son in New York was just the kind of human interest story that old man Trump figured would double the sales of his newspapers.

Bubbe and Charles sat quietly on one of the long wooden benches that lined the inside of the enormous room. Murphy and a black porter wrested the baggage to one of the officers who sat behind a marble counter. The man glanced at Murphy's passport and then at those of Charles and Bubbe Rosenfelt. He smiled.

"Oh! So you're the fella they're all after. I thought they'd be here to interview the captain after *Queen Mary* broke the record. Or maybe to interview Ford or Cantor or . . . that government man. But you're the bigwig of the hour. You and that kid."

"What?"

"Fifty guys out there—all want a picture of the little boy with the harelip." The customs man tapped Charles' passport and visa papers. "Big news, I guess. 'Course, you oughta know. You're a newsman too, huh? Your boss is out there. Mr. Trump himself. Asked if we could move you through in a hurry so they could talk to the kid about his folks being killed."

Murphy grimaced. Talk to Charles? Take his picture? Plaster his face all over the front page before surgery? The child was not a circus side-show freak.

The customs officer did not bother to search the luggage; he stamped Murphy's documents and waved him through. "Your public awaits," the officer said with a grin.

Murphy stepped away from the counter and doubled back to Charles and Bubbe. He slipped the old woman her papers and Charles' visa. "Look," he said in a low voice. "Half the press corps in New York is out there waiting for Charles. It's nothing the kid needs right now. Those guys are a mob. They would interview their dying grandmother if it would make a story." He glanced back toward the doors that led to the lobby.

Murphy paused and exhaled loudly, remembering the fiasco when he had left Charles in the playroom on the *Queen Mary*. He was growing fond of the boy—almost as if Charles were his own son. He didn't want to leave him, didn't want to subject him to any danger. They were in America, after all. What could happen to a child and an old lady in New York City? And the decision had to be made *now*. "We've got a suite at the Plaza Hotel, across from Central Park. I'll meet you there with your luggage, and then—"

Bubbe wrapped her arm protectively around Charles. "Would you like to go in a real New York taxi with me?" she asked cheerfully. Murphy didn't need to say any more.

"Uh-huh," came the muffled reply.

"Okay. I hate to leave you, kiddo, but I think it'll be best." Murphy patted his knee. "I'll meet you at the Plaza Hotel." He slipped a twenty-dollar bill into Bubbe's hand. "Give me five minutes, then make a run for it." He winked and gave Charles the thumbs-up sign, then slipped out through the crowd of departing *Queen Mary* passengers to pull the hounds from the scent.

᭐

"The Plaza Hotel, you say?" the round-faced businessman smiled pleasantly at Mrs. Rosenfelt from the bench at the taxi stand. "That's my hotel also." He tossed his suitcase into the taxi. "A pity for you to wait here. Would you care to share the cab with me? split the fare?"

Bubbe started to refuse, then looked over her shoulder toward the doors of the customs house. Any minute a hoard of reporters would storm through those doors and engulf her and Charles. Murphy could hold them back only so long.

"Such a gentleman!" She herded Charles to the car. "Our luggage will be along. Yes. A friend is bringing—" The sound of voices echoed from behind. Bubbe nudged Charles hard into the rear seat.

"Come on, Murphy! You gonna keep the story all to yourself?"

"Where's the kid?"

"We just want to ask him a few questions! Get his picture!"

"And where's that old lady? The one with kids on the coffin ship! Level with us, Murphy—you made it all up, huh? Nuthin' to do on the ship, so you've taken to writin' fiction!"

"Mr. Trump ain't gonna like this, Murphy!"

The plump businessman climbed in after Bubbe and slammed the door. "Celebrities." He jerked a thumb at the mob trailing Murphy.

Bubbe pretended not to notice the clamor sweeping across the sidewalk. She smiled wanly and drew a deep breath. "So. New York."

The taxi lurched into traffic. The real world. Cabs and government cars. Freight trucks coming and going from a hundred piers. Smokestacks of other liners blocking out the sun on one side, while towering buildings hid the sky on the other.

Bubbe was thankful that their fellow passenger seemed quite uninterested in small talk. He scanned a fresh copy of the *Wall Street Journal* like a hungry man needing nourishment. Bubbe whispered explanations of landmarks and city sights to Charles, who gaped with wide-eyed fascination.

The journey from the piers to the Plaza Hotel seemed surprisingly quick. But when the entrance of the hotel came into view, Bubbe saw they had not escaped quickly enough. She could tell the press corps by their cameras. Pencils behind ears. Notebooks in pockets. Crushed fedoras pushed back on curious heads. They were waiting like vultures squawking and cawing among themselves.

"I have changed my mind." She leaned forward and tapped the cabby on his shoulder. "I would rather go to Brooklyn first."

"Suit yourself, lady. It'll cost you. Gotta run the meter from the Plaza. Like you was ridin' from the Plaza to Brooklyn, see?"

Now the businessman looked up from his paper. He seemed surprised. "Brooklyn?" he said.

"I have family there," she explained. "I think I will see them before I check in." She checked the meter. Three dollars. She would pay half regardless. It was only right.

"You will be coming back here?" the businessman asked, his round cheeks like apples when he smiled. "Then perhaps I shall see you. Such a nice, quiet little boy you have." He lifted his hat and tipped the cabby, who shrugged and started the meter ticking all over again.

"Brooklyn, huh? You Italian, Irish, or Jewish, lady?" Her answer would determine exactly where he would take her in Brooklyn.

❦

It was obvious that Mr. Trump had expected more news in the arrival of Charles Kronenberger and the old grandmother. The suite at the Plaza was decked out with hors d'oeuvres and drinks and an assortment of reporters gathered for the story.

Trump took Murphy by the arm and escorted him firmly through the double doors into the bedroom. With a patronizing smile, he closed the doors behind him and then, red-faced, he exploded.

It was a quiet, whispered explosion. "Where the blankity-blank is everybody? Look, Murphy, Trump Publications—that's me—has gone to a lot of expense with this one . . . breaking a great story here. We're out in front on this German refugee thing, and now you've hidden the witnesses! And where—you didn't even bring your wife! I thought she could play the violin for us. I've got half the bigwigs in New York out there. A couple of senators who might even *care* about these refugees!"

Murphy let him wind down. He nodded agreeably with every point Trump made. "You want these people to talk to Charles, right? ask him about the death of his father? his mother?"

"That's right. Is that too much to ask?"

"The boy can't talk."

"You could interpret for him."

"I mean . . . he can't talk, Mr. Trump. He has a severe cleft palate, remember? Everything that has happened, everything he has witnessed, the child is unable to talk about." Now Murphy dug through his briefcase, finally producing the paper-wrapped scrapbook that Timmons had rescued in Paris. He passed it to Trump. "It's all in there. You need documentation of racial theories and practices by the Reich? mercy killing? abortion? persecution of the church? parochial schools? It's all in there."

Trump worked his mouth, opening and closing it but not saying anything. "What about this Mrs. Rosenfelt? the *Darien*? eight hundred refugees?" he said at last.

"She has Charles. Somewhere. I told her to come here and meet me, but she's a good old gal. Knows the kid doesn't need a press reception."

Murphy shrugged. "I'm sorry, Mr. Trump; the boy has been through more . . . stuff . . . than most people see in seventy years of living. I appreciate all this; I know you've done it with the best of intentions, but—"

Trump opened the book. His expression softened, and he flipped through the pages for a long time. "My grandson is five," he said finally. "The same age as Charles. Looks like him, too." Suddenly Trump looked up at Murphy, his eyes filled with tears and blazing with anger. "What if it was him, Murphy? What if it was *my* grandson who was condemned as subhuman for something he couldn't control?"

Murphy gaped at Trump, astounded. Something in this story had pierced beyond the crust of this tough old newsman and struck a nerve. "It *could* happen here, Mr. Trump," Murphy answered quietly.

"Not if I can help it!" Trump roared. He stuck out his lower lip. "I did it to sell papers, Murphy." He looked up. "Every one of these hounds is out of my own kennel, so to speak, and I'll call them off. He's just a boy. And if it were my grandson—"

"Mrs. Rosenfelt will have plenty to say to the press. Can we give her a go at it in a day or so? There are iron bars around the Statue of Liberty now, Mr. Trump. Iron bars keeping a lot of desperate people out. She can speak of that. So can I. She can speak about people—real people, not just numbers and quotas."

"Are you up to filling in the details, Murphy?" Trump was not only calm but apologetic. "People, not numbers. We can't send the senators away empty-headed, like they came. Set the stage, Murphy. It's a terribly blank stage for us over here. And we'll do it because it's right—" he closed the scrapbook—"and not just to sell papers."

Murphy exhaled loudly with relief. "I don't even know where to begin."

"We'll need public support, something to show the State Department that America is for these people—petitions and such." Trump was fired up. His steps quickened. "You have a mother, Murphy?"

"Everybody has a mother."

"She go to church?"

"Sunday morning, Sunday night, Wednesday night, and Friday sewing circle. Why?"

"Call your mother. Ask her to call every other praying woman from every other church she knows of. Ask her to tell them to call everybody they know. That's where we'll begin—your mother's sewing circle. We'll need signatures for petitions to the State Department. Food—tons of it. Clothes. Medicine and the like. Christians who know how to pray with their hands and feet, Murphy. That'll do it!"

⊂⊃

By the beginning of the second week aboard the *Darien*, Maria joined a rotating shift of women who had taken over the job of cooking meals. The large oblong loaves of black bread, which had been hung in hammocks from the pipes in the galley, had now become hoary with white mold. "Fuzzy white rabbits," Maria called them. "Fetch us another white rabbit, will you?" When the mold and crust were peeled away, the inside of the loaves was hard but edible—especially when dipped into a fine simmering stew of fish.

Once meal preparation had been taken out of the inept and frantic hands of a male cook hired on for the trip, tasteless food somehow became delicious. While the men and children labored to catch fish with improvised lines and hooks, the sea herself provided the salt to season the daily fare. Fish was boiled, fried, baked and poached. Like the manna in the wilderness centuries before, fish fed these wandering children of Abraham. Fish with potatoes. Fish with beets. Gefilte fish— almost. Breaded fish fried in the crumbs of the white rabbits in the hammocks.

More than once Klaus was called to help haul up a particularly large fish only to find that the line was snipped and the catch devoured by one of the sharks that patrolled beside the freighter. There were sharks everywhere. Their malevolent presence made mothers cling tightly to their little ones, and more than one passenger awoke in the night to a horrifying dream about snapping jaws and black eyes rolling back at the kill.

It was the sharks that Maria feared—more than storms, more than waves as big as a house, more than Nazis. The sharks could not have haunted her more if they had put jackboots on their fins and tattooed swastikas on their noses. She had seen them snap a dangling fish in two. Somehow they seemed like demon shadows in the water—skimming along, waiting. Waiting. Waiting for one false step. One slip of a foot. One careless child playing on the rail. For now, only the leftover entrails of fish satisfied their hunger.

Fish guts also aided in the harvest of more fish from the Atlantic. A fish head on the end of a hook was like seed sown in fallow soil.

"'Y' calls it boit!" Tucker explained to the rabbi of Nuremberg.

Maria knew that it should properly be called *bait*, but there was something literary in Tucker's cockney pronunciation. *The fish should bite the boit.*

"More boit! More boit!" The rabbi would snap his fingers impatiently after landing a big, flopping something on the deck with the aid of six of his Torah school pupils. Then he blessed each glop of fish entrails and tossed the loaded hook into the water. The learned rabbi of Nuremberg became the finest fisherman on the ship. "Perhaps it is the prayers," shrugged the less fortunate fishermen.

Contests were organized. The Orthodox Jews pitted their skills against the nonreligious Jews. The fishing was not so good that day. Bankers fished against shopkeepers. Doctors against lawyers. Boys against girls. The girls won easily, having overcome their squeamishness about all things slimy. There was a certain pride when the biggest catch of the day was announced. Of course, sliced, diced, and stewed, the fish never looked as magnificent as it had looked slapping against the deck. But it was good. Better than porridge and plain black bread with cheese or black bread with potatoes or black bread with beets.

When the last white rabbit was taken down from the hammock in the galley, no one noticed that there was no more bread. Most would have been relieved, since the white fuzz on the black bread had been a subject of concern for them. The sea would not run out of fish. This seemed a miracle to most. The landlubber rabbi of Nuremberg had taken to stretching his gnarled hands out to bless this source of manna every morning and every night.

"Blessed art thou, Lord God of the universe, who bringeth us . . . *fish.*"

23

Command Performance

The morning sun glinted on the white silk and silver thread of the prayer shawl. Like a carved figurehead on the prow of a sailing vessel, the rabbi stood in the bow of the ship as he prayed. This was the first time in his life he prayed facing west. The wind billowed beneath the folds of his tallith, and the tied fringes extended like the feathers of a seabird reaching for the current of air.

The scent of America was in the spray and on the breeze. The name of America was laced in the prayers of every praying man and woman, and even on the lips of those who did not pray at all.

The rabbi of Nuremberg raised his voice above the winds and recited Psalm 92 for the Sabbath Day: *"It is a good thing to give thanks unto the Lord, and to sing praises unto Thy name, O most High: to shew forth Thy lovingkindness in the morning, and thy faithfulness every night."*

As the congregation prayed with the old rabbi, little Ada-Marie stood up and staggered forward on the gently rolling deck. Maria reached for her daughter, but already the child stood at the feet of the rabbi. He was their Torah schoolteacher. Their friend. Their storyteller and fish catcher.

Oblivious to the worship ceremony, Ada-Marie raised her arms to be picked up. Without missing even one syllable of the psalm, the rabbi chuckled with delight and hefted the child into his arms. *"For Thou, Lord, hast made me glad through Thy work: I will triumph in the works of Thy hands."*

As if on cue, Ada-Marie stretched her arms up toward God. The fringes of the silk tallith were tangled in her fingers, and for a moment she too looked like a little bird longing to fly up into the heavens. She laughed and repeated the words of the rabbi: "*How . . . great . . . are Thy works, O E-ter-nal.*" She was delighted that the grown-ups had come to join the children in Torah school.

⌒⌒

Elisa awoke to the sound of birds chirping in the tree outside her window. The tree was ancient and tall and in full leaf. Sunlight dappled the new green of the top branches and filtered down to warm the window panes.

Here, in this massive old house on the outskirts of London, she had been allowed to rest and read for two days. But she still felt herself a sort of prisoner. The mansion was some sort of training area for men under the command of Tedrick, and she was allowed freedom only in her bedroom and the sitting room that adjoined it.

Tedrick had turned out to be a colonel. Two women who served on the house staff referred to the fact that Colonel Tedrick would be back in a day or so to begin her briefing. In the meantime, she had been promised that soon after that she would be allowed to place a transatlantic phone call to Murphy at the Plaza Hotel in New York.

They seemed quite concerned that Murphy remain docile and placated. She had been warned that any indication of trouble from her would result in the communication being cut off. Colonel Tedrick would provide a script for her to fill in the details. Whatever personal assurances of her well-being and affection she wished to give Murphy would certainly be allowed.

Elisa resented the efficiency of Colonel Tedrick and his British Intelligence Service. They had left no detail unattended to, no avenue open for her to refuse to cooperate with them.

A young woman named Shelby Pence was assigned to question her regarding her life in Vienna. Shelby, who spoke fluent German and had spent two years as a secretary for the British Embassy in Berlin, had a remarkable ability for making what might have been a dull task quite interesting.

Where Elisa lived and shopped and went out with friends were the innocuous sorts of details Shelby seemed most interested in. Names and descriptions of orchestra members, their habits and peculiarities, became subjects that made both women howl with laughter.

If it had not been for Shelby, Elisa thought she might have passed the time in tears instead of laughter. Shelby, with her light red shoulder-length hair and ready smile, was two years older than Elisa and had already been married once and divorced. Often the interviews that were meant to garner details of Elisa's personal life dissolved into personal conversation between the two women. Over endless cups of tea they discussed Berlin as it had been before such absolute evil had consumed it. Shelby squealed with delight when she discovered that Elisa's father had been the owner of Lindheim's Department Store—it had been her favorite place to shop. They might have passed each other in the aisles!

At this point, Shelby forced herself back to her assignment. She was not to interview Elisa Lindheim . . . but rather, Elisa *Linder*, holder of the Czech passport who played violin at Vienna's Musikverein.

This morning, Shelby knocked softly on the door before Elisa had climbed out of bed. "It's me, luv." She opened the door a crack and then, seeing Elisa gazing out the window, she entered, wheeling a clothes rack behind her.

Elisa smiled and sat up, her eyes wide at the sight of a rack of lovely dresses with the tags still on them. "What . . . ?"

"I picked them out myself. The colonel noticed we're nearly the same size, and so I got all the fun of shopping for you. Try them on. What you don't like I'll gladly wear for you!" She winked. "Well, today is the day, isn't it? Colonel Tedrick promised a phone call to New York."

Elisa had jumped up and was eagerly looking through the clothes. "Shelby!" she said at last. "They're beautiful—all of them!" She gave Shelby a quick hug. "You've made this almost bearable."

"Well, pick out something pretty and run take a bath. You have to look lovely when you talk to your husband."

☙

"The problem with the Czechs, of course—" Colonel Tedrick lit his briar pipe and studied the wreath of smoke—"is that they offered you no real training. Totally unprofessional. Plop you down in a jail in Vienna with the instructions that you must keep your mouth shut." Puffing on the pipe, he considered the lack of instruction Elisa had received. "It is no wonder you were unable to follow through when you met with Le Morthomme. We shall do better with you, Elisa. Give you a taste of the sort of training Himmler gives his Gestapo and Canaris gives the Abwehr." He stuck out his lower lip and cocked an eye to question her. "Ever fired a gun?"

Uneasy with the line of questioning, Elisa shrugged and shook her head. "But you told me I had only to make contact with Thomas in Paris, and then—"

"Of course, yes. But the Nazis may not take kindly to your involvement. If that is the case, a weapon may well come in handy."

"What use—?"

"Might have been some use to you if you could have simply shot that fat fellow who cornered you and your friend in your Vienna apartment, eh?"

Elisa exhaled loudly, then remarked dryly, "I suppose if I had known how to fire a gun, I would be in New York right now with Murphy, and you would have two less men on your payroll."

Tedrick laughed, then waved her anger away with the smoke from his pipe. "Quite! Well, well, well—technicalities! That was simply a matter of—"

"Abduction."

"I was about to say *necessity*, Elisa! How else might we have wrested you away from John Murphy without a scene?"

"You wouldn't have! And I would not have had any need at all for learning to fire a gun."

"You have need *now*." He cleared his throat and became serious. "Shelby reports that you were the last person, as far as you know, to see Rudy Dorbransky alive."

Elisa focused her gaze on the burled walnut desktop. She did not want to look into Tedrick's probing eyes. She did not want to discuss that night in Vienna again. "Yes . . . Rudy."

"And he gave you *this*—" Tedrick tapped the battered violin case that held the priceless Guarnerius.

Elisa nodded. "He told me where it was. I waited, and then . . . later . . . I got it out from behind the display case with Haydn's skull . . . in the Musikverein. I told Shelby about it. And then my friend Leah Feldstein . . ."

Tedrick absently thumbed through the typed transcript. He raised a hand to stop her. "We know all about that, and the point is, you *saw* Rudy—what they had done to him."

"Yes." Elisa whispered her reply. "His hands were—"

"Quite." Tedrick shifted his massive bulk uneasily in the leather wingback chair. "Rudy was one of our own fellows."

"I assumed he was . . . that his work was simply smuggling passports to those in need."

"Passports . . . and other things. We often provided passports to him in exchange for favors. A message here . . . a document there. We knew long before the Nazis marched into Austria what Hitler's plans were."

Elisa flushed with new anger. "Then why didn't you stop him? Why?"

"We were able to communicate with Chancellor Schuschnigg on the matter. He took it into his own hands and called for the vote in Austria. A rash move on his part. Made the Führer angry."

"But why did Britain sit back and—"

"My *dear girl*, you have wandered from the point!" An edge of irritation laced Tedrick's words.

"And what is the point?" Elisa was accusatory. Her fists were clenched in her lap and her blue eyes radiated anger as she thought of the violence that had come to Vienna and all of Austria from the Nazis.

"We are an organization meant to gather information." Tedrick sniffed defensively. "Our information is relayed to His Majesty's government, where decisions are made—or *not* made. We are simply here to provide perhaps a glimpse into the minds of the other players in the game. Help our team to guess future moves."

"And do the opponents also have the capacity to read your moves?"

Tedrick smiled with relief. "Quite. Which is why it is important that you carry a gun and know well how to use it, my dear. You see, the same fellows who tortured Rudy Dorbransky are still out there and willing to do the same to you as they did to him."

"But Albert Sporer is dead."

"Come now, do you think he was alone?" The fire in the pipe died, and Tedrick poked at the tobacco with the end of a match. "I am certain that your . . . *husband* . . . Mr. Murphy was informed in Prague that the Gestapo is quite interested in you. We relayed that information to the Czech government some weeks ago. Murphy was notified. Did he not tell you of the danger?"

Elisa frowned, remembering the night of the party at Hradcany Castle when Murphy had seemed to sense some terrible darkness on the Charles Bridge. He had not been the same from that moment. Until they reached England, he had always seemed to be looking over his shoulder for an unseen threat. "Not in words. He did not want to worry me, I suppose."

"The danger is real, even for a short detour across the Channel into Paris. Even with something this simple, much hangs in the balance. Believe me, the Gestapo will not let you go so easily." Again he tapped the violin case. "After all, you were the one Dorbransky chose to take his place. They killed him. They killed him in order to get the information he carried here. They were not clear about what they were after, or you would have been eliminated while you were walking around with the violin in Vienna." He sat back to let that thought penetrate Elisa with a cold knife of fear. "Now I think they know what they want." He changed the subject suddenly. "Your photograph—slightly altered—has been run in the major European newspapers. We will see to it that another photograph appears in the London *Times* announcing that you will solo on the BBC radio over the next few weeks."

"But Paris?" Elisa was alarmed. When would she be allowed to leave

London for Paris? When could she get this job finished and leave for America?

"Paris is certainly on your agenda, my dear." He struck another match and held it to the bowl of the pipe. "But most certainly John Murphy will understand that you cannot turn down a chance to play with the BBC Symphony Orchestra in London. The Gestapo may even listen in—who knows?"

"You are telling me—" Elisa sat back as she tried to comprehend exactly what Tedrick's agenda was—"that I will be here longer than—"

"Longer than we thought originally." He smiled without emotion, a cold, determined kind of smile that told her she had no choice in any of this. "Long enough to perform several times with the BBC. You must explain it quite clearly to Mr. Murphy. Any musician would jump at such an opportunity. No one could refuse such a contract."

"I could."

"That is where you are mistaken, Elisa." Tedrick was certain of the power he held over her. So certain that he would not bother pretending to be sympathetic. "You see, the moment you picked up *this*—" he shoved the violin case across the desk to her—"you signed a contract to perform. And so, you *will* perform, and you will begin that performance with a phone call to New York. *Then* we shall provide you with the rest of the script."

⟳

Charles knew that it was very late at night—or very early in the morning—when the phone in the hotel suite rang.

Murphy was still dressed. He had never undressed. Never gotten into his pajamas. Never been to sleep the whole night long. He had paced the room and stared out the window at traffic. Once when Charles had gotten up to go to the bathroom, Murphy had explained, "Elisa is going to call, see? The time is different between London and New York. When it's daytime there, it's night here. When it's night here, it's day there."

Charles suspected that this strange difference in the time was why Murphy never seemed to sleep more than a few hours. Since they had arrived in New York, the typewriter had continued to *clack* and *ping* far into the night. Charles would awaken to find poor Murphy asleep at the desk, still in his clothes. Murphy would then shower and shave and start all over again with endless interviews on the question of refugees and appointments at the medical center and still more interviews. The hours of darkness were passed writing. Sometimes Murphy would eat, but not always. Charles was worried about Murphy—more worried about him than he was worried about the surgery he was to face ten days from now.

Tonight, or this morning, Murphy's voice boomed into the telephone as if he were trying to shout across the Atlantic all the way to London. Charles listened quietly from his dark bedroom. At first Murphy sounded excited and happy. Moments passed and the voice took on an edge of unhappiness. Charles had heard the sound of unhappiness in the voice of his father before. He knew what it sounded like.

"Speak up, Elisa! Elisa? Darling, I can barely hear you. What? What are you saying? The BBC orchestra . . . what?" A long silence followed those words. And then, "But how *long*?" Charles heard something like a groan. Soft and barely audible. Certainly Elisa could not have heard the groan all the way to London. "I . . . but I thought you were coming right away. If I had known about this I would have turned right around and come back to England. Now Charles is scheduled for surgery, and I . . ."

The voice sounded angry now. It made Charles feel sad that his own name was recited with anger. He wished that Murphy would go on back to England, leaving him in the care of Bubbe Rosenfelt. He should go back to be with Elisa so he would not be angry. Maybe if he was with Elisa he would sleep in a bed and eat breakfast and lunch and supper.

Murphy sounded exhausted. "No . . . yes. I suppose I'll survive. Work? Sure. I've gotten myself smack in the middle of the refugee problem here, but—" Murphy sighed loudly. Charles could see Murphy's long legs stretch out from where he sprawled on the couch. "If I had known . . . no. Well, of course I see how important . . . what a break it is for you, but . . . but . . . sure, yeah. I'll give Charles your love. Sure. Yeah. I . . . love you too, Elisa. Next week. You'll call next week? Same time. Sure. Fifty bucks for three minutes. Sure. Good-bye, darling."

Murphy had trouble replacing the receiver. It banged and rattled.

Through the crack in the door, Charles could see Murphy was lonely. Charles knew about that. He climbed out of his warm bed and tiptoed quietly to the doorway. He stood very still for a long time and watched, but Murphy did not move. He only sighed a lot and exhaled loudly as if he might breathe deeply enough to relieve some terrible pain.

At last Charles coughed—a soft cough to let Murphy know he was there.

Murphy looked up. His eyes were red-rimmed and he appeared to be sick. "Hi ya, kiddo," he said. It was not the usual happy greeting. "You need something? Water? Bathroom? You have a bad dream?"

Charles shook his head and walked slowly toward Murphy. Three feet from him he stopped and waited patiently.

"What?" Murphy asked again.

In reply, Charles put out his arms. *A hug.*

With a muffled cry, Murphy enfolded him in an embrace. "Me, too, Charles," he said. "Just what I was missing."

24

Do-Gooders and Jew-Lovers

America's Loss Is England's Gain!" The headline on the entertainment page of the London *Times* ran just above the photograph of the lovely blond violinist performing with the renowned BBC Symphony Orchestra. The article read:

> *A fortnight ago, a beautiful young violinist named Elisa Linder-Murphy fainted on the docks of Southampton and missed sailing to America aboard the Queen Mary. Those of us privileged enough to have heard Elisa Linder perform in her native Vienna were delighted to hear that her bout with influenza is over and that she has been signed to perform with the BBC Symphony Orchestra as a soloist over the next several weeks.*

The article continued with reference to her daring escape from Nazi-occupied Austria and the incident in the Czech National Theatre when the assassination of President Beneš had been thwarted by her warning. No mention was made of where she was staying in London. It was assumed by Colonel Tedrick that the Gestapo would pick up such details easily enough on their own.

Several different versions of Elisa's agreement to perform with the BBC were published in dozens of publications in England and even across the Channel in France, where the BBC was listened to as well. Most of the news accounts published the photograph. However, Colonel Tedrick considered that his goal had been accomplished merely by the publication of the information. He made certain that a copy of the

article was cut out of one of the lesser newspapers and tucked into an envelope with a personal letter for Murphy from Elisa. The letter was
placed in a mail pouch bound for America onboard the *Queen Mary.*

⤫

Murphy was in good company on the express train from New York to
Washington, D.C. Eddie Cantor and Rabbi Stephen Wise represented
the American Jewish perspective along with Dr. Nahum Goldmann, the
hard-driving founder of the World Jewish Congress. On the Christian
end of the spectrum, Dr. Henry Lieper, secretary of the Federal Council
of Churches, had come as spokesman of twenty-two million church
members and twenty-four Protestant denominations. Catholic Bishop
Bernard Sheil had come to represent Cardinal Mundelein of Chicago.

Along with the two hundred thousand signatures favoring assistance
to the refugees onboard the *Darien,* these leaders of the American religious communities made up an impressive roster for the meeting scheduled with Secretary of State Hull in Washington.

True to his word, Secretary of the Interior Ickes had helped arrange
the meeting. He had not forgotten his offer to help, which he made
onboard the *Queen Mary.*

Secretary of State Hull was over seventy years old. He was a handsome, tall Tennessee congressman, who had become a senator, and finally Roosevelt's secretary of state. He was known for his keen political
sense—a real horse trader, some said with admiration. His political
savvy, then, tempered whatever personal feelings he might have acted
on in regard to the immigration policies. His wife was Jewish, yet Hull
still had not been persuaded to soften the immigration restrictions that
prevented so many desperate and qualified applicants to flee Nazi persecution.

Secretary Hull sat behind his desk and scanned the stacks of petitions
as if he might somehow recognize the names. The distinguished committee sat silently before him, waiting for some reply.

"Impressive," Hull drawled at last. "A moving show of unity. Jews.
Catholics. Protestants. But the law of the land is still the law."

Each man in the room took a turn at appealing to factors beyond the
government, beyond restrictions—humanity, the cause of right and
wrong, standing for what was right.

Bishop Sheil concluded quietly, "In providing these people sanctuary—especially the children—where they can grow up in the ways of
peace and walk in the paths of freedom, we will help not only them but
ourselves. If we suffer little children to come unto us, we will demonstrate to the world our own devotion to the sanctity of human life."

Hull nodded thoughtfully and then replied to the men who had gathered to plead for those onboard the *Darien*—and for those who remained behind in the Reich. "At this point we cannot grant those refugees asylum."

"Can they not remain anchored until the matter is explored more fully?" asked Doctor Goldmann.

Hull swung around in his chair and pointed to the American flag behind him. "Doctor Goldmann," Hull answered gravely, "I took an oath to protect the flag and obey the laws of my country. You are asking me to break those laws."

Made bold by the desperation of the refugees, Goldmann cleared his throat and replied, "Several weeks ago a number of anti-Nazi German sailors jumped overboard as their ship was leaving New York. The Coast Guard picked them up, and now every one of those sailors has been given sanctuary on Ellis Island by the United States government. Those German sailors are still there, under the authority of the State Department. Now, as secretary of state, might you not send a telegram to those people onboard the *Darien* and suggest that they jump overboard in New York Harbor? Certainly the Coast Guard would pick them up. Certainly they would not be allowed to drown because they are Jews without papers. Then they would be safe."

Secretary Hull's mouth turned down angrily at Goodmann's words. "You are the most cynical man I have ever met," Hull replied angrily.

Undaunted, Henry Lieper answered for the group: "We ask you, Mr. Secretary, who is the cynical one—we Christians and Jews who wish to save these innocent people, or you, who are prepared to send them back to Germany to their deaths?"

Nothing further was said. Hull dismissed the delegation and refused to shake the hand of Dr. Goldmann. On this melancholy note, Murphy returned to New York with the others in the hope that public opinion might have the last word in this matter.

Ⓒ⅁

Himmler adjusted his glasses nervously as he read the latest decoded message from Gestapo agent Hans Erb in New York. How the old Jewess Trudence Rosenfelt had come to be so closely allied with John Murphy and the Kronenberger child was unexplained. It was, however, a fact that the old woman had accompanied the boy to the hospital when Murphy had been working. She had taken him to meet her family in the Jewish district of Brooklyn. While John Murphy had busied himself rousing support for the Jewish scum onboard the freighter *Darien*, the old woman had cared for the boy.

Himmler scratched his head and grimaced with irritation. "Sewer water flows down the same gutter," he muttered. It was inevitable, he supposed, that persecuted people would somehow band together. This was not what troubled him.

Perhaps the most annoying fact in the recent dispatches was the matter of American public response to the plight of the refugee ship. One announcement over the radio by Eddie Cantor had led to thousands of letters offering assistance to individuals and families onboard the *Darien*. The U.S. State Department had been inundated with phone calls and wires. Christian ministers had joined with rabbis around the country to organize committees for gathering food and clothing and medical supplies for the passengers when they arrived in New York.

Only one week had passed since the arrival of the *Queen Mary*, and yet already Trump Publications and John Murphy had managed to create a stir of sentimentality that might well destroy all that the Führer had in mind by releasing the Jewish ships from the Reich.

With a sigh, Himmler placed a phone call to Joseph Goebbels and then one to Hitler himself, asking them to meet with him at the Reich Chancellery. It was past time to discuss a strategy against the tide of do-gooders and Jew-lovers who had suddenly materialized in America.

⟨∞⟩

Adolf Hitler was surprisingly calm as he listened to Himmler's assessment of the latest difficulty in New York.

"And so you see there is quite a stirring among the religious population to allow the Jews from *Darien* to leave the ship when it reaches New York. The Quakers have joined forces with the Jews—"

"Strange bedfellows, eh?" remarked Goebbels dryly.

A look from the Führer silenced his remarks. Hitler was quite relaxed. He sat back in his favorite overstuffed chair and pressed his fingertips together as if he was considering the possibilities of an American movement to open immigration to Jews—beginning with the Jews onboard the coffin ship *Darien*. At last he sighed. "It will not happen, of course."

"But . . . but, mein Führer, it *is* happening."

Hitler smiled—a rare smile. "Great noise. It means nothing. Have you been with me so long, Himmler, and you have not learned that the way to destroy opposition is simply to shout louder?"

"But what power do we have in America?"

"For years we have been supplying that Fritz Kuhn fellow with funds to build his German-American Bund. We have Father Coughlin who quotes Goebbels' anti-Bolshevik propaganda to the American masses every week.

A priest! And he uses our propaganda quite effectively, I understand. And then there is the Christian Front—dedicated anti-Semites."

"What difference can they make?"

The Führer was uncharacteristically patient with Himmler. He instructed him gently tonight. He was confident in his principles. "Our goal—" Hitler gazed at the ceiling as though a script had been written there. "Our goal in matters such as these is to simply demonstrate that the democracies are really hypocrisies. They hate the Jews as much as we do. They will not take them in, either."

"But there is a movement to do just that."

Hitler laughed. "But you see, America is a democracy. Nothing at all can be done for months. Congress will simply sit in hearings and worry about being reelected if they make the wrong choice in this matter. By the time they decide what they are deciding, the *Darien* will have been forced to return here, or will be run aground or sunk somewhere! You have panicked, Himmler. Here in Germany my word is law, and so things get done. But America is a land of committees; most choices are so watered down that they become useless."

Himmler considered the Führer's assertion. It was true. The machinery moved like a snail in American politics. "Well, it seems that we are still the ones with the advantage—after all, your word is law. So what is your law in this matter, mein Führer?"

Hitler did not hesitate. The choice was simple. The enforcement of his command would also be simple. "Wire Hans Erb in New York. Then wire Fritz Kuhn. He is politically strong in New York, I believe. Have these men organize opposition to the pro-refugee movement. Rallies in New York with the German-American Bund and the Christian Front. When the *Darien* arrives in the harbor make certain that these groups are on hand as a counterdemonstration to the *Darien*'s supporters. Such a demonstration should shake up the politicians a bit. After all, it is an election year." He waved his hand languidly in the air. "You will see. I am right about this. I am always right. President Roosevelt may be a secret Jew, but he is also a coward. He would hate to see his Democratic Congress voted out of office. The fellow is a politician first and a humanitarian second—when it suits his purposes. He will let the Jews perish before he will let his career suffer for helping them. You will see, Himmler. I am right about this."

Himmler nudged his glasses back on the ridge of his nose. He nodded grudgingly. "And what about the journalist John Murphy? It was he who first published the Kronenberger document. He who somehow got the mutant Kronenberger child out of the Reich. And now look what he is doing with his columns and stories in America."

Hitler yawned and rubbed his eye as he considered the problem. "Yes. My own life is an example of how the diligence of one man can change the course of events. Of course, I had nothing to lose and therefore nothing to fear." Hitler smiled a second time. "That is why I am here and my opponents are not. So, it is time perhaps to let this American experience real fear, Himmler. Send that message to Hans Erb. The American will have to be silenced."

Elisa Murphy was even more beautiful in person than she was in the news photograph. Blond hair curled softly at her shoulders. Her lips seemed a bit fuller, her figure slightly more voluptuous. She wore dark glasses as she entered the lobby through the revolving door. She carried a battered violin case. If she indeed had been ill, nothing in her appearance now gave the impression of a woman stricken with influenza.

She gazed absently at her watch, and then as the folds of her navy dress floated around shapely legs, she descended the steps and entered the news and magazine shop just off the lobby.

Georg Wand was only steps behind her. He picked up a German language newspaper describing the latest turmoil in Czechoslovakia and, with a shake of his head, muttered in Yiddish, "*Oy*, so terrible. Terrible what those Nazis are doing!"

She looked at him sideways and purchased her own newspaper. Hers was a copy of the London *Times*. She put her coins on the counter as Georg stared disconsolately at his handful of change and said in German, "How much? I will never figure out these English coins."

The ploy worked. Helpless. Confused. Ordinary. And the beautiful blond woman smiled sympathetically and pointed out the correct change. "Here," she replied in her native tongue. "It will take a while, but you will catch on." Then she inclined her head. "You are German?"

"*Danke*! No, I am Austrian . . . or at least I *was* Austrian . . . until there was no more Austria."

She frowned. He could see the pity in her eyes even through the dark glasses. "A terrible thing."

"*Ja*. What they did to the Jews there . . . my wife . . ." He let his tone express his grief. "One day she goes out, and then I do not see her again." He shook his head as if to shake off the memory of something horrible. "You are German also?"

"I lived in Vienna for a while." She was careful. Evasive. Her feeling of sympathy had not yet caused her to lower her guard.

Georg nodded toward the violin case. "A musician!" he exclaimed.

"Ah, how my wife and I loved the concerts at the Musikverein!" Here was the point of connection he had hoped for.

"They are not the same any longer. Sad times have fallen on Vienna, Herr . . ."

"*Bitte* . . . my name is Georg Krepps. And your name?"

"Elisa Murphy." She extended her hand to shake his. "Very good to meet you." This first interview was over.

"Good luck," he said, bowing humbly. Then he added the Austrian farewell, "*Grüss Gott.*"

"*Grüss Gott,*" she replied, sweeping out of the little shop.

Georg was quite pleased with this first contact. He would not crowd her. He would take things slowly. Progress with caution so that sympathy did not sour into annoyance.

He watched her cross the lobby. She swung the violin case with a lighthearted air as she stopped at the desk. "Messages for Elisa Murphy?" she asked. The clerk checked her box and slipped an envelope across the counter.

Shaking his head, Georg read the news as he walked slowly back to his chair in the lobby. From the corner of his eyes, he saw the woman glance at him as she boarded the elevator.

It had been months since Shimon had eaten so well. Throughout the day, visiting Yiddish mamas presented him with various meals and chastising tirades if he did not eat every last morsel.

"So what's wrong? You don't like the way we cook? You turn your nose up at good Jewish cooking? You don't want to get well or what? So eat, already! *Oy!* Doktor Freund, tell him he should eat it all so the ladies down in the kitchen will not think he does not like our cooking, *nu?*"

Morsel by morsel, strength returned to Shimon until one day Dr. Freund pronounced, "If he has not died by now, he is going to live. A miracle!"

"Not such a miracle. Just good Jewish cooks!" argued a hefty matron as she ladled broth down Shimon's throat. "A good Yiddish mama can make chicken soup out of pickled herring. True, Shimon Feldstein? Of course true! So eat! *Eat!*"

The rabbi of Nuremberg came to see the miracle of the almost-dead man they had pulled from the vent shaft like a grouper from the sea. It was a good sign that this fellow lived, he pronounced. Then he raised his hand to proclaim the promise of Psalm 91: "*Er hut mir tzu fridden gemacht* . . . He has satisfied me with long life."

Hope coursed through the veins of Shimon, and new hope bubbled up among the passengers of the *Darien* as they drew nearer to New York, America.

Torah school students made pilgrimages to see that the man who should be dead was very much alive. The five daughters of Klaus and Maria Holbein came once a day to sing him a song or tell him about the very largest fish they had helped the rabbi haul over the rail. He learned their names: Trudy, Katrina, Louise, Gretchen, and Ada-Marie.

The burns and open wounds on Shimon's back began to heal, and each day he took a few more steps along the narrow corridor and back again while Aaron and the clean-up brigade cheered him on.

Bit by bit he recited the story of how he had come to be here: The arrest in Vienna on the first day of Nazi invasion. On to the labor camp. Then to Germany and Dachau, where the strongest were chosen to work in the steel mills of Hamburg. Searing heat that killed lesser men. Hours of brutal work to produce the armored steel plate for the battleship *Bismarck*. The explosion. The water. There his memory failed him. He could not remember climbing onboard the *Darien*. He could not recall hiding in the ventilation shaft. Even the night of his discovery remained a mystery to him.

Again the rabbi offered the explanation of a miracle. Perhaps an angel had carried Shimon to the ship! Such things were not unheard of, after all. Perhaps the hand of the Almighty, blessed be His name forever, had reached down and lifted Shimon from the explosion and then helped him into the water and onto the ship. *Oy!* Such a miracle that he survived. And then, of course, the Almighty would deem it necessary to block the event from the mind of Shimon!

There was no other logical solution to the question. It was settled. An angel had done the deed. Even those who were not religious could not help but marvel over the fact that Shimon was here and that he was not only alive but also talking and smiling and eating and laughing and now walking.

Often Shimon spoke of his wife, Leah, whom he had not seen since that first morning of the Anschluss. She was his angel, he often said. He asked the rabbi to offer a prayer for her since he had no way of knowing what had become of her.

In the next breath Shimon would speak of Zion: "We had visas, you see. Certainly they are expired by now, but we had them. Even our dishes were shipped to Palestine. No doubt they are still wrapped in newspapers from the Austria of Chancellor Schuschnigg. Ah, me. How we hoped that all that news was true! We discussed it as we packed the dishes. We hoped that Schuschnigg would make a strong Austria. That Hitler would never be so brazen to cross the frontier of our little country.

Maybe someday Leah and I will be in Jerusalem and unpack our things together. Then we will read those pages again and marvel at how our hopes were so completely smashed, even though a set of china remained unbroken."

Quietly the doctor discussed Shimon's case with Captain Burton. The captain feared that no country would ever accept Shimon for immigration. He had no identification. No proof he was not a man imprisoned in Germany for murder or embezzlement. How could he prove such a thing? As for Shimon's wife, Captain Burton knew of no way at all to reach her with word that her husband was alive. One word sent through the official censors of the Reich, and most certainly the Nazis would demand that Shimon Feldstein be extradited to Germany and charged with sabotage in the explosion of the steel mill.

Such deductive reasoning made sense. The man was an escaped prisoner. Might that fact not also imperil the rest of the passengers? Such a thought made the good Dr. Freund shudder. Talk of miracles and angels could provide no solution. Perhaps it would simply be best if Shimon was listed as a crew member. Indeed, when he was well enough, he could work on the *Darien* to pay for his passage. The rabbi had ranked the presence of Shimon as a signal of blessing from God. The captain saw him only as a danger. He was sorry he had not convinced the British coast patrol to take him off their hands.

25

Human Interest

The offer of one hundred dollars by old man Trump to the first vessel or airplane sighting the *Darien* had given a holiday-like anticipation to the arrival of the coffin ship.

It was Tuesday morning when the captain of a small commercial fishing boat arrived in Trump's Times Square offices with the information that the *Darien* was a mere two days from New York and right on course. The captain's name was duly taken with the promise that if he was correct, he would be paid the one hundred dollars. When the talkative man went on to describe in detail the wretched boat, Murphy was certain that the freighter had indeed been sighted.

Trump had lunch catered for Murphy and the rest of his New York staff. He toasted the sighting with champagne. He toasted the boost of his nationwide newspaper circulation with yet another bottle of champagne. While Hearst Publications and Craine Publications and that old Colonel McCormick in Chicago had twiddled their ink-stained thumbs in the matter of refugees, Trump had managed to awaken America.

He thumped John Murphy on the back and right then and there gave him a raise of fifty dollars a week and the position of head of European operations. "Those ol' blankity-blanks don't know a good newspaperman when they see one, my boy!" he exclaimed. "Human interest— that's what sells newspapers! Get people involved in something that makes them feel good!"

Tons of food had already been collected and assembled at the New York docks. People were indeed doing something. The granite towers of the bureaucracy had even begun to crack, it seemed. The State Department was already issuing the order that no refugees would be allowed to disembark from the *Darien*; private sources, however, were reporting that the ship would probably be allowed to anchor in New York Harbor until the matter was settled through proper channels.

Trump hired a biplane and sent his staff photographer out to search the gray waters and photograph the ship. He would run the photo on the front page of his newspaper with the estimated time of arrival. Hundreds, if not thousands, would no doubt turn out for the event. And old man Trump would host the party. A real American party it would be, too. Trump personally called Eddie Cantor and a dozen other celebrities who had climbed onto the bandwagon the past few days. "Bands and speeches and fireworks," the old man promised.

That afternoon Murphy left the offices of Trump Publications feeling almost intoxicated with the joy of it. In Germany there had been such a sense of despair and helplessness in the face of Nazi inhumanity. But here, something was indeed happening. There was more to it than selling newspapers. Trump's heart had begun to thaw over the story of Charles Kronenberger, and the warmth was spreading fast.

A glimmer of sunlight had managed to penetrate the canyon of skyscrapers that lined each side of Broadway. Murphy threw his head back and laughed at the sky. A raise and a promotion! He wished he could call Elisa and tell her what was happening here. Instead he found a pay phone and called the Plaza Hotel where Bubbe stayed with Charles.

"Catch a cab to the Woolworth Building! Bring Charles and we'll celebrate with a movie tonight, Bubbe! That's right! They've spotted the *Darien*! You heard right! *Oy vey*, huh? And yippee! I'll meet you at the top of the Woolworth. We can see all the way to England from there!"

⌘

Murphy stepped out of the phone booth and laughed at himself as he made his way through the throngs of pedestrians toward Woolworth's sixty stories of Gothic granite and steel.

Taller buildings had been erected since Murphy had left America for Europe years before. Like a giant hypodermic needle, the Chrysler Building towered over City Hall a thousand feet above the pavement. The Empire State Building had recently been completed, adding another two hundred feet to the record. Murphy had not yet made his pilgrimage to the tops of either of those towers. He decided he would see them first with Elisa.

This afternoon, however, he felt too good to stay on the ground. Like a seasoned bull, he was following an old and familiar trail back to his beginnings as a rookie reporter in New York—back to sack lunches on the Woolworth Building when he had looked out over the world with a sense of innocence and hope. He had long ago lost that innocence. In Germany, in Spain, he had seen what men were capable of. He had stared into the eyes of the Nazi Medusa and felt his heart grow hard and hopeless. He had stopped believing that he could make a difference. For a time he had stood over the broken bodies of Spanish children killed by German bombs, he had seen Jewish blood on the sidewalks of Berlin, and he had shaken his fist at the dark and silent heavens and yelled inwardly, *Where are You, God? Why have You allowed this to happen?*

The answer had come back as a whisper, but the message was as clear as it had been the night the farm boy from Pennsylvania knew that he must become a writer.

Where are you, John Murphy? Have I not given you a voice and hands to hold a candle? What I tell you in darkness, speak in the light! What I whisper in your ear, preach on the rooftops! Fear not them which kill the body but are not able to kill the soul! Only fear him who is able to destroy both body and soul in hell!

Today John Murphy entered the polished marble-and-granite foyer of the Woolworth Building. The shiny copper doors opened like a strongbox, and an elevator carried him up to the top of the world. Murphy stepped into the wind and stood at the railing to gaze at the sun-silver Atlantic. He was so high up that he thought he should be able to see Europe—or at least spot the little coffin ship struggling through the waters.

From this high vantage point he replied to God's whisper, "Here I am, Lord. Use me."

He had indeed lost his youthful innocence since he had last stood here. But once again hope sang in his heart.

Ada-Marie lay with her head at one end of the hammock and her little feet snug against Maria's feet. Maria gently rocked their hammock as she sang a lullaby to the steady rhythm of the *Darien*'s engine.

"Mama? How long until New York?" Gretchen asked from across the narrow aisle. She reached out her hand and Maria held it.

A child at her feet, a tiny hand in hers, and a baby in her womb— Maria sighed with the contentment of being surrounded by her little ones. All safe. All snug in their hammocks. She was overwhelmed with a sense of well-being.

"Two days," she answered. "The captain says if the engine stays well, we will enter the harbor in two days."

Ada-Marie stretched and yawned and rubbed her eyes. "How many more sleeps?"

Maria laughed, loving the way her youngest daughter counted the passing of time. "Only two more sleeps, Ada-Marie, and we will see Bubbe."

"Will she have surprises for us?" asked Katrina through a yawn.

"Bubbe always has surprises," Trudy answered.

The baby moved within Maria, making her smile. *Another little girl?* she wondered. *Or a son for Klaus to hoist on his shoulder and take to the park? A son would be nice. Klaus would like to sail toy boats on a pond or play catch or . . . all the things fathers do with sons.*

Young voices buzzing around her and the baby kicking within, Maria drifted into a contented sleep. Only two more sleeps, and then *New York*!

⟨◯⟩

Bubbe Rosenfelt shielded her eyes against the glare of the sun on the Atlantic. She, too, seemed to be searching the horizon for a glimpse of the *Darien*. Murphy held Charles up to peer over the edge of the chasm at the shiny line of the East River. A row of metallic bridges spanned the water, looking like miniature railway models. Beyond the bridges the city of Brooklyn sprawled. Bubbe pointed out distant landmarks that defined her old neighborhood.

All around them the highest buildings seemed like staircases that climbed upward to nothing. Water tanks capped the roofs, and here and there feathers of smoke rose like plumes on helmets. Murphy pointed out the tops of the Ritz Tower and the Paramount, where they would later go to see *Snow White*. Charles felt dizzy as Murphy held him to lean toward the steel-colored North River and the smokestacks of the New Jersey bank. Everywhere the waterfront was fringed with docks as busy as the traffic in Times Square, but there was one pier waiting for its most prized cargo—the seven hundred and seventy-six lucky Jews onboard the *Darien*.

⟨◯⟩

It was Charles who first noticed the three strong young men who lounged against the stone railing of the observation deck. They were not looking at the vast panorama beyond. They simply stared at Murphy. Their lips curved in disdain, as though their faces had been drawn by the same artist. Eyes were narrowed. The winds whipped at their clothes, giving the three a sense of violent movement even though they were standing still.

"Two days," said Bubbe Rosenfelt. "I can hardly believe it. If I could stay here and watch, I would."

"Mr. Trump has gotten word out to most of the New York fleet. He sent out a plane this afternoon. You may not be the first to know when they arrive, but I guarantee I'll call the minute I hear anything."

The three strong men exchanged glances. Charles had seen such looks before. In Hamburg. In Vienna. The men straightened and continued to stare at Murphy.

Charles tugged on Murphy's jacket sleeve.

"You ready for the movie?" Murphy mussed his hair. "Which one of the Seven Dwarfs are you, anyway?" The pained look on Charles' face made Murphy's smile fade. He followed the child's glance toward the three young men.

They smiled back menacingly. The man in the center flexed his hands.

The voice of Bubbe Rosenfelt became high and tense as she tried to ignore the three. "*Oy!* We'll be late, Charles. Here is the elevator. Come on, come, come, come—"

The copper doors slid open slowly. A couple got out and walked between Murphy and the three strongmen. Murphy nudged Bubbe and Charles onto the elevator, only to be followed by the three men.

One, stockily built with a bull-like neck, grabbed the elevator attendant by the collar. "Out!" he shouted, sending the man sprawling onto the roof.

Murphy tried to push past the other two. Iron hands grabbed his tie and shirtfront and slammed him up against the wall. Bubbe was shoved screaming from the cubicle, and Charles was thrown out on top of the sputtering elevator attendant.

"What do you want?" Murphy shouted as the doors silently closed out the wind and the screams and the startled faces of the couple who had come to see the sights.

A fist slammed into his mouth as the moving strongbox dropped with a moan and then lurched to a stop between the thirty-first and thirty-second floors.

"Hey, we got us a little Jew-lover here!" Like a driving piston, a fist exploded into Murphy's stomach. He moaned and tried to double over. Hands pinned him tight against the wall. The men shared him—driving a blow and then passing him on. One holding, one beating, one jeering. "You think you're gonna bring them Jews here? Huh, Jew-lover? You think you're gonna fill New York with freaks and fiends and commies? Huh?"

Murphy gasped for air, but there was no air. He was suffocating, choking on his own vomit as the blows moved from his gut to his face. Blood spurted from his nose onto his tormentors and onto the sterile interior of the elevator.

"You think you're gonna be a big shot, huh? Yeah? Well, if we can do this here, there ain't no tellin' what we might do to your wife. Get it? She's in London, ain't she?"

Murphy's eyes widened. Now he struggled to fight back, straining against the vise that held him. *Elisa!* How did they know?

"This ain't even rough, pal." Another blow to Murphy's eye. "You ought to see what kind of guys we have in London. Savoy Hotel, ain't it?"

Murphy cried out in unbearable anguish. *They are here! They are here! They are even here!*

"Word is—" a slap to the cheek—"you better wise up. Better lay off the commie propaganda. We can take care of scum like you, Mr. Writer. I hear your wife's real pretty. A shame to mess her up."

A knee to Murphy's middle sent him to the floor as the elevator resumed its downward slide to the lobby.

Murphy's tortured lungs gasped for oxygen. Blood and vomit mingled beneath his face. There was darkness . . . darkness! *Fear not them which kill the body—*

"This is just a little reminder. A kind of down payment in case you don't take our advice." The elevator stopped and one more kick was delivered to his back as the doors slowly opened, and the three men stepped over him to stride, laughing, from the building.

A woman screamed. Footsteps ran toward the open door of the elevator.

"Somebody call a doctor!"

"Is he dead?"

"Call a doctor!"

"Get back, everybody!"

"Pull him out of there!"

"Careful! Easy . . . give him a little room! Let him breathe!"

"Okay, pal. That's it. Take a breath. You ain't gonna die, buddy. Another breath. Slow and easy-like."

It was an ordinary pair of pliers, and yet Georg Wand knew well what such an ordinary tool in his hands could accomplish. He removed the price tag and placed the pliers on the desk beside the radio. Tonight Elisa Linder-Murphy played a violin concerto by Dvořák. No doubt this was played with some sense of sympathy toward the floundering Czech government with whom she had such ties.

Georg smiled. Such a foolish gesture on her part. After tonight he would make certain that she played no more songs for the pygmy race. As a matter of fact, she would be unable to play anything at all ever again.

He toyed with the pliers, turning them over and over again. He had used such a tool on Rudy Dorbransky in Vienna as well. Dorbransky had remained silent, but Georg and Sporer had made him suffer longer because of that silence. In the end it had been of no benefit to the Jewish violinist. He had died anyway. A long and slow death. It served him right, Georg reasoned. Things might have been easy for the fellow if he had only been reasonable and shared his information. They might have killed him more quickly.

Georg was certain that Elisa Murphy would not be so unreasonable. The moment he clamped the pliers onto the knuckle of her index finger, she would talk. She would beg him to listen and she would tell him everything he wanted to know. Getting information from women was easy for Georg Wand. Elisa Linder-Murphy would be no different than all the others in the end. She would be a much simpler project than Rudy Dorbransky had been.

The final applause echoed from the radio into the hotel room. Elisa would be taking her bows now. He could imagine her holding her instrument in long, delicate fingers. He could almost see her smiling at the audience that had listened in the studios of the BBC.

She was an extraordinary musician, indeed. This fact gave Georg Wand the ultimate power over her. To crush those extraordinary fingers one by one with such an ordinary tool—who would think of such a thing? If he held a gun to her head, she might well smile and tell him to shoot; it would be over so quickly. But these pliers . . . to make her watch the destruction of her own life one joint at a time—now that was where the genius of Georg Wand lay.

☙

"*Oy*, such a place this America is!" exclaimed the rabbi of Nuremberg as Captain Burton switched on the freighter's PA system to broadcast the orchestra of Tommy Dorsey playing at the Algonquin Hotel live from New York!

There was reason to smile and laugh tonight onboard the *Darien*. Men and women sat spellbound in little groups as the music echoed over the dark waters. Periodic interruptions were enjoyed as quartets of harmonic voices sang love songs about detergents and jingles about cigarettes and the honking of an automobile horn was interspersed with excited jabbering about the newest Ford automobile!

Maria, her group of five future American debutantes around her, translated every word of the advertisements as well as song lyrics. Ada-Marie danced with Trudy, Gretchen with Louise, and Katrina with Klaus. A sprinkling of stars lit the moonless night sky like tiny lanterns. Even the grim faces of the ultraorthodox looked more relaxed.

"To hear America is almost like being in America," Aaron pronounced as the program emcee described the pretty girls on the dance floor. Other young men looked wistfully at the girls who giggled in their own group across the stern from them.

Klaus leaned over to kiss Maria on her forehead. "A cruise on the Atlantic, my love," he grinned. "A million stars. A warm breeze. An American orchestra. What more could we ask for?"

Maria reached up to stroke his cheek. "A bed? Something to sleep in, maybe? You and me together, perhaps?"

Klaus threw his head back in laughter. "I have almost forgotten what that is like." He kissed her on the cheek and settled down beside her to gaze up at the stars and remember.

26

Drag Hunt

Georg Wand traveled to Portland Place on the top of a big red omnibus. The quiet Victorian square was lit by old-fashioned streetlamps that illuminated the large white stone headquarters of the BBC.

The bus moved on in a cloud of exhaust. Georg stepped back into the shadows to study the entrance of the prominent building. It seemed out of place here, like a dry-docked ship set among the ornate houses of an older age.

Things seemed so very still tonight that it was almost impossible to imagine that within that white ship of a building the voice of a nation reached out to millions of houses. Here Churchill convinced the listeners of the dreadful threat of Germany, only to have Prime Minister Chamberlain cast doubts on his assertions. Then perhaps another minister threw opinion in this direction or another. Strange that these Britishers allowed so many opinions to be broadcast. It was no wonder that everyone was confused.

The English could not even agree on what music they should listen to. Highbrows demanded classical. The lowborn clamored for American jazz.

Tonight the listening menu served up classical. Elisa Linder-Murphy was the main course. First she would play her music; then she would emerge from the BBC, and Georg Wand would begin carving. Slowly and carefully he would do his work: separating information from flesh and bone.

It was exacting work, exhausting work, but Georg was adept at it. He absently clicked the pliers in his coat pocket. They sounded like teeth, hungry for a meal.

It was not the deep cough of Ada-Marie that woke Maria from sleep but the heat of the child's fever. Her little feet radiated against Maria's legs, causing her to climb from the hammock and grope toward the stairs to find the doctor.

Wringing her hands, she followed Dr. Freund up the steps as he carried Ada-Marie to the infirmary. Trudy was sent to fetch Klaus. The other children still slept, unaware of the seriousness of their little sister's condition.

Shimon watched quietly from his cot as Dr. Freund checked the child's uneven breath with his stethoscope. Klaus and Maria hovered in the background, their faces shadowed with concern.

Dr. Freund straightened slowly. His expression was grave, almost angry as he spoke. "Pneumonia. Both lungs."

Maria cried out and put a hand over her face. Klaus seemed almost ghostlike as he stood supporting her.

"What can we do?" Klaus managed to say.

"*Here?*" There was something in the tone of the doctor's voice that answered the question with hopelessness. He touched the little girl's face. Her lips were tinged with blue and her breathing labored. "Keep her as comfortable as possible. There is very little else."

Maria shook her head in disbelief. What was the doctor saying? Did he mean Ada-Marie might die? that she *would* die? She pulled free of her husband's arm and walked slowly to the bedside of Ada-Marie. Smoothing the child's damp hair from her forehead, she whispered the beloved name. Ada-Marie stirred at the touch of her mother and then convulsed again with coughing. A sprinkling of freckles stood out against the pale skin.

"Only two more sleeps until New York." Maria's voice quavered. "Only two more sleeps and then a hospital. Medicine. Mama is right here, Ada-Marie. Hang on for Mama."

The doctor turned away from the scene as if he could not bear to watch. His features were tight with frustration. He was a physician without even the barest tools to work with. Klaus read his expression. *Hopeless.*

"Surely we can do something?" The voice of Klaus cracked. He spread his hands in bewilderment. How could this happen so *suddenly*?

There was room for only two cots in the infirmary. Shimon watched the pale faces of Maria and Klaus as they hovered over their child. He heard the dull despair in the tone of Dr. Freund. His heart ached for the child. For the family.

Slowly, his wounds still tender, Shimon sat up and swung his legs over the side of his cot.

"What are you doing?" asked Dr. Freund almost angrily.

"It is time that I go up with the other men," Shimon answered quietly. The truth was that he simply could not bear to see such grief enacted before him. "Maria—" Shimon leaned against the watertight door— "you may have my bed. She will like you to sleep by her."

Maria glanced up in gratitude at the big man. She did not refuse his generosity.

"You are not well enough for this," Dr. Freund protested.

"I am. You are a good doctor." Shimon managed a sad smile through his ragged, new-grown beard.

The doctor replied with resignation, "Not good enough." He accompanied Shimon to the stairs leading up to the outer deck. "Ask the rabbi to come," he whispered. "They will need him before morning. The child is breathing by sheer will, breathing to please her mother. The rabbi should be here."

⟋⟍

Murphy looked and felt as if he had been hit by a truck. His nose was broken. The doctor had packed it with yards of cotton gauze. "Hey, Doc, are you sure one of those guys didn't leave a fist up there?"

His eyes were swollen to mere slits. "One of 'em had to be Joe Louis in white makeup."

Two ribs were cracked. "Why don't you wrap that tape a little tighter, Doc, so I can't breathe at all? It will save them from coming back for the second round."

Now Murphy lay back on the sofa of his hotel suite as Trump paced the length of the room and back. "Other than this, I'm fine," Murphy replied dryly. Talking made him wince with pain. Even wincing made him wince. "I'm not worried about me."

"We contacted Scotland Yard in London immediately, of course. By the time we phoned the BBC there was already a bodyguard at the studio with her. We left a message. She'll call you as soon as she finishes the broadcast."

"Thanks." Murphy sounded as if he had a cold. "Somebody needs to be with her twenty-four hours a day until we can get her to America."

"Or until you join her in Europe." Trump rose up on his toes as if he had something important to say.

"I'm hoping she'll join me here."

"Actually, I just got a phone call from the president's press secretary."

"Which president?"

"Roosevelt, of course. You've stirred things up a bit, you know." Trump managed a smile. "Turned up the heat. Anyway, President Roosevelt has settled the date for the conference of the Western Nations—the refugee conference in Evian. No matter what happens here with the *Darien*, it seems as if the Evian Conference ought to be your story."

Murphy tried to frown. The effort was too painful. He exhaled loudly as he thought about Charles, who slept soundly in the next room. "I need to stick around for the boy's operation. I owe him that. I brought him here and—"

"We can see to it he's taken care of." Trump brushed away Murphy's objection. "And there is always Mrs. Rosenfelt."

"She'll have her own family here if things go well in the State Department mire."

Trump paced a few steps more, then turned. "You are my new chief of European operations, Murphy. Evian is the place I want you to start. The issue I want you to start with. If Hitler does indeed invade Czechoslovakia, there will be tens of thousands more people like the ones on that little ship. The fate of eight hundred is insignificant when you look at what is happening to the multitudes." He was determined. Murphy would not stay in the States any longer than necessary. "Charles Kronenberger will survive without you. The assignment is yours. My new head of European operations needs to be in Europe. That is you."

"What about the *Darien*? Who will cover the story?"

Trump scratched his chin and peered thoughtfully at the ceiling. "Well, to tell the truth . . . I thought I might like to take this assignment myself."

Murphy tried not to look surprised. How could this man, the head of a multimillion-dollar publishing empire, take time to cover the plight of the *Darien*? Murphy did not ask that question. Instead he answered diplomatically, "That is a real relief to me, Mr. Trump," knowing that the story would have a guarantee of front-page coverage on every one of the Trump empire newspapers.

Trump smiled, pleased at the approval of Murphy. "I got myself tangled up in this one, son. Those blankity-blanks down at the State Department got my dander up again. We'll need to work real close on this. You at the conference and me for the ship."

"And what about Charles? and Mrs. Rosenfelt?"

"I'll see to both of them; don't you worry. I've already hired a lawyer to look into the fact that Mrs. Rosenfelt's family was refused visas unfairly. Did you know she has enough in her bank account to support them all for several years? The State Department contention that they might become public charges just doesn't hold water in this case!" He banged his fist on the table. "There has been an abuse of the law here, and I'm gonna see to it that we turn the State Department so blasted inside out that they're looking at the world through the soles of their feet!"

Murphy tried to smile, but the effort was too painful. He liked this gruff old man. He liked working for him. Trump was sending him to Europe because this story had the man so up in arms he wanted to attend to the details himself. Old man Trump was determined this would have a happy ending—and he would write it!

⚮

Georg Wand strained to see the dial of his watch. It was 10:17 PM and still Elisa had not exited the building of the BBC. She was later than usual. He toyed with the clanking pliers impatiently. Had she slipped out another way?

At 10:20 a black, official-looking sedan pulled up in front of the entrance. Two men stepped out and waited beside the car. Perhaps an important government official had broadcast. Someone who needed bodyguards. The prime minister?

Again Georg glanced at his watch. Then he looked up and gasped as Elisa emerged, laughing and chatting, from the BBC. The men stepped to either side of her. One opened the door for her as the other took the violin case from her and stepped in after.

Even in the darkness Georg could feel himself redden with disappointment and anger. Had he waited too long to move in? Or was this perhaps a temporary arrangement? Two fellows sent to pick her up for some engagement Georg had not anticipated, perhaps?

Georg cursed as the black sedan moved away from the curb and immediately turned the corner out of sight.

The omnibus would come in another ten minutes. He would simply return to the lobby of the Savoy to wait for her.

⚮

"The hook is set." Tedrick leaned far back in his swivel chair and pressed his fingertips together. He was pleased with the latest development.

Elisa gazed miserably at the telephone on the broad walnut desktop. How could she say anything at all to Murphy with Tedrick sitting in the room? Who could know who else might be listening? And now this terrible news that Murphy had been beaten up by thugs in New York. Yet she could not even ask him about it.

"What about the Savoy?" Elisa asked, disturbed by the news that the New York thugs had mentioned her name as well as the Savoy Hotel.

"Shelby knows what she is doing." Tedrick was reassuring without a hint of warmth in his voice. "A drag hunt," he said cryptically; then he realized the obscurity of his allusion. "Ever ride the hunt?" he asked with a smile. "Fox hunt?"

"The sort of sport you would enjoy," she snapped. "I am a musician. Foxes and hounds are not my style."

He laughed. "A drag hunt is when the scent of the fox is laid even when there is no fox. The hounds simply follow the scent; the riders follow the hounds. Everyone has a jolly good time and no blood is spilled. The fox is usually grateful." He leaned forward. "Why aren't you grateful, little fox? The hounds are baying only at your scent. Tonight only at your scent. Tonight you are off to Paris."

"And what do I tell my husband?"

"Tell him you're fine, which you are. And you are certain to stay that way in such a bloodless hunt. No details. Tell him you have a bodyguard. His publisher has arranged for that. Tell him you are eager to see him, if you like. Sooner or later you might slip him the news that you will have to repeat your vows—unless you would prefer to remain legally unattached. That might also be of benefit considering your past relationship with Thomas von Kleistmann."

"You are despicable!" Elisa flared.

Again Tedrick laughed at her anger. "Probably," he answered. "But more practical than despicable. Say what you like to Murphy, within the limits you know we will enforce. Really, I would *not* mention von Kleistmann, however. John Murphy may suspect that you have stayed in Europe just to visit your old friend."

Enraged, Elisa stood and moved to the opposite side of the room. The room was not big enough. She had grown to despise Tedrick over the past few days. She had felt this strongly about the Nazis, but to carry such anger for an Englishman was somehow even more unpleasant.

The phone rang. Tedrick did not move. He motioned with his head for Elisa to pick up the receiver. Murphy was to think she was at the Savoy Hotel. The switchboard operator had been well coached. "Your move." Tedrick smiled as the phone rang again.

Elisa picked it up. The long-distance crackle brought tears of frustration to her eyes. "Murphy?" she asked desperately.

Seconds of delay. His voice echoed through wires and half a dozen connections before finally arriving. "Elisa—you're all right. Thank God!"

"I'm fine, darling. Except I miss you terribly." Tears streamed down her cheeks. She could hear her own voice tumbling across the hollow chasm that separated them. "Are you all right?"

"If I wasn't so busy with all this . . . refugee stuff. . . . Ship will be in tomorrow evening. . . . Got it all ready for . . ."

There was a long pause. Had she lost him? "Murphy?"

"Yeah! Right here. New York. Charles is scheduled for surgery. I got a raise. Stay where you are. . . . I'm coming to Europe. . . . Chief of Euro . . . oper . . . I'm coming to get you."

Elisa's heart felt as if it were in a vise. She had forgotten that Tedrick observed and listened a few feet away. "Oh, Murphy! That man at the consulate who married us—"

"Yeah?"

"He's been fired."

"For what?" There was dread in his voice.

"Performing illegal wedding ceremonies."

Waves washed over Murphy's reply. Bits of words popped out like startled, angry squeaks. Then, "I still respect you."

Elisa laughed. It felt good to laugh. "We'll just have to do it all over again."

"As often as you like."

"I mean get married!"

Murphy laughed. The familiar sound of his laughter lifted her past her rage and past her fears. She could do what needed doing and then Murphy would come. It would be all over.

A roaring punched through the receiver and a woman's voice broke in. "I am so sorry. We seem to have lost your connection."

⬭

Mile by mile the *Darien* moved closer to port. Seabirds swirled and cried overhead. Seaweed floated past. Other boats were sighted nearly every hour.

Shimon had found refuge beneath a tarp shelter among the young men of the ship. Aaron looked after him, bringing him cups of water and meals from the galley and word from the infirmary. "The child is still with us! Ada-Marie is fighting back!"

As the sun climbed high above the ship, men and women who had been exuberant only the day before now talked in low tones about the fierce battle taking place belowdeck.

"Surely she will not die!"

"We are so close to New York, America, now! There are hospitals there. Doctors who will help her."

"My cousin lives in Brooklyn. He says that children in America hardly ever die of things like pneumonia anymore!"

"*Oy,* but look at Doktor Freund. Up there. He is going to see the captain. Look at his face. So sad. So hopeless."

"Maybe he wants to know when we will arrive tomorrow. If she lives through the night, then surely she will not die."

The late-afternoon air cooled into a soft evening of pastel skies. Shimon sat up and watched as a group of men gathered on the bow to offer evening prayers.

"Help me up," he asked Aaron. "I want to join the minyan. I want to pray for Ada-Marie."

The plaintive cry of the evening psalms rose up as the seagulls circled back toward land.

"Blessed be the Eternal forever! Omaine! Blessed from Zion be the Eternal, who dwelleth in Jerusalem. Hallelujah! Blessed be the Eternal God, the God of Israel, who alone performeth miracles. . . ."

"If only we could have a miracle, Rebbe," said Aaron as he helped Shimon to stand. "If only we could put little Ada-Marie on the back of a seagull and fly her to New York, America!"

"Ah well, that is the Lord's business," said another sadly.

"Who says God is still not in a business of miracles, *nu*?" asked the rabbi of Nuremberg. "Look here! Each one of us is here! And look there—" he stretched out his hand to Shimon—"a miracle. Who would think Shimon could have lived that night we pulled him from the vent!"

Everyone agreed that Shimon's presence in the minyan was indeed a miracle. And now one was very much needed for little Ada-Marie, whose four sisters huddled unhappily on the steps that led to the infirmary.

"If she lives through the night, she will not die. We will come to New York, and there . . . you will see."

⚭

Throughout the second night Ada-Marie still clung tenaciously to life. At the mention of her name she would open her eyes and squeeze Maria's hand. The rabbi of Nuremberg had come several times to read to her a lesson from Torah school or sing her a song. One by one, her older sisters came to stand beside her cot and tell her stories about the happenings on the upper decks. All of this Ada-Marie acknowledged with her eyes; she could not speak.

For Maria and Klaus such signs were fragments of hope that they clung to even though the child's fever still soared and each breath was drawn with exhausting labor. The face of Dr. Freund showed no such hope.

"If we can get her to New York in time . . . ," Klaus ventured.

"Yes. New York," said the doctor. His tone was flat and without encouragement, as if to warn the grieved father that even a modern hospital in New York could not perform the miracle needed here.

Still Maria whispered words that praised each labored breath. She sang quietly the lullabies that were Ada-Marie's favorite. She spoke of Bubbe, waiting for them in New York. "She will be right on the docks, Ada-Marie. After we sail by the big statue of the lady in the harbor, we will see Bubbe. Yes, yes, another breath. Yes, Mama knows it hurts, but you will get well. Yes, another breath."

27

Her Soul Has Flown Away

It was nearly closing time at the café. The usual crowds had thinned until only a handful of persistent regulars remained around the table with Thomas. The topic of conversation had ranged from music to the latest political turmoil in the Czech Sudetenland. On the last, Thomas did not offer his opinion or the knowledge that the riots there were financed and led by men from Germany. He simply listened with fascination to the way opinions had begun to swing against the government of Prague over the last few weeks.

In the corner, a young man named Michael played the last sad love song on his accordion. Two more men from the table drifted out and wandered across the street to le Panier Fleuri. They entered the bordello almost at the same moment a young, lively black-haired prostitute emerged and walked across the street toward the café.

Thomas recognized her. Her name was Suzanne, and she came from a farm in the south of France. On more than one occasion she had provided him with companionship, so he was not surprised when she swept through the door and lowered her chin to fix her seductive gaze on him. She winked and waved and moved toward him when he smiled and shrugged. *Why not?*

She sat down beside him, barely noticed by the dozen diehards who still argued around the table.

"Things are slow tonight," she whispered. "I was hoping you would be here."

"Me . . . or someone, eh, Suzanne?" He had no illusions. If he had not been here she would have found someone else to sit with.

"No, *mon chéri! You!*" She brushed her fingers lightly against his cheek; then she pressed a note into his hand beneath the table. Her mouth against his ear, she whispered, "Something for you, Thomas. And I'm told you will pay me well for it. Why did you not tell me you are in love with a married woman? Then I would have understood when you do not come around anymore." She kissed his ear and then sat back with a coy smile.

Puzzled, Thomas looked down at the small white envelope. His name was written on the outside in handwriting he recognized instantly. *Elisa!* He tried to hide his surprise. A thousand questions flooded his mind, but he would not ask the woman across from him. Suzanne was a messenger, nothing more.

Thomas shrugged. "Affair du coeur, Suzanne. I can only manage one at a time." He pocketed the envelope and slipped twenty francs into her hand. "Is that enough?"

Suzanne glanced at her payment and smiled. "Enough for the note—and more, if you like."

"Another time, perhaps."

"If things do not work out for you, then?"

Thomas nodded and kissed her on the cheek. He wanted only to be rid of her, to tear open the envelope and read the words from Elisa. The thought of seeing her crashed through the fog of his wine with a sobering impact.

"Well, then—" Suzanne shifted her attention to a bearded student who was listening to the discussion with apparent boredom. "How about you?" she asked, moving from beside Thomas to smile into the student's eyes with rapt attention.

Unnoticed, Thomas left the table and staggered to the washroom in the back of the café. With trembling hands he hooked the latch on the door and pulled the chain of the lightbulb above his head. He took the envelope from his pocket and stood with his back against the brick wall as he stared at the finely written script. A thousand times he had seen his name written in that hand. *Thomas . . .* Always before he had cherished the thoughts that had come within. *"I love you. Today I thought only of you. I could hardly practice because the music made me think of you."*

And then there had come a time when he had feared to open the letters—feared that they had already been read, and that his love for her might end his hopes for his career.

Tonight he opened the envelope carefully, afraid to tear even one word that her hand had written. Inside the envelope was a tiny white square of paper. Written upon the paper were an address and a date and a time. Nothing else. No signature. No personal words. Only pertinent facts in her distinct handwriting.

He exhaled and pressed his lips to the writing. How clever she was. She had no doubt that he would know at a glance who had sent the message.

One more look before Thomas held the paper under running water until the ink ran together and finally disappeared. Then he tore the envelope and the note and flushed the fragments down the toilet.

☙❧

Gaining entrance into the hotel room registered to Elisa Murphy had been laughably simple for Georg Wand. A skeleton key inserted in the lock. A moment of concentration, and the mechanism had clicked and opened.

He waited behind the louvered doors of the closet. The soft fabric of her dresses touched him. He could smell perfume. The hour of waiting there in the dark was not at all unpleasant.

His pistol, equipped with a silencer, was in his right jacket pocket in case the bodyguard came into the room with her. In his left pocket he still carried the pliers. The idea of using them had stuck with him. He would not abandon the idea because of a little inconvenience.

Light from outside streetlights bathed the room in a soft glow. He could make out the dial on a clock that ticked on the night table. It was after midnight. He heard voices outside in the corridor. A man's voice and that of a woman. Elisa Murphy.

The rattle of the lock. A man's laughter. "I'll just give the place the once-over for you."

"Freddy, I know you. Why Tedrick assigned you to me is a total mystery. No, on second thought, it's no mystery. He did it to annoy me."

The door opened and the light clicked on. Voices were strong and clear as they stepped into the room. "Actually, I'm paying *him* so I can guard your body, honey."

"You're worse than an adolescent." Her voice was playful as she shoved the man away.

"Just once around the room!"

"Leave!" she ordered, shoving him back. "I'll scream if I need anything."

Georg grimaced. Yes, she would scream. That would be a problem in the hotel. He would have to think.

"I'm going to the corner for a sandwich and a pint. Would you like me to bring you back a snack?" The man sounded hopeful.

"Do you know how long I've been up? Goodness, Fred, don't you ever give up?"

"Just trying to be friendly. Make sure you're taken care of."

Georg watched through the slats as she stepped aside and swept her hand over the empty room. "As you can see I am quite alone and will remain so quite happily, thank you. Tell Tedrick I'm sleeping with my revolver under my pillow. That is the only protection I need tonight."

She gave the man one gentle shove and sent him, sputtering a protest, into the hallway.

She shut the door and locked it. With a sigh she walked slowly to the bed and tossed the violin case onto a pillow before she sat down. Georg's hands perspired in his pockets. He would have to wait; he would need to remain very quiet. If she screamed, her companion might still be close enough to hear her. At any rate, the scream of a woman in the Savoy Hotel would certainly be investigated. Someone would hear her.

He watched her kick off her shoes and rub her foot a moment before she rose and walked into the bathroom.

She turned on the bathwater and began to sing softly, "I can't give you anything but love, baby. . . ."

Georg smiled and took the gun out of his pocket. He would not use the weapon, but it would serve to silence her at a glance.

"Room service!" he called as he stepped from behind the closet door.

Her angry voice replied, "Go away! I didn't hear you knock, and I'm—"

Georg had already moved to block the doorway of the bathroom. "Do not scream." He leveled the barrel of the gun within an inch of her head.

She froze, horrified. She opened her mouth as if to speak.

"I have come for your autograph," Georg whined. "Come to hear you play the violin."

"Please," she managed. "Please, don't—"

"Come out, very quietly, please," he replied, stepping away from the door.

She followed him, her eyes wide with fright. "You're the man in the lobby . . . the Jew."

Georg laughed. "I am no Jew." He glanced toward the violin case. "Now show me what kind of musician you are, eh?" He placed the cold black steel of the gun barrel along the line of her jaw. "Such lovely unblemished skin," he crooned. "And manicured nails. Polished. Very pretty. Will you play the violin for me . . . Elisa?"

"But—"

"No, no. I insist. The 'Blue Danube Waltz,' perhaps? Or something easier?"

"What is it you want?" Her voice was level, serious. Perhaps they could talk.

"I want to hear you play the violin." He moved back. "That is all. You, with your jaw unmarked from the chin rest of your instrument. Your uncalloused fingers. Elisa? Elisa Linder-Murphy? No. I don't think so. A good likeness in the papers. Quite good. But you see, I have seen a real photograph of her. And I have also heard her play. They should have chosen a real musician to play this role. Who are you, eh? I have been wondering that. And then I decided that it did not matter because you will tell me who you are. And then you will tell me where she is, won't you?"

The woman before him hardened as he spoke. She had not expected to meet with anyone as bright as himself, Georg reasoned. Bleached blond hair, a phony photograph planted in the papers and published with the name of Elisa Linder-Murphy beneath. The whole scheme was adolescent in its conception.

"I don't know what you are talking about," protested the woman.

"Well, then, I will continue to call you Elisa, if you like." He nodded his head slightly. "Put your shoes on."

"Why?" A shadow of fear crossed her face.

"We are going for a ride."

"No. Get out of here. I have bodyguards, and—"

"If your feet are too sore, what is that to me? Leave your shoes off if you like . . . Elisa. But if you do not come with me, I will blow your brains out all over the lovely silk bedspread."

The woman was trembling as she put her shoes on. Her skin was pale, as if she were already dead. "You will not get three yards from this room," she threatened.

"You are quite wrong. Fred is enjoying his sandwich and beer, remember?" He motioned for her to go ahead of him to the door. He took her arm and held the gun concealed but aimed with deadly accuracy into her ribs. "Now remember as we walk down the service stairs . . . Elisa . . . I have only to pull the trigger and the bullet will explode through both lungs. You will drown in your own blood."

She stiffened and pulled back. "My name is Shelby," she whispered hoarsely. "Let me go. I don't know anything about her."

"Of course you do." Georg pulled her toward the door. "Shelby—a very nice name. You are quite lovely, Shelby. British, eh? Tell me, are you embarrassed to be seen with such an ordinary-looking fellow as me, eh?" He was smiling and nodding now, chatting to the terrified woman as he opened the door and emerged into the empty corridor. "I want to know all about you, Shelby . . . everything. We have all night." The pliers in his pocket were waiting to do their work. "We have hours to talk. You can tell me whatever you want, and I will listen attentively. I am a man of patience, Shelby. I enjoy the company of a pretty girl as much as the next fellow."

Again she balked as he shoved open the door of the service stairs. "Let's stay here." Her words were husky with terror. "We can talk here."

"No. It is a warm night. A good night for a drive in the country. Shelby. Come along. Just a little chat."

How long had it been since Bubbe Rosenfelt had worn any other color than black? Today she wore a blue dress with an orchid corsage pinned to her left shoulder. Mr. Trump had purchased the dress for her. It was not pale blue or medium blue, but a dignified navy with a white lace collar and white lace sleeves. No longer was she like Rachel, mourning for her children.

The hotel suite was once again crowded with reporters and dignitaries. Bubbe Rosenfelt sat erect before the eager group and answered their questions as best she could. Her answers were tinged with hope and gratitude for the outpouring of public support from across the country. A press conference, Mr. Trump had explained to her, would be just the thing to let the readers capture what she must be feeling on such a day as this, this glorious day when the *Darien* would be arriving in New York!

"How do you feel, Mrs. Rosenfelt, after all the heartache the Nazi government put your family through?"

Her head raised slightly. She tried to find words. "I have been home only a little more than a week, and yet over two hundred thousand people have signed a petition asking for special consideration of my granddaughter and her children and husband. How do I feel? *Oy!* Such a question! We have come from bondage to the Promised Land. The Red Sea has opened once again!"

The reporters chuckled gently at the old woman's allusion. She was a great interview, the stuff great stories came from—a tough old lady who had faced the Nazis and now was facing the formidable immigration laws of the United States.

"Are you aware that there are sixty-six bills before Congress to limit immigration?" the sobering question was asked.

Mrs. Rosenfelt cleared her throat. "Such bills, if passed, *will be paid in human life*—by the suffering of millions, by children like my grandchildren and great-grandchildren." And as the weight of her words was pressed from pens to notepads, she smiled. It was the smile of a grandmother. "Would you like to see their photographs? I have them. Yes. Right here." She pulled half a dozen snapshots from her new handbag. "Here are Maria and Klaus. And their little ones—Trudy, Katrina, Gretchen, Louise. And this—this littlest—is my heart, Ada-Marie. You should interview her when she comes to New York!"

Much laughter. Typical grandmother. Pictures and everything. There was a murmur of questions. Could copies be made of the photos for publication? Trump answered that soon enough the kids would be in the harbor, and a photo session could be arranged.

"What does the State Department say about bypassing the quotas for the *Darien's* passengers?" The question seemed harsh after seeing the photos of the children. But it was the issue after all—it was reality.

"The State Department—Secretary Hull and Undersecretary Wells—have not yet responded to the petition about my family or the other refugees onboard the ship."

"Will the *Darien* be allowed to stay in New York Harbor until the issue is decided?"

Mrs. Rosenfelt frowned a bit at that one. She glanced at Murphy for help and answered, "In the absence of any word to the contrary, we are hopeful that the harbor authorities will be allowed to be hospitable."

So. It wasn't settled yet. But who would protest the anchoring of a freighter full of desperate people? With that question bobbing around the room, the next question seemed to be, "Who beat you up, Murphy? If there is no opposition to this, why were you clobbered?"

Murphy waved away the question. He did not want to be any part of the focus this afternoon. "I owe a couple of guys money from a poker game." His colleagues laughed good-naturedly. He had fended them off. *No. There was no opposition or protest against the refugees.*

"Mrs. Rosenfelt, how do you feel about the upcoming Evian Refugee Conference?"

"God bless President Roosevelt! Thirty-three countries should be able to decide how to help, *nu*? There will be doors opened for many like my own dear family by this conference. These are good men who will think of others. Yes. This is a very good idea! Tell the president I think so, will you?"

What a woman! *Tell the president!* Just then the telephone rang, the phone call they had all been waiting for. There was silence as old man Trump picked up the receiver.

"Trump here . . . yes. Yes. Thank you." It was that simple. He hung up the phone and leaned to whisper to Mrs. Rosenfelt. It was a whisper loud enough for the reporters to hear. "The *Darien* has just passed Sandy Hook Lighthouse. We should leave for the pier now."

☙

Shimon stood at the rail of the *Darien* with the others. The sulfur yellow sun was sinking behind the immense bulk that was America. The swelling tide had turned to carry the freighter easily up the estuary toward the harbor.

This should have been a moment of joy. But it was not.

"Tell them we are here," Shimon instructed Aaron. "They should know that we have arrived in America."

Aaron nodded silently. His face reflected the agony in every heart onboard the *Darien*. Thirty minutes before, as the Atlantic waves dashed themselves against the jutting spur of purple rock, the whispered word had swept through them. Hope had shattered like the waters, and then had receded into the low, undulating moan of collective grief.

"Ada-Marie is no longer with us. The soul of Ada-Marie has flown away. Ada-Marie is dead . . . is dead . . . is dead. . . ."

The words were repeated on every mouth as if it must be said in order to be comprehended. "Could this be? So close to New York? We are so close . . . if only . . . if only . . ."

Two hours before, the sisters had been called below with Klaus and Maria. The family had not come up yet. The rabbi of Nuremberg was with them when Dr. Freund had climbed wearily to the upper deck and shook his head in silent confirmation of tragedy.

As the great green statue of Liberty loomed ahead of them, the waters became suddenly cluttered with small boats bobbing alongside the *Darien*. Curious onlookers had come to see the arrival of this desperate cargo. Shimon could recognize reporters on the upper deck of a sightseeing vessel. These men waved and snapped their cameras into the faces of men and women who could not find the strength now for even one smile.

The faces turned away from the statue. "They are coming up now, coming up to see America. They are coming, and look! Look how gently Klaus carries Ada-Marie in his arms! You would think she was only sleeping, only sleeping. See how the wind ruffles her hair."

Klaus emerged first with the child's body in his arms. Maria followed after him. Trudy and Gretchen held her hands. And then Louise and Katrina came, holding tightly to each other.

The horn of the *Darien* bellowed. No one looked at the green statue. All eyes moved with the family. The passengers parted like the Red Sea; Klaus held his head high as he made his way with Ada-Marie to the bow of the ship.

"You see, my little one," he was heard to whisper. "We are safe at last. . . . America. There will be a place for us here. A place for you where we will come. You see, Ada-Marie? Bubbe will be waiting. Like Papa said, we are safe."

28

In the Hour of Our Death

By the time the tugs had nudged the *Darien* into its berth, a crowd of three thousand supporters had gathered outside the chain-link fence. Christians and Jews alike sat or stood on the enormous crates of canned goods and necessities that had been gathered over the last ten days.

Mrs. Rosenfelt stood at the front of the happy crowd with her sisters and nieces and nephews and a host of little Rosenfelts—including the infamous Franklin D. Rosenfelt! Charles sat on the top of a crate beside Murphy, who wanted very much to remain out of the range of excited elbows and jostling participants in this evening's welcome.

A band from Brooklyn played a full repertoire of Jewish songs as if the occasion were a bar mitzvah or a wedding reception. Pastors from every variety of Protestant church led their little flocks among others led by priests and rabbis. For this one evening, at any rate, theological disputes had been laid aside and warring factions remembered together the parable of the Good Samaritan and the miracles of Christ. The loaves and fishes of God's love had suddenly multiplied beyond the laws of immigration, to reach out to the immigrants as human beings.

It was, Murphy concluded, really something to see. Jesus was out there right in the middle of it—loading canned peaches onto a pallet, carrying boxes of clothing and blankets to the dockside, counting out vials of aspirin and sulfa pills. Loaves and fishes! A miracle in New York City!

There were, of course, the modern Pharisees who watched the miracle from the sidelines. Government officials from the State Department, uniformed officers from the port authority, policemen, and lawyers—all stood together with sour, disapproving faces. These were the fellows inside the chain-link fence. These were the authorities who were nearest the silent refugees peering down with emotion-filled eyes. These men were placed there to keep any of the refugees from disembarking. Murphy had been warned of this. Everyone knew that the law of the land was still much stronger than the law of love as far as the government was concerned. This show of authority was not a surprise. Twenty officials, it seemed, still had more muscle than three thousand prayerful well-wishers this evening.

Lines were secured. Murphy watched from his perch as Bubbe Rosenfelt clutched at the chain-link and searched the crowded deck above for some sign of Maria and Klaus. For Trudy, Katrina, Gretchen, Louise and . . . Ada-Marie! He knew their names now. Everyone in America knew their names.

And now the question filled his mind as it must have filled the minds of all the others who had come to do what was good and right: Why were the faces of the *Darien* passengers so sad? Why did tears stream down their faces? Could joy have overcome them with such emotion?

The clarinet played a lively tune, something to dance to. The crowds continued to call, "Welcome to America!" Signs of greeting were waved, and yet . . .

Charles tugged hard on Murphy's sleeve. The boy's eyes suddenly became a mirror of the sadness Murphy saw in the *Darien* faces. Charles pointed up—up to the deck of the wheelhouse. And there they were: Maria, Klaus, Trudy, Gretchen, Katrina, Louise. *And Ada-Marie!* The reason for the tears was plain now. Chalk-white and limp, the child in her father's arms was dead. Murphy had seen dead children before. He had seen the tears of parents as they held their children like this.

"Ah, no!" he muttered. A knife tore through his heart. "Ah, Jesus, no! Not the little one . . . not Ada-Marie." He did not move. He could not. It seemed that no one on this side of the fence had noticed the tragedy on the bridge. No one except . . . Bubbe Rosenfelt.

"Maria!" cried the old woman. "Oh, Maria . . . my little ones! I am here! Maria . . . Oh no! Ada-Marie? Is it? Can it be? Dear God, tell me it is not so!"

Through the fog of her pain, Maria followed the sounds of her grandmother's grief! She saw Bubbe Rosenfelt pressed against the chain-link, crushing the orchid corsage against the blue dress she had worn on this day of such great joy. "Bubbe!" Maria cried. And then, "Oh, Bubbe, she is gone! She is gone!" Her arms stretched out as if to span the cruel distance with an embrace. Fingers spread and reached from the ship, and the hands of Bubbe Rosenfelt strained gnarled fingers through the wire squares.

The music still played. Why did they not stop? Happy music and speeches of welcome suddenly had no place.

Another melody filled the air. From beyond the docks Murphy could hear the sound of men's voices singing . . . *what*? Their feet tramped upon the pavement and then the wood of the docks. They rounded the corner of a huge warehouse. They marched rank on rank with torches in hand. They carried signs. They came and came until the three thousand well-wishers fell silent at the thunder of the newcomers. *Three to one the ranks number, at least*, Murphy thought. *Maybe more. Probably more.* Some wore uniforms. And they sang as they carried their torches and their signs:

> "God bless America, land that I love!
> Stand beside her and guide her!
> Through the night with the light from above!"

And with that well-known song the light of the torches illuminated the signs:

> *America for Americans!*
> *No More Jewish Scum in Our Country!*
> *Ban Christ-killers from Our Shores!*
> *Tighten Immigration Laws!*
> *Let Them Sink!*
> *Roosevelt—Remember We Vote Too!*

There was violence simmering just beneath the surface as nine thousand men, led by the Nazi Fritz Kuhn, were joined by another two thousand men and women from the other directions.

Silence fell as three thousand Christians and Jews stood together among the crates and the boxes and the slack-jawed musicians. The silence was angry. Fire from the upraised torches reflected in their eyes.

Murphy could hear the sobs of Bubbe Rosenfelt. He saw the policemen move out through the chain-link gate and place themselves between what had become two angry mobs. Another official hurried into a corrugated tin office. Framed in the window, Murphy watched as the official picked up a telephone and dialed. His shouting voice radiated through the glass panes of the window: "Send a riot squad down here! Quick! There's going to be bloodshed over this! Hurry! Thousands! Hurry!"

Bubbe Rosenfelt seemed not to notice. She held her hand over her mouth. In her eyes was the reflected image of Ada-Marie.

A policeman raised his hands as if to silence the already silent mob. "Ah, now. Why don't you all go home!"

The suggestion of reasonable behavior pried the lid off Pandora's box. A chorus of angry shouts and boos came up in a wave to cover the dock and the buildings and the ship and the mourners.

"We don't want them here!"

"Why doesn't Roosevelt feed America's hungry?" This was shrieked as the mob gestured wildly at the crates of food that had been gathered from the churches.

"Hitler has the right idea!"

"We don't want no stinking Jews in New York!"

"We got the laws on our side!"

"They all got syphilis! Typhus! No foreigners! Tow 'em outta here, or we'll tear 'em apart!"

From far away the faint sound of sirens could be heard. Closer and closer they came to the docks. How would they ever penetrate the hatred of this mob?

At that moment some brave young man in a Salvation Army uniform stood up on the crates and raised his arms like a choir director. He began to sing,

> "I was sinking deep in sin,
> Far from the peaceful shore,
> Very deeply stained within,
> Sinking to rise no more."

Others joined him until the sound of the sirens and catcalls was drowned for an instant, only to rise up again with new fury. A barrage of rotten vegetables exploded from the ranks of Kuhn's followers. The young song leader was splattered with the stinking mess and knocked from his perch.

As if by signal, the flashing red lights of the riot squad spun to a halt at the rear of the cursing, hostile legion. Now shrieks and wails erupted and the mob burst into violence. Torches and placards were hurled, crates overturned. The two groups blended into one raging sea of fury as the men and women and children of the *Darien* looked on.

And Bubbe Rosenfelt wept.

꩜

There was nothing to be done now. There was nothing to do but watch.

As Leah and Louis sprawled exhausted on a flat boulder below Father Prato, he crouched behind a fortress of stones and peered through the binoculars across the Italian border into Austria. He longed to turn away from the scene being played out there, but still he stared in horror as the Wehrmacht soldiers pursued Henri, the stocky young Austrian guide who had led Leah and Louis here, and then had stepped back across the unseen line into the danger of his homeland.

"Pray for us now and in the hour of our death." Father Prato whispered the words as soldiers with guns and dogs closed in on the Austrian. From boulder to boulder the brave man leaped, as dogs strained against short leads and bared their fangs in snarls that the priest could see but not hear. "Why did he not flee to Italy?" the priest muttered as the Austrian climbed higher along the face of a cliff that had no escape route to the top. The priest could see the trap. The Austrian could not.

Face taut with fear, lips tight with exertion, the Austrian clambered up a slope of loose shale and slipped backward. He was an easy target for the rifles of the German border patrol, and yet they did not shoot. Why?

In horrifying fascination, the priest turned the binoculars onto the face of the Nazi pursuers. There were seven of them—young, hard men. They were no older than the man they now hunted. That was it. This was a hunt, a sport for them, and all seven of the Nazis were smiling with pleasure at the game. No doubt they had hunted before. No doubt there was coming a moment when they would turn the dogs loose on their prey like hounds on a fox.

"Now and in the hour of our death . . ."

Father Prato's binoculars swung across the face of the shale, back to where the Austrian scrambled up once again in vain and then slid back. His face was ashen, covered with dust, reflecting the color of death even before he knew his life was ending. Still he struggled. The priest prayed louder now, cheering and encouraging the Austrian across the distance of the small valley.

Leah and Louis seemed oblivious to the fate of their savior. It was just as well. Hadn't they been through enough? Days and miles of hiking over crumbling mountain paths. Hiding from the German border patrols. Sleeping cold and hungry for days. The priest would not direct their attention to the inevitable end of the man who had brought them to safety. He would not remind them that a man was going to die for them. They had lost enough; it would not be fitting.

"Why do they not shoot him?" the priest muttered again. The dogs leaned against the grips of their masters. The priest gasped as the leader of the patrol raised a whistle to his lips and blew hard. Delayed by distance, the sound reached the ears of the priest. Hard young men reached forward to unsnap the leather leads of their fierce dogs. Like wolves, the animals sprang forward and moved toward their victim as though he had called them to him.

"No!" shouted Father Prato as the animals covered the distance to the Austrian. They converged upon him in effortless violence, leaping upon him as he tried to shield his face with his arms. Seven wolves. One man. He fell beneath the force of their weight. The soldiers in the patrol cheered and laughed in exultation at the spectacle. No doubt they had enjoyed this sport before. Father Prato crossed himself at that evil thought.

Far above, two eagles circled and screamed. Or was it the voice of the Austrian that filled the mountains and caused the heart of the priest to go cold? A stream of red spurted up into the air. The dogs formed a circle around the Austrian. The guards still cheered them on. The struggle seemed to go on forever; it was, in fact, only a moment before the Austrian ceased to fight. Father Prato wept and shook his head. The soldiers did not call off the dogs even when it was over.

෨෩

It was like a jewel box. White enamel trimmed in brass that gleamed like gold, the inside lined with white satin.

"A lovely little thing. One of our finest children's caskets," said the mortician as Murphy wrote out the check from the account Theo had set up for them at Chase-Manhattan.

"You will deliver it to the dock."

"Within the hour, Mr. Murphy."

"The negotiations are continuing, of course," Murphy said grimly. "We thought that perhaps if the arrangements were already made the State Department could not refuse to let the child be buried here by her grandmother."

"Heartless, these government regulations." The mortician shook his head as he looked at the check. "They are quite strict even about American citizens who die abroad. The casket is airtight, of course. That is their main requirement. Rumors are the little girl died of typhus."

"Pneumonia." Murphy wanted out of this pale blue office. Away from this place that smelled of carnations. He was bone-tired. All of this somehow felt like his responsibility. If only he hadn't publicized the arrival of the ship.

"A pity." The man smiled a saccharine smile. "Quite brutal the way the demonstrators smashed everything."

"The State Department has given us twenty-four hours. We can salvage most of it. Load it before the *Darien* has to leave New York Harbor."

"And where is the ship going to next, Mr. Murphy?"

Murphy did not answer the question. He did not have an answer. "Just make sure the casket is there within an hour. Nobody in the government can refuse to let Mrs. Rosenfelt give the child a proper burial. There can't be laws on the books that would be so heartless."

"We will be happy to help in any way," said the mortician.

Murphy wanted to say, *I'll bet. As long as you get paid.* Instead, he shook the man's too-soft hand and hurried back to the tin office at the docks where the end of the matter was being negotiated.

29

What Can We Tell Them?

The tiny bistro was tucked into one of the many alleys that criss-crossed the Left Bank neighborhoods of Paris. *Elisa chose this meeting place well*, Thomas thought as he studied the faded sign above the entrance.

He had to duck his head as he entered the door. As he descended a flight of narrow stone steps, he held his head at a slight angle to keep from brushing his hair against the low ceiling. A place for ferrets and moles, he mused. Like the ancient Christians in the catacombs, this seemed an appropriate setting for them to meet again.

The aromas of garlic and wine drifted up with the noisy hum of French voices and the clatter of dishes. Thomas was hungry. It was lunchtime, and he had skipped last night's dinner and breakfast this morning in nervous anticipation of this meeting. He had closed his eyes to sleep and had still seen Elisa's distinct handwriting on the white paper. The name of the bistro. The date. The time. Nothing else.

A heavyset woman in a red-checked apron and wild wisps of gray hair met him at the foot of the stairs.

"This way." She greeted him pleasantly and led him across the sawdust-covered floor past several empty tables to a scarred wooden table in the far corner. "Here is a good place for you, monsieur." She winked as if she knew him, then rattled off a list of the day's fare. "You think about it, no? I will come back when the lady comes."

"Thank you." Thomas smiled and nodded as if he knew what the gnarled old woman was talking about. Had he ever been here before? He tried to remember. Paris was thick with little bistros like this one. He had visited dozens. They looked so much alike. Sausages dangling from the ceiling, sawdust, bad lighting. *Lady?* Had Thomas brought a lady here? or been brought here by a lady? Perhaps this meeting was not what he had imagined it to be.

He rested his arms on the table and listened in on a conversation between two French peasants over the need for a change in government. "Remember what the revolution was all about, eh? Well, we are still poor and the rich are still rich! I tell you the spirit of Marie Antoinette still lives in France!"

"And you think the Socialists will change that? I say we are doomed to poverty! So it makes no differ—"

Such conversations were common on the menu during French mealtimes. *There is hardly a more unsettled country in Europe than France,* Thomas thought with amusement. This sort of open hostility toward government—any government—would make it impossible for a dictator like Hitler or Mussolini to succeed here. Sooner or later someone would throw a glass of wine in the face of the opposition and then the slinging of salami would begin. Politics was entertainment to the French. The freedom to argue was what mattered most to them. Unlike the Germans, they were not easily led.

Thomas searched the room for a familiar face. He recognized no one, and yet he recognized the crowd as exclusively French. Dark eyes and skin. Berets and full glasses of wine. Thomas looked at his watch. Thirty minutes had passed, and still no *lady* had come to join him. His stomach rumbled a protest. He would wait a few more minutes and then he would order.

Could he have made a mistake about the handwriting? For a time he had made love to any woman who was beautiful and willing in an effort to forget Elisa. The therapy had failed miserably, and he was now haunted by the angry and curious looks of those he had convinced of his love. This mysterious meeting might be somehow related to one of those unhappy affairs. And yet the note had looked *so much* like Elisa's handwriting.

The old woman who had seated him passed by the table. He touched her arm. "Pardon, madame."

"Your lady friend has not come? You wish to order anyway?"

So that was it. He ran through a list of the women he had disappointed. Broken dinner engagements. Calls that were not returned. Someone was playing a game with him. "Do you know the woman I am supposed to meet?" he asked.

"Do you not know her?" The old woman laughed.

"Yes . . . I mean, no. I got a note, you see, to meet her here—"

"Well, she comes to me and says, 'I am meeting my lover here this afternoon; please give us this table, and if I am not here you will know him because he is very tall with black hair and blue eyes, very handsome.' " The old woman chuckled at the last, revealing a nearly toothless smile of appreciation. "You see anybody else in here in my bistro who looks like that? Only you! I know who you are the moment I see you try not to bump your head!"

"Well, yes." Now the crowd of Frenchmen turned their eyes to see what the old proprietress was cackling about. Thomas lowered his voice. "I am just not certain who I am meeting. She did not sign, and I am not sure—"

The old woman slapped his back and laughed even louder now. "Ah yes, monsieur. You look like the type who will have more than one! Two or three in every neighborhood, yes? You be careful you don't get yourself shot!"

Thomas put his hand to his throat nervously. "Exactly. Did she give her name?"

"No name. She just tells me about you. Handsome. Black hair. Big and strong." She squeezed the muscle of Thomas' arm playfully. "Oh, that I was young again, monsieur—I would steal you right away from her!"

The smile on Thomas' face wavered. "Thank you, madame. Perhaps I may let you spirit me away out the back all the same. Can you describe her to me?"

The old woman doubled over in laughter as she pointed toward the stairs. "Oh, but you see, monsieur, she is here. Too late! Too late!"

Thomas followed her gaze to where the woman stood with her back to him as she removed her coat. He resisted the urge to groan in disappointment. The woman had light auburn hair cut short at the neckline. She wore a brown tweed suit like an English tourist. A nice figure, very nice. But even from the back he could tell that it was not Elisa.

And then the woman turned around. Thomas blinked in amazement. It was not Elisa, and yet it was indeed Elisa! From the top of her head to her low-heeled walking shoes, she had been made over. Her smile was the same. Her clear blue eyes radiated relief and happiness to see him, but even her eyebrows had been darkened.

He held up his hand and stood as she moved through the close tables toward him. Her eyes were bright with emotion, silently begging him for understanding without explanation. She reached her hands out to him and embraced him lightly as if it had not been months since she had last seen him.

"Sorry I'm late, darling," she said casually, brushing her lips against his.

He helped her with her chair. He could not take his eyes from the familiar yet unfamiliar face. "You have changed your hair, love."

Her eyes warned him that all must seem natural, easy, and routine. "You like it? Colette asked me if I might not need a change. Like the American film star Myrna Loy. Are you starving? I am so sorry I'm late. Traffic was dreadful coming in. Have you waited long?"

He wanted to reply that he had waited years. But he looked at his watch. "Thirty minutes. I came early . . . so anxious to see you." His voice was strained with emotion. Strained from this charade. For whom were they performing? Had she been followed? Had he been followed?

"You should have ordered, darling." She studied the menu. "Or have you ordered without me?" She smiled brightly.

"No." He feigned irritation. "I should have. Why didn't you sign your note?" This he said for the benefit of the old woman who shuffled toward them, pencil and pad in hand, to take their orders.

"I wanted to surprise you." Elisa laid her hand on his. The hand was still beautiful. Delicate but strong. Thomas lifted her fingers to his lips and kissed them.

The old woman leaned forward with a conspiratorial whisper. "Now you know her, eh, monsieur?"

They were old friends. Old lovers come to meet for lunch. Elisa played the part with an ease that astonished Thomas. He wanted nothing so much as to take her by the arm and whisk her out of the crowded bistro so they could find some place to be alone. But then, perhaps it was better to be alone this way. In the middle of a crowd.

Elisa rattled off her order to the still-chuckling old woman; then, looking at Thomas for approval, she asked, "And what wine, darling? You like burgundy, yes?"

He nodded, unable now to take his eyes off her. She looked quite different, but even a change in hair color and a British tailored suit could not conceal her beauty. He recited his order, mimicking hers. The old woman placed a long loaf of bread and fresh butter before them. Then wineglasses and wine. Thomas noticed none of that until Elisa lifted her glass to him. His thoughts had run the course of a planned escape from Paris to Marseilles. From Marseilles to . . . somewhere. They would leave together, build a life together away from the darkness of Europe. Surely that must be why she had come. She had left that American husband and had come to find him, Thomas reasoned. Just as he had looked for her in the face of every woman he had been with.

"What shall we toast?" he asked hopefully.

A soft, loving smile curved her lips. Anyone looking on could see she loved him. "Keep looking at me that way, Thomas. No matter what I say."

He reached out to touch her hand. "No matter what happens, I want to spend the rest of my life looking at you."

Her smile did not waver. "I hope you live longer than that."

A cloud passed between them. Why had she come? He held himself in tight control. He did not allow the look of a man in love to pass from his face, although suddenly he realized she had come with other matters in mind. "Tell me."

She touched her glass lightly to his. "To the Abwehr and British intelligence, Thomas." She took a sip. Words became quiet whispers.

Fleeting surprise crossed his face. He mastered it with a sip of wine and then he held her fingers to his lips again. "This is not what I hoped."

"It is not what I wanted, either. But it seems there is no other alternative." How did she maintain such an expression of adoration on her face? "There has been utter silence from the German High Command. The only voice heard is that of Hitler. I have come to ask . . . are there other voices that must be considered?"

"So they have sent you." He took another drink of wine.

"Who else? They tell me you will not speak to anyone else."

"I trust no one."

"Can you trust me?"

"Of course." Disappointment weighed in his voice and colored his performance now. Were they being watched? If so, then the watcher might catch a glimpse of the deprived lover in the countenance of Thomas. The emotion was real. The ache was authentic. Thomas von Kleistmann in love with a married woman. His childhood friend. The first love of his young manhood.

"They must know what is happening."

"You need not explain the reason for your visit to me. I understand clearly now."

She brushed her fingers against his cheek. The performance again. The gesture caused him pain. "Then you will help?"

"The question is, will the British listen when we talk? Chamberlain comes to the throne of the beast and serves him Europe course by course like dinner. And the beast roars now that he is hungry for the Czech line of defense. The line cannot be taken by force by Germany. The Czechs are too strong if Britain and France stand with them."

"The English will listen. Churchill—"

"The only intelligent statesman in Parliament. One man."

"There are others."

"Did they listen to Churchill when he recited the vast sums Hitler is spending on rearmament? Did they listen when Churchill urged them to stop the German march into the Rhineland? And of course you saw what happened to Austria—what still happens there. A vile plague of evil and death. Mass suicides by Jews refused visas in Vienna. Worse than Germany. What will happen if the Sudetenland is also served up to the beast?"

Through all of this Thomas had buttered his bread and spoken with a fixed smile on his face. What would the watchers surmise from such a look? Were the lovers discussing the husband? her divorce?

"If we spend the present condemning the past, then we will lose the future, Thomas. There is much that can be done. It is not too late. Not even for Germany."

"And what about for ourselves?" He had not meant to ask the question. It had simply fallen from his heart; there it lay on the table between them, like the bread.

Elisa did not answer as the old woman arrived with her arms laden with food. Thomas continued to gaze imploringly at Elisa throughout small talk about the veal and the vegetables. Steam floated up between them until at last Elisa answered him quietly.

"For myself . . . I would not choose to be here." She smiled sadly now. "I did not choose this." She waved a hand over the issue as if it were steam from the veal. "But here it is. And here I am. What can I tell them in London, Thomas, that might change things?"

⟨ᴄꞬᴅ⟩

"Burial *here*? Well it's . . . it's simply out of the question!" The State Department representative tugged on his bow tie and stretched his neck out as if the whole discussion was too dreadful for him to think about.

Rabbi Stephen Wise hesitated. He would be cautious now as he broached the next subject. "And what about the women among the refugees who are pregnant? Certainly the United States could grant them at least temporary asylum?"

The official coughed loudly in disbelief at such a suggestion. "My good man, this is none of our affair. Quite out of the question. Then we would have to face an issue of the citizenship of the child. Absolutely not—out of the question!"

"No room at the inn," remarked Dr. Henry Lieper of the Federal Council of Churches. "Can it be?"

"What? What's that you say?" Now the indignant official leaned forward. His face reddened. "This has nothing to do with sentimental hogwash! This is the law! No room at the inn, indeed!"

Wise and Lieper exchanged looks.

Murphy swallowed hard, imagining how Bubbe Rosenfelt would react to the news. He glanced at Mr. Trump, whose face showed that the headline of this story would be: "NO ROOM AT THE INN"—a 36-point banner headline on the front page of the evening edition.

The government official checked his watch against the clock above the door of the dusty shipping office. "We have already extended their time limit by six hours. Time enough for Burton to have the radio fixed. Time enough to load additional supplies. That is time enough, if you ask me. I will notify the captain that his ship will be escorted out of the harbor within the hour." He shoved his papers into a well-worn briefcase, and without another word he left the delegation in stunned silence.

"Well," began Lieper in a choked voice.

"The law of Germany makes them homeless." Trump spoke up. "The law of the United States keeps them that way. Strange edicts, these things that feed on the lives of the innocent and the helpless, the dead—even the unborn."

Lieper attempted to speak again. " 'I desire mercy, not sacrifice,' saith the Lord."

Rabbi Wise ran a hand over his face in frustration. "Then we should consider how we can best show mercy to these people until we can find a way to get around the immigration statutes."

"Evian is a start." Trump nodded toward Murphy. "Murphy will be there. And I know the Jewish Agency will have representatives there as well. Until we can find a permanent solution, I suggest that we continue to publish the plight of the *Darien* as well as set up a supply line for food and medical needs as they come up."

"Mr. Trump." Murphy tugged his ear thoughtfully. "I would like to suggest that perhaps an observer join the refugees. A reporter. I would like to volunteer to go along."

Without a pause, Trump refused his offer. "You have other things to cover. The fate of this ship will be decided at Evian. We already know what sort of misery these people are living through. No, Murphy. I had the feeling it might come to this the other night. This is *my* story, son. And it's not gonna be the *Darien* that gets blown out of the water by the time I'm finished!"

And so it was settled, irrevocably. Murphy might as well pack. Trump was on the phone within minutes of the final decision by the State Department. Points of contact would be established. Committees would need to be formed from the Jewish and Christian groups who had been so vocal about this issue. That evening the *New York Times* editorial spoke eloquently:

> It is hard to imagine the bitterness of exile when it takes place over a faraway frontier. Helpless families driven from their homes to a barren island in the Danube, thrust over the Polish border, escaping in terror of their lives to Switzerland or France. These things are hard for

us in a free country to visualize. But the exiles of the Darien *have floated by our own shores. We have seen their faces, shared their grief at the loss of one little girl. Perhaps some of them may be added to the American quota list and return here. What is to happen to them in the meantime remains uncertain from hour to hour. We can only hope and pray that some hearts will soften somewhere, and that some refuge will be found. The rejection of the* Darien *by our government cries to high heaven of man's inhumanity to man!*

◌ᄋᄋ◌

The U.S. Coast Guard cutter accompanied the *Darien* far beyond Sandy Hook Lighthouse, finally turning back twelve miles out to sea. They did not want the body of a dead Jewish child accidentally washing up on a beach somewhere. The burial of Ada-Marie would have to take place far from shore to prevent such a possibility.

◌ᄋᄋ◌

Maria and Klaus sat in the cluttered office adjoining the captain's cabin where the tiny jewel-box coffin of Ada-Marie had been placed. Maria's eyes were dry now, dull with grief. Her child was to be immersed in the terrible ocean after all, cast loose among the sharks and fish and cold swirling currents of the Atlantic. What would they do with the tiny coffin now?

Captain Burton's voice was low and yet gruff, as if he resisted the grief that threatened to founder his ship. "Go on now, Tucker. Cut a square of canvas for a shroud. There is nothing else to do . . . nothing else."

Klaus held Maria's fingers limply in his own. His eyebrows were slightly raised, causing his brow to furrow as he stared through the door at the casket. The last comfort had been demolished. There had been one glimmer of relief in the thought that Bubbe Rosenfelt might have been allowed to give their little one a proper burial. To imagine coming to stand beside a small headstone on a grassy knoll, to whisper sweet words of memory at such a place—somehow that thought had eased the broken heart of Ada-Marie's father. But now . . . *Cut a square of canvas for a shroud!* Could no one see the sweetness that had been little Ada-Marie? Was the world so heartless that bright eyes and shining braids and laughter and little hands reaching up could now simply be stuffed into a square of canvas and dropped into the sea?

Klaus squeezed Maria's hand and then stood to walk into the cabin where Ada-Marie lay.

Captain Burton would not—could not—look into the face of the grieving father. He could not bear the scene.

Klaus stood over the open coffin. Lovingly he traced the curve of his child's smile with his eyes. Had he ever taken time to count the freckles on her pale skin before? Had he noticed her soft lashes when she slept? the small button nose that seemed always to be pointing up as she craned her neck to look into his face?

Her hair still shone. The ends of her honey brown braids curled on the pillow where she lay. Klaus touched her forehead. *Cold.* He let his tears fall onto her pudgy little hands. All the ocean could not contain more grief than those tears.

"How can Papa say good-bye, Ada-Marie?" he whispered, smoothing back her bangs. "How many sleeps until I see you again?"

His breath was shallow as he tried to keep himself from breaking. His hands trembled. He turned to Captain Burton, who stared out through a porthole at the flat gray sea. "Do you have scissors?" Klaus managed to ask. "A lock of hair . . . for her mother to . . ." His voice failed him.

Captain Burton fetched scissors from a drawer and then turned quickly to the porthole again. Klaus carefully snipped the curl on the child's right braid. He let himself smile for a moment at the memory of Ada-Marie trimming her own hair a year before. It had only just grown out.

The door to the cabin opened suddenly. Tucker stood in the doorway. He seemed suddenly awkward at the sight of Klaus beside the little girl's body. In his hand was a frayed square of canvas from a tarp. Tucker tried to conceal the material. It was stained with oil.

Klaus let his eyes linger on the canvas. "She deserved so much more," he said at last. Then he closed his fingers around the lock of hair.

Captain Burton cleared his throat uncomfortably. "I . . . am ashamed today to be an American."

For a long time no one spoke. Behind them the sound of Maria's heavy sighs drifted through the door. At last Klaus nodded. "I will take Maria below now. Thank you for . . . trying." There was nothing else to thank the captain for. He had tried. They all had done their best.

The face of the rabbi of Nuremberg appeared behind Tucker in that instant. He wore his white silk prayer shawl and carried his prayer book in his gnarled hand. The ancient eyes were red with grief. He had seen much in his lifetime. This act was a new kind of heartlessness. He bowed slightly to Tucker and inched past him into the cabin. "They say we must bury the child at sea." He addressed Captain Burton but put a hand gently on the arm of Klaus.

Burton nodded once. "There is no choice."

The rabbi looked into the sweet face of the child. "Sleeping," he murmured. Then he examined the dirty square of canvas that would be her shroud. Carefully he removed his prayer shawl, its white silk and silver thread gleaming in the dim light. He placed it gently over the body of Ada-Marie, tucked it around her chin like a blanket, and bent low to whisper something.

His eyes shining, he straightened and turned to face Klaus. "She loved my tallith. Silver and silk. And so this shall be her shroud."

Klaus closed his eyes in gratitude at such a gesture.

Then the rabbi of Nuremberg reached out his hand to take the canvas from Tucker. "And this—" the old man draped the canvas over his head where silk and silver had been— "this shall be my prayer shawl." He lowered his eyes, and his lips moved silently behind his beard. He shuffled toward the door of the office. "Maria." His voice was gentle. "Look at me, Maria."

She raised her eyes and cried, "Oh, Rebbe! She is so little. To leave her in this dark sea . . ."

The old man nodded. "When our fathers crossed the Red Sea from bondage to freedom they took with them the coffin of Joseph as he had instructed them." He sighed and glanced toward the child. "They wandered forty years without destination until all that generation was gone. And when they crossed the Jordan at last, the bones of Joseph were also carried to the shores of the Promised Land." Now he gazed imploringly into the face of Captain Burton. The question was clear even before words formed on his lips. "How can we leave Ada-Marie behind? If all of us should wander homeless, still this child should have a plot of ground; a very small piece of soil will do."

The stern facade of the captain cracked at last. His eyes were bright with emotion. He gave the order quietly to Tucker. "Make the casket airtight. A lead seal. The child will have a proper burial."

The rabbi smiled as Maria wept tears of relief. "Like Joseph, Ada-Marie shall go with us and before us, wherever our Promised Land may be."

◌

From the first hour after the *Darien* was escorted from New York, the shadow of U.S. Coast Guard cutter 177 was never far away. Sometimes it was a small gray shape on the horizon between the ship and the vast land of America. Other times it was near enough to the *Darien* that the shapes of men could easily be made out. But always, the cutter stood guard on American soil. Day and night it crept slowly behind the rusty hulk to make certain that none of the refugees jumped into the water or attempted to swim to shore.

30

Wait until Morning

Dressed in new pajamas, Charles sat cross-legged on the hospital bed as Murphy tried very hard to explain it all to him. English wasn't working, so Murphy tried German:

"Doc says the surgery won't be tough at all. Maybe you'll feel like you had your tonsils out. I had my tonsils out, and it wasn't so bad. Got all the ice cream I wanted, and after a week I was home."

To this last statement, Charles looked curiously at Murphy. Home? Where would Charles go after a week in the hospital? He had no home to go to, and now that Murphy was returning to Europe, who would come to visit him?

Murphy cleared his throat uncomfortably. The cello case stood open in the corner of the small, sterile room—a reminder of Louis, of Leah Feldstein, of Vienna. Murphy scratched his head and ran a hand over his face. *I'm not handling this very well*, he thought. He felt guilty about it all, but what choice was there now? How could he explain? "Mrs. Rosenfelt . . . Bubbe Rosenfelt . . . can't be here, Charles, because she's . . . in mourning. You know what mourning is?"

Charles nodded his understanding. Murphy blinked at his own stupidity. Of course Charles Kronenberger knew about mourning. He had spent his entire life in mourning.

"Well, I wish I could stay. You know I just wish I could put this off long enough—but I know you're going to be okay. Take it like a man, and pretty soon you'll be saying 'hot dog!' And 'Let's go to the movies,' and all sorts of great stuff." The combination of German and American slang sounded funny, but Murphy didn't smile.

"Uh-huh," Charles said quietly. He wanted to ask when Murphy would come back. Or when Murphy would send for him. And if Murphy would find his brother, Louis, and tell Leah that her cello was in New York with Charles.

"Okay." Murphy patted the shoulder of the frail little boy. "And I'll be praying for you, Charles." The promise fell flat. Murphy could see the brave front was only a front. Both of them felt it. "Mr. Trump and the rest of the guys from the newsroom promised to come visit. I don't know how long Bubbe Rosenfelt will be out of commission. Poor old lady; she took it pretty hard. But I want you to understand that all this . . . with the ships . . . is the reason I have to leave, Charles. You understand? They're having this big meeting in Evian to see if maybe some country might not have a place for them."

"Uh-huh!" Charles said enthusiastically. It *was* important. Charles knew Murphy would not leave him to face the surgery all alone unless he had to go. The child sighed. It *was* important, and yet did Murphy know that Charles was afraid? Could he see it? Could Murphy see that the cello in the corner was not enough to keep him company?

Ah, well, Charles was also aware that the ache in his heart could not change things. And so it had to be.

Good-bye, Murphy. I hope you come back, Charles' heart said. *I hope you find Louis and come back for me. Will you forget about me, Murphy? Please come back.*

"Okay then," Murphy said with a buck-up smile, "we're gonna make it fine." He glanced at his watch. "I've got a ship to catch. I'll call as soon as I reach France. Mr. Trump will wire me on the ship. It's all going to go fine, and next time I see you I want you to say, 'Hi ya, Murph,' okay?"

A quick hug. No tears. Another quick hug, and then Murphy was gone.

Everything was quiet now except for the hollow echoes of city sounds. Charles crept from his bed and tiptoed to the window of his hospital room. He leaned against the cool glass of the pane and gazed in wonder at the vast display of New York City lights that surrounded the hospital compound.

Suddenly the big brick building where he stayed seemed very small. Charles felt very small and insignificant as well. The ache of loneliness and fear filled him as never before. If he closed his eyes he could almost remember what Mommy had looked like—the sound of her voice, the touch of her hand on his head when she held him. She had been soft and had smelled like flowers—always like flowers. His head had just fit beneath her chin, and if he sat very still he could hear her heart beating.

Charles put his hand to his mouth. By tomorrow at this time the operation would be finished and he would be on his way to looking like other boys. Like his brother, Louis. He would learn to talk and laugh and even sing the songs Mommy had sung to them so long ago. Could he make those words come as clearly to his mouth as they were in his heart? And if Louis never came back, whom would he sing with?

Tonight the city was a study in electric geometry. Neat lines of yellow light. Bright boxed grids of unpeopled windows. Headlights reflected in puddles on the street. The bright orange line of the elevated train as it inched like a caterpillar along a narrow, leafless stem. It was as if mankind had envied the bright chaos of the stars and had sought to arrange a more orderly image below.

From beneath the blackened tin roof of the massive New York train sheds, engines whined and squeaked. The clank of metal against metal sounded like the little brass bells Mommy had hung outside their bedroom window in Hamburg. Summer breezes from the Aussen-Alster had made them ring gently. Often she had sung Charles and Louis to sleep accompanied by the formless melody of those bells.

When winter had come the bells had banged against the glass of the window. No longer pretty, they had blended with the sound of fists against the door. The men had broken down the door and taken Father away. Taken him to the prisoner trains—the trains of Germany that had cried and moaned and carried Father where he did not want to go. Then Mommy had been taken . . . where? To heaven, they told him.

And then the Nazi doctors had strapped Charles onto the cold, shiny table and hurt him. He would never forget their words:

"They should have tossed this one into the Aussen-Alster and let him drown. Well, this will make sure he does not spawn a tribe of monsters like himself."

"Who would ever love such a beast anyway?"

"Better to make certain he is armed with blanks just in case he puts a bag over his head and marries a blind girl!"

Their laughter had drowned out his screams. He had been sore for a few days and then he had forgotten the physical pain, although the memory of their laughter rang in his nightmares.

Even when summer had come gently on the breezes of the Aussen-Alster to ring the bells Mommy had hung outside the window, Charles could hear that terrible laughter in his dreams. And the formless melody mocked him as the white-coated doctors of the Reich had mocked him.

As Charles leaned against the window and stared out on the lights of this unfamiliar city, tears formed and fell silently onto the windowsill. Murphy had left. He was alone. And tomorrow the doctors would again strap him onto a cold steel table and reach toward him with their knives. There was nothing he could do; he could not even tell anyone how terrified he was. He could only cry and wait for morning.

Silence reigned in the Brooklyn home of the Rosenfelt family. The old clock at the foot of the stairs ticked off the seconds and minutes and hours of mourning that cloaked the house in grief for little Ada-Marie.

During the seven days of mourning, old friends and neighbors had brought meals for Bubbe Rosenfelt and had sat with her to grieve in silence for the little girl they had never known. It seemed that all of Brooklyn observed shiva that week; every Jew grieved for the dead child and for the ship that had been turned back out to sea. Old men shook their heads sadly as if the great-grandchild of Bubbe Rosenfelt had been their own, as if their own sons and daughters were packed into the holds of the decrepit freighter.

In every synagogue across the country kaddish was recited:

> *"Magnified and sanctified be His great name in the world which He hath created according to His will."*

And with the words of that ancient prayer the question echoed in a thousand hearts: *Did God create such a cruel world? Did He close the gates to these few refugees? Why has this evil come upon them?*

For every one of those onboard the *Darien*, a thousand homes now begged to give them shelter—Jewish homes and Christian as well.

> *"May He establish His kingdom during your life and during your days, and during the life of all the House of Israel, even speedily and at a near time; and ye say, Amen!"*

In the pulpits of churches across the nation, pastors and priests stood to recount with shame the denial of the U.S. government against the people of the *Darien*. Families from farms and cities stood and asked if they might take even one Jewish child into their homes until the persecution had passed over the Jews of the Reich.

> *"May there be abundant peace from heaven and life for us and for all Israel; and ye say, Amen!"*

As the silence of shiva continued in the little home in Brooklyn, the public outcry swelled at the sight of the photograph of the tiny coffin on the deck of the ship. That image of grieving father and mother touched a chord in the hearts of parents that transcended all considerations of race and religion.

Letters to congressmen filled mail pouches with seething indignation. Christian ministers stood beside rabbis to question the inhumanity of the government's decision.

Politicians raised their eyebrows in surprise at the public outcry, then quietly raised their fingers to test the shift in political winds. Was this response the opinion of the majority of Americans or only a very vocal minority of religious fanatics? Would the interest in the refugees onboard that ship die out as the vision of the photograph faded from memory? Often that was the case in such matters. One big hullabaloo, and then it was over. Washington would wait a bit and take a reading later on. After all, it was election year.

After the seven days of shiva, Bubbe Rosenfelt stood slowly and removed the black cloth that covered the mirrors in her room. She opened her mouth with slight surprise at the image of the old woman who gazed back at her. She did not remember being so very old. Had she aged so very much in seven days?

"It is possible," she muttered to herself. "God created the whole world in six days. A lot can happen in a week."

With a shake of her head she washed her face and combed her hair and put on comfortable shoes. It was time to return to the real world, to see if the world had also grown older and wiser in one week. She had not read the newspaper or listened to the news on the radio in all that time. She had asked no questions until now. Answers were one phone call away.

❧

A voice in the familiar accent of Hamburg reached out to Charles in the darkness. "It is late, Charles. Tomorrow you have an important day, *nu?* Why are you still up?"

Charles turned from the window to face Bubbe Rosenfelt. She had come after all! Even though Murphy had told him she could not, *would* not come, she was here!

He opened his mouth with a cry. Bubbe did not bother to turn on the light but moved quickly toward him and gathered him up in her arms.

Charles had resigned himself to his loneliness; his tears had dried an hour ago. Now he wept softly again as Bubbe Rosenfelt sat down with him in her lap and pressed his head beneath her chin. She smelled like a garden . . . like flowers . . . like Mommy. She stroked his hair and hummed to him as he wept.

His feet dangled awkwardly over the arm of the chair. Maybe he was too big to be rocked, but he did not resist. He rested his head against her and absorbed her nearness like parched soil soaking up rainfall.

He wanted to say, *"Bubbe. Thank you, Bubbe. Thank you for coming. Thank you for hugging me. Thank you for speaking in the same sweet accent as Mommy and Father and Louis."*

But he could not say these things. He had to sit his own silent shiva and be content to let her comfort him.

And then she began to tell him stories about her own little boys. She spoke of her house beside the Aussen-Alster, of sailboats and picnics in the very same places Mommy and Father had taken him and Louis when they were very little. She reminded him of church bells and markets and the big ships in the docks. She spoke of blue skies above Hamburg and white clouds that looked like rabbits and sailing ships and other things.

After a time Charles no longer remembered the banging of fists against the door or the cruel laughter of the doctors in Hamburg. Only happy memories filled his thoughts until at last he became sleepy. He closed his eyes and his fingers became limp. He would tell Bubbe Rosenfelt tomorrow . . . tomorrow, when his mouth was fixed; then he would tell her, "Thank you."

Charles fell fast asleep in her arms, yet still the old woman rocked him far into the night. Long after his breathing was deep and even, she continued to talk to him. He did not feel the dampness of her own tears against his hair.

"Of course, my son was a little smaller than you then—just a baby, really. And I held him for hours and hours while the artist worked. And I remember thinking that Mary could not have been any happier holding her son than I was holding mine. Just like I am holding you now, sweet kinderlach. Don't you know? It is you who comforts my heart tonight." She pressed her lined cheek against his soft forehead and laid her hand over his ear. "Sleep now, Charles. You are not alone."

◌◌

Things had been quiet in the Czech-Sudeten city of Eger for nearly three days. The Sudeten-Nazi Free Corps headed by Henlein and Frank had been dispersed with clubs and bayonets by the Czech military. Broken glass, burned-out buildings, and littered streets were the marred reminders of the riots and violence that had rocked the Czech-Sudetenland. Martial law and curfews now prevailed, and the Nazi Brownshirts seemed to disappear into the woodwork.

This afternoon Colonel Ludwig Segki of the Czech Reserve Air Corps had at last found a moment to relax his vigilance. This luncheon with his officers at Hotel Eger was more than a social visit, however. Events of the past days and weeks were discussed. The readiness of the new air cadets was evaluated. The ominous future was probed.

All the men under his command remained silent when officer Theo Linder spoke. They knew that he had once been a hero for the German Luftwaffe. He had been on personal terms with Luftwaffe Reichsführer Hermann Göring.

"As long as we do not negotiate away this territory in the Sudetenland, we will remain safe," Theo said. "The Maginot Line in France is not even as strong as our line of defense in these mountains. Concrete bunkers, machine-gun emplacements—even from the air, the Luftwaffe could not disable us."

"And if the Germans fly over our heads to bomb Prague?"

On this issue Theo could not comment with encouragement. He shook his head and let a more senior officer answer.

"I say we arrest the Free Corp Nazis here who cause the violence and jail them all around the city of Prague. Then if the Germans bomb civilians, they will also be bombing their own compatriots."

The plan met with general approval, but Theo saw the flaw. "With such an idea you are presupposing that Hitler cares what happens to the Aryans in our territory. I do not believe that he cares even that much—" Theo snapped his fingers.

"Then why does he rage so about them? Why send terrorists into our country? Why?"

Theo had a theory about that. He hesitated, hoping one of the dozen others would speak. Instead they all looked at him. "Because if he can somehow cross these fortified mountains and possess the Sudeten defenses he will simply roll into Prague, then into Poland and maybe all the way to Moscow. Five miles from the border of the Sudeten territory he desires is the Skoda arms factory in Pilsen. Only five miles, gentlemen, from Hitler to the finest munitions factory in the world. No, Hitler does not care one whit about the Germans who live in the Czech territories. He cares about the ground they live on."

Such reasoning made sense. Colonel Segki had heard just such matters discussed in staff meetings in Prague, and now from the mouth of a former German-Jew who had once been well connected with the German members of the High Command.

Confident that all of this was true, Colonel Segki instructed his men not to relax their vigilance. Three days without violence in the Sudetenland made it certain that violence was just around the corner.

The colonel left Hotel Eger with Theo. There was much he wanted to ask the man. Perhaps Theo had some personal insight that might help the colonel deal with the unexpected.

"My car is just there around the corner," said the colonel. "I will give you a ride back to the airfield."

Flattered, Theo agreed, then stopped at the edge of the sidewalk. He had forgotten his hat in the dining room. "I'll just be a moment."

The colonel walked briskly across the street and rounded the corner with two other officers who had ridden with him. He would pick up Theo in front of the hotel.

Theo had just retrieved his cap when the blast ripped through Colonel Segki's automobile. Plate glass was shattered a block and a half away. The force of the explosion knocked Theo to the floor and sent a waiter tumbling down a flight of steps. Pieces of the officer's car mowed down seven civilians, later determined to be German-Czechs.

Just around the corner, violence had returned to the Sudetenland with a fury that made headlines halfway around the globe.

∽⟨ᑫᑫ⟩∾

Penniless, hungry, and still dressed in their Austrian traveling clothes, Leah and Louis arrived in Paris in the cab of a stuttering old pickup truck. The driver of the truck was a farmer from the provinces on his way to the Marché aux Puces, the flea market of Paris. He was a drop-cloth peddler prepared to spread the finest of his wares out on a canvas sheet for browsers to observe and perhaps purchase.

Among those wares was a selection of needlepoint as well as an assortment of cabbages and fine apples from his orchard. In a moment of kindhearted weakness, he offered each of his ragged passengers one of his apples and watched with astonishment as they devoured everything, even the core. Smoothing his thick mustache thoughtfully at the sight, the peddler reached back through the glassless window and retrieved two more apples.

"For later," he explained to Leah. "For you and your son." The man had seen a thousand refugees from the Rhineland and Germany and now Austria on the dirt roads of France. Occasionally he had given them rides, although most did not know where they wanted to go. This young woman he had picked up because of her child. A more weary, underfed little boy he had not seen in a long time. The woman spoke fluent French and even produced a French passport. She must have spent her last franc on the document, he reasoned. At any rate, the village priest would be pleased to hear of this good deed, and penance for his sins would perhaps be less because of it.

The peddler had fully intended to drop the woman off amid the stalls in the flea market. But instead, she had made a strange request that piqued his curiosity and caused him to steer his vehicle into the crazy traffic of central Paris with its canted streets and boulevards and hordes of taxis and bicycles.

The brakes of his truck squeaked in amazement as the peddler finally stopped before the ornate and elegant facade of L'Opera.

Leah took his hand in gratitude. Tears of appreciation gleamed in her eyes. "I am a musician," she explained, and now the accent of Austria tinged her French. "I have played here many times. Perhaps I will again, and then I will see that you and your wife have tickets, monsieur."

The farmer laughed, revealing great gaps in his teeth. *The poor woman has gone mad from her hunger,* he thought. *Poor thing.*

With a shrug, he watched as she and the boy darted across the street to the towering edifice of L'Opera. Holding the child's hand, she dashed around the corner of the building and up the stage-door steps.

⌒⌒

The two sisters hovered over Leah and Louis like hens over chicks. After each sip of hot tea, Leah's cup was refilled. Mounds of bread and cheese and cold cuts were spread out on the table in the one-room Paris apartment. Sonia fixed a salad: fresh lettuce, carrots, broccoli tossed with herbs, and vinegar-and-oil salad dressing. It was a feast even without the pastries that they stacked on a plate and placed within view but out of reach of the half-starved child.

And all the while Leah and Louis ate as if it were something new to them. They had nearly forgotten about tables and forks and knives during their long journey across the Alps from the Wattenbarger farm. How long ago and far away Austria seemed now!

Leah looked at her fingers as she tore a piece of bread from a long loaf. Her hands were cracked and sore from rocks and brush and the icy cold winds that had stalked them in the highest passes. But they were safe. Her fingers would heal. They would find Elisa and Charles and Murphy and perhaps, God willing, she would hear some word about Shimon.

"For you just to show up like that!" cried Magda, adding fresh milk to Louis' empty glass. "The doorman thought you were beggars. Imagine you, a beggar, the finest cellist in Europe. We thought you were lost to the Nazis. Herbert—you remember him? Bass fiddle. He was in Vienna last month, and he said none of the old gang remained except a few who were able to play to the Nazi tune! Shimon was arrested, he said—"

Leah nodded. "On the first night they took him. I heard there were almost one hundred thousand arrests in Vienna during the first two

days. Many were freed. I am hoping—" she furrowed her brow—
"*praying* that he has somehow gotten free."

"Herbert told us about Elisa Linder, too. Of course we were frantic
about you all! And then we turned on the BBC, and as clear as anything
there is Elisa with the BBC, playing that sweet fiddle of hers! It is a miracle! First Elisa, and now you. Oh, Leah, we have been so worried!"

Leah swallowed hard. She had not allowed herself to show any emotion before this moment. But now at the mention of Elisa . . . "She is . . .
performing? In London? Oh, Louis, do you know what that means? They
made it, too! Murphy and Charles must be with her!"

Louis laughed brightly. Life and color returned to this thin face.
"Charles! Wait until I tell him everything—about the mountains and the
guides, the Nazis on the border, and the avalanche! I will have so many
stories to tell him, won't I, Aunt Leah? How the angels hid us and the
dogs passed by. He will be glad to see me."

Through all of this burst of excitement from Louis, Leah found herself unable to do anything except hug the boy and nod at the miracle of
their arrival in Paris—and the miracle that Elisa was just across the
Channel from them!

Then Sonia cried, "We'll have to have a party, you know—to celebrate!"

"Have you got your cello across the border somehow too, Leah?"

Louis answered for her. "My brother, Charles, has it. He took it out of
Austria for her, and now he has it."

Magda frowned. "Well, we'll just have to get you another one for
now so you can play. The maestro will want you to begin immediately, I
know. We will have to borrow a decent instrument for you until you are
reunited with Vitorio."

It was all happening so fast. Food, real food. Talk of parties. Now
playing for the maestro. Leah suddenly felt very weak. She could let herself ease up for a few days. "No party." She put a hand to her churning
stomach. "Only . . . a bath now. Only a little sleep. And then we'll see . . .
we'll see." She stumbled, reeling, from the table and sat on the small sofa
for a minute until she closed her eyes and instantly fell asleep.

31
Life in the Shadow of Death

The broken body of Shelby Pence washed downstream from London until the pilot of a garbage scow found her floating like a discarded mannequin.

She had not been in the water long enough for time to conceal the brutality of her end. Colonel Tedrick had personally gone to the morgue, and with one glance at the young woman's hands, he was convinced that she had told everything she knew. No doubt she had given her tormentor the information he wanted within the first moments of her torture. That was the horrifying thing about it all. What had been done to Shelby Pence must have been done for the sake of pleasure, a dark and evil sort of cruelty.

The body was cremated. The case was suppressed. She was listed as unidentified by Scotland Yard. The prerecorded performances of Elisa continued to be broadcast weekly over the BBC. The room at the Savoy was still registered to her name, although Tedrick was confident that the Gestapo was quite aware that Elisa Linder-Murphy was now in France, making contact with another agent. Shelby had not known where in France or who the German contact was. If she had known, she certainly would have begged her attacker to let her tell him.

Tedrick decided at once that it was not in the best interests of the British Intelligence Service for Elisa Murphy to know what had happened to her double. The bloodless drag hunt had become quite bloody indeed. Letters and telegrams from John Murphy had continued to arrive at the Savoy while Elisa was in Paris. Now that she had returned, she sat in Tedrick's office and read them each again and again. Even with the distance of the Atlantic between them, she could feel his frustration and grief at the events he had witnessed with the *Darien*.

Tedrick allowed Elisa an hour of privacy before he resumed his place behind the desk. "So, you see, John Murphy will be in Europe soon. On his way to Evian he will want to see you."

"You read every telegram, every letter?"

"We have taken the liberty of—"

"Too much liberty."

"Of arranging for you to meet him. A few hours only at the BBC. We need a little time, and no doubt he will be watched. We do not wish to have your cover blown."

Elisa shrugged with smoldering resignation. As always, she had no choice in the matter. "How is Shelby?" she asked, folding the love letters on her lap.

"Playing the role quite effectively," Tedrick lied. "A splendid job of drawing the hounds."

Elisa sighed. She was weary from her trip. "Give her my best . . . and tell her . . ."

"What?"

"Just hello. And to be careful. Colonel Tedrick, I . . ." She searched for a way to communicate the importance of what Thomas had told her.

"The meeting went well, I assume?" He lit his pipe and leaned back with a calm detachment that did not betray the excitement of what he was feeling. "He had something of importance to say?"

Elisa closed her eyes and mentally conjured up each minute detail that Thomas had given her to carry back to England. "Yes."

"Then we were right to send you."

"If there was no one else, then yes."

"What news, then, from the German Chancellery, Elisa? Will there be a war over Czechoslovakia?"

She smiled, a faint smile of pleasure that she could bring this news herself. "All that you hear from Berlin is only a brazen front. Hitler is all bark and very little bite. Thomas has firsthand information that General Beck, chief of the Army General Staff, is profoundly alarmed about Hitler's plans.

"And what are those plans?"

"He would have not only the Czech-Sudetenland but all of Czechoslovakia along with it."

"I can read the papers and know that. I want details."

"All right, then. After the invasion of Austria in March, General Beck sent a memorandum to Hitler arguing that a program of conquest would lead to a worldwide catastrophe and the ruin of Germany."

Tedrick coughed impatiently. "This is not news. We got a copy of that memorandum through Le Morthomme months ago. What is the latest?"

"Details." Elisa searched her memory for the details Thomas had told her were most important. "Beck is universally trusted by the military staff and by the army itself. He plans to confront Hitler personally this week. He refuses to share the responsibility with the Führer for plunging the world into another war. Beck will demand assurance against further military advances against the Czechs."

"We have known of opposition of the war ministry to Hitler's escapades."

"Beck himself will answer your questions and those of Prime Minister Chamberlain as to whether there will be a German-instigated war over Czechoslovakia."

"How will he do this?"

"If the Führer does not listen to him, if Hitler insists on following through with his deadline for an October first invasion, then Beck will resign. You will have your insight into the mind of Hitler in the London *Times* if a man like General Ludwig Beck resigns."

"Is that all?"

"For the moment. Thomas asks that I inform you of this. The resignation of Beck would mean that the path of reason has been utterly forsaken by Hitler. If this is the case, then there may be another path that the leaders of the German Army might take."

"Details?"

"Nothing yet. Everything depends on whether Hitler listens to Beck."

"When is this meeting between Beck and Hitler to take place?"

"This week. During the party rally."

"Well, then—" Tedrick puffed his pipe in thought as he swiveled back and forth in his chair—"we'll just have to sit it out for a few days. That will give you a little time with John Murphy." He smiled at her astonished reaction. "Then he will be off to Evian, and you will return to Paris. The conference in Evian will keep your Mr. Murphy occupied long enough for us to complete our business."

Elisa put a hand to her bobbed, dyed hair. "Murphy?" she asked weakly. "Soon?" He would hate her hair. She hated it. And he would ask her a thousand questions. He would know somehow that from the beginning nothing had been right. The thought frightened her.

Tedrick read her thoughts. "Of course you will not be able to let him in on our . . . arrangement."

"He'll know. It is one thing for me to pretend when he is thousands of miles away, but . . . how?"

"I doubt that he will think much about anything after he sees you. You will have to change your hair color back for the time being."

She frowned at his patronizing smile. "I want the passports in the hands of my family in Prague. I want them there now!" She looked down at the telegrams and then lifted her eyes in the stony demand that Tedrick keep his promise. "If Beck resigns, they will need them immediately."

"My dear girl—" Tedrick tapped the bowl of his pipe—"we can't have you running off to Prague on a family visit before this matter is concluded. You still have a great deal of performing to do. Recorded concerts to run on the BBC."

"If you won't trust me with them, then at least let me give them to Murphy. He can take them to Prague, give them to my parents and my brothers. Surely you see what an invasion would mean to them—"

"Of course we understand." Tedrick reconsidered. Giving Murphy fresh British passports to carry to Prague would delay him even longer, leaving Elisa just that much more time to work. "Yes," he said after a moment longer. "I think that will work. Providing you do not slip and somehow let him know what it is you are involved in. If he should catch wind of it, I'm afraid the entire arrangement would be canceled, Elisa."

She lifted her chin angrily. This man was adept at manipulation and blackmail—perfect for his job. She detested him. "Then I want one more thing from you."

"Adding to the contract?"

"Haven't you?" she shot back. Her eyes narrowed. "I want three days with him alone. I mean *alone*! No tails. No microphones. No men in the shadows."

Tedrick smiled slightly. Elisa was not only learning the ropes of the espionage game, she was learning the language as well. Then his smile faded as he considered her demands.

"How can we do that? The Gestapo might well follow him . . . straight to you. And you know what that means." He drew back; he had come too near the revelation of Shelby's gruesome demise. "I mean—"

"No! I mean it! You arrange it. You're the expert in such matters, aren't you?"

He exhaled loudly in disapproval. "Is that all?" he asked sarcastically.

"No." Now it was Elisa's turn to smile. "I was married to Murphy in Vienna."

"I told you that was invalid."

"I want it made valid. Legal. However that is done. You seem to be a wizard of such matters. You have undone my marriage, thinking that it would give you more control over me. Now I am telling you, Colonel, I quite enjoy being Mrs. John Murphy."

A muscle in Tedrick's cheek twitched. He had hoped the woman would perhaps fall into something with von Kleistmann. He had been misinformed about the reason Elisa had married Murphy. "Of course, we will do as you wish."

"Three days. I want to spend them with my husband, Mr. Tedrick."

Tedrick nodded curtly. Her insistence irritated him. He cleared his throat and returned the conversation to his own realm of power. "Quite. Well, regardless of what General Beck does, Chamberlain has sent Lord Runciman to study the riots in the Sudetenland. He will serve as a mediator between President Beneš and the Czech Nazis Henlein and Frank. Perhaps a peaceful solution will be found and all this worry about your family will have been needless, eh?" He flashed an insincere smile. "Hitler's reaction to the British mediator is something we are quite interested in—something you should discuss with Thomas von Kleistmann when you are next in Paris."

He flipped open one more file on his desk. The folder was nearly empty, but he produced a letter from it with a French postmark. It, too, had been opened.

"Leah!" Elisa gasped at the glimpse of the handwriting.

"She is safe in Paris—" Tedrick began to explain the contents of the letter as Elisa snatched it from him.

"In *Paris*! She made it out!"

"Yes. She apparently heard your BBC broadcast and wishes to have some contact with you. She is . . . will be performing with L'Opera and is curious about her cello."

This dry report was lost to Elisa as she scanned the emotion-laden page.

> *And so, my dear sister, this Jesus whom I have come to love has guided us safely here. I am to have a job with L'Opera and perhaps will be able to move into a little flat with Louis. I know how your schedule is; mine will be tight for a while also. But please write me and let me know when I can hope to see your face again. I think often of our last night in Vienna and pray that those fears of our last good-bye will now be forgotten! Of course, I have no word from Shimon, but I pray hourly that he may live and come to find our Messiah as I have and that we may raise our children to serve our loving God! Can I ever doubt His miracles again? I was safe long before we crossed the border. Marta Wattenbarger told me and showed me all I needed to come to this great peace in my heart! I long to see you soon! There are so many things I want to tell you, my dear Elisa—*

Tedrick coughed loudly, interrupting this gentle flow. "You cannot see her, of course," he barked.

Elisa looked up. Her smile slipped away. "How can I not see her? She is in Paris. I will be in Paris—"

"You must not see her. You may be followed—or at least the Gestapo may be on the lookout for you."

"But Shelby is playing me . . . quite well, you said."

Tedrick's scowl deepened. "Until this matter is finished, until we have obtained our information from von Kleistmann, you cannot run the risk of seeing her. You could jeopardize everything."

Elisa looked down at the final lines.

> *Pray with me for Shimon. For all the others still in the shadow of the darkness. If you hear any news of him, call me at L'Opera. Until I see you again, dear sister, here is my heart in gratitude.*
>
> *Love, Leah*
>
> *P.S. How is Charles and how is Vitorio? Write soon.*

It was obvious that something in the letter disturbed Tedrick. His expression was a sour contrast to the emotion in Elisa's eyes. "Not surprising. A Jewess converting to the Christian religion. They are doing it by the thousands in Vienna, I hear. Not that it will do them any good. Hitler is hanging priests right along with rabbis." He said this in an arrogant tone.

How could she answer this man's resentment against Leah, a Jew, claiming Christ as her Savior? She decided that she would not give him the satisfaction of an argument. Like Hitler and the Nazis, Tedrick somehow equated Christianity with race, not with the Jewish Messiah. "I will not see her until my duty is finished." Elisa folded the precious letter. It was something sacred, and she feared a man like Tedrick would somehow profane it if they talked further. And so she had given her word, but with the hope she would be free soon to walk into L'Opera and embrace her friend.

⊘

Murphy had wired ahead to London with the date and time of his arrival in Southampton. Traveling on the *Queen Mary* had been Trump's idea— a chance for Murphy to relax a little and at the same time tap into public sentiment concerning the *Darien* controversy and the immigration issue.

Theoretically, Trump may have been right. But Murphy neither rested nor mixed with the other passengers. He had spent his days and nights onboard the liner alternately obsessed with thoughts about the refugees onboard the *Darien* and thoughts about Elisa. Two days from England, the vision of Elisa had managed to drive away even his ability to make coherent conversation. The ache of longing for her returned with almost overwhelming intensity, until, at last, Murphy understood the words in the Song of Songs: *I am sick with love.*

He was the bridegroom returning for his bride. At night he dreamed of the softness of her skin and the sweetness of her smile. Throughout the day he lounged in a deck chair on the sun deck and placed a newspaper over his face as if he were sleeping. He was, in fact, wide awake and dreaming of her. He should have hung a *Do Not Disturb* sign on his broken nose. Passengers wishing to make small talk soon found they were talking to themselves, anyway. Murphy was capable of such profound utterances as "Huh? Oh, yes. Is that so?" Even the phrase "Is that so?" was a fraction too long.

At least in New York he had been unbelievably preoccupied with the crisis of the *Darien*. He knew now that his work had been a merciful distraction. If he had been forced to endure the pain of separation he was feeling right now, he might have languished away. For the moment he had let go of the immense frustration surrounding the refugees and had found himself faced with another. Why didn't the ship go faster? Had the *Queen Mary* slowed her crossing time simply because she already held the transatlantic speed record?

Why didn't I fly? Murphy thought to himself as he gazed over the side at the glistening white hull of this moving island. *I could have stayed longer with Charles and found Elisa sooner.*

Then he remembered the rust-streaked hull of the *Darien*—the men and women and children who now sailed with no hope, no destination at all. The memory made him ashamed of his own impatience. *What must the father of little Ada-Marie be feeling?* Murphy wondered. The man was bound and gagged and impotent to protect his family against the forces of governments and the hatred of mankind.

Murphy inhaled the fresh salt air and slowly exhaled again. "I am a selfish man, Klaus," he whispered. "I do not know you, and yet I want to know you. I want to write the happy ending of your story. Forgive me, Klaus. Forgive me, God. My own unhappiness is so small next to this."

Letting his eyes trace the lacy wake of the superliner, Murphy closed his eyes and prayed again, "Here I am. Use me."

✆

The wind-weathered lifeboat onboard the *Darien* made an improbable crypt. But there, beneath a tarp, the tiny casket was reverently placed.

The days of mourning passed. Life went on. Two babies were born as the freighter limped southward shadowed by the Coast Guard cutter along the coastline. There was some reason to smile again. Life renewed itself, even here.

Children squealed and played tag beneath the shadow of the lifeboat, the small reminder of man's frailty and mortality. On occasion the philosophers among the passengers would quietly speculate on the symbolism of a lifeboat sheltering death. Some commented that such a paradox was unnatural and must certainly contain some prophecy of their own fate. When this sort of talk was whispered, the more sensible from among the passengers would wave a hand in the air as if brushing off a fly.

Maria grieved nobly for her lost child. Her head high and her shoulders squared, she resumed her role among the cooks. She caressed the faces of her other four daughters with more tenderness, but the only time the ache in her heart became evident was when she would turn around to look for her little one. "Ada-Marie? Where are you?" Then she would catch herself midthought. Her head would jerk back as if she had been slapped in the face. A moment of anguish, of memory; a fleeting glance at the lifeboat, and then she would return to the task in front of her.

Klaus seemed more visibly stricken by the death of Ada-Marie. There was no place for him to find privacy, so when the tears welled up in his eyes he made his way to the bow where the spray washed his face and gave him an excuse for the salty dampness of his cheeks. Gaunt already, Klaus appeared to stoop even more. His shoulders bowed and he seemed to have no strength left to look up. The rabbi could not offer him hope. Maria could no longer make him smile. A part of the soul of Klaus Holbein now lay still and cold in the lifeboat. He could not focus on now; he could only look backward in bitterness and forward to a dark and uncertain future. His grief for the lost one had stolen whatever joy he might have shared with his other children. His eyes could not focus on their hopeful faces.

And so Maria decided to live for her family, because life *must* continue! With this brave heart she placed her hand on the arm of Klaus one warm night beneath the starry skies.

"Klaus. It is time. Klaus, make your heart look at me."

Slowly the eyes of Klaus turned toward her. He did not speak. There was no question in his look. There was only dull obedience in his gaze. "What is it?" he asked wearily.

"It is time," Maria said again. "Awaken your heart, my dear husband, and help me to the infirmary. It is time for our baby."

❦

Tears of joy now erased the lines of grief from the face of Klaus Holbein. A lusty, angry, indignant cry erupted from the mouth of the child.

"You have a son!" Dr. Freund exclaimed, holding the bleating baby up for Klaus and Maria to marvel at. "Healthy and perfect!"

"A boy." Maria lay back exhausted but content.

"Ten toes and ten fingers." Klaus laughed. "And look! What is *that*? Well, I've never seen anything quite like *that* on one of our babies before!"

"Something to carry on the Holbein family name in the future," quipped Dr. Freund. "Such a handsome little fellow. The first boy baby we have had onboard ship. Two girls ahead of him. He will have his choice of pretty girls when he grows up!"

The baby was gently cleaned, his thick black hair washed. Dr. Freund wrapped him in a soft flannel blanket, one of those presented to the ship in New York; then he offered the baby to Maria.

"No," she said quietly, watching the new life that surged through Klaus. "Let his father hold him first."

Had there ever been a father's heart so tender? Klaus reached out awkwardly for the diminutive bundle. He cradled the baby in his long arms and let the tears fall on the blanket. "Oh," he said, and then again, "Oooooh! He is so . . . ooooh, Maria, *look* at him!"

"What will we call him, Klaus?" she asked gratefully.

Klaus turned slowly around in a circle as he placed his cheek against the soft head. "His hands . . . he has hands like hammers, so big on such a little boy." Klaus laughed. "*A son,*" the laughter seemed to say. "*The makings of a man who can wrestle an angel. Like Israel.*" "Yes, I think this one is an Israel!"

"Israel," Maria repeated. "A strong name."

"*Mazel tov*, little Israel." Dr. Freund shook the flailing fist of the baby. "Long life and happiness to you!"

In reply to the 36-point banner headline "NO ROOM AT THE INN," the *Darien* broadcast this joyous message:

> For unto us a child is born; unto us a son is given; and his name shall be called . . . ISRAEL! A healthy son is born to Klaus and Maria Holbein tonight just off Norfolk, Virginia, in American waters. We onboard the Darien face each day with hope for the future of our little ones! We pray that mercy will be found for us among the council of Evian. Destination: Havana. Supplies of canned milk and fresh fruits and vegetables are desperately needed . . . Darien.

No sooner had the birth announcement been wired to Trump than the Coast Guard cutter turned and made course directly toward the *Darien*.

In the distance Shimon and Aaron spotted the huge tower of a naval battleship heading out to sea from Norfolk. The little cutter seemed to be moving much faster than the battleship, and certainly faster than the *Darien*.

Sailors in white uniforms waved and shouted greetings as the cutter crossed the wake just behind the *Darien*. A cheer rose up from the passengers. *So these fellows were human, after all.*

The cutter slowed, and half a dozen American sailors held up a crudely painted sign: *WELCOME, BABY ISRAEL!*

Tucker translated the meaning as the cutter turned and sped away toward Norfolk. Eyes grew moist at even this small show of kindness. How different than Germany, and yet the infant was not truly welcome anywhere. Cutter 177 had not yet vanished from sight before another Coast Guard cutter was spotted coming out of the channel behind the battleship.

Moments later, it resumed the duty of shadow for the *Darien*, taking a position flanking the *Darien* between ship and shoreline.

"I cannot even swim," Aaron said unhappily. "And I would not jump for fear they would let me drown."

32

A Toast to Israel

Thousands upon thousands of Nazi Party members had swarmed to the great field of Nuremberg for the rally. Now where the Great Synagogue had once stood, troops of SS marched with awesome precision. Hour after hour, battalions of young men drilled before the spectators on the platform.

When at last the hazy dusk faded away, 130 searchlights were switched on. These lights, borrowed from a grudging Göring, were placed around the field at forty-foot intervals. Sharply defined beams rose straight up to a height of twenty thousand feet where they merged into a glowing, heavenly canopy. It seemed as though the field was a vast auditorium surrounded by mighty pillars of crystal and ice. Clouds moved like spirits through the wreath of light as a hundred thousand voices joined in songs of praise to the Aryan god who had united them in this fierce pride and an even fiercer hatred.

> "Adolf Hitler is our savior, our hero!
> He is the noblest being in all the world.
> For Hitler we live!
> For Hitler we die!
> Our Hitler is our lord
> Who rules the brave new world!"

Thomas sat among a group of twenty other Abwehr officers along the wall of Nuremberg Castle. The ancient walls of the old city seemed to glow like canvas backdrops in an opera. *Soon,* Thomas thought, *the build-*

ings of Nuremberg will be leveled like the old synagogue. If the war Hitler desired actually began, there would be ample open space for such hysterical demonstrations. But many from these multitudes would find the words of their evil hymn had come true: "For Hitler we die."

Spotlights now illuminated the platform as Adolf Hitler emerged from behind a red curtain. The song dissolved into a wild roar of ecstasy that made even the stones of the castle wall tremble. Thomas trembled with them as minutes were consumed by chants of "Heil Hitler!"

In his simple brown uniform, Hitler played out the parody of a modest leader of the plain folk of the Reich. Here was evil in imitation of goodness. Like the occult painting by Franz von Stuck, this new god lowered his chin and glared down upon his hysterical worshipers. He knew well what plans he had laid for Czechoslovakia. Now he would publicly justify his actions and receive the voiced approval of his minyans!

The Führer stepped up to the microphone, and before the listening world, he laid the guilt for his coming trespasses upon the neck of the innocent. The spell was formed and cast upon these who worshiped at his feet and upon those who merely listened: "Prague bears the responsibility for everything that happened and may happen still in Czechoslovakia!"

A roaring followed. *Yes! It is not us but the Czechs who are responsible! One Folk! One Reich! One Führer!*

"For every blow in the face of a Sudeten German, for every clubbing, for every bayonet pointed at the breast of a Sudeten German"—the voice continued to rise in a frenzied crescendo as the eyes of the audience widened and men swayed in its power—"for every shot fired, for all German tears shed, and for all German blood which has flowed! That is the awful accusation, and the entire German nation raises it!"

Once again the hysterical wave of approval swept the mass. Thomas watched in hopeless terror. *Are they listening in the government of London,* he wondered, *and are they terrified as well?*

"For every blow in the face of a Sudeten German is also a blow in the face of seventy-five million Germans in the Reich of Adolf Hitler! It is a blow in the face of a great, proud nation! It is seventy-five million persons who today accuse Prague before Europe, who once more appeal to the conscience of Europe." The Führer swept back his forelock and stepped aside.

Cheers and shouts and screams for revenge against the Czechs filled the crystal auditorium with a more virulent form of hatred.

How many of these seduced here tonight would still cry out if they could see the future? Thomas wondered. How many of these would soon lie still and cold in some distant field for the sake of this madness tonight in Nuremberg?

Profane in his glory, Adolf Hitler crossed his arms and paced across the very place where the rabbi of Nuremberg had once recited praise to the one God. The Führer seemed pleased by the adulation. The people of Germany were in his hand. Victory would bring him even greater praise; a failure could be blamed on the people themselves. After all, could he turn his will away from their desires?

Ein Volk! Ein Reich! Ein Führer!

ꙮ

Before news of the birth of Israel Holbein hit the front pages of the newspaper, Mr. Trump wanted to deliver the message to Bubbe Rosenfelt personally.

He dressed for the occasion, tying his red polka-dot bow tie with great grumbling and choosing a suit that had been pressed only last week.

From his office high above Times Square, he had a pretty good view of the world. He had kept the electric marquee that ringed the building supplied with small items about the progress of the *Darien* and the stubborn refusals by the State Department to consider anything until after the Evian Conference. The birth of the Holbein baby—Israel, no less— was going to make for some much-needed human interest.

He picked up the phone and shouted for his driver. "I have to go to Brooklyn. That's right, I'm going to Brooklyn."

Trump did not approve of flaunting wealth by hiring a chauffeur; but on the other hand, since he could not drive an automobile himself, it seemed sensible. He never admitted the fact that he could not drive. He simply pointed to the chauffeur when asked and stated that the man had needed a job.

He gave the bow tie one final tug. "How do I look?" he asked the mirror. Then he answered himself, "Like an old fool."

Before he left the building, Trump put the technician to work setting the pattern of lights for the Times Square electric headline that would flash tonight at rush hour:

> "Baby Boy Born to Grieving Darien Family . . . State Department Still Mum on Fate of Desperate Passengers!"

The story was written for the late edition with the strict orders that not a word of the event was to be breathed outside the building lest the *New York Times* be scooped by Hearst or Craine.

He had not called ahead to the Brooklyn home of Bubbe Rosenfelt. He did not want to get her hopes up about the U.S. visas, and he also did not want to scare her to death. She was, after all, probably almost as old as he was and had undergone quite enough grief and worries these past weeks.

As the sleek black car drove across the Brooklyn Bridge, Trump now was sorry he had not called. Suppose the appearance of a black limousine at her doorstep in Brooklyn shocked her? "Pull over at a public phone," Trump ordered his driver. He would call her—warn her that he was in Brooklyn and just wanted to stop by and see Charles.

This seemed a sensible plan. The limousine of Harold Trump glided down into the flat, vast immensity of Brooklyn. It elicited respectful stares from the Italians, who assumed a gangland meeting was scheduled; from the Irish, who assumed a bishop was traveling to visit a local parish; and finally from the Jews, who could only assume that someone had died and the mortician was on his way to make arrangements.

When at last Trump decided on an appropriate filling station from which to make his call, he found that he was in the heart of the Jewish district and merely a block away from Bubbe Rosenfelt's boxlike brownstone.

He called her. A young woman answered. There were squeals of laughter in the background. Children. Lots of them.

"*Oy!* Such a racket! I can't hear you!"

"Mr. Trump calling for Mrs. Rosenfelt, please!" he replied loudly since the din of traffic and street vendors was also deafening on his end of things.

"Children! *Oy!* Quiet! Somebody for Bubbe, I think! You want Mrs. Trudence Rosenfelt? *Who* are you?"

"Harold Trump. Publisher of the—"

"*Oy vey!* Mr. *Trump!* Why didn't you say so? She's out at the bakery. Just down the street from here. Can you call back in a few minutes? It's Friday, and we're getting ready for Shabbat, so—"

Trump looked out through the glass of the phone booth. There was a bakery across the street, crowded with women. Trump recognized the black dress. The cane slung over the arm. The ramrod straight back. Bubbe Rosenfelt was in front of the bakery with six other women. Her arms were full of bags. She was admiring a baby in a black pram. "Thank you," Trump said to the young woman on the phone. "I found her." He hung up the receiver and stepped out. He called her name across the clamor of cars and buses between them.

"Mrs. Rosenfelt! Mrs. Rosenfelt!"

Some of the women had seen the black limousine and were wondering who had died. Then Bubbe Rosenfelt spotted Mr. Trump in his semi-rumpled suit and crooked red polka-dot bow tie. *Such a fine-looking man!* Her eyes widened. She raised her pince-nez up to be sure. Then she smiled and waved and cupped her hand, "Are you lost?" she called, and then again, "Are you lost, Mr. Trump?"

This was not as he had planned it. "It's a boy!" he shouted back. "Maria has a baby boy! Named *Israel*!"

ᕽ

Like an elephant calling for her mate, the whistles of the *Queen* bellowed her arrival to all of Southampton and beyond. Murphy could picture the men of southern England gathered in their little pubs tonight. No doubt they paused at the deep vibration of the ship's horn and remarked with an air of proprietorship, "Well, the ol' garl's come home."

There were lights everywhere in the harbor. Lights on tugs. Lights on the docks. Lights leading up to High Street. The liner floated on a dark pool reflecting the stars, and the shoreline was a galaxy of stars where sky and water met. Murphy enjoyed the sense of magic the late-evening arrival provided. Somewhere in all that galaxy Elisa was no doubt watching this bright island gliding toward its berth. Again the ship's horn bellowed.

Murphy turned away from the rail now and moved through the press of passengers and the wood-paneled shopping deck of Picadilly Circus and out to where the boarding ramp would soon be locked into place. The galaxy now consisted of streetlamps and windows and shiny asphalt. Murphy wanted to be the first man off the ship, the first through customs, and the first out through the gates to where a crowd of two thousand well-wishers waited. Elisa would be there, where he had last seen her on the quay, and they would start all over again tonight.

ᕽ

"John Lee Murphy?" The sour-looking man in the ill-fitting pin-striped suit flipped open his badge folder. He had the look of a plain-clothes policeman; Murphy would have guessed his occupation even without the badge. There were two other men flanking him. All three were thick-soled stereotypes right out of a bad Dashiell Hammett story.

"John Lee Murphy?" the big man in the center asked again.

"Only to my mother. When she's unhappy with me." He managed a grin. The men did not smile back. The small fellow nearest the counter nodded to the customs officer who stamped Murphy's passport and waved him through without bothering to inspect his tan pigskin suitcase or Elisa's steamer trunk.

"Come with us, please," the big man in the center ordered curtly. *The Marx brothers in pin-striped suits*, Murphy thought as he was surrounded and led off toward a door marked *Cunard Lines Information*.

"What is this?" Murphy asked, suddenly fearful that something terrible had happened to Elisa. Maybe these men had been sent to tell him. *One to give him the bad news and two to hold him down?*

The door of the office closed behind them before the big man answered. "We are quite certain you have been followed."

Instinctively Murphy put a hand to his taped nose. He had thought the Fritz Kuhn gang had finished with him in New York. "Where's Elisa?" he asked. A real sense of dread settled upon him.

"Your Mr. Trump has paid quite handsomely for bodyguards for her. You certainly cannot imagine we would have allowed her to come *here*?"

Murphy simply blinked at them, then sighed. These guys had taken his beating on the roof of the Woolworth seriously. He was grateful. "Then she's okay?" he responded with relief, then frowned. "And you think the heat is still on? I was tailed on the ship?"

The three exchanged looks. *Americans! Will they never learn to talk?* "We thought it best to make certain of her safety because of your involvement with the Jewish refugees and her involvement with the Czech government. Especially at this moment in world affairs. There is no way to accurately gauge her vulnerability. We take matters of protection seriously."

Murphy felt overwhelmed with gratitude. These fellas had really taken care of Elisa—made sure she was okay, not taken any chances with her. He couldn't have done any better himself, he mused. Their measure of concern probably far outweighed the possible threat. So she had been in good hands, after all.

"Where is she now?" he asked.

"An hour's drive from here." The big man stepped back and opened a door that led to a long corridor with rooms opening off either side. At the far end he warned Murphy. "In, and then out the other side—"

No time to question. The door opened to the honking of horns and voices of passengers screaming for cabs. A long black Rolls-Royce waited three steps away with the door open. The big man preceded Murphy and then a little shove moved Murphy into the car. The door slammed behind him at the same instant the big man opened the opposite door and stepped out into yet another black automobile pointed the opposite way. Murphy slipped into the second car and closed the door behind him. The first Rolls sped away to the east as Murphy's car slipped out into the westbound traffic.

The windows were curtained with green velvet. Murphy resisted the urge to look out. He grinned at the unsmiling big man who seemed irritated by the very presence of Murphy.

"Quite a little shell game you've got here," Murphy said as the traffic thinned and the car bumped over a series of railroad tracks. "You know— hide the pea under the walnut shell and move the shells around—"

The big man cleared his throat and ignored the comment. He removed a pipe from his vest pocket. "Mind if I smoke?" he asked. Without waiting for a reply, he filled his pipe and lit it.

An hour in the back of this curtained car with this surly grouch? Murphy tried again. "I appreciate the way you fellas have taken care of Elisa. I don't think I caught your name." Murphy extended his hand.

"Tedrick. Amos Tedrick," came the reply and the handshake. This was better. A bit more human. "Quite all right. That's our job, making certain a woman of your wife's notoriety remains safe."

"Notoriety?" Murphy repeated. "Not a word I would have chosen for Elisa."

Tedrick shrugged. "Shall I say fame, then? Of course, you must have known that a woman could not foil an assassination plot against the president of Czechoslovakia and not arouse curiosity, at least, on the part of the Gestapo." Tedrick puffed his pipe, filling the interior of the car with smoke. "I am surprised you did not arrange for this sort of protection for her *before* you were attacked in New York." He frowned. "Certainly you are not considering taking her with you when you go on to—"

"Evian," Murphy replied, suddenly feeling the weight of a veiled accusation from Tedrick. "I had thought . . . if her schedule—"

Tedrick's eyebrows went up in astonishment. Then he let them slide back down in thought and cocked one in a gesture that said, *What an absolute lunatic! This man must want his wife dead or maimed . . . or kidnapped and taken to Germany to prison!* "Well, well," Tedrick said at last.

Everything Murphy had decided about never letting her out of his sight now seemed foolish. How could she go with him to Evian with this Czech crisis in the headlines every day? Might the Gestapo still consider her to be some sort of link, just as Beneš had warned him in Prague? At least here she was under the watchful eye of professionals; under the care of the BBC, no less. Murphy coughed from the smoke. "Evian will probably be crawling with Gestapo agents," he said. "I . . . think you're right about that. She's better off in England. Under protection."

Tedrick nodded once. He smiled from behind his pipe. "Now *here's* a sensible man." He congratulated Murphy, even as he inwardly congratulated himself in the handling of this inconvenience.

൭

That evening at the Shabbat meal, Trump sat wedged tightly between Charles and Bubbe Rosenfelt. There were fourteen altogether around the table. A big family. Nieces and nephews, the youngest of whom was two-year-old Franklin Delano Rosenfelt.

"A pistol," Trump declared upon meeting the child.

"Our little kochleffl," declared his young mother with a laugh.

"Like a cooking spoon," explained Bubbe, "always stirring things up, *nu?*"

The entire joyous evening was spent in translation and counter-translation of the Yiddish. Occasionally Charles tested the sounds against his lovely new mouth. Nothing yet seemed to come out quite right; it would be a long time, Bubbe warned, before Charles was speaking perfect Yiddish.

Here in Brooklyn and beneath the electric headlines in Times Square, toasts were raised to the birth of baby Israel. Bubbe Rosenfelt expressed only one regret. "If only I could see the bris milah of my great-grandson."

"Circumcision," explained a niece. "For Jewish baby boys this is a ceremony on the eighth day, which is very important."

This wish, expressed after one of the finest meals Trump had ever eaten in his life, was a request that he considered seriously. Within thirty seconds after the words had fallen from Bubbe's mouth, Mr. Trump had already written the headlines:

> "Great-Grandmother Travels by Fishing Vessel to Witness
> Dedication of Infant to God!"

Ah, yes. This might be too good to pass up. A few photos, plus a story about the ceremony, and within the time it took to read the article, this little boy would belong to all of America!

Trump narrowed his eyes in thought as he remembered the Coast Guard cutter assigned to keep all other vessels away from the little freighter. Might he take Bubbe Rosenfelt with him to Cuba? Out of the authority of the Americans?

Trump dabbed his lips on the white linen napkin and addressed Bubbe over the racket of fourteen voices that all seemed to be talking at once. "Well, I'm no fairy godfather, but if you'd like to go to Cuba—"

"Cuba?"

"We have arranged for the ship to be resupplied there. We are also attempting to acquire temporary landing certificates for the passengers—"

"Cuba?" Bubbe Rosenfelt raised her pince-nez to her nose in disbelief. "Could I see them there? The *baby?*"

All conversation stopped midsentence. Thirteen sets of eyes locked on Trump. He could do that? He could take Bubbe to Cuba to be with Klaus and Maria and the children?

"We are still negotiating with the Cubans—a little awkward, since all the immigration big shots are in Evian. But we can do our best, if you'd like."

Bubbe's eyes shone brightly in the Shabbat candles. "The Lord is good," she whispered. "I'll pack. Right after I help with the dishes."

33

Snow White's Cottage

The Rolls-Royce crept slowly over the rutted land. They had, in fact, traveled much longer than the promised hour—not because they had covered a great distance, but because of the condition of the roads. At last Tedrick pulled back the green velvet curtain on his side of the car and opened the window slightly. Murphy followed suit, grateful to be able to breathe fresh air at last.

The roadsides were lined with stands of beech tress for miles, and then the gnarled trunks of giant oak trees gleamed like silver sentinels in the reflection of the headlights. The countryside rolled gently. *More gently than the Rolls*, Murphy thought wryly. He had the sense that they would come upon the characters of Shakespeare's *A Midsummer Night's Dream* just around the bend.

"Are we lost?" he asked at last.

"Only to the world, Mr. Murphy. Actually you are in the center of New Forest."

"Crown lands." Murphy searched his memory for whatever musty textbook information he had about this section of England. *Ancient Royal Hunting Grounds* was all he could come up with. As if to confirm his memory, they heard the distant, ghostly baying of hounds. Murphy shuddered slightly as he remembered tales of Sherlock Holmes and *The Hound of the Baskervilles*. "You have a flair for the dramatic, Mr. Tedrick," he joked.

"Purely unrehearsed, I assure you," Tedrick answered. "We just passed the kennels of the New Forest hunt. The hounds tend to bay if an automobile passes on the lane at night." He dumped the ashes of his pipe out the window. "Natural alarm system against poachers or intruders."

The driver maneuvered the car over increasingly bad roads, turning onto lanes that were little more than old carriage tracks. Crossing over a barren ridge, Murphy looked out over a dark, wooded valley below. Other names returned to his memory: *Boldrewood. Mark Ash Wood. Knightwood, where ancient oaks measured twenty feet in girth.* Indeed this man Tedrick enjoyed the drama of the mysterious, the sense of the medieval.

"How much longer?" Murphy asked, trying not to sound like a kid in the backseat.

In answer to his question, Tedrick raised a massive arm and pointed to the edge of the wooded valley. A single light shone. And then as the car moved closer, Murphy could see that the light was one window, then two.

"Elisa's requirement was privacy," Tedrick explained. "We have tried to meet that requirement. A small hunting cottage. Quite remote, and yet comfortable—except for a lack of electricity. There are ample oil lamps. I doubt you will notice the lack."

Murphy considered how he might reply to that, but thought better of it. "If there is no electricity, then I assume there is no telephone. No radio."

"Privacy," Tedrick repeated. "Three days, and then we will send a car for you. You'll make it back to Southampton in time to catch your steamer to France."

Murphy considered that he would be able to jog to the cottage much faster than the car was moving. He did not take his eyes from the lighted windows. There, within that solitary halo, was his galaxy.

The cottage was of white stone with a thatched roof and heavy, time-blackened beams. Windowsills and doorjambs were all crooked; Murphy could see the light emanating from the cracks as if the cottage could not hold it. Yet another car was parked to the side of the cottage, and at the sound of tires the door opened and Elisa stepped out.

She stood framed in the doorway. A cream-colored cotton skirt and blouse gave her an almost golden glow in the lamplight that shone behind her. She put her hands on her hips like a farmwife waiting for her tardy husband to come home. Murphy felt as if he could not breathe until she was in his arms. Before the wheels stopped, he was out. She moved toward him, and they met somewhere between the darkness and the light. Kisses and tears mingled together, and Murphy forgot that anyone was with them, watching this reunion in the woods of Titania. Here was magic. He buried his face in the nape of her neck and inhaled the sweetness of her skin. She kissed his ear and tangled her fingers in his hair with careless, joyful passion.

"Elisa." He managed to say her name at last.

She laughed. "You missed me." This was a fact, not a question. Then she pushed him back a bit and looked around. No one remained outside with them. Murphy could see four men gathered in the front room of the low-ceilinged cottage. There was a fire in the open hearth, although it was not cold outside.

Murphy drew a deep breath of frustration. "How do we get rid of them?"

"I have arranged everything." She stood on tiptoe and cradled his chin in her hand as she kissed his mouth again. Then she stopped short. "Your nose!" she cried.

"Your hair!" he replied. "You cut it. Like Myrna Loy. I like it."

"Does it hurt?" She seemed overwhelmed by the green and purple blotches that were only now fading from his face.

"Only when I try to kiss you too long."

At the sound of their laughter, Tedrick ducked and put his head out to call them. "We'll have to be going soon," he remarked in an almost military manner. "The rector is already three hours later than we told him."

"Rector?" Murphy asked.

"Remember I told you Tedrick said our wedding ceremony was not legal," Elisa responded. "We're not officially married."

Murphy shook his head, trying to clear his mind and comprehend what she was saying. Maybe they *had* entered an enchanted forest after all. There certainly didn't seem to be any other rational explanation.

"You don't think I would spend three days alone with you without being married, do you?" Elisa smiled up into his eyes.

He was lost. Nuts about her. Anything she wanted. He would marry her again and stay in this cottage as royal game warden if she wanted. "Since we've already had our honeymoon, do you mind if we go for the short version of the ceremony?"

❧

Only embers remained glowing on the hearth. Night sounds surrounded the little cottage. The hooting of an owl. A million crickets. The song of a nightingale.

"It sounds like this back home in the woods," Murphy said quietly as Elisa lay in his arms. "When I was a kid, we used to go out camping. There are woods just beyond the farm. My brother Terry and I would pitch Pop's old pup tent and camp out there like we were Yukon explorers."

Elisa answered with a sigh and smiled in the darkness as if they were there now, a few hundred yards from Murphy's house. "And then what did you do?"

"Roasted hot dogs and pretended it was big game. Told stories. Talked about the places we wanted to go when we grew up. Funny, I feel closer to home tonight than I ever have before. Clear across the ocean with you beside me, Elisa, I am closer than I ever was last week in New York or fifteen years ago in that tent with Terry." He kissed her forehead and stroked her hair. "You are home to me."

"And the two shall become one flesh," Elisa whispered. "And you are *home* to me, Murphy." She lifted her face to kiss his chin and then pressed herself against his side. She ran her fingers gently across the tape that still encircled his ribs. "Does it hurt?" she asked.

Murphy put his hand on hers. "Eve must have asked Adam the same question."

"And how did he answer?" She punctuated the question with a lingering kiss.

"Nothing hurts anymore," Murphy replied, his lips still close to hers. "Not as long as you are near. Nothing hurts."

❦

Maria could hardly repeat the message Captain Burton presented to her that morning. The paper fluttered in her hand as she held it up to Klaus.

"Please," she whispered as the girls gathered around her and the baby in concern.

Klaus cleared his throat.

> "GRANDMOTHER ROSENFELT EN ROUTE TO MIAMI STOP REQUESTED ATTENDANCE AT CIRCUMCISION CEREMONY OF ISRAEL IN OPEN INTERNATIONAL WATERS STOP ARRANGEMENTS BEING MADE FOR THAT POSSIBILITY STOP FURTHER DETAILS WILL BE SENT AS THEY DEVELOP STOP BUBBE SAYS MAZEL TOV STOP LOVE TO ALL STOP TRUMP"

"Bubbe?" squeaked Trudy. "She is coming *here*, Mama?"

They all turned to gape at Captain Burton, who could only smile and shrug. "Trump has a reputation for getting his way."

"So does Bubbe Rosenfelt." Klaus grinned and reached down to touch the cheek of his nursing son. "Well, little Israel, what do you think? You are about to become an international incident."

Captain Burton laughed. No one had ever seen him laugh before. He nodded slightly toward Maria. "If we are to have guests, perhaps I should tell the rest of the passengers. They may wish to plan something special for the occasion."

"Of course it is possible!" Shimon almost shouted to the dozen men who sat beside him near the anchor chain.

"Well, something certainly must be done in honor of such an occasion," agreed a middle-aged ex-bank clerk named Fredrik, who seldom agreed with anything at all.

The rabbi of Nuremberg nodded in approval. "They say the choir in the Temple sang entirely without instruments, *nu*? What do they call that, Shimon?"

"A cappella," Shimon answered. "The Vienna Boys' Choir sings all the time in the great cathedral of St. Stephan's. Beautiful. *Beautiful!*"

"You have heard this?" asked the rabbi. "In a cathedral?"

"He is a musician," Aaron defended. "Sometimes they have to go into such places to listen to or play music."

"Well, then," the rabbi concluded, "if those goyim boys can perform this in such a place as St. Stephan's, why can we not do the same in honor of the child's circumcision?" His lower lip protruded slightly. "The Eternal, blessed be He, has given the Holbeins a son after the loss of their little one. And now this son is to be circumcised and named *Israel*! *Oy!* Such blessing! A little prince of God has come to our ship of suffering!"

"Well, then," said the bank clerk, "what symphony shall we perform for our little Israel?"

"Schubert!" cried Aaron. "A Jewish composer, *ja*?"

Shimon furrowed his brow in thought and shook his head. "I will tell you something. In Germany, the prison where we have come from, it is not lawful for a Jew to sing or play anything except what is written by Jewish composers. I myself saw a fellow beaten to death because he hummed a few bars of Beethoven's Fifth." He demonstrated. "*Bah-Bah-Bah Baaaaaaaah!* Just like that, he was dead. So all the time when I am shoveling coal into their furnaces like a man caught in hell, my mind is singing over and over again. I am quietly dreaming of all the music I used to play and listen to and hum! *Now* I say . . . we are free men, free to roam all over this ocean and free to sing whatever we wish to sing. And my heart can shout Beethoven's Fifth, and they cannot stop me."

The bank clerk disagreed. "Too severe. The Fifth is too . . . noisy for a circumcision! We will have little Israel squawking like a cat with his tail in a door."

"No, no, no," Shimon corrected. "Not the *first* movement."

"Listen to Shimon. He is from Vienna!" said the rabbi.

"Yes. Our maestro from the Musikverein, *ja*?" Aaron chuckled, and the fellows in his work crew joined him in an infectious laughter. They would become an orchestra—bass fiddle and oboe and violin and tympani and cello would soon come from their throats. Such joy, and all for little Israel!

"Yes!" The rabbi of Nuremberg was also laughing. Others came around and they laughed, too, although they were not quite certain what they were laughing at. "Shimon is the maestro! If he has Beethoven swimming in his brain, then it is time we rescue poor Beethoven!"

And so the matter was settled. "All right, then, we will perform the second movement of Beethoven's Fifth Symphony! *Andante con moto!* It is perfect for our little prince Israel! Probably it was performed in Solomon's Temple, Rebbe! And Beethoven found the old score and copied it!"

"Don't tell the Nazis!" hooted Aaron.

"Well, good music is good music," said the rabbi. "And the Eternal, blessed be He forever, will enjoy our concert also, even if the composer was not a Jew!"

∽

Elisa's report that Leah had arrived safely in Paris lifted yet one more pain from Murphy's heart. He would wire Charles in New York. He would tell him his brother was safe, and that he and Elisa had spent three days in Snow White's cottage like in the movie!

The timbers of the cottage had been hewn and shaped by hand some time before the Spanish armada had been demolished by the ships of Elizabeth's navy. The ceiling was low enough that Murphy had to duck his head as he walked across the room. Everything looked like a Beatrix Potter painting inside. Cups hung in an open sideboard. Plates were lined up on a plate rail. The sink had a hand pump for water. A wood cookstove provided warmth for heating the teakettle and cooking meals with the ample supply of canned goods Tedrick had provided. There were apples and wine and an assortment of breads and pastries to last them three days or longer, even if they did not take a breath between bites. Perhaps a yeoman farmer had built this place before the Tudors ruled England. Generations of gamekeepers had lived here, protecting the red deer against poachers.

There were carpets of primroses and bluebells just beyond the first stand of trees. Hazy sunlight dappled the branches and gave each color a thousand varied shades.

Murphy dried the breakfast dishes as Elisa washed. It had been a Beatrix Potter sort of breakfast, too—coddled eggs and melon and black bread with unsalted butter. Elisa hummed as she rinsed the plates. She looked out the window over the sink. The light bathed her with gold and shades of blue from the flowers. Such beauty made Murphy's heart ache with the joy of it. He had seen her in sequins at a castle; he had marveled at her in the footlights; he had reeled at the moonglow on her ivory skin; but here, in this plain place, yet another dimension was added to his love for her.

After a time she looked up, surprised at his quizzical smile. "What?" she asked, blushing.

"I was just thinking. . . ." He touched her cheek lightly. "I used to wonder how I could take you away from all the glamour of your life. You know, how could I ask you to go back to a farm in Pennsylvania—"

"And now?" Her hands immersed in dishwater, she waited, unmoving, for his answer.

He kissed her gently. "I think you'll do fine."

He drew back and still she did not move. Her eyes closed, she stood dreaming of all the things he had told her about through the night. "If only we could be there now," she whispered at last. And when she opened her eyes, they were filled with tears.

Murphy laughed lightly. "Well, you're the one who wanted to play for the BBC," he said, and instantly their peace was shattered.

Elisa did not answer. She did not dare reply. Mechanically, she turned back to her task.

"Well, didn't you?" Murphy asked a little more harshly this time. Her lack of response somehow irritated him. "It could have been just like this, you know. We would have gone on to Pennsylvania, and—"

Her eyes flashed angrily at him. She thrust a plate into his hands. "Did you come here to fight with me? If you knew—" She stopped short. Any more of this and she would answer his challenge with the truth. She could not do that. She would not.

"And I can say the same to you—if you knew what I have been going through with you over here and me over there. The nights without you. And little Charles! The poor boy has had to put up with me all the time. What do I know about kids? If it hadn't been for Bubbe Rosenfelt—"

Elisa was crying. Angry at Murphy for not knowing, and angry at herself because she could not tell him! "What do you want from me, Murphy, what? It's done now. Finished! We have been together less than twelve hours, and we're fighting!" With that, she stormed from the house and retreated down a footpath blending into the shadows as Murphy watched miserably from the doorway.

He banged his head on a timber. "Right, Murphy. Really nice. Really bright. You're a swell guy, Murphy," he chided himself as he sank into a rocking chair beside the cheerless hearth.

What must have been a roaring stream in the spring was now only a trickle. Elisa sat on a stone beside a little pool where stranded guppies hoped for rain. The weight of all the world beyond New Forest rested heavily on her.

If only Murphy knew. She had been forced to miss the ship, bullied and ordered and coaxed and coached. If only Murphy knew. She had even been taught how to use a gun. What would he say if he knew all this? if he found out she had gone back to Paris and had met Thomas again?

But of course Murphy could not know. Not now. And if the Gestapo caught up with her, maybe he would never know the full truth. For now, until her family was safely out of the path of danger, she dared not tell him. Tedrick would bring the passports. Murphy would carry them to Prague for her. Czechoslovakia would stand or fall, and then she could tell him.

Tedrick, she thought, *is very polite in his blackmail. He held my family hostage by simply threatening that they could not get away. He held no gun to their heads like the Nazis. His way was civilized and urbane. He used his power without conscience, but at least he had no blood on his hands. Not directly, anyway.*

Her only consolation was the hope that she might really be doing something to help. Certainly Thomas had been grateful to see her, anxious to tell her everything.

If she had not fallen in love with Murphy, this would all seem right and easy. But she was in love—*one flesh*; not being able to tell him everything was a cold, sharp blade between them.

Elisa gazed heavenward through the fluttering leaves. "Tell me what I should do," she prayed. But there was no answer. No answer. Only silence in her heart. The knife remained painful in her as she walked back to the cottage

Murphy had finished the dishes. He looked up when her shadow crossed the floor in front of his chair. Neither of them spoke for a long time. She walked toward him and sat down on the floor, laying her head against his knee. He touched her head gently.

"Forgive me?" he whispered. "You must have had a reason."

Thank You, Lord, that he didn't ask. "You know I would have gone. I would not have stayed here for anything without you. It just *happened*. Forgive me, Murphy."

"No more about it, huh?" He pulled her up until she sat in his lap like a little girl. "We have three days now in Snow White's cottage." She looked puzzled and he laughed. "I forgot you haven't seen the movie. It's all the rage in New York. I took Charles to see it, and—"

Murphy rattled on as if no harsh words had ever been spoken. Bit by bit he told her the details of everything that had happened in New York, from the wonder of Times Square to the arrival of the *Darien* and the death of the little girl. And then he spoke of his hope for those people and the importance of the Evian Conference next week.

The dam of his silence had broken, and he hardly noticed that Elisa had no real news to tell him—no concerts to report or trips shopping. She listened to him silently, wishing she could have been part of it all.

Later they walked hand in hand back to the stranded pool where the stream had been. They made love on a blanket beneath the trees, and he quoted Song of Songs to her again, *"This is my beloved, and this is my friend."*

If only you knew, she thought. *Oh, darling, if only you could know!*

34

United Voices

The sun beat down on their heads as men and women lined up to try out for the *Darien* Symphony Orchestra. An entire orchestra was required to play Beethoven's Symphony No. 5 in C minor, op. 67. Of course, only the second movement would be performed, but who could know what occasion they might have to perform yet another symphony?

Those with the quality of strings in their voices were selected in groups of first and second violin, viola, cello, and bass fiddle. Brass and woodwinds were also divided into groups, and then Shimon spent an hour alone with each group in the bow daily as he rehearsed their parts.

"How does he know all this?" asked Aaron's younger companion, who was a cello.

"He played the kettledrums," Aaron the oboe explained with authority. "He learned everyone's parts while he waited for his turn to play."

So great was the response at the auditions that Shimon doubled the size of the orchestra. When others came and asked to join, he discarded the thought that the orchestra must be a certain number of this or that. In the end he had fifty-seven cellos. Fifty-nine first and second violins, and so on. Those who were passable musicians themselves became first and second chair and coaches who helped rehearse the passages and the particular sound of each vocal instrument. Morning, noon, and night the 214 members of the *Darien* Symphony Orchestra could be heard humming their parts as they worked, stood in the dinner line, washed dishes, or cleaned latrines. At night as the hammocks swung easily in the dark holds, the cacophony of unmatched notes competed with the sounds of the engine and the groaning hull. Nothing at all seemed to fit together. Each part was different. Each instrument had a different sound. Each musician hummed the part with a little different shading.

"*Oy!*" remarked the rabbi who had been excluded from the orchestra because he was a rabbi, after all, and so he had to perform the circumcision. "If such a racket makes *one moment* of sense, then I shall declare the miracle of it before the congregation."

"You will see, Rebbe," came the constant reply. "You will see."

On the fourth day, Maestro Shimon Feldstein began rehearsing sections of musicians together on the stern. All the string players came together jabbering and excited. Violinists without violins. Cellists without cellos. Bass fiddle players came with empty hands, yet with voices tuned and all the notes memorized completely.

They sat as a proper orchestra would. "Cellos and bass fiddles there to my right. Yes, *that's* it. Fredrik, you are first-chair cellist. Yes, as my wife, Leah, was in Vienna. Violas and second violins here in front of me. First violins to the left—such a *big* string section. Are you ready?" Shimon's hands were damp with perspiration as he lowered his head for a moment and found the pitch. And there it was. He raised his arm and all the other voices found their notes. And then he began. "Cellos—ah, yes, *cellos!* Mellow, *beautiful.* Now, violins—yes, yes. Can you hear?" The melody and counterpoint rose to the heavens as Beethoven must have conceived it, as God must have sent it to him in the night. It was no longer the sound of 150 string players each singing alone, but an orchestra to rival those young goyim fellows at St. Stephan's. "Build the music; think of our little prince Israel. Play *boldly* now—"

By evening the horns and woodwinds had joined together. No one seemed to want to stop when the dinner bell rang. It was, indeed, beautiful!

The signal from the German War Ministry was clear. General Beck was informed by Hitler that the army was an instrument of the state, and that Hitler was the head of the state, and therefore Beck and all the forces of the army owed him unquestioning obedience. On this discordant note, General Beck retreated to Munich and placed his signature on a letter of resignation.

If the heads of the British government and the French government shuddered at this news, it was not visible to the outside world. This defiant signature by a German of honor and integrity quietly confirmed the worst fears of those men of power who had been enlightened by the message carried by Elisa.

One day later, England and France announced that they would stand by their commitment to defend Czechoslovakia if she was attacked. To this gesture, Hitler responded by replacing Beck with General Halder and raising the level of his fury against the Czechs. He did not tremble, so sure was he of the hesitance of Chamberlain and Daladier to go to war.

⚭

It was well past 1:00 AM by the time the last of the conspirators left the home of Canaris. There would be one final briefing for Thomas before he returned to Paris.

His eyes animated, Canaris paced the length of the office, then back again like an expectant father in a waiting room. Indeed, the plot against Hitler conceived so many weeks ago was about to be given birth.

"The divisions are in place, Thomas. Hitler's own military plans against the Czechs have placed him where we need him to be. The date he has given for the acceptance of the ultimatum will be his last day in power." Canaris held up a clenched fist in exultation. He jerked his head toward the map of Berlin and the surrounding countryside. With a snap of his fingers he indicated the area south of Berlin where the Führer had placed General Erich Hoepner's Third Panzer Division.

"The Third Division will be no more than a night's march from here!" Thomas exclaimed, catching the fever of Canaris' enthusiasm.

"Exactly." Canaris gazed happily at the map. "Hoepner and the Third Panzer will occupy Berlin while the rest of the army is occupied on the border of Czechoslovakia."

"Only one division. Is it enough?"

"General von Witzleben has joined with us. With his division here as well—" he rubbed his hands together—"Count Helldorf has made meticulous arrangements to arrest Hitler, Göring, Goebbels, and Himmler here in Berlin. Witzleben's Berlin garrison will storm the Chancellery at the signal. Tanks and artillery will be moved into position to hold the Ministry of Propaganda and the Chancellery SS units at bay until von Brockdorff and the Pottsdam garrison arrive. We take over the Ministry of Propaganda and immediately we hold the power of the nation in our hands. General Halder will begin his broadcasts then. He will read the document we have prepared that states the peril Hitler has put us in. The people have great respect for our military leaders." He frowned. "I only wish that General Beck might have been with us at this moment. The document will have been presented to Hitler beforehand, and no man can accuse us of treason."

Thomas smiled doubtfully. "As long as we pull it off we will not be traitors, you mean."

"Quite." Canaris rubbed his chin thoughtfully. "The military take-over will be in effect long enough to restore the Constitution. We will offer the German people a glimpse of the truth in the meantime. Publish the facts. Adolf Hitler is indeed the German god of creation, and now he begins his efforts to destroy what has been created. They will listen and will understand how he has deceived them. Ultimately, a war in Europe will destroy us. They must listen. . . ."

Mentally, Thomas ticked off the impressive list of military leaders involved in the plot. Canaris was right. The people would acquiesce when the deed was accomplished and the fallacies of Hitler's plans were brought to light. The troops of the SS units might dare to fight the coup, but their numbers were small in comparison to the regular army. And without Himmler, they would have no diabolical leadership to follow. Would this result in civil war? The question had been asked a thousand times over the last desperate weeks. There was a possibility, of course, but the bloodshed would be minimal compared to what devastation might lay ahead for Germany if Hitler carried out his threats.

"And so—" Canaris patted Thomas on the back—"what is the mood in England?"

"Trenches in Hyde Park, and gas masks are being issued."

"Good. They are expecting war. Expecting Prime Minister Chamberlain to hold by his commitments to the Czechs. These are matters which I will make certain Hitler hears. Such news will cause even his black heart to question his wisdom. If he wavers—if he pulls back—then we are saved a lot of trouble and bloodshed. Not to mention the fact that his public prestige will be damaged here in Germany. Yes, this is all good news." Canaris sat down in the enormous leather desk chair that dwarfed him. "You must get word to your contact. Do not tell her everything that is happening here. No names. No details, of course. If the Gestapo should catch her, such information would be easily extracted from her. Then all would be lost." He tapped his hand on the desk blotter. "Make no mention of a coup."

"What can I tell her that she can offer to the British leaders? What can we give them that will strengthen their resolve but not give us away?"

Canaris chewed his lip as he swiveled to stare out the window at the hazy autumn sunlight. "Just this. The German military is utterly opposed to further aggression against the Czechs or any land. She must tell them that the words of the Führer are pure bluff."

"But they are not bluff!" Thomas protested, as certain as anyone that Hitler did indeed intend to invade the Czech territory.

"His threats are not a bluff simply because the man is utterly mad! Given the condition of our armed forces, we would not last three months if the English and the French joined forces with the Czech divisions. Even alone, the Czechs could last for months against us. The bluff, Thomas, is in the fact that we are not invincible, as Hitler proclaims!" He slammed his fist on the desk. "Can't you see? He has deluded the world as he has deluded the German people. We are not a master race, Thomas. We are men! As such we will bleed and die, and in the end after so much blood and so many millions of corpses, the bluff of Adolf Hitler will be discovered! Let us save the world a lot of misery and reveal the lie now, eh? So tell your contact that Hitler is bluffing. Tell her that the British must also bluff or we shall all lose the game." He frowned. "You have in your mind the figures of the document we have prepared to show the Führer?"

"Yes." Thomas ran through the information dealing with the unreadiness of the German Army to face a major conflict.

"Good. Then give her that information as well. It is no secret. Let the British agent carry that to the British Intelligence Service and then to the prime minister. If that does not stiffen the backbone of Chamberlain, I cannot think what will."

In the musty-smelling file room of Berlin's Gestapo headquarters, Georg Wand huddled over the report like a college student studying for an exam.

He had a list of items that he had extracted easily from the British agent Shelby Pence. She had been a willing and eager informer. Still, there was not much she told him that he had not already known. Every fact about the Vienna existence of Elisa Linder had been gathered already by sources in Vienna. Her friendship with Leah Feldstein, the Zionist. Her relationship with Rudy Dorbransky. Her aid in hiding the Kronenberger twins, and the fact that they had obviously managed to escape the Reich. None of that seemed to be of any importance. Only one small item had surprised Wand. "Lindheim's Department Store. Elisa Lindheim. Daughter of Theo Lindheim. Christian-Jew Theo Lindheim!"

How was it, Georg wondered, that the connection had not been made before this? It was no wonder that Elisa Linder was actively assisting Jews! She herself was a Jewess—not a resident and citizen of Prague as she claimed, but rather a German citizen. This information was not only startling, but made all the time and effort he had spent in London suddenly worthwhile. There was nothing else of substance that Shelby Pence had offered. But this was *everything* he needed.

This scrap of information led Wand to another file. At one time Elisa Lindheim had been in love with a young Wehrmacht officer. The Gestapo had investigated him. He was now a member of the Abwehr staff of Admiral Canaris and stationed in Paris. *In Paris!*

Wand smiled at the thoroughness of the investigation of Thomas von Kleistmann. The young officer had been careful about covering his tracks if he was an anti-Nazi, but all the details of his love affair with this Jewess were still on record. Might they not still be lovers? The thought was intriguing. The past association with this woman at least made von Kleistmann worth another look.

Closing the file cabinet, Georg glanced at his watch. Paris was only a few hours away.

The last quiet morning in New Forest, Elisa lay beside Murphy as he slept. Once again she traced his body with her eyes as she had done their first morning together in Prague. *Is this to be our last morning together?* she wondered.

She had felt foreboding in the predawn hours as the distant baying of hounds shattered the peaceful song of the woods. The hunt. Was it really so harmless and bloodless as Tedrick had told her? She had seen too much to believe that with her whole heart. Perhaps the British liked to imagine that there were no teeth in Hitler's hounds, but Elisa knew differently. She knew, as Thomas did, that their duty placed them on the crest of a tidal wave headed for a stone wall.

As the light filtered into the room, Elisa wanted to beg Murphy to take her with him to Evian. But when he awoke and they made love once more, she did not ask. She could not ask.

Tedrick had kept his part of the bargain. She and Murphy had had these three days together alone. Now Elisa must keep her agreement as well.

Strangely, Murphy did not ask her to go with him. It was as if the possibility did not enter his mind. Several times he had mentioned that he did not particularly like this guy Tedrick, but that the man seemed to know his job pretty well. "As long as you're safe," Murphy would say. And Elisa wondered silently what he would do if he knew the truth. The Bargain kept her from saying more. The Bargain meant British passports presented to Murphy by Tedrick when he came with the car.

"Here you are. Just as I promised. Mr. Murphy, you will want to take them to Prague to the Linder family as soon as possible."

"Why so soon?" Murphy stopped. There was something grim and dark on the edge of Tedrick's words.

Tedrick cleared his throat nervously. "Looks like war is a certainty. The mediation of the Czech problem by Lord Runciman has failed to solve the problem. Hitler has issued an ultimatum. Our Prime Minister Chamberlain has flown to Germany to meet with Hitler privately in Berchtesgaden."

"Chamberlain? To Berchtesgaden? This sounds a lot like the way Hitler took Austria, if you ask me. First the Führer issues an ultimatum; then he calls a conference to reply to it."

The news was astonishing to Elisa. *General Beck must have resigned,* she thought. She could not discuss any of it with Murphy, so she played her role—the concerned but uninformed musician.

A lump in her throat, she stepped into the cottage with Murphy for the last time. She could not speak as he kissed her good-bye.

The engine of the Rolls-Royce hummed impatiently. Tedrick ducked his head through the low doorway. "We are keeping Elisa under wraps, Mr. Murphy. Would it be more convenient if she called you at your hotel in Evian to check in?"

"Right. I'll be at the Royale." One quick kiss, a lingering look, and Murphy was out the door.

☙

An interesting man, this Tedrick. He had not been in the car five minutes with Murphy before he announced that due to the extraordinary circumstances and political developments in Prague, he had taken the liberty of rearranging Murphy's travel plans.

"Steamers are such ghastly slow things, anyway. I simply got you a plane ticket to Prague. You can drop off the papers with Elisa's family and three hours later catch another plane to Geneva. From there it's a steamer on to Evian."

Maybe this gruff man was not such a bad guy after all. Yes, indeed, he knew his business. That thought made Murphy frown as a question entered his mind. "You weren't kidding when you said the Linders needed their passports as soon as possible, were you?"

Tedrick leveled a steely gaze on Murphy. "No, Mr. Murphy. The events in Czechoslovakia are nothing at all to joke about. Not that I'm an authority, but—" he reached for the newspaper next to him and pointed to a photograph of a long line of people waiting to receive instruction in the use of gas masks— "in Prague, Hitler would not hesitate to use gas on the population if this comes to war. He considers the Czech race to be only one notch above the Jews. And you know what he thinks of Jews."

⊂⊃

At Heathrow, Murphy sent wires first to Charles about Louis, and then
to Hradcany Castle in Prague. The thought of an interview with the besieged Czech president was too good to pass up. There would be time,
Murphy reasoned, after he stopped to give Theo and Anna the passports,
for an hour with President Beneš. The little man still owed him a small
favor.

⊂⊃

The airfield outside Prague was a beehive of activity. Modern fighter
planes were lined up along the tarmac and covered with camouflage net-
ting. Murphy stepped from the passenger plane and strained his eyes to
see if Theo might not be among the officers and men who congregated
together by a Quonset hut.

He sighed loudly and inhaled the fresh air. It was a strange feeling to
come back without Elisa by his side. He half expected to see her and little
Charles, even though he had just left her in England. He shook himself
back to reality as he noticed the fortifications all around the buildings.
Gun emplacements. Searchlights. Antiaircraft cannons on the far end of
the field.

While the British and French had been talking about the defense of
Czechoslovakia, President Beneš had been doing something about it.
The images of such fortifications were at the same time terrifying and
comforting. What Hitler coveted would not be easily stolen, Murphy
thought as he flagged down a green taxi and gave the grim driver the address of the Linder house.

No one answered Murphy's knock, so he pushed the door open and
stepped in. He hardly recognized the little house of Mala Strana. There
were people everywhere. The music room where he and Elisa had shared
so many happy hours with Theo and Anna was now strewn with mat-
tresses; a young mother sat nursing a baby while three other children
played beside her. The magnificent piano was shoved off in the corner
and covered with a quilt.

Two men excused themselves and walked quickly past Murphy in the
hallway. He stopped long enough to peer into the room that had been
his and Elisa's. An old woman sat in the chair beside the window. An old
man sat on the edge of the bed and read the latest reports in the Czech
newspaper. A younger couple played cards at the foot of the bed, and
two toddlers scrambled back and forth in play.

The old woman looked up. "You are looking for someone?" she
asked.

Murphy nodded, suddenly frightened that something had happened to Theo and Anna. "Yes. The Linder family."

"Linder? Linder? A German name. We are mostly Czechs here in this house."

"Anna and Theo Linder *own* this house!" Murphy exclaimed.

"Ah yes! Anna. You mean you are looking for Frau Anna!" The old woman laughed. No one else in the room even looked up. It was as if Murphy was not there. "Everyone is always looking for Anna!"

"I am her son-in-law. I have very little time here before I have to catch a plane."

"Well, if that is the case, God bless you. Anna is down in the cellar with Bette, counting sacks of flour and bags of lentils."

The cellar. Murphy scarcely remembered that the little house had a cellar. He hurried back down the corridor and through the kitchen, where six peasant women tended steaming cauldrons of soup.

"Wait! Wait! Who are you? You can't go into the cellar! Is he from the government? Hey you, come back here!"

The cellar. Murphy had guessed right. He threw open the door and clattered down the stone steps into the cold, musty-smelling cubicle. Anna stood beneath a bare lightbulb, a clipboard in her hand. Her hair was tied back in a scarf like the women who called after him in the kitchen. Her face was intense with thought.

"At least another ton of lentils," she was saying to the plump, broad-faced woman who examined the sack in the corner.

Murphy waited politely on the bottom step. Anna checked her figures once again. She must have sensed his presence because she looked up, then back down, and then her eyes widened and she dropped the clipboard as she whirled around. "John! Oh, John, you are here! God is good!"

They were both laughing now. "Anna, Anna!" Murphy embraced her with relief. "I was beginning to think you had already fled the country!"

"Is Elisa with you?" Her eyes were bright with emotion.

"In London."

"Thank God. I would not want her here now. You can see—"

They walked arm in arm up the steps and then she led him through the crowd of strangers, stopping to introduce him to each one in turn. At last she led him up the steep stairs to the attic where she had moved some personal things to make a place for herself.

☙

The British passports lay between them as they sat on the sagging bed. Anna absently traced the embossed emblem with her finger. "We had

almost given up, you see," Anna said wearily. "Weeks ago we were notified of the rejection of our visas by the American consulate."

"Weeks?" How could this be? Murphy had placed himself as spon-
sor, and he had not been notified.

"And then I got Elisa's letter saying that it would be all well. She had
contacts in London who were arranging for the passports—and here
they are. God is good to us!" But there was a hesitance in her words. "It's
just that there are so many others now . . . more every day. Most of the
men who are able have dug in on the front. But you can see what has
happened here in Prague. We are expecting the worst. Preparing for the
worst and trying to live day by day."

"Theo and the boys?" Murphy asked, feeling that it was crucial that
plane tickets be purchased immediately. "You can join Elisa in London?"

Anna shook her head slowly. She absently flipped open the cover of
first one document and then the next. "They are at an airfield near Eger.
They won't come, John. Not until the last fortification of Czechoslovakia is smashed. Theo is committed. He believes that the Nazis must be
held here, or—"

"Right." Murphy needed no further explanation. "Theo and Churchill would get along nicely together."

"But at least we will have these—just in case."

"Anna, you can go. You must. Come with me to Evian, and then we
will go back to London together. Elisa needs you."

She smiled a sad, wise smile, and Murphy thought what a beautiful
woman she was. How much like her Elisa would be someday! "Elisa
does not need me. She is safe. She has you, John. My husband needs me
to be here when he comes home. And my sons, Wilhelm and Dieter.
And then there are all these others. There is so much yet to do. And I
must stay here to do it." She took his hand. "But tell Elisa we are just fine.
Tell her I have the passports kept very safe and close at hand in case we
must fly away." She laughed at herself, at her foolishness for turning
down such an offer. "Evian. The French resort of Geneva. Theo and I
went there on our fifteenth anniversary. Ah, me, how very far away such
elegance seems now from the real world of Prague!"

Murphy could hear the clamor of voices and smell the aromas from
the soup kettles. Yes, Evian seemed very far away from reality indeed. "I
have to go. You're sure?"

"Quite sure. My place is here." Her eyes clouded now at the thought
of Elisa. "Tell her I love her, will you?" She stood and tucked the passports beneath her mattress. "And tell her we'll be together again soon.
She must not worry."

Anna escorted Murphy down three stories from the garret, out among the busy women who worked to prepare for the evening meal. Murphy hugged Anna on the front step and then as he neared the corner, he turned for one last look. Anna stood with her hands on her hips, joking and giving orders in alternate breaths as long tables on the sidewalk were laden with food.

⌘

Sandbags and trenches were everywhere in Prague. Sacks of sand surrounded the statue of St. Nepomuk on the Charles Bridge. Candles burned before the sandbags. Windows were taped and boarded up in the shops of Old Town. The windows of hotels and businesses were covered with black cloth.

Murphy caught a trolley car crowded with Czechs who scanned the newspapers and angrily discussed Hitler's ultimatum. These people were strong and indignant, Murphy thought. They would fight for their freedom if they were called to do so!

Stepping from the trolley in front of Hradcany Castle, Murphy shook his head in wonder at the changes Hitler's threats had brought. Where once the lights of thousands of candles had beckoned him and Elisa to the castle, now sandbags and armed guards were everywhere. Every window had been carefully blacked out. Even the window of President Beneš's office.

Soldiers challenged him as he walked toward the entrance. "I am John Murphy. American journalist. I wired President Beneš of my arrival in Prague. He is expecting me."

Someone recognized the name. The American who had saved the life of the president. First one officer was called and then another, and finally the face of the colonel who had been wounded appeared.

The colonel did not smile, although he seemed glad to see Murphy. The man looked visibly aged and not nearly so splendid as he had in his dress uniform the night at the ball.

"Come in, come in." He opened the bronze door for Murphy as if he were inviting him for coffee. But inside the marbled hallway, grim and worried men hurried from one office to another. "President Beneš mentioned you would come today," he said. "Of course, the schedule is full. We are, you may see, on a full-war footing. Ready for what may come." He was walking quickly toward the back staircase that led to the private offices of Beneš.

On the first landing Murphy stopped him. "I will not intrude," Murphy said, putting a hand on the officer's arm. He was throwing away the scoop of a lifetime, but there was a sense of importance here that did not allow the thought of an interview to be taken seriously.' "This is not a social call." Murphy pulled out a white envelope from his coat pocket. "I came first of all to wish President Beneš—all of you—" Murphy stopped, feeling trite and foolish. "I am praying for you," he finished. "And I came to ask a favor." He handed the envelope to the officer. "It is explained very briefly. You will see that he gets it?"

The officer clicked his heels and bowed slightly. "Gladly." Then he smiled. "We are men besieged, Mr. Murphy—hardly in a position to grant favors now." He laughed bitterly. "But I will give our president your letter, certainly."

"I can find my way out. Long life!" Murphy spoke the words of Czech farewell, and as he said them, he hoped they were true.

35

Closed Doors

Leah, my heart,

When I read your letter I could not speak for the joy of learning you and Louis are safe and only a short swim away from me across the Channel. How good is our Lord, and how merciful He is to spare your lives! There has not been a day since we parted that terrible moment in Vienna that I have not thought of you a thousand times. And now you are in Paris staying with Sonia and Magda, who I know will care for you and make certain you are well fed and happy. Soon I hope to join you there. I have some performances yet to finish, but pray for me that I will finish soon. Then I will take you to tea at the Eiffel Tower, and you can tell me everything—and I will tell you everything, too. Words and letters are terrible little things—trifles, so stiff and unmoving. Not at all like my bow. And so, I want you to try very hard to catch the 7:00 PM performance on the BBC radio on the 17ᵗʰ. I will play Mozart's (who else?) Violinkonzert Nr. 4 D-Dur, and my heart will be singing the Rondeau especially for you. Loving sister, you will hear my joy. Until then, think of me, and I will be very near to you.

All my love,

Elisa

Elisa lay back on the bed of her darkly furnished Left Bank Paris hotel room. She could see her image in the dim mirror of the dresser. Short hair. Serious eyes. *I look years older,* she mused. *Weary, and even frightened.*

It was hard to believe that less than eighteen hours ago she had been with Murphy, but then everything seemed to be moving so fast. They had been away from a radio for only three days and when they surfaced, the news was startling. Hitler had demanded the evacuation of all Czechs from the Sudetenland. They were to take nothing with them—not furniture or livestock or weapons!

Of course, Elisa knew that multiple thousands had already fled to Prague from the territories even before Hitler's ultimatum. But this Diktat from the Führer made the situation seem all the more ominous.

Elisa rolled over and switched on the radio, turning the knob until the voice of the BBC crackled into the room. She did not want to hear news. Tedrick had filled her in with information that she was certain was so explosive that not even the BBC would know of it. Her assignment was to meet with Thomas, find out if Hitler's ultimatum against the Czech citizens in the Sudetenland was the certain indication that an invasion was on.

Tonight Elisa only wanted some comfort. Tonight the BBC was scheduled to broadcast a violin concerto by a certain young violinist named Elisa Linder-Murphy! Elisa smiled as her name was announced. All the way from London to Paris, and she could hear herself. It seemed almost humorous now. She looked toward the corner of the room at the brand-new case housing her Guarnerius, and she wondered how Shelby was making out hefting around the old case and the ten-dollar violin it contained.

There was the rousing sound of applause—canned, certainly. There had been no audience when Elisa had recorded the concerto. Then the music began, sweet and poignant. Within the notes all her longings were carried.

She wondered if Leah was listening right now, a few miles from her in Paris. How she wanted to see her again! And Thomas—was he able to listen to a BBC broadcast in the German Embassy? Or was that forbidden? Perhaps she would ask him tomorrow when they met at the bistro. How would they feel listening to a Jewess play Mozart's happy bright music?

She did not feel happy or bright tonight. She wanted only to be finished with all this before something inside her broke forever. And she wanted to be with Murphy on a farm in Pennsylvania where someday their sons could camp in the woods and dream of faraway places.

❧

Thomas resented the appearance of this rather greasy-looking little Gestapo agent at the embassy. Playing on the rivalry between Himmler and

Admiral Canaris, this newcomer seemed to have found a thousand ways to needle Thomas.

Thomas guessed that Georg Wand had come to Paris to gauge the effect of the Czech crisis on the French. Not until this moment did he finally understand the reason for the man's encampment at the embassy.

It was after dinner, and as was the custom, the staff members adjourned to the lounge where most of the Führer's tirades were listened to and discussed. But tonight, Wand did something remarkable according to the standards of the German Embassy. He turned on the large upright radio and played with the dials and the volume until at last the distinct music of a violin and orchestra filled the room.

He smiled. His tooth glinted gold, "Ah yes!" he cried with delight, rubbing his hands together. "Mozart! *Violinkonzert, D-Dur!*"

"Is that not the BBC?" asked Herr Trodt, third assistant secretary.

"Indeed it is," Wand answered. "But the violinist is one of our own. At least she *was* . . . an Austrian, I think. Or perhaps Czech. Or maybe she was German-born! It is all confusing. Her name is . . . it escapes me." He looked directly at Thomas. "*Elisa*, is it?"

Thomas stared at the toe of his spit-polished boot as he lounged back in an easy chair. He did not answer the gaze of Georg Wand, but the hair on the back of his neck prickled. What did this creature know? Probably nothing—nothing more than what had been in the Gestapo files. *Silence, Thomas!*

"Elisa!" Georg continued. "*Ja.* I think that is the first name. Married to an American journalist, John Murphy. Very much anti-Nazi, I'm afraid. Very dangerous to us." He slapped his hand on his skinny thigh and sat down. "But all the same, the music is quite remarkable, don't you think?"

<hr />

The skies above Lake Geneva were as deep blue and transparent as the lake itself today. Murphy looked out the window of the Pan American passenger plane, past the spinning props to where steamers plied the waters like tiny toy boats.

To the north, rolling hills were crisscrossed with the geometric patterns of vineyards and orchards sloping to the shoreline. South and east, the mountains of Valais and Savoy reared up, only to be dwarfed by the peak of Mont Blanc shimmering in the distance.

Tucked between the mountains and the lake was the resort of Evian, a village that existed for the sake of wealthy Frenchmen who came to drink its famous waters and bathe away the aches and pains of age. The hotels were opulent and expensive, and this week they would be

crowded. He was confident that there would be more reporters and ob-
servers than participants in the refugee conference. Those who were not
included had much more at stake than those who took up their suites in
the Hotel Royale and studied the alarming reports of homeless thousands clamoring for a safe heaven.

Were they discussing the *Darien*? Murphy wondered. Or were those
few hundred onboard the freighter too few in the scope of the millions
to consider right now? Fewer than eight hundred people. The refugees of
the *Darien* represented no more than a ten-thousandth part of the millions now clearly within Hitler's gunsights. *Merely a drop in the proverbial
bucket,* Murphy mused, and that realization made him shudder. How
many could be saved? Each hour that passed was already too late for
some. Each day, how many more were being pushed closer to the brink
of . . . *of what?*

Murphy shook his head, unable to believe that the threats in Hitler's
speeches could be taken literally. *Annihilate? Exterminate? Eliminate?*
These were words used for bugs not people! And yet it was happening.
Even now. Even as this council of wise and humane representatives of
the nations gathered to enjoy the spas and thermal springs of Evian, people were dying. People were waiting, hoping, praying that there would
be an answer for them and their families.

The plane banked to the southwest, giving Murphy a clear view of
Geneva, glistening on the shoreline where the swift blue waters of the
Rhone River exited the lake.

Murphy had loved Geneva when, as a young reporter for Craine and
the INS, he had been sent to cover the fall sessions of the League of Nations. He had been a naive kid then. He had believed somehow that the
assignment was his big break. While other reporters abandoned the sessions for visits to the Casino Municipal or strolls in the steep lanes of the
Left Bank's Old City, Murphy had stuck it out.

By the end of the session he had learned one important fact: The Palais
des Nations was nothing more than a whitewashed tomb filled with the
bones of dead men! What had been created as a covenant between nations to keep the peace of the world had become a platform for banal platitudes that accomplished nothing at all. When Hitler as new chancellor of
Germany had pulled out of the League, Murphy broke the story. This
event was the only thing that woke anyone up during the session. The
journalists who had dropped their wages at the roulette wheel during that
momentous day shrugged and said, "We don't want to be here either."

For his effort, Murphy had gotten a raise of five bucks a week and a
transfer to Berlin. The League of Nations pretended not to notice that the
Germans had gone. When Mussolini left, when the Japanese attacked

Manchuria, they looked the other way. They shrugged when the Italians invaded Abyssinia. They yawned when Hitler marched into the Rhineland, when Hitler stirred up the civil war in Spain, when Hitler invaded Austria. There were a thousand other little offenses that had also been ignored by the rattling bones of Geneva's great tomb. There was finally nothing left for a journalist to cover. Any insult, any breach of common decency, could easily be written up by a reporter who spent his day at the casino while the League discussed the crisis.

In response to the Japanese execution of a thousand civilians, in response to the imprisonment of Baron von Rothchilds by the Germans, the League of Nations said, "My goodness, how dreadful! What a pity! Oh, dear me! Well, what can we do? It's finished and best forgotten!"

The bump of wheels on the airstrip pulled Murphy from his unpleasant reverie. Those same old codgers were over at the Palais des Nations right now. No doubt they were all very much insulted that this Evian Conference had been called and no one had invited them! After all, they enjoyed the spa as much as anyone!

It was a short ride on the tram from Cointrin Aerodrome to le quai du Mont Blanc, where Murphy would catch the express steamer up the lake to Evian. He was edgy, anxious to get there. This time, he was certain, the nations would not fall into the pit of apathy as they dealt with the present issue. This time, surely, the thumb-twiddlers and sleep-talkers would be hooted out of the assembly. Something would be done. Something *must* be done, Murphy thought as he boarded the lake steamer among a bevy of other reporters. As they greeted him and slapped him on the back, he wondered if they could see the intensity of hope he carried with him to Evian.

〰

Thomas stepped from the Metro into the Left Bank neighborhood. He had already walked two blocks toward the bistro before he realized that he was being followed.

Georg Wand. Across the narrow lane. Hat pulled low over his forehead. Eyes downcast. Yes, it was the Gestapo agent.

Thomas glanced at his watch. He swallowed hard and hurried toward a confectioner's shop around the corner. Purchasing a small box of chocolates, he left the shop and hurried back toward the River Seine and rue de la Huchette. Wand stayed with him, moving discreetly through the crowds of students on the sidewalks.

At the corner, Thomas looked first toward the Bureau de Police and then toward le Panier Fleuri, "The Basket of Blossoms." He walked briskly toward the bordello and entered.

The madame, a woman of education and culture, recognized Thomas and smiled through her dark red lips. "You have come back, monsieur!" she exclaimed. "And you have brought a box of bonbons? Not every man brings candy to a place like le Panier Fleuri."

Thomas could feel the presence of Georg Wand at his back. Threatening. Breathing death. He half expected the bell above the door to ring, but it did not. Wand would take his station outside. Possibly in the very café where Thomas spent his time.

"Is Suzanne occupied?" he asked.

The woman laughed, tossing her head. "You look desperate, monsieur. And *oui*, she is occupied. But only for another twenty minutes. But if you do not care to wait, there are others who will be happy to have the bonbons."

He shook his head, trying to appear nonchalant. "No. Suzanne, I think."

"Then sit down. Have some wine."

"I want her all night," he blurted out.

She looked at him sideways. "Monsieur Thomas! You should have bought a bigger box of chocolates!"

He ran a hand over his face. "She is not busy for the rest of the night, is she?" he tried again, feeling foolish and frightened at the same moment.

"No. You will fill her hours nicely."

"Good," he said. Then again, "Good."

⌘

Twenty minutes passed slowly. Georg Wand did not venture into the bordello. Thomas considered all the different angles of this building that might be observed from across the street. Wand was only one man, but might he have called in other watchers to follow Thomas?

"*Mon chéri!*" cried Suzanne as the madame whispered to her. "I am to have you all to myself for an entire night!" She took his hands and led him up the stairway. "And *chocolates.*" She said the word seductively. An astonishing girl, this Suzanne.

Thomas closed the door of the bedroom. The air was heavy with perfume. The bed was made. Lace lingerie was draped across a chair. Suzanne put her arms around his neck and kissed his ear.

"I want you to stay here," Thomas said. "All night."

"But of course, Thomas."

He looked at the window. He could make out the iron grid of a fire escape. "You will have to stay alone, though, my darling."

"What?" She pulled back slightly and looked quizzically into his eyes.

"I am being followed, you see."

Her mouth turned down in a pout. "But, Thomas—"

"You will be well paid." He pulled a sheaf of bills from his pocket. "Double for your time?"

She smiled and opened the chocolate box. She sat down on the bed. "A detective?"

"Yes. He is out there now. He has followed me all afternoon, hired by the husband of my mistress. The fellow says he will kill me if we are caught together, and I do not fancy being killed."

Suzanne shrugged. Her mouth full of candy, she put a finger to her lips. Yes. She would stay alone in the room. She had been given stranger assignments. "And you will come back?"

"About eleven." He opened the window and peered out. There was no one in the alley below the fire escape. He could see the Seine. "I'll tap on the window. You'll let me in?"

"Of course, *mon chéri*." She blew him a kiss. "Don't worry about me. I will be faithful to you."

⊘

Four times Elisa had met with Thomas at the bistro to gather bits of information to take back to London. But this meeting was different. There was something desperate yet hopeful in his voice. She knew there was more behind what he was saying.

"General Halder is one of us!" Thomas whispered urgently to Elisa from across the table in the dim Paris café. "You must tell them that! Hitler's ultimatum is nothing to fear! Halder is one of us!" Thomas sat back as if to consider that he might have gone too far in mentioning Halder's name as an anti-Nazi. Beck's replacement was as ardently opposed to Hitler as General Beck had been. The question was how to make a man like Chamberlain understand that at this moment Hitler was only the howling of the wind!

"But you told me that if Beck resigned, that meant Hitler was intent on war." Elisa's hands were trembling. Had she somehow mistaken the meaning of Thomas' first message?

"Hitler is only one man! And now this Prime Minister Chamberlain has gone to Berchtesgaden to meet with him! It is folly, Elisa! It is too much like Schuschnigg and Austria. Hitler will bully and flatter and see that Chamberlain is a man so blinded by hope of peace that he will set the table and serve up Czechoslovakia like a roasted lamb. Hitler will have only to carve."

Elisa sighed. The news of that meeting between Chamberlain and Hitler was not at all encouraging. "What do I tell them? What word from the High Command?"

"You might tell them that Adolf Hitler spent an hour and a half ridiculing Chamberlain after he left. Then others of his lackeys took up where the Führer left off. There is no respect, no fear." Thomas took her hand in his. "Now you must listen very carefully. Tell them this in England. There are things being done. I cannot say all. The generals have written a document that they will present to Hitler. In this document they show that the Czechs have between thirty and forty divisions that they are deploying right now on Germany's eastern frontier along their fortified line in the mountains of Sudetenland. The weight of the French Army in sheer numbers is eight to one against us along the western wall. Daily, Churchill speaks of forming an alliance between France and England and Russia. Russia might use Czech airfields against Germany. The British Royal Navy is unsurpassed—"

"This is true? Then it is madness for Hitler to want to fight."

"*Madness!* Every member of the High Command knows he is insane. Our Siegfried Line is not finished yet. We are in need of no fewer than forty-eight thousand officers and at least one hundred thousand NCOs to bring the army up to strength! With France and Britain allied with the Czechs, we would face a war on all sides. We could hold out a few months at best. Even if the Czechs fought us alone, it would take us three months to break through."

"Then why does Hitler persist?"

"Because he believes the French are cowards and Chamberlain is a doddering old fool. Elisa, *listen!* Czechoslovakia is the key. If the Nazis are stopped on this side of the Czech mountains, they will go no farther! If those Czech lands are lost, there is nothing that can stop Hitler. The land is level clear to Moscow!"

"Can I tell the British that Hitler thinks Chamberlain is a fool?"

Thomas smiled. "No, I suppose not. Tell them that this document telling of the fearful condition of the German Army and our inability to fight on so many fronts will be presented to Hitler at the Chancellery. He must listen to the generals in Berlin, or—" Again Thomas stopped himself. He could not say too much. Not now. Until the English showed themselves to be men of honor, he could not risk the possible betrayal of Halder and Canaris and the rest. He clenched his fists and gazed at his untouched food. He wanted to tell her everything. *If Hitler refuses to listen to reason again . . . if he gives the insane order to march against the Czechs, then he will be jailed and made to stand trial on charges of bringing Germany to the brink of destruction!*

"Thomas?" Elisa said his name gently. "Are you all right?"

Thomas raised his head and looked into her eyes. "I can only hope that Hitler is indeed a madman and that Prime Minister Chamberlain is not a fool. Tell them in London that Hitler claims he can have it all without a shot being fired. That is his argument against the generals who oppose him. He says they are props, only props, like the backdrops in one of his Wagnerian operas. Oh, Elisa"—he squeezed her hand—"if only a man like Churchill were at the helm of England—if only."

Thomas sat silent and ashen-faced as he studied Elisa. *Still beautiful. A heart-wrenching beauty.* He took her hands and held them to his lips. This was not part of the performance. *Fingers calloused and strong. Red mark along her jawline.* The thought of Georg Wand made his heart race.

She did not pull her hands away, but there was no response in those sensitive fingers. The fingers that could sing such glory to God were without energy in his hands. "What is it, Thomas?"

"I heard you play again last night."

She smiled, pleased. "You listened to the BBC? Blasphemy in the German Embassy, is it not?"

He nodded. "The man who turned on the radio was a Gestapo agent, Elisa. And when he pretended not to know the name of the violinist he looked at me and said, 'Elisa, isn't it? Elisa something?'"

A cold knot of fear settled in Elisa's stomach. "Why . . . did he ask you?"

Thomas shrugged. "No doubt everyone in the Gestapo knows I was once . . . in love with—"

"A Jewess."

"I still am."

Elisa withdrew her hands. "Then I am sorry for you. She is not in love with you, Thomas." Her voice was sharp. "While you were in Germany, I spent three days with my husband. I love him. I cannot even permit you to speak such words to me and let them stand unchallenged."

"Sorry," he said quietly. "Yes, well. It is all my own fault. But that is not what we are speaking of. I just wanted to warn you to be very careful. I have heard this fellow Georg Wand is the very best they have. Which means the most efficiently brutal. I went two hours out of my way today before I met you." He frowned. "Of course, this may be nothing more than the fact that his boss, Himmler, hates my boss, Canaris. It may mean nothing more than the fact that this little weasel read each file on every man in the embassy before he came here. Making the connection and using it against me is the most natural thing for him to do. But all the same, be careful. When you go back to London, be very careful. He mentioned the fact that your husband is anti-Nazi."

"Murphy has stated that in a thousand ways." She tried to reassure Thomas, although she could not reassure herself. "Why would he think twice about me in connection with you?"

Thomas gave a tight-lipped smile of consternation. "Only one thought with a man like Georg Wand is enough for action. These people have their methods. Not very pretty."

"I know that," Elisa answered quietly. "That is why I am here, remember? The British have set up a lovely decoy. They will handle him if he comes that way. I technically do not exist. This person you see here has no real identity—except to meet with you."

Thomas reached up to touch the mark on her jawline. "Your music stays with me, Elisa. Last night I—"

Elisa lifted her chin defiantly as he began again with a hint of his love. "I have to leave now," she said abruptly.

"Elisa?"

"No. I will come here Thursday at five o'clock. I will tell them what you said." She gathered her handbag and gloves and left the bistro.

Thomas stayed for thirty minutes longer. He gazed at the place where she had been, and in his mind he said everything he wanted to say to her.

36

Innocence Lost

It was only a small box on the entertainment page of the *Paris Daily Herald,* and yet Georg Wand had reason to study each item on those pages now. Logic had told him Elisa was here in the city. Instinct told him that she was indeed somehow connected with Thomas von Kleistmann. The question remained: Where might a musician wish to spend her spare time?

Perhaps at a concert? He had ruled that possibility out. She would not be so foolish to go to a concert in Paris where she might be recognized, not after all the trouble of arranging BBC broadcasts from London. But then again, if this was a concert given by a much-loved friend . . .

<hr />

The cello Leah played was a three-hundred-year-old Tecchler. The sound was superb. The grain of the wood looked like the dark varnished hide of a tiger. It was truly a beautiful instrument, but it was still not Vitorio.

In exchange for free concert tickets, she had rented the instrument from an old instrument repairman who had a shop three blocks from L'Opera. During rehearsals, Leah could see the wizened old Frenchman sitting alone in the empty auditorium as he listened with pleasure to the sound of his instrument.

Today there was someone else sitting with the old man. A small-boned man with a long head and dark eyes and eyebrows that met in the middle. Perhaps this was another person the instrument makers brought to hear the instrument—a cellist, the father of an eager student intent on buying the best. Ah well, it was part of the bargain. And no one could better show the fines tones of a cello than Leah Feldstein.

The maestro had warned her that the old fellow had run an ad describing the instrument and the fact that Leah would be playing it.

> *"Interested parties please contact Bernard at 14-009 Paris exchange, and a demonstration of tone and excellence will be arranged."*

So this was the demonstration. The small client of Monsieur Bernard nodded with vigor in time to the music. Bernard sat proudly beside him. *Indeed, this is the finest cello in the world. Listen to her play, will you?*

Well, there was a price for every favor, and now Leah must pay it. After the rehearsal, the maestro rolled his eyes and raised his arms in a shrug of apology. She remained at her music stand while Bernard and his client hurried forward to the stage.

"Beautiful, mademoiselle!" cried Bernard with his hands spread wide as if he would embrace both the cello and Leah. "What do you think of my instrument?" He had asked the question before and now she answered as she always had.

"A treasure, monsieur. Priceless."

"Is it not the finest you have ever played?"

"It is a joy to play, indeed," she replied, choosing her words carefully so she would not lie. The instrument was not so fine as her own Pedronelli, but he would not want her to say so right in front of the client.

The client. He seemed to be looking more at Leah than at the instrument. Noticing her questioning gaze, he smiled a brief smile, showing a glint of gold on his front tooth. "Pardon me for staring." He bowed humbly. "It is just that I have heard you play so many times before. First in Salzburg, and later when you were in Vienna at the Musikverein." He touched his chest as if she had affected his heart.

Bernard exclaimed, "Forgive me—my manners! The excitement of the music was so—" He kissed his fingertips for emphasis. "And now I must introduce you. This is Herr Krepps. Also late of Austria. He has also managed to escape from the Nazis."

Again the flash of gold. The smile. "*Bitte*, Frau Feldstein. My escape from those people was not so exciting as your own with the child. The news accounts say you came over the Alps on foot?"

Cautious, Leah replied politely but vaguely. "I'm afraid my hosts exaggerated when they spoke of it to the reporters. I would have rather it not be mentioned at all."

"I see. Yes. An ordeal, then." The man bowed a slight apology. "My wife was left in Vienna. I was here on business when the Anschluss took place. She killed herself the first night."

At such a story even the exuberant Bernard fell silent. At last Leah spoke. She felt pity for this ordinary little man. He seemed helpless and somewhat lost. He was no musician. She could tell by his hands. "Well, this is a fine instrument if you are thinking of buying a cello."

"For my daughter," the man said again. "She is in Geneva now. A fine cellist. She has not been quite the same since word of her mother."

"I can understand why." Leah lapsed from French into the soft tone of Vienna. "You have heard me play in Vienna?"

"And Salzburg. You and—Elisa Linder was her name? The violinist. I remember seeing the two of you giggling onstage. Fast friends." He smiled at the pleasant memory. The flash of gold. "Is she still in Vienna?"

"In London," Leah answered readily. "Playing for the BBC. I heard her just last night."

At this the man frowned slightly, then replied, "Well, this is good news—both of you safe. I suppose you still see each other."

Suddenly there was a cold stirring inside Leah. Too many questions. The smile. A touching story, but . . .

"Would you like to hear a little more? I have an engagement shortly. I would like to chat about old times—they were good times, too—but I must be on my way."

"I can't think of keeping you." Krepps backed up a step as if horrified that he had detained such a great musician with small talk. "Perhaps I might be allowed to come back and listen again. If I could hear something a bit slower, perhaps."

"Oh! Yes, yes, yes, monsieur!" Bernard promised. "She will be happy to play for you! Yes, mademoiselle?"

Leah nodded, not at all certain that she liked the use of the Tecchler cello, after all.

☙

There were a dozen stops where Elisa could have gotten off the Metro. But she found herself still riding the subway as if she had someplace to go. A goal. A destination where she would squeeze past the other passengers and step out into the light.

Then the conductor cried out, "Opera, next stop! All out for Opera!" She blinked and edged past the others, waited until the doors slid back, and stepped off the train.

The doors slammed behind her after the warning bell sounded; the train roared off through the tunnel. Elisa stood in the dim light of the underground station and stared dully at the light that streamed down from the steps. She could hear the sounds of traffic on the boulevard des Capucines above her. Could Leah also hear the same horns? Did Leah take this very train home from rehearsal each day?

Someone bumped her. "Pardon, mademoiselle; are you unwell?" She looked up into the concerned face of a blue-uniformed gendarme.

"No. I . . . might have gotten off at the wrong . . ."

"Metro Opera." He lifted his hand toward the sign.

She tried to smile. *"Merci."* She moved mechanically toward the stairs. Toward Leah. The din of traffic became louder, and the great facade of the famous building was framed in the opening.

Elisa looked at her watch. Rehearsal would just be over. She could find Leah; she could wait at the stage door and surprise her. They would have tea together, and Elisa would confide in her. There was nothing she couldn't tell Leah!

Elisa ran up the last few steps and then, as the full light fell on her, she felt suddenly as if a hand had seized her and shaken her. A warning flashed in her mind. Why had Tedrick forbidden her to see Leah? What did he know that he had not told her?

Through the open doors of L'Opera, Elisa could see the grand staircase. A janitor was sweeping the steps. Leah was inside. Just through those doors and down the aisle to the stage where they had once performed together. All the orchestra from Vienna. All of them like a family—she and Leah and Shimon and Rudy. The memory brought her no joy now. She shuddered as if the building were a tomb filled with ghosts.

Turning at the sound of the bell that warned of an approaching train, she ran back down the steps and deposited her coins to take the train back to the Left Bank.

❧

"Murphy?" Elisa's voice sounded so near. It was wonderful. Just what he had needed after a round with the hard cases and the cynics!

"Elisa! I've been to Prague already, seen your mother!"

"Oh, darling, what good news! I have needed to hear good news all day! This meeting between Hitler and Chamberlain seems so . . . scary. How are you? Is everything all right in Prague? Did you give Mother a hug for me?" A dam had burst inside her. She sounded so lonely for him, almost desperate—maybe as desperate as he felt to see her right now.

He laughed. "One thing at a time. Anna sent a hug back. She is single-handedly feeding half the refugees in Prague—of whom there are a legion."

"Mother?" Elisa seemed astonished. "And Papa?"

"He is still in the Sudeten. With your brothers."

This news was met with silence. Then, "Murphy, they will be all right. There won't be a war. I know it."

"Yeah," he replied doubtfully. "We'll keep our fingers crossed."

"Is everyone in Evian still fat and rich and satisfied?" she asked.

"All of the above. Except for me. Tomorrow is the big debate. Everyone is so calm about this—too calm. Not one word of the *Darien*. I guess there are not enough of them to worry about in the light of all the rest of this mess."

"Oh, Murphy, talk to people. Tell them about it like you told me. They will listen. They will open up a small crack for the *Darien* to float through. And then soon everything will be right in Germany again—you will see. They will be able to go home again, and then we can go home too and be done with all of this."

Murphy listened, bemused by her burst of optimism. She had not seen Prague. She had not understood the seriousness of Chamberlain's visit to Hitler after all. He sighed. He wished he could be so happily naive again.

The minutes of hurried conversation passed like one breath, and when Murphy hung up the receiver, he felt even more lonely than he had before. He was lonely for more than Elisa . . . he missed his own sense of innocence and hope. There was much he had lost over the years, and somehow he wanted to find it again here in Evian.

❧

"*Ha-van-a, Cu-ba.*" Maria pronounced their destination very clearly for the girls. Very precisely and properly.

"But, Mama," Katrina protested, "First Mate Tucker says we should say, 'Av-an-er, Cu-Ber.' That's the way he says it."

Maria raised one eyebrow as she wondered what Bubbe would say about the Englishman's mutilation of the English language. "Well, First Mate Tucker says a lot of things I would not want you to repeat. You must not drop the sound of the *H*. Havana, Cuba. That is where we will be tomorrow."

Trudy sighed and sank down on the blanket beneath the tarp. Her pale skin was pink from the reflection of the sun on the water. Her lips were chapped and smeared with a greasy mixture Dr. Freund had found in the American supplies. Nearly everyone had become tender from the sun in the last week, and now the entire ship smelled of the pungent balm.

"Will we be able to get off the ship in Ha-van-a, Mama? Or will we still have to stay onboard? I would very much like to run on real ground again. Roll in the grass, even though it is not ladylike." Trudy shaded her eyes and looked across the endless blue.

Maria held little Israel close; he sighed with contentment and smiled so that a drip of milk spilled from the corner of his mouth. *Just a little piece of ground to rest on, Lord.*

"I don't know if that will be possible right away, Trudy," Maria answered honestly. "But Captain Burton says that there are men trying very hard to help us now. Tonight we will hear the news from Evian, where there are very wise and good men from all the nations working for a solution."

Gretchen made a face. She was tired of hearing about wise and good men. She wanted to walk on real ground again. "I hope they let us off in 'avaner."

"Havana," Trudy corrected.

"Whatever." Gretchen shrugged. "Tucker says we will all swagger like sailors when we get off the ship."

"I don't want to swagger," Louise said softly, laying her head in Maria's lap.

"I liked being a landlubber better," agreed Katrina. Then she frowned. "But I do like everybody being together. Will they take us all different places when they let us in?"

"Maybe they won't let us in because we're Jews," said Gretchen.

"We're only very little Jews," Katrina said indignantly. "And little Israel is hardly a Jew at all!"

Maria turned her head away, grieved that her children had to grow up with such things on their minds. But here it was. And it was truth. Even very little Jews were not welcome in this world.

⌒⌒

Perhaps only Adolf Hitler had guessed just how unwelcome even little Jews were to the world. Perhaps that is why he scoffed so openly when he heard of President Roosevelt's refugee conference.

> *"We cannot take seriously President Roosevelt's appeal to the nations as long as the United States maintains racial quotas for immigrants and as long as the quota for Jews remains unfilled. We see that the Americans like to pity the Jews as long as this pity can be used for agitation against Germany, but they are not prepared to accept a few hundred Jews into their country, let alone a few thousand! Thus, this conference will only serve to justify Germany's policy against Jewry!"*

In the lobby of the Hotel Royale, Murphy, along with Johnson, Timmons, Amanda, and a dozen other familiar faces from the European Press Corps, listened to the latest radio tirade of Hitler.

"Thus spake der Führer!" Timmons shouted irreverently in the posh setting.

"And the conscience of the world stirreth not," Johnson concluded, stirring his whiskey and soda with his finger.

Amanda, looking a bit more hardened over the months, sighed and gazed thoughtfully at the gilded ceiling. "Well, here's one for the record, fellows." She smiled slyly. "I just heard that our glorious British representative asked the American representative to exclude both Golda Meir and Chaim Weitzmann from the meeting."

Murphy leaned forward. This news was more than just the usual cynical wisecrack. "And?"

"They agreed. No one from the Jewish Agency of Palestine will be admitted or allowed to speak."

Philkins stretched laconically and drawled in his Southern accent, "That's no surprise, Amanda, honey. Weitzmann would be calling for more Jews to come into Palestine. Like on Murphy's pet freighter . . . the *Darien*? Why, nobody's gonna let those folks in, especially not in Palestine, where the Arabs are rioting and blowing things up. You remember Cedric Taylor? He got himself posted over there in Jerusalem and broke the story when the blanket-heads crucified those British soldiers! How'd you like *that* for an assignment?"

"You're a jerk, Philkins," Timmons mumbled into his glass.

"Personally, I like this assignment just fine," Philkins continued. "Nice hotels. Friendly natives. I plan on enjoying this story to the limit of my Hearst Publishing expense account!"

Amanda smiled sympathetically at Murphy, who seemed more troubled than the others by this latest development. "How did you get yourself involved with that ship, Johnny?" She exhaled with mock exasperation.

"It was a story. I fell into it." He smoldered at the apathy of this exclusive little corner of the press.

Amanda smiled sadly as the sarcastic banter continued over their conversation. "Are you really expecting anything to get done here?"

"Yes. Yes, I am," he replied angrily.

She raised a hand in surrender. "Just asking, Johnny. No need to jump down my throat. But—" she hesitated, then tried again— "haven't you noticed that this is exactly like every other conference we've ever covered in Geneva? Same players. A few different faces. Johnny, this is not going to be the great solution to all our problems, I'm afraid."

"You're all so cynical."

"No. I'm a realist, Johnny, and so are you—usually."

"What are we supposed to do then? Sit back and let Hitler do what he wants? Talk about it? Deplore it? Then do nothing?"

Amanda shrugged again, a one-shoulder shrug that seemed to imply there might be something else that could be done. "As for me, I gave my press pass to Golda Meir and arranged for Chaim Weitzmann to get in as an observer."

"Well, good. I mean, that's nice of you, Amanda."

"Not at all. I just don't believe in the big show anymore. So I'm leaving for Prague after tomorrow's session. That's where the next phase of the refugee story will be played out, you know."

Murphy sat silent and glum, affected by the hopeless cynicism around him. Could Hitler be right about everything? Was his heart so dark and evil that he could see himself reflected in the chilling apathy of all the world?

Amanda touched his arm and looked over his shoulder to where a small group of delegates chatted together near the elevators. "That fellow right there—" she nodded at a small Latin man dressed like a gangster in an Italian suit—"his name is Cabrillo. He is third assistant secretary of the Cuban foreign office," she whispered. "He has his hand out for all sorts of bribes, I'm told."

Murphy looked at her with a strange admiration. "How do you know such things?"

"I'm a newsman, remember? And my ex-husband knows him. Both are the sleazy types." She flashed a broad smile. "If things do not go as you hope . . ." She paused as if to say she was certain they would not go well. Instead, she narrowed her eyes knowingly as she sized up the little Cuban official. "Maybe you should talk to Cabrillo. You would be amazed how a little money might help your ship come in, Murphy."

37

A Candle of Hope

The distant lights of Miami glistened in a thin, bright line off the stern of the *Darien*. Tonight some onboard stared back at those lights with the sense that they would never see the shores of America again.

"That is the last of it," said Aaron. Then he turned his eyes toward the cone of the speaker where the flat, banal tones of the radio broadcaster called the roll of Evian. And again Aaron said, "And there is the end of our hope."

Once again the Holbein family sat at the base of the ventilation shaft. Klaus held baby Israel. Maria sat flanked by Trudy and Katrina. Gretchen and Louise lay on a blanket at Maria's feet.

> *"Argentina, which has a population one-tenth that of the United States, has declared that it has opened the doors to nearly as many refugees as the United States and cannot be expected to take any more."*

"Mama," Katrina asked, "does that mean we can't go there?"
"Yes, darling. Shhh, now."

> *"Australia, a continent of vast unpopulated areas, has likewise announced that since they have no real racial problems in their country, they do not wish to import one."*

"What is a race problem?" Trudy asked.
"Little Jews," Katrina answered, only to be shushed again.

"Canada, Colombia, Uruguay, and Venezuela have announced that their nations are interested only in the immigration of agricultural workers."

"I picked apples once," commented a friend of Aaron's.

"The honorable delegate from Peru has given the example of U.S. prudence and caution as the reason his nation has such strict immigration restrictions. Peru has further stated that it is opposed to all classes of intellectuals such as doctors and lawyers, lest their social structure be disrupted."

"Is that why they don't want us in the United States? Too many doctors and teachers there? I wonder."

"The British Colonial Empire, according to Sir John Shuckburgh, contains no territory suitable for the large-scale settlement of Jewish refugees."

A racket of boos rose up from the *Darien* passengers. Chants of "Palestine! Palestine! Palestine!" drowned out the next few moments of the broadcast.

Then a hush came over the congregation as Shimon stood and shouted. "Be quiet! We've missed what he said about Cuba!"

"Cuba?"

"Cuber? Did he say something about Cuber?"

"Nicaragua, Costa Rica, Panama, and Honduras have issued a joint statement saying they would not accept merchants or intellectuals."

"That means everyone."

"France, which has already absorbed two hundred thousand refugees and included three million aliens in its population, states that it has reached the limit of saturation."

The list of nations progressed slowly and painfully for the nearly eight hundred Jews onboard the *Darien*. There were bright spots among the tedious roll call. The Netherlands and Denmark stated that they would, in spite of terrible overcrowding, continue to offer their countries for temporary sojourn. The United States promised that it would accept its full legal quota of Austrian and German immigrants. No more. No less.

If there is disappointment among these here on the Darien, Klaus thought as he looked up at the stars above them, *how many millions of others have also waited in hope for an answer from the wise men of Evian? How many uncountable hearts tonight are despairing? How many have raised their voices to cry out, "Where shall I go? Oh, where shall I go?"*

Were those numbers as many as the stars? or as great as the sand on the shores? If they were as many as the stars, then perhaps only heaven would hold them now. And if they were as the sands, then surely the sea would draw them in and pull them forever away from the land and the light and the air. But of those millions, this family numbered only seven.

"I am only one grain of sand," Klaus whispered to Maria as they slept side by side on the deck tonight. "And you are one bright star. And there—" he swept a hand over the children—"these orbit around you, so small, so bright. Can it be that there is no room for us?"

❧

It was four in the morning. The sound of waves on the Miami breakwater was the most lively sound in the predawn darkness.

Three boats had been chartered by Trump Publishing. The largest was a seventy-foot fishing boat that carried cases of canned milk and fresh vegetables. The vessel had set out ahead of the others, bound for Havana, where the cargo would be loaded onto the *Darien.*

The two other boats were also fishing vessels. One was a sixty-foot commercial craft and the other was somewhat smaller, used as a charter boat for tourists wishing to fish off the coast of Florida.

The docks were crowded with photographers and reporters dressed like fishermen without the fishing gear. In the place of rods and tackle boxes were cameras and notepads and thermoses of coffee and bags of donuts and sandwiches. It was going to be a long trip—straight out to sea for eight hours. The sea was rough this morning, and the most hardy of newsmen were having second thoughts about bobbing around on the swells to get a story about a kid's circumcision.

But Bubbe Rosenfelt was undaunted. She had dressed warmly for the early-morning trip. She wore a sweater and a riding skirt that Mr. Trump had purchased for her. On her feet were her most comfortable walking shoes, but she also carried the lovely blue dress she had worn to the docks of New York. This time there truly would be reason to rejoice. She would go below to the little cabin Mr. Trump set aside for her, and she would change into the dress. This was her first great-

grandson, and she vowed she would not attend his bris milah in a riding skirt and old shoes. She also brought a hatbox containing a lovely
round hat with gold and blue pheasant feathers and a veil—and of
course she hadn't forgotten a picnic basket filled with treats for the
children. The only thing she did not have for the occasion was sponge
cake and coffee for all the guests. But she was too excited to worry
about anything so trivial.

Mr. Trump, who looked more like a fisherman than any of the others, held her arm firmly as he helped her onto the boat. Her boat. The reporters were assigned to ride in the larger of the two vessels. They packed
in like sardines, while Bubbe Rosenfelt was graciously seated inside the
wood-paneled cabin and served coffee by a man in a white smock.

Bubbe had ridden on small boats before on the lakes in Hamburg,
but never on the ocean. The whole ship seemed to vibrate with the rumble of the smelly diesel engine. She smiled as Trump shouted for the reporters to get aboard the press ship if they were going. *He is a good man,
this Mr. Trump.* Indeed, throughout the long journey to Miami he had assured her comfort and privacy on the one hand, while he barked at his
reporters on the other.

"It's a long trip," he said as the engine revved and the vessel idled
away from the dock. "You can have breakfast now if you'd like, or go
sleep awhile in your cabin, Mrs. Rosenfelt."

"So now it's breakfast, Mr. Trump?" She smiled. He looked so very
concerned that everything be right for her. "You have thought of everything."

"My way of saying thank you for the best supper I've eaten since my
wife passed on in 1929."

"That's a long time to be without supper, Mr. Trump," Bubbe answered. "If I had known, I would have asked you over long before now.
Of course, you would have had to travel to Hamburg, but—"

The boat lurched forward and the engine settled into an even pulse.

Trump frowned slightly. He had not told her about the disastrous
broadcast from Evian last night. He had warned the newsmen not to
bother her with questions about it on pain of being thrown to the
sharks. Things were not going as he had hoped. They were not going well
on other fronts either. He was determined, however, that Bubbe would
be spared as much of the painful news as possible.

"If I had known there was such good home cooking in Hamburg, I
assure you I would have been there long before this. Now, breakfast, or
sleep, or something else?"

Bubbe raised her chin in thought. "More coffee, perhaps? And . . . do
you know how to play canasta, Mr. Trump?"

◯

Still an hour from the proposed rendezvous point with the *Darien* a message clattered over the wireless.

An agitated radioman handed the scrawled message to Trump in the galley.

> *DARIEN* SURROUNDED BY TWO CUBAN GUNBOATS AND ONE U.S.
> CUTTER STOP CUBANS DENY ENTRY TO HAVANA STOP AMERICAN
> COMMANDER DEMING DEMANDS BOARDING STOP *DARIEN*

With barely a moment to absorb this news, Trump was then presented with a second message.

> *DARIEN* FOOD CARGO CONFISCATED IN HAVANA STOP PLEASE
> ADVISE IMMEDIATELY

He felt the blood drain from his face.

"Mr. Trump?" asked Bubbe Rosenfelt. "Are you all right? Is something wrong?"

He frowned, suddenly furious and determined at once. "Party crashers, my dear. But they won't stop us." He ran a hand over his head. "The Cubans and the Coast Guard have sent a few overzealous officers to gum things up." Now he sounded almost light. "We'll be there soon. You should probably get dressed."

◯

Anna Lindheim walked as quickly as she could along the dark sidewalks of Prague. She felt blind as she passed her hand along the stone facades of the buildings for direction. More than once she touched a human form in the shadows; then she moved out to the edge of the sidewalk again to grope her way toward the Anglican church, where she had an urgent appointment with the rector.

Czechoslovakia's capital was the darkest city in Europe tonight, blacked out against the probability of an air raid. Streetcars crawled along, a faint blue glimmer replacing the usual headlight. Within most of the old houses there was no light at all.

Gendarmes stood at a few of the downtown street corners to hold blue lanterns for those who, like Anna, had some urgent business pertaining to this last, terrible crisis. It was said that these blue lanterns were invisible from an altitude of more than a few hundred feet. Any German bombers or fighter planes attempting to make an unannounced call on

the city of Prague would find themselves lost over the countryside beyond.

The citizens of Prague obeyed the urgent edict of their government:
total mobilization. President Beneš insisted that the country must be
ready for any eventuality—especially now that the ultimatum of Hitler
had been put in such plain terms. Now there was no question what he
intended:

1. *Withdrawal of the whole Czech armed forces from the Sudetenland, including police, gendarmes, customs officials and frontier
   guards from the area to be evacuated as designated by the Führer
   on a map attached. This entire area to be handed over to Germany
   on October 1.*
2. *Evacuated territory to be presented to Germany in its present condition—farms, mines, industrial sites intact.*
3. *The Czech government to discharge at once all Sudeten Germans
   serving in the military forces or the police anywhere in the state
   and allow them to return home.*
4. *The Czech government to release all political prisoners of German
   race.*
5. *The Czech government to extradite on demand any criminals who
   have fled Germany for Czechoslovakia.*

This last point struck fear in Anna's heart. Theo was considered a
criminal by the Nazi government. The thousands of Jews who had fled
first from Germany and Austria and now from the Sudetenland were
also criminals. Anna carried the precious documents wrapped in cloth
and tucked inside her blouse.

At least Theo had a passport. The others of the frightened multitudes
had nothing. Most had fled without any sort of identification papers.
For this reason Anna had promised to speak with the Anglican rector tonight. She carried with her a list of nearly a thousand names—Jewish
names, names that were no doubt also on some Gestapo list.

She quickened her pace as an army truck rumbled past. She still had a
long way to walk and it had become impossible to get a taxi. All cabs had
been requisitioned for transport of officers and men. There were no filling stations open, and wherever Anna passed small groups standing
near an automobile, there was talk about gasoline. How far would this
much or that much take them?

"The trains are packed. Everything on wheels is moving somewhere—only who knows where?"

International trains, however, were not crossing the borders. Passengers wishing to continue on from the border had to carry their baggage and cross on foot, in hopes that another train would pick them up.

Most American, French, and British visitors had left over the course of the last week. Still, some hotels contained small cliques of determined journalists who would cover the ominous coming of the dawn. Anna was glad Murphy was not among them. How grateful she was that he and Elisa were safe! How desperately she wished the same for Theo and Dieter and Wilhelm tonight!

She stopped beside a gendarme, who looked strangely cold in the blue light of his lantern. "Pardon," she asked. "It is so dark, and I am afraid I have become lost."

"Madame," came the sad reply, "who is not lost in Prague tonight?"

"Can you point the way to the Anglican church for me?" she asked.

He chuckled. "Do you see that streetcar?" He lifted a dark arm to point at the slowly moving blue headlight. "Wait until it passes, and then cross the street. There you will find the Anglican Cathedral."

Anna thanked him. She was too relieved to feel foolish as she ran across the street to the back entrance of the church. She felt her way around the rough stone wall to the corner, groping for a door she knew was there. She had walked through it a hundred times since she had come to Prague, but always it had been in the light of day.

She stepped into a flower bed she had forgotten. Still, she felt the stones until at last she found the smoothly carved door. She half expected the door to be locked, but when she pulled on it, it opened easily. And inside was a glimmer of light. Candles shimmered a welcome to her, and the rector looked up from where he sat in the first pew and waved a greeting.

"You are here!" Anna closed the door behind her.

"As I promised." The graying hair of the rector gleamed silver in the light. The reflection of the candles obscured his eyes, but he smiled, genuinely pleased to see Anna again, even under such circumstances.

"I thought maybe you might have to leave suddenly, like the rest of the British." She sat down wearily beside him.

"Not yet." He looked up at the ceiling where shadows danced on the beams. "I still have a tiny flock, Anna. Any word from Theo?"

She shook her head. "Not since Tuesday. There has been no time, I am sure."

"Why haven't you left yet, my dear lady?" the rector asked seriously.

In reply, Anna pulled her list of one thousand names from her pocket. "I still have some flock to care for as well. I need your help. *They* need your help, Reverend Carwell."

Puzzled, he took the sheaf of papers and glanced through it. "Names?"

Anna paused, uncertain how and where she could begin to explain. "Names. Yes, Jewish names with Jewish faces attached to them. If Theo were here, he would say they were relatives of Mary and Joseph and Jesus, fleeing for their lives from Herod."

With that beginning, Anna spent the next few hours explaining until, at last, she left the church carrying a candle of hope back to the little house on Mala Strana.

♋

The Cuban gunboats idled off the port and starboard sides of the *Darien*. The Coast Guard cutter remained moored to the port-side bow.

The vessel full of newsmen bobbed in the distance. There would be no slipups here. No refugee would dive over the side and swim to either of these two private ships.

Trump stood scowling beside the captain of the small fishing boat. "Go on!" he ordered the ashen-faced man. "They would not dare blow Trump Publishing out of the water! One shot fired, and I'll make that little Spanish-American war Hearst started look like a turkey shoot in Nantucket!"

The captain nodded, not sure why he was obeying Mr. Trump. After all, there were cannons trained on his craft as he bumped against the *Darien*. Commander Deming of the U.S. Coast Guard cutter stood on the deck of the *Darien* with six armed men.

Trump took the bullhorn in his hand and stepped out of the wheelhouse. "You are in violation of international law, Commander! These are international waters, and you have no right to board the vessel! No right to prevent Mrs. Rosenfelt from boarding the *Darien*!"

Deming replied without benefit of the bullhorn. "We are under orders to prevent the exodus of these refugees onto American soil! We intend to obey those orders, newspapers or no newspapers!"

The bulbs of cameras flashed and popped, capturing the confrontation.

Bubbe Rosenfelt, now changed into her blue dress, held the basket of gifts on her arm. Her face was concealed by the veil of her hat. The expression of grief was only hinted at in the slight droop of her shoulders.

"There is only one woman going to board the *Darien*, and you have no right to stop her, Commander," the voice of Trump bellowed. "By all that is holy, sir, I offer you this warning: If Mrs. Rosenfelt is touched or detained in any way, if she is kept from seeing her family or boarding the *Darien*, you will pay for your mistake with your career!"

The cutter commander did not reply for a long moment. His men stood ready behind him. But ready for what? Ready to shoot an old woman? Ready to arrest her for trying to visit her great-grandchildren and her granddaughter?

Trump called down to Bubbe and a crew member who stood beside her. "Go on. They won't stop you! They won't lay one finger on you, Mrs. Rosenfelt! Maybe we don't live in a free country anymore, but nobody owns the ocean." He raised the bullhorn to his lips. "Get off the *Darien*, Commander! You and your men and the whole blasted State Department have no legal right to be there. President Roosevelt couldn't come onboard uninvited. You want to end up sailing a desk around Norfolk, pal, then just stay there another minute."

The commander was beaten. Arrogant and angry, he climbed down the narrow iron steps on the side of the freighter. His men followed as the passengers of the *Darien* cheered with a deafening roar.

The faces of Maria and Klaus, along with Trudy, Katrina, Louise, and Gretchen, appeared high above at the rail to shout and wave at Bubbe. The veiled face was uncovered. Bubbe was radiant with joy and relief. Like a female Moses, her face shone with a great light. She was laughing, reaching out to grasp the metal rails even as the crew of the little boat tied it off to the *Darien*. She climbed easily the steep steps. The nearness of her family swept the unsteadiness of age from her legs.

"Bubbe! Bubbe!" shouted the children, jumping up and down.

Bubbe called their names as she climbed. Above her the passengers still cheered. Arms reached out to pull her up—familiar arms. The loving arms of Maria and Klaus and Trudy and Katrina and Gretchen and Louis. Only Ada-Marie was not here.

Bubbe did not let them see the momentary pain that knifed through her heart. She had not really believed it. Not until now. And then Klaus took the basket, and Maria laid the new little Holbein in her arms. Bubbe let her tears fall on him. Tears for joy and yet for loss. Tears for the realization that this reunion was only for one hour, and yet . . .

Baby Israel squalled his hello. So much noise! So much commotion! Had he not yet learned the difference between happiness and grief? Maria clung to her, laying her head on Bubbe's shoulder.

"Oh, my Kinderlach!" cried Bubbe, touching every face and then touching again. To lay a hand on each sunburned cheek, to feel the fine soft braids, to hold the baby—it was like breathing again after being underwater for a long time. She filled her lungs with them. *My family! My family!*

The Cuban gunboats were forgotten. The arrogant American officer with his inhuman idea of duty to his country was forgotten. No one no-

ticed the endless clicking of cameras or the flashes of light that blinked
against the scarred hull of the freighter. This was the hour of joy; this
hour was all they had hoped it would be.

And so began the bris milah of little Israel. Carried in the arms of
Bubbe Rosenfelt, he was placed before the rabbi of Nuremberg, and all
the men onboard the *Darien* stood and cried with one voice: "Blessed is
he that cometh!"

Although Mr. Trump knew those words were meant for the infant Israel, he still could not help but smile when he heard them. *Blessed is He
that cometh. . . .*

⟨♋⟩

All noise and confusion subsided when Shimon stood before his orchestra of voices and began to conduct Beethoven's Fifth Symphony. The
voices blended together, singing the instrumental parts with a precision
no one, not even Shimon, truly expected. The *Darien* Symphony Orchestra, in perfect harmony and counterpoint, was fulfilling the rabbi's
prophecy of a miracle.

But beyond the decks of the *Darien*, a greater miracle was happening.
On the decks of the Cuban gunboats, armed men lowered their rifles to
their sides and stood transfixed as the music swelled to a crescendo, en-
hanced by the percussion of the waves slapping against the hull of the
ship. Coast Guard officers—even Commander Deming—stood still and
listened. The press corps stopped their picture-taking and waited, awe-
struck, as the music reached its end.

No one had ever heard anything like it. A boatload of refugees, wandering the seas in a coffin ship, produced the most beautiful music
imaginable. This was no coffin—it was an opera house, a symphony
hall, a place where life and love and creativity still flourished in the most
adverse circumstances. And not a few among the listeners wondered
who was truly alive—the occupants of the coffin ship or those who refused them sanctuary. One thing was certain: No prince of Israel ever
had such a circumcision ceremony.

As the foreskin of the child was cut and the blessing recited, baby Israel howled; all the men aboard the *Darien* grimaced and the ladies
closed their eyes. Maria felt faint. Klaus was grateful that his son would
not remember this moment. Trudy, Gretchen, Katrina, and Louise felt
very sorry for their baby brother and very glad they had not been born
sons! And if there was any reminder of grief on that day, it was the
stained canvas prayer shawl worn by the rabbi of Nuremberg.

The steady voice of the rabbi intoned the final blessing: "May the lad
grow in vigor of mind and body to a love of the Torah, to the marriage

canopy, and to a life of good works." A single cup of wine was held up and blessed before the congregation, and the name of Israel Burton Holbein was pronounced. Captain Burton flushed slightly at the surprise. He smiled and nodded as a drop of wine was placed on the baby's lips.

And so it was accomplished. Beautiful and hopeful, another little life was sealed in the Covenant. Heads raised and *Mazel tov*s filled the air as Captain Burton led the little family off to his private quarters for what short time remained of the visit of Bubbe Rosenfelt.

38

Running before the Winds

A wind stirred the sea from the southeast. Choppy waves battered the hull of the smaller craft against the *Darien*.

The commander of the cutter blasted his horn impatiently. *Time enough; the visit is at an end.* The Cuban gunboats imitated his impatience, also letting go with shrill whistles.

The newsmen, who had shouted questions up to the refugees and scribbled down their answers, were surprised when exactly one hour passed and Mrs. Rosenfelt appeared at the top of the steep steps. Her veil now once again covered her face. The little girls clung tightly to her. They were crying. They did not want to let go, and Mrs. Rosenfelt held them as long as she could. Maria had not come to the deck with her. Was such a parting too painful to be made in public? With a drawn face, Klaus Holbein embraced her and then placed the picnic basket back over her arm. Mrs. Rosenfelt reached out for him again. She held him tightly, and at last he took her arms in his hands and gently stepped back.

There were tears beneath that veil. Anyone with eyes could see that there had never been a more painful parting. One hour. Only one. Such a tiny fragment of time to crowd in such joy and such sorrow.

Mrs. Rosenfelt descended the steps slowly—with infinitely more care than she had gone up to meet her loved ones. At the bottom, Mr. Trump stood with one foot on his little boat and the other on the metal mesh landing. He reached to take the hand of Bubbe Rosenfelt to help her off the *Darien*. She looked back over her shoulder and waved to the sobbing children. She held the basket and stepped away.

Trump heard her weeping from behind the veil.

"Mrs. Rosenfelt? Can I get you anything?" he asked as the engines sputtered and the boat drifted from the freighter. He hurt for her. Perhaps this had been more painful; perhaps it would have been easier for her not to have seen them.

Bubbe Rosenfelt shook her head. She did not speak; she looked back one more time and raised a hand to Klaus, who was also weeping. Then she descended the steps and retreated to her cabin, closing the door behind her.

⚬

It was astonishing to Murphy as he walked through the lobby of Hotel Royale this morning that none of the expressions on the faces of the conference participants seemed changed. Still vague and pleasant, they had spoken their first round of sympathetic platitudes last night, and then proceeded to explain why they would *DO NOTHING*!

It was the League of Nations all over again. *Oh my, how sad. Perfectly dreadful situation, these refugees; but you can see how our hands are tied.*

The *Darien* and her passengers were not even mentioned. They were so small in the horrible scope of desperation, why should anyone think of them? There were, Murphy learned, dozens more ships just like the old freighter leaving Germany any way possible. How could these busy, important men think of eight hundred when there were millions at stake? And how could they consider millions . . . so many . . . too many! And so the conference of Evian was lost to the thumb-twiddlers and the sleep-talkers, after all.

A bellboy in a round gray cap and gray uniform walked past the restaurant. "Paging John Murphy! Cable for Mr. John Murphy!"

On an etched silver tray lay a telegram from Havana, Cuba. Murphy tore it open, hoping for some word of good news from Trump.

> MURPHY STOP *DARIEN* TURNED AWAY BY GUNBOATS IN HAVANA STOP MUCH-NEEDED FOOD CONFISCATED STOP HAVANA OFFICIALS SAY PAYOFFS REQUIRED TO LIBERATE STOP ALSO MAY BE POSSIBLE TEMPORARY LANDING CERTIFICATES IF RIGHT MEN ARE BRIBED STOP ALL IMMIGRATION AUTHORITES IN EVIAN STOP GET BUSY STOP TRUMP

Murphy read the cable; then he read it again. Good news, bad news, huh? The *Darien* is turned away and the food confiscated; however, certain officials told Trump that the right amount in the right pocket of a Cuban immigration official at Evian would at least buy a little time! A Cuban landing certificate!

Amanda was long gone, but she had essentially told Murphy the same thing. There were ways to get around the reluctance of men to do the right thing. Money might stir hearts to action on behalf of the down-trodden much sooner than lofty words and ideals.

"Welcome back to the real world, Murphy," he muttered to himself as he strode quickly to the desk. He had plenty of money in the account Theo had set up in New York. Hadn't this been the very sort of thing he had intended the funds to be used for? He would talk to Theo about that some other time. Now he had people to meet.

He rang the bell on the lobby counter. "I would like the room number of Cuban representative Cabrillo, please." He spelled the name for the French clerk. "C-A-B-R-I-L-L-O. He's Cuban."

⟨ೞ⟩

Anna made her way back through the crowded kitchen. "What did he say?"

"Did he agree?"

"Was he insulted, or angry with you?"

There were a thousand questions that seemed to need answers at the same moment.

Anna answered hopefully. "He says you should come and see." And that answer was passed from one to another in the house and down the food line.

In the midst of the noon meal a harried-looking messenger boy arrived on a bicycle in front of the heavy-laden tables set up outside. He had a telegram for Anna Linder marked *Urgent*.

Women exchanged glances. Could this mean that Theo or her sons had been injured or killed? A small boy went to fetch her from the kitchen.

Wiping her hands on her apron, Anna hurried down the steps to where the messenger stood guarding his bicycle. She paid him the charge; then with trembling hands she tore open the envelope.

The whole street seemed silent as they watched her. Tears filled her eyes, and she smiled. "They are being called home to Prague," she said at last. "Theo, Wilhelm, and Dieter are to be stationed here at the airfield. *Sunday!* God is good to me! They are coming home!"

⟨ೞ⟩

"So, Señor Murphy." Manuello Cabrillo studied Murphy from across the table. "You are buying time for these people, no?" He toyed thoughtfully with the silver knife at the edge of his plate. "Time is a very expensive thing. I have spoken to my superiors. In this case . . . time will cost one million dollars."

Murphy simply blinked at him in disbelief. *One million!* "Nobody has that kind of money," he replied unhappily.

Cabrillo shrugged as the waiter in the tearoom poured their glasses full of the famous Evian water. "You see those two men over there?" Cabrillo now leaned in to whisper as he jerked a thumb toward two iron-jawed Germans across the room at a window table.

"What about them?" Murphy had a distinct distaste for this unctuous little Latin with his slick hair and Italian silk suit and two-toned shoes. He looked like a casino manager and displayed the greed of a Chicago bank robber.

"These men are Germans, Señor." He shared a fact that Murphy had easily guessed. Evian was packed with members of Hitler's tribe this week.

"So what?"

"They are here to *sell Jews*, Señor Murphy!" Cabrillo grinned and sat back in amazement at the thought. "Yes! They are *selling* their Jews for two hundred and fifty dollars a head! And you know what?" He paused for effect. "Nobody wants to buy their Jews, Señor! No one at all is in the market for Jews. Have you not noticed? No country wants Jews! Even when Hitler offers them free, no one will take the German Jews!" He spread his hands in a broad gesture. These were the facts. "Since no one will even take free Jews, like your Jews, well then, it only makes sense that maybe Hitler will have to pay to get rid of them, no? Or maybe you—the company you represent—maybe you will pay such a little amount to the government of Cuba to keep your Jews on the Isle of Pines for six months? Such a little amount considering our risk."

"What risk?" Murphy was inwardly fuming but did not show it.

"What if after six months you still cannot get them on the quota list? What if the U.S. government will not take them then? What will we do with them? Tow them out to sea and let them sink?"

"One million is . . . impossible." Murphy glanced toward the Nazi flesh peddlers who lunched on quiche washed down with white wine. They accepted their failure as Jew salesmen rather pragmatically. They looked totally carefree. Perhaps they had found another use for their unwanted merchandise. *So this was Evian. Council of the great and merciful nations.*

Murphy cleared his throat in an effort to hold down the sudden revulsion he felt. He considered the account Theo had set up in New York. He estimated what might be raised from other sources. "We are prepared to offer you two hundred dollars for each Cuban landing certificate for the people aboard the *Darien*."

Cabrillo smiled a wide-mouthed, incredulous smile. He shook his head at such a ridiculous offer. "We all know that the rich Jews can pay much more than that. Sears and Roebuck, Loeb and Kuhn—they say, 'I'll give you fifty thousand for this or that. One hundred, two hundred thousand.' We all know about these rich bankers. These Jews! They can come up with a million dollars in one hour!"

"There are no rich bankers aboard the *Darien*. These people paid passage with their last cent." Murphy controlled his outrage. "This might be their last hope."

"Ah, well. Pity them. But they do have rich relatives in the United States, do they not, Señor? Everyone knows the Jews control the press. All the banks in America. Such a small amount will be simple for them to arrange, no, Señor? That is our final offer. We can give you twenty-four hours to consider it. That is all we can do."

Twenty-four hours to raise one million dollars. All for the privilege of camping on Cuban soil. But what other options were there? Could Trump and the others manage to raise that kind of cash?

Murphy met the man's impudent gaze with a slow nod. He glanced toward the Nazis and suddenly had the sickening sense that the man he was dealing with was just as dark in his soul.

～⠀ᏀᎧ⠀～

There were no little shiploads of news reporters. No one to denounce or threaten. Now Commander Deming could do his job. He radioed for support from a second cutter as the *Darien* again came within American waters. Together these two American vessels flanked the *Darien* even as the skies above them grew darker with the approaching storm.

Bullhorn to his lips, Deming issued the warning, the ultimatum: "YOU HAVE ENTERED AMERICAN WATERS! TURN ABOUT, *DARIEN*, OR WE WILL BE FORCED TO FIRE ON YOU."

Captain Burton answered: "There is a gale approaching. We ask for anchorage."

"NOTHING DOING, *DARIEN*. SMALL-CRAFT WARNINGS ONLY ARE ISSUED AS OF NOW. NOTHING YOU CAN USE AS AN EXCUSE TO MOOR IN AN AMERICAN HARBOR."

"Check your barometer!" Burton shouted back in frustration.

In reply, the crew of the cutter fired a round above the bow of the *Darien*. "YOU WILL WISH YOU HAD A LITTLE WIND TO SAIL THROUGH IF YOU DO NOT TURN ABOUT IMMEDIATELY!"

Burton looked at the small, timid radio repairman from Berlin who now manned the transmitter. "Send word to Trump. Tell him we're being forced to turn out to sea. Keep sending word of our position."

❦

First Mate Tucker stood defiantly beside Captain Burton. Together they stared down the barrel of a revolver. It was not a large weapon, but it was enough.

Five other crewmen faced them almost apologetically. "This ain't mutiny, Captain Burton. We done more than we signed up for, and now we're finished with it, that's all." The leader jerked a thumb toward the lifeboat. "We ain't more than eight miles from shore, and I ain't much of a man if I can't row eight miles."

"You see, sir," his second offered, "we signed up from Hamburg to New York. We been on this stinking tub for weeks, and now it looks like you're gonna have to go back to Hamburg. I don't fancy another trip across the big pond, not with the weather comin' up the way it is."

Tucker drew himself up angrily; he took a step toward the man with the gun. "If this ain't mut'ny, they why y' got a gun?"

"Just to make sure we get off."

Burton had remained silent throughout the confrontation. He placed a hand on Tucker's chest as if to hold him back. "We can run the ship without them."

"But, Cap'n . . ."

"No," Burton said, "I mean it. If we are forced back to Hamburg, then I will at least have a reason to keep a few of the men here onboard as crew. Go on, Tucker. Pick out a few from among the single passengers and let these gentlemen have the lifeboat." He smiled a thin-lipped smile. "Payment for the lifeboat?" he asked. "I want the marine cards of every one of you. Keep the rest of your papers, but I want your Merchant Marine cards."

"You can't keep us from picking up work on another ship. We can get those cards replaced, you know."

"In Hamburg your cards will be identification for my new crew, that's all. You are free to go."

The lifeboat was lowered after the casket of Ada-Marie was gently removed from it. The little coffin was taken to the bow of the ship and secured, then covered with a tarp as the five crewmen rowed toward shore. Fifteen minutes later they were picked up by Captain Deming in his Coast Guard cutter. After showing their papers as proof of American citizenship, they were given a lift into Norfolk even as the *Darien* turned out to sea for the last time.

❦

Shimon stood for a moment with his back to the giant mountain of coal. Captain Burton did not look back as he clattered up the metal steps and ducked through the watertight door.

Well, perhaps it is only right, Shimon thought as he turned to face the broad, flat shovel. After all, the fires of the Thyssen Steelworks had brought him here. Now the coal and the shovel and the fires of the boiler would take him home. Wherever home might be. *Leah is where home is.* He grabbed the shovel and plunged it into the coal, then tossed the load into the furnace. He would find her somehow. If this ship was ever brought into a port, he would find a way to reach her. Was she still in Vienna? he wondered. Had the Nazis expelled her from the orchestra, or did her cello still sing sweetly from the stage of the Musikverein night after night?

He could picture her most easily at her music stand. *Yes, Leah, I see you there, nodding as the crowds applaud you. You are more clear to me than these fires I feed. My heart glows more warmly than these flames.*

Shimon had not yet regained all his strength; the doctor was correct about that, but still he was stronger than he had been working in the steel plant. Good food, laughter, hopeful Jewish hearts and words had brought him back to life again. He did not mind this work at all. His muscle fueled the fires that turned the engines that would somehow take him home. Home to the only thing that mattered to him. Home to his dear Leah.

As he worked he sang the melodies of a hundred symphonies that they had played together. The clanging rhythm of the engine boomed like the kettledrums. He had not been allowed to sing when he had been under the thumb of the Nazi overseers. Music made the burden of work seem lighter, and always ringing in his ears was the clear sweet melody of Leah's cello. The music never left him as he labored deep in the belly of the ship. And always she was there: a smile, a nod of thanks to the audience, and then a knowing wink for Shimon across the stage.

☙

For a hundred miles into international waters, the Coast Guard cutter of Deming pursued the *Darien* out to sea. In the distance lightning split the black sky like veins on the hide of Satan.

The storm was more than a danger to small craft. Burton could smell it coming, even if the bottom had not yet dropped out of the barometer. The Coast Guard cutter at last turned away to rip back across the water to safe harbor. The lumbering *Darien* had no such advantage.

"Secure lifelines," Burton instructed Tucker. "Get everyone below deck. I'll bring her around and head for shore in an hour, when I'm sure the cutter is long gone."

☙

From the first assault of the storm, it had been difficult to stoke the boiler. The ship rolled from side to side until the men who manned the engines could not stand up. And then when the *Darien* turned to climb the towering waves like mountains and slide down into the deep valleys, the task became nearly impossible.

Aaron, Fredrik, Klaus, and a dozen others held on to ropes and one another as they manned the pumps. A few inches of water in the bottom of the ship had risen to eighteen inches. Their faces reflected terror. They were pumping as fast as possible, and yet . . .

The moans of the others were covered by the winds until Shimon could no longer tell if the sounds came from humans or from the whole world.

He picked up his shovel as the bow of the ship raised to ascend the face of a wave. "Open the boiler!" he shouted to the terror-stricken young Orthodox man who helped him. "Open, and then close it after I toss in the fuel!"

The man nodded. If he did not move quickly enough the fire would spill out. Shimon braced himself and struggled to stand as the iron door swung back. White heat emanated. It swallowed the black chunks of coal. The Orthodox man slammed the door, looking relieved.

"More men on the pumps!" Klaus shouted. "We need shifts."

Aaron struggled toward the steps to climb up and raise the cry for more help to combat the mounting seawater.

⚭

Maria cradled Israel in her arms as the floor of the *Darien* sloped away and another moan rose up from the refugees trapped below the howling storm.

There was sickness. The air smelled of vomit and fear. Somehow the four little girls managed to sleep through this hideous rolling and lurching. And Israel nursed calmly and then paused, turning his wide dark eyes to gaze at his mother. Something in those peaceful, innocent eyes calmed Maria's own heart. So at rest he was, not aware of the waves that towered over the highest masts of the *Darien*, oblivious to the howling of the winds and the shouting of men who tried to pump the water from the hold of the boat. Slowly but surely, the waves that tumbled over the decks were winning the contest against the men who manned the pumps below.

And yet Israel was not frightened by the shouts of fear and hopelessness that echoed around him. In the arms of his mother he was content.

39

Birds in the Eye of the Storm

In this same hour, all of Europe seemed to be running before the winds. The howling of the gale had drowned out the cries of the *Darien*. Entire nations lost resolve and bent as the gale approached their borders.

Tonight in the home of Admiral Canaris in Berlin, General Halder sat among the other conspirators to listen to Hitler's speech over the radio. Twenty-five thousand faithful party members cheered the Führer as he spoke to them from the Berlin Sportspalast. Millions of others listened with dread to his words. Only this handful among the German High Command knew that this was the Führer's last speech, his last threat.

"We have him where we want him." General Hoepner rubbed his hands together. "Here in Berlin we will bag the whole lot of them at once."

"Tonight the people hear the voice of Hitler and tremble. On Saturday, when the Führer gives the order to march, it will be General Halder who speaks," said Canaris quietly. "And then the world will see that this madness is Hitler's alone."

Straight and tense, General Halder gazed out the window as the tumult of the crowds at the Sportspalast filled the room. "Perhaps we should not wait until Saturday," he interjected. "Perhaps we should arrest them all tonight. Himmler. Göring. Goebbels. My Regular Army divisions could march within the hour. We could take Hitler after his speech, even as he leaves the Sportspalast."

The men looked questioningly at one another. Would it not be easier

to accomplish the coup tonight? Three days before the army was scheduled by Hitler to invade the Czech-Sudetenland?

"No, no," Hoepner concluded. "The plan is right as we have conceived it. There are twenty-five thousand Nazis in the Sportspalast. We
do not want to contend with them as well. Better for us to bide our time.
Arrest Hitler in the staff room as he hovers over his maps like a vulture."

Others among the conspirators nodded. The coup against Hitler
must not become a massacre. It must not be announced until it was accomplished. Hitler and his head henchmen were in Berlin. The plan of
the army staff officers could not go wrong!

The roaring of the broadcast fell to silence. The Führer was about to
state his final ultimatum to the Czechs and to the world.

The voice of Adolf Hitler reached into the room.

> "On February 22 of this year, I made a fundamental demand calling
> for the uniting of German minorities and the return of German colo-
> nies lost in the war. My nation heard it and understood what I
> meant. One statesman in Austria, Schuschnigg, failed to understand.
> He has been removed, and my promise has been fulfilled. For the
> second time I made my demand at the Reich party's Nuremberg
> convention. Again the nation heard!"

Once again the spell was conjured and cast. The whole world could
hear the tumultuous applause of those in the Sportspalast. The Führer
held them by the throat as he began to build one statement upon another. His volume increased, and with it, the volume of applause.

> "Today there must be no vestige of doubt in the world. It is not a
> Führer or a man who speaks, but the whole German people. And if I
> am now spokesman of the German people, I know at this hour that all
> the listening millions of these people are one, that they endorse these
> words and make them their own testimony. Let other statesmen search
> themselves and see if it is the same with them."

Thomas knew these words were spoken directly to Chamberlain who
paced, alone and frightened, in his offices in London. The people of
England were torn and resentful at the thought of fighting a war for the
nation of Czechoslovakia. In France, the leaders were besieged with opposition. This claim of Hitler that he alone had the full assent of his people must have galled other leaders of nations. Those men could not fully
know the depth of opposition against the German leader! They would
not know until Saturday, when German divisions ordered to march

turned their guns instead on the Chancellery and marched back to Berlin.

"Hold firm!" Thomas whispered to Chamberlain and Daladier as if they could hear. "Do not waver in your commitment." Thomas looked around the room at the pensive faces of Germany's finest men. Some had closed their eyes as if they prayed. All seemed determined to go through with the plan.

> *"The question that has been agitating us most deeply for the past months and weeks has been well-known to those leaders. Its name is not so much Czechoslovakia. Its name is rather Herr President Beneš. This name unites all that is agitating millions today and drives them to despair and fills them with fanatic determination!"*

Shouts of "Bloodhound!" and "Viper!" echoed from the hall.

> *"German foreign policy is distinct from the democracies. It is fixed on our philosophy of life. The new Third Reich is based upon safeguarding the existence of our German people. We are not interested in oppressing other peoples. We do not wish to have other nationalities among us. We want to live after our own patterns and let others live after theirs. This racially bound conception leads to limitation of our foreign policy. We want only what is ours!"*

Halder and Canaris exchanged glances. Halder had heard enough. He sighed and shook his head. He had seen the plans of Hitler's conquest of Europe. Every word the Führer uttered tonight was a lie. From the Czech borders, Poland would be next—then Russia, then France. Even England.

> *"There is a limit beyond which I cannot go. How right I was is proven first by the peaceful union of Austria with the Reich. Now we must confront this last problem to be solved. This is the last territorial demand I have to make in Europe, but it is also a demand on which I shall not yield. Herr Beneš refuses to withdraw from this territory. He refuses to give legal title to an area populated by racial Germans and being raped by the Czechs. The Germans want peace; the Slovak people want peace! This tyrant Beneš will rush us into war. This territory will come under German rule because it is essentially inhabited by Germans! The final boundaries, however, I will leave to a vote of the people there."*

Canaris smiled bitterly. Such a vote of approval in Austria had been rigged from the beginning. It would be no different if Hitler took over the Sudetenland from the Czechs. How could the French and British leaders believe such words?

> *"I have now addressed a memorandum to the British government with this last and final German proposal. Territory that is racially German and wants to join Germany is to go with Germany."*

The military men gathered in the room tonight knew what acceptance of such a proposal would mean to the nation of Czechoslovakia. If that mountainous region that defended the Czechs from Germany was simply handed over to Germany, then it would only be a matter of time before Hitler marched on to Prague. The defense lines of the Czechs were strong and impenetrable. To turn them over to Hitler would be pure suicide. Beneš would never consent. In his words tonight, Hitler had as much as declared war. Even Chamberlain must admit this now! British treaty obligations would have to be recognized and conciliation abandoned.

General Beck had resigned his commission after he had explained that the Czech-Sudeten line of defense was too strong to break through without months of fighting. The Führer had scoffed at him and insisted that he would have Beneš served up on a plate the day after invasion.

Tonight's speech was more reason then ever why Adolf Hitler would find himself in a cell by Saturday morning. In his cry to rescue the Sudeten-Germans, he was willing to sacrifice thousands of young German soldiers. These were facts that Halder would explain after the coup.

The tirade against Beneš continued for an hour and a half. By its end, the thousands in the Berlin Sportspalast were in a hysterical frenzy of hatred against the Czechs.

The conspirators sat beside the radio far into the night as they waited for the opinions of other world leaders to whisper back in answer to the howling. Their jaws set with determination, they strengthened their resolve that Hitler would not again stand before the microphone and shout his threats.

⟨∅⟩

Shimon was grateful when two men came to relieve him at the boiler. Beneath the roaring of the winds, they could not hear his voice and so he nodded and demonstrated the method of loading the fire without spilling hot coals out of the furnace.

A pat on his back. His replacement mouthed the words "Get some sleep."

Shimon crawled toward the steel ladder leading to the passenger decks. The *Darien* rolled a full twenty-five degrees to starboard and thirty-degrees to port, sending men toppling over like dominoes. The pumps flailed uselessly as men clung to one another and struggled back to grasp the handles.

Shimon climbed three steps and then was tossed back, managing to hold on to the handrail with his left hand while the rest of his body twisted around. Aaron grasped Shimon's leg and pulled himself up with the man's help. Aaron's hands were bloody and raw from the hours on the pump. His features seemed frozen with the effort, like a runner pushing himself to finish the race.

Shimon emerged onto the passenger deck and reached back to pull the young man up after him. Together they sprawled on the pitching deck in exhaustion.

෨

As Murphy paced the luxurious suite at Hotel Royale, he could feel the eyes of Timmons on him.

"Ah, Murph—" Timmons scowled— "I don't know if I want to work for you. I mean . . . it's been great working with you. I don't know if I want to ruin our friendship."

"I'm not asking you to marry me, Timmons!" Murphy roared. "I want you to go to work for the Trump European operations. I need a journalist in Munich."

"But . . . I started as a sportswriter." Timmons thoughtfully probed his ear. "I'm no political reporter. Munich? You want me to cover Chamberlain and Daladier going to bed with Hitler and Mussolini? Huh? Cheating on Beneš in Prague?"

"Exactly!" Murphy exploded. "You can do it."

"No. *You* can do it."

"I *can't* do it; that's the point." Murphy whirled around and picked up the sheaf of papers with the list of *Darien* passengers. "I can't leave now, not until this is settled. I've got nearly eight hundred people in my hands."

"Yeah, well, when the Big Four get finished with their hanky-panky, we're going to have a few million more."

"I need you to go to Munich for me. Go to work for me on this, Timmons. I can't give you a raise, but at least you'll know you're working for a good, straight-thinking man like Trump instead of Craine."

"Or Hearst," Timmons concluded.

"This is the biggest story of betrayal since Judas kissed Jesus in Gethsemane. And I can't leave. What do you say, Timmons?"

Timmons exhaled. His breath blew his tousled hair like feathers. "Yeah, I guess you're right. You're right." He grimaced. "But you're the only man I'd go back into Germany for. I've come to hate that place, Murphy. Really hate it."

Murphy smiled. He was actually pulling together a team. Yesterday he had hired Johnson and sent him to cover Prague. The day before he had lured Phipps away from INS and had pulled together one of the best crews in London.

"Now all I have to do is get the rest of that million bucks, and we've got it made!"

❧

Manuello Cabrillo studied Murphy with a doubtful look. "We cannot give you any more time, Señor."

"Raising a million dollars takes time. The *Darien* is still north of Cuba. We can recall her when we get the money. Mr. Trump has personally donated several hundred thousand. There is another account that we have access to. But it is not nearly as much as you are asking for. We could put the money up as a bond, a guarantee—"

Cabrillo shook his head. "We have offered you our terms," he said with an air of unconcern. "It is, of course, your responsibility to meet them. Or we simply cannot do business."

"We are asking for a few days. That is all."

"The government of Cuba is not prepared to extend our deadline."

"These are *people* on this boat—"

"There are more where they come from, Señor." Cabrillo smiled sarcastically. "You remind me of my sister. When we were small, a boy in our neighborhood kept snakes. He fed birds to his snakes, and my sister would buy the baby birds from him to keep them from being eaten. He would sell them, of course. She was a fool. The boy always had many more birds to feed his snakes, Señor. The snakes did not care which bird they ate." He shook his head. "Yes. The Nazis have millions of birds. Why do you wish to save these? Why not the others?"

Snakes and birds. Nazis and Jews. A good comparison. "Because these are the ones I can help . . . maybe. They are on the shores of my homeland. And I don't want—" He did not finish his thought that America was also full of snakes who would watch with cold eyes as the jaws of Nazi Germany opened wide and swallowed whole.

Cabrillo did not really care. His question had been purely rhetorical, as he must have asked his sister why she bought the baby birds. "I can do nothing more for you, Señor. If you do not have the money, then—" He shrugged. "You should save it up, however. Who knows how many more refugees will sail by your country, no?"

Was this it, then? Cabrillo was ending the negotiations? "Wait!" Murphy tried again as the little Cuban snatched his hat and moved for the door. "Wait." He put a hand on the silk suit. He was begging. "Just a few days; we'll get it."

Cabrillo looked at the hand touching his suit. There was scorn in his eyes. "Perhaps another time, Señor. I have a train to catch, then a steamer back to my homeland."

And that was the last of it. The end of options. Murphy had already sent feelers out to most of the Latin American countries. Nothing doing. Nobody was in the market for Jews. Nobody wanted Jews. Not even if you paid for them to take one little boatload.

Cabrillo retreated down the hall as Murphy sank onto the sofa with his head in his hands. What was left? Where could he turn? How could he look at himself in the mirror in the morning when the situation of the *Darien* grew more desperate each day?

⟨♾⟩

The wind was up, hard and strong, as Trump left his Times Square office building. He held on to his hat and squinted up at the four-foot high letters that flashed the news:

VICTORY FOR DARIEN *REFUGEES? . . . STATE DEPARTMENT MAY ISSUE QUOTA NUMBERS FOR 1940.*

It was only a partial victory, but it was something all the same. Those families aboard the *Darien* might be allowed into the United States in the quota of 1940. Two years from now. That guarantee might open the door for a temporary refuge somewhere else now that Cuba had refused.

The chauffeur held open the door of Trump's automobile as he contemplated the news that now overshadowed everything else:

CHAMBERLAIN FLIES TO HITLER'S SIDE IN MUNICH. . . . BIG FOUR POWERS TO DECIDE FATE OF CZECHOSLOVAKIA.

The last item of the moving lines of news was, for Trump, the most chilling:

CARIBBEAN HURRICANE MOVES UP COAST TOWARD CAPE HATTERAS.

Since early morning there had been no communication from the wireless of the *Darien*. At every publishing outpost along the entire Atlantic seaboard, Trump had issued orders that all radio transmissions must be directed toward contacting the ship. There had been no luck.

Trump shoved his hat down hard on his head and ducked into the car. What would he tell Mrs. Rosenfelt today? She had not spoken since they had returned by plane from Miami. She had not seemed to hear when he told her about the protests and the thousands of letters that had swamped the offices of the secretary of state and President Roosevelt. She had not listened when he told her how the wife of the president had spoken out against the heartlessness of this policy.

What news could he offer her? *Rejoice; your family will be on a quota list for immigration two years from now.* Would she not reply that two years was a long time to wait for a woman of seventy-eight?

He must not let her know there had been no word from the *Darien* since last night, that they had been unable to contact the ship that was last reported a hundred miles out and directly in the path of the worst hurricane to hit the Carribean and New England in a hundred years.

With a sigh, Trump gritted his teeth. He would tell her only the first headline:

VICTORY FOR DARIEN *REFUGEES.*

◁꩜▷

Klaus crawled over the bodies of his shipmates toward where he knew Maria and the girls huddled. He had stopped thinking long ago about whom he would save. He had little hope now that anyone would live unless Captain Burton managed somehow to drive the *Darien* up on land very soon. One of the pumps had broken. The rolling of the ship made repair almost impossible, although a crew of men worked together to do so.

Klaus had never heard such noise—the wind wailing like a million souls trapped in hell. A hundred miles an hour, Tucker had guessed. He had never been on seas so rough. But Captain Burton would see them through. He had turned the ship toward land. There would be no Coast Guard out now to stop them.

Maria reached out for him as he neared their corner. She grasped his soaking shirt. She pulled him against her, and only then did he notice that she was cold. Shivering. Teeth chattering. He laid his head against her, although the ship tried to roll him away.

"How much longer?" Maria shouted over the howling gale. "How long—the storm?"

He could not answer. They had survived twenty-eight hours thus far. How much longer could this listing hulk last? And if the *Darien* did indeed make it to a shoal, how could anyone escape this steel shell? Would the winds not tear them to pieces and the waves break each body on the rocks?

Klaus squeezed her arm in reply. There was not a sound from his children. *Trudy. Katrina. Gretchen. Louise. Little Israel.* Had he brought them here to end like this?

He then thought about the little coffin lashed to the deck like a figurehead. *Ada-Marie.* Perhaps soon they would all be together again. He hoped and prayed for the sake of his children that the terror would not last too long, that the pain of death would be over quickly.

40

Who Will Buy the Little Birds?

Elisa could not believe her ears. She wanted to snatch the pipe from Tedrick's smug lips and throw it at him in frustration. "What do you mean 'None of this is significant'?" She was almost shouting. She had carried the startling defiance of the German High Command across the Channel to this office, and now Tedrick was telling her a document presented to Hitler on the eve of his announced invasion was without significance.

"I am not making policy," Tedrick said patronizingly. "The prime minister and the cabinet make policy, and the policy is to prevent a war in Europe if possible!"

"But . . . he told me . . . General Halder opposes a move against the Czechs."

"General Halder is under Hitler's authority. As are the other members of the High Command. Our own PM is presented with documents a hundred times a week that state opinions about this or that. Hitler may very well disregard such a document and march anyway, you see."

"But they won't let him ignore it."

"They *who*?" He smiled skeptically.

"The generals."

"Oh? You have information that they—the generals—are planning a coup? They will assassinate Hitler, or arrest him? What?"

"No. Not in so many words."

"Well, then." Tedrick had lost all patience. "Have you so thrown yourself into this work you detest that you have become a prophetess?"

"No. But there was something else. I could hear it in his voice. I know him so well—"

"We are aware of how *well* you know von Kleistmann, but unless you can give us more to go on than this document that will somehow make Hitler change his mind, then I am repeating to you what the whole world already knows. Herr Hitler is traveling from Berlin at this moment to meet with Chamberlain and Daladier of France and Mussolini. There they will attempt to settle the Czech problem between them." He struck a match and sat back. "You and the generals have not been invited to the conference. Neither have the Czechs. They will accept whatever peaceful decision is made; I am certain."

Elisa felt like crying. Had she ever been so angry? "You will pass this information on to Chamberlain?"

"When he gets back from Munich."

She sat in anguished silence. Hitler, leaving Berlin. Drawn away from Berlin by this meeting. Would the document still be presented? she wondered. Or would the High Command simply submit to the Führer once again?

"Are you finished with me, then?"

"Finished?"

"What has been the use of this if you won't listen?"

"My dear girl, the government listens. And the government makes decisions based on many different factors. Our ambassador in Berlin is the one who was personally requested to relay the Führer's willingness to negotiate a solution. You are only a messenger. A courier. One of hundreds, I might add."

"Then you are finished with me."

"We would like you to return one more time to Paris. To set up von Kleistmann with a new contact. A meeting time. Recognition signal. But, yes. I'm sure you're relieved. Your part is over."

She simply stared at Tedrick. He was discharging her without a word of thanks, like the dismissal of an incompetent secretary.

"You mean, I can—"

"Go where you like." He smiled. Was there something behind that smile? Some knowledge? He opened a drawer and tossed her a key. "The Savoy Hotel tonight? We've kept your room for you."

"And the need for Shelby? for my protection?"

"Nothing at all to worry about. You can once again be Elisa Murphy."

"Just like that?"

He puffed his pipe. The smoke rose up before his face. "Just like that."

Elisa nodded and extended her hand for the final message she was to relay to Thomas. A name. A date. A time. She would remember. She gave the paper back to Tedrick, who touched it to his tobacco and let it burn.

☙

From Argentina to Venezuela, Murphy checked off the lists of Western Hemisphere nations. A few, rumor had it, were already involved in under-the-table transactions to take in a paltry few refugees. But no one was interested in the *Darien*. Too high profile. Too much interest. People might start asking questions like, How much was paid? and to whom?

There were other shiploads of refugees. One had been anchored in Istanbul for two months. Two others had been blockaded from entering Palestine by the British. The refugees onboard those ships had been taken by the British to Mauritania, where they were now held behind barbed wire and watched by guards in machine-gun towers. A leaky barge filled with Jewish children destined for Palestine had sunk in the Adriatic. A handful of others had set sail and never been heard from since. *A pity. But one cannot save everyone.*

With all of this a matter of record, these delegates whom Murphy approached one by one simply looked at him with the same pitying smile he had seen on the face of Cabrillo. *Why buy these little birds when there are so many?*

Each morning Murphy asked himself that question. He tried to harden himself against the disappointment as each delegate shook his head and answered, "No, we cannot change our laws for a few, or we will find our country overrun by many."

So. In the interest of fairness to all of the persecuted, was it more just to let everyone perish?

The coldness of this civilized reasoning pushed Murphy to a raging frustration like nothing he had ever experienced before—not even in Spain, not even when German bombs had dropped with arbitrary brutality on schools and homes and churches. Until now he had not fully understood that apathy was the glove into which evil slipped its hand. Apathy protected the fist of evil from skinning its knuckles as it slammed babies against a wall. The searing of a man's conscience was, in the end, just as deadly as a machine gun fired into a classroom of children, just as final in the end as the sinking of a ship.

The horrible weight of this knowledge did not lift from Murphy's heart. It was dusk. The end of another day in Evian. The room was dim, but Murphy did not turn on the light. He picked up the list of *Darien* names and sank down onto the sofa.

Skimming his finger over the list, he began to pray. Each name was a person, a face, an individual with hopes and fears and a certain number of years to live on this earth, and then an eternity to face. These were not numbers or statistics—they were living, breathing, hurting, hoping souls.

Why these birds when there are so many others? "Why, Lord?" Murphy asked aloud. He waited, expecting an answer.

And in his heart the answer came to him. *Everyone is on the* Darien, *Murphy. Every man. Every woman. Every child. They wait. They hope for a word that will give them life, and no one speaks. No one reaches out.* "Not *now! No time! No room!*" *In the end it will be the same for everyone, and I will judge apathy and evil side by side. They will hear My words and remember: I was hungry and you gave Me nothing to eat, I was thirsty and you gave Me nothing to drink, I was a stranger and you did not invite Me in, I needed clothes, and you did not clothe Me, I was sick and in prison and you did not look after Me. Whatever you did not do for one of the least of these, you did not do for Me!*

So, this was the answer. *Emmanuel, God with us.* Was Jesus also on the *Darien?* Was He among the lost sheep of Israel? By this, did He weigh the nations and the hearts of men?

Such thoughts were too great for John Murphy. He bowed his head and wept with grief—not just for the people on the *Darien* anymore, but for everyone.

After a time he switched on the light. The list of names still lay on his lap. His eyes focused on one name in the center of the list: *SHIMON FELDSTEIN, AGE 29, ORIGIN VIENNA, AUSTRIA.*

Murphy gasped and touched the name. Why had he not seen it before now? He jumped up and ran to the telephone. He had to call Elisa. She had to know! But where should he call? The Savoy? She seemed to get her messages from there. Yes. He would call London. Savoy Hotel.

He closed his eyes and prayed that she would be there.

◌◌

Rough hands shook Shimon where he lay on the deck below. The storm had not abated. How had he slept? How had anyone slept? He raised his head, and Tucker put his mouth against his ear and shouted over the roaring of the storm.

"Captain needs you! Wheelhouse!"

Shimon nodded and struggled after Tucker, who seemed somehow to be able to walk upright in rhythm with the bucking ship. Up the metal steps. The force of the winds was deafening. Tucker turned to Shimon as if to warn him he was about to open the hatch. They would have to fight the water, cling to the lifelines.

"Ready?" Tucker shouted.

One nod. Shimon was not certain he was ready. Up until now he had only heard the force of the gale and felt the rolling of the ship. Was it day or night? He did not know anymore. The hatch opened; the screaming winds jerked it out of Tucker's hands, sucking him out onto the deck. There was a wail of anguish from below as the fury increased and penetrated the belly of the ship. Shimon ducked and followed, grasping the metal of the hatch and helping Tucker slam it back and secure it.

The *Darien* was a toy boat among mountains of moving gray water. Shimon could see only the water. Walls of water. Sprays of water stinging him until he felt blind as he held desperately to the slippery lifelines. Inch by inch Tucker pulled himself forward. Shimon followed hand over hand. His legs did not matter any longer. They offered barely any support on the slippery, churning foam that covered the planks.

There was a dim light in the wheelhouse. The two men strained against the force that pushed against them, threatening them to make even one false step. A slip. One instant of error and the waters that towered over the hull of the *Darien* would suck them in forever. At the sight of such force and fury, Shimon wondered how they had stayed afloat so long.

Tucker kept one hand on the lifeline as he reached to open the door of the wheelhouse. Lightning flashed, illuminating the face of Captain Burton. He strained to hold the wheel in control, his face contorted with the effort. Tucker lunged forward to help him hold it, and Shimon jumped after him, falling to the floor and kicking the door shut with his feet as a twenty-foot wave crested and broke against the port side.

There was no need for explanation. Burton could not hold the wheel alone. Shimon struggled to stand and grasped the wheel with the other two men.

Shimon could see the face of a wall of water ahead of them. Gray, undulating force. In a corner of the wheelhouse, a middle-aged man continued to tap urgently on the telegraph. Was anyone listening? And was there any way of helping even if a message might penetrate the storm?

"Fifty miles!" shouted Burton. "Fifty miles to shore! If we can—" His words were lost to them, but there was hope in his voice. And he had brought them so far already.

⊂⊃

Murphy left his message for Elisa with the operator at the Savoy; then he hurried downstairs to grab a sandwich before she called.

Luggage belonging to the Evian delegates was piled everywhere in the lobby. The conference had ended so hopelessly, yet the faces of the men looked rested and pleasant as they chatted in little groups. Murphy was the last journalist remaining in Evian. Everyone else had rushed off to Munich or Prague or London or Paris. Tomorrow Murphy would leave.

An overcoat on his arm, the representative from Holland stood beside a marble column as he waited for his luggage to be brought down. Murphy had tried half a dozen times to contact Pietr Vander without success or response. The small portly Dutchman raised a hand to hail him.

Murphy changed his course, trying to suppress some small light of hope.

"Ah, Mr. Murphy," Vander said warmly. "Have you found a Latin port for that ship of yours?"

"No," Murphy replied. "And I have been hoping to talk to you about the possibility of—"

"Temporary haven?" Vander nodded. "I thought perhaps you might. Are these people on a quota list? Have they been issued quota numbers by the American State Department yet?"

"We are working on that now. Nothing yet. A few stirrings."

Vander nodded as the bellman approached with his trunk. "We are only a country of temporary sojourn. But if there is proof that these people will be moving toward immigration in another country, perhaps we can discuss a short period for them to come to Holland. It is all hinged on those quota numbers, however." He smiled and handed Murphy his card. "When that happens, you will call me?"

Murphy nodded. It wasn't much, but this was at least a small glimmer of hope.

⟨∾⟩

The ornate spires of the Houses of Parliament reflected in the water of the broad Thames River. If Elisa had not seen the trenches in Hyde Park and St. James, if it were not for the sandbags now around Buckingham Palace, it would be difficult to believe the sense of freedom she felt walking out of Tedrick's office for the final time. Only one duty left. One more short lunch with Thomas and then pass him along to someone else. Poor Thomas. Caught between generals and Gestapo agents. She hoped for his sake that his generals won. She hoped that for everyone.

A train steamed across Charing Bridge to the station. There were telephones there; she would call Murphy and tell him she was finished forever with the BBC. No more British broadcasts. She could meet him in Paris after she saw Thomas, and they could go somewhere together. Anywhere. A place like New Forest, where there were no radios, and the only reminder of civilization was an occasional airplane buzzing overhead or the distant whistle of a train—like the one now lumbering into Charing Cross Station.

Inside the vast hall of the old Victorian station, newsboys were hawking their papers—competing with one another as they shouted the latest news about the Munich conference:

"Big Four Powers in Munich to Settle Fate of Czech Nation! Chamberlain Hopeful for Peace! Deadline Looms!"
"Munich Conference Promises Peace for Our Time!"

A strange contrast to such cries were the men and women carrying gas masks at their sides. Until the peace treaty was signed, they would take no chances.

Elisa waited in line for a telephone. Conversations buzzed around her.

"Personally, if the Germans drop gas, I'm just going to walk outside and take a deep breath."

"Ah, it won't come t' that now! This will settle it. Chamberlain's not going t' get us into a war over a little territory in Czechoslovakia. He'll give it t' Hitler."

Elisa wanted to put her hands to her ears. Was the whole world filled with noise just a few steps from the Thames? She was sorry she had not waited to call Murphy. She stepped into the phone booth, then realized she had no change.

Leaving Charing Cross Station, she walked briskly toward the Savoy. How long would it be until Tedrick canceled the reservation held in her name? How would the staff feel after so many weeks of Shelby's charade to have another Elisa Murphy appear on the scene?

But no one seemed to notice that this Elisa had short hair—blond once more, but still cut short, like Myrna Loy. She ran a hand self-consciously down the nape of her neck. "Any messages?" she asked the clerk.

A message from Murphy was handed to her:

Call Evian at once.

She thought no more of the fact that not one curious look had been given to her. She hurried to the gleaming copper elevators and returned to her room.

It was nearly half an hour before Elisa heard Murphy on the other end of the line.

"I was about to give up on you!"

"I'm in London," she said, nearly forgetting that Murphy had never known she was anywhere else. "I'm all through. I want to meet you, Murphy. Can you come to Paris?"

"I got a ray of hope from Holland!" he cried. "They'll consider giving the *Darien* temporary refuge! And Elisa, get this—the list of passengers?

Shimon Feldstein is among them!" He was laughing with relief and exhaustion. "*Shimon is on the Darien!* You bet I'll meet you in Paris! Name the time and place."

Time and place. She must still meet Thomas. But after that she was free. "Leah is performing at L'Opera tomorrow night at eight thirty! I'll meet you there, darling. We can tell her together about Shimon!"

41

The Sacrament

The winds had swung around now, driving the *Darien* away from land. Up the wall of water, then like a bobsled down the other side into the trough. Never forward, only shoved back by the next wave.

As a wave crested and broke over the bow, Shimon could see the white casket of Ada-Marie Holbein still tied there. The symbol of the coffin ship *Darien*!

For an instant Shimon thought the ship would be lifted up and flipped over backward, but then the swell abated and the *Darien* slid forward again.

"Any messages?" shouted Burton to the frantic-looking radio operator.

A wide shake of the head answered him. No word. Eighteen hours since the last message. Probably no one was receiving either. They were alone, and moving out to sea.

❧

The assignment of trailing John Murphy twice across the Atlantic and now to Evian had been pleasant for Hans Erb. He had experienced three days of recrimination from Himmler after he lost Murphy in England, but his performance in Evian had more than made up for it. He had tapped every phone call. Had followed every attempt of Mr. Murphy to unload his Jews somewhere—anywhere. And then he had presented Himmler with the trump card.

"He is meeting his wife in Paris."

"Georg Wand is quite certain he is near to finding her in Paris. He has made contact with her friend, and—"

"Yes, Reichsführer Himmler, her friend Leah Feldstein. And the Feldstein woman's husband, it seems, is one of the Jewish swine aboard that ship that has caused so much uproar. Elisa Murphy will meet with John Murphy at L'Opera tomorrow night at eight thirty. I heard it plainly. No attempt to conceal it. They both sounded quite relieved. She says her duties with the BBC are complete, and she will meet him."

There was silence on the line as Heinrich Himmler considered the words of his agent. "Well, then. This simplifies things. I will call Georg at the embassy. He will be pleased to have this handed to him so easily."

"Would you like me to continue following?"

Another silence. "No, Hans. You have done well. But it would not hurt to let him know we have not been asleep. Don't harm him. He is a fool and a nuisance, but she is the one we are after. We do not want to drive her underground again. Step back, and we will present this to Georg as nearly completed, *ja?*"

৩৩

Murphy recognized the German walking toward him on the quay where the steamboat back to Geneva waited. He was one of the men Cabrillo told him was there to sell the Jews of Germany for two hundred and fifty a head.

The man was big. Close-cropped blond hair, a thick neck, and hands like a football player. He was smiling at Murphy. "Hi," he said. Just like an American!

"You talking to me?" Murphy instinctively ran a finger against the side of his slightly crooked nose. This was the kind of man who might have been on the docks with the Nazis in New York. He looked as if he could do damage if he wanted to.

"Yes. You are John Murphy, aren't you?" American. No doubt. From Chicago maybe? or Detroit? What was he doing selling for the Nazis?

"So what?"

"My name is Hans Erb," he said brightly. Friendly.

"Like I said, so what?" Murphy spurned the man's hand and started to walk past him.

"I just wanted to let you know we're watching. Found a place for those Jews of yours yet? They can always go back to Hamburg!" he called as Murphy kept walking.

The *EVIAN* sign on the dock was plainly reflected in the polished brass of the steamer door. Murphy frowned as he read the mirror-image of the name in the brass: *NAIVE* the name now cried. *Evian* spelled backward read *naive*. The big German stepped beneath the sign. Murphy could see him grinning at his back.

The Evian council for the aid of refugees had come to an end.

ᘓᕉ

It must be daylight by now, Maria thought. They had been enclosed in this metal coffin for so many hours. The rolling of the *Darien* seemed to have eased some.

No one had eaten since the onset of the storm. The children who had been sick through the night now put their hands to their empty bellies. There would be no way to eat until they were out of danger, if they did manage to pass through this sea.

The rabbi of Nuremberg sat cloaked in his canvas tallith near the door to the infirmary. His lips moved in silent prayer. Had he ever stopped praying through this long and terrible ordeal?

Little Israel still had not opened his mouth to cry. He cooed and now turned his mouth toward Maria's breast. At least he would be able to eat. He alone would be fed.

Like the rabbi of Nuremberg, Israel had lain untroubled in the midst of the night's terror. Maria lifted her blouse and let him nurse. To eat, to sleep an untroubled sleep, to wake and never know the dark fear of death that surrounded them. Maria smiled. It seemed strange that she could smile now, but Israel nursed and looked at her with eyes so trusting and content that she had to smile back at him.

ᘓᕉ

The blackness of night moved into deep gray as the sun rose somewhere. Captain Burton and Shimon were still at the helm, still pointed west, although they had not moved forward more than one or two miles throughout the long night.

The radioman was asleep. As the wheelhouse brightened, Burton kicked him awake. The winds that had seemed to be abating shifted again to roar in from the southeast. Waves broke against the stern, pushing the ailing freighter forward toward the Cape. The seas had tamed from fifty-foot swells to twenty-five and thirty-five feet.

With the dawn, some hope was renewed in the wheelhouse. They had survived the worst! There was more storm racing in behind them, but if the *Darien* could make it to shore. . . .

ᘓᕉ

A long line of young airmen stood at attention as Theo took his leave of them. There had been no official explanation why Theo and his sons were being transferred to the Prague defenses. Most believed that it was because the name Theo Linder had undoubtedly been placed on the list of criminals Hitler wished returned to Germany for justice.

Wilhelm and Dieter both resented the fact that they would not be at the front with the units they had trained for. Whatever the reason for this transfer, Theo did not question it. The seal of President Beneš himself marked the document.

With a final salute, Theo strode from the field. These were good men. They had learned quickly, and they would give the Luftwaffe something to contend with.

All of the Sudetenland seemed deserted now. Entire families had fled their homes, leaving food on the tables and livestock untended in the fields. The train into Prague was crowded with remnants of the Czechs who had waited until the last possible moment to leave. Word that France had placed one and a half million men along the Maginot Line from the English Channel to the Swiss frontier had finally convinced most of them that this was indeed the end of peace.

Theo breathed a sigh of gratitude when he heard of the French move. Then he, like others, had felt a twinge of resentment at the news that Prime Minister Chamberlain was flying once more to meet with Hitler—this time in Munich; this time with French leaders as well as with Mussolini and Hitler to discuss the possibility of a peaceful solution to the Czech crisis. Why had President Beneš been excluded from the conference that was to decide the fate of his own country? The possibility of a betrayal of Czechoslovakia by France and England seemed very real at this moment, in spite of the French Army along the Maginot Line.

The train rumbled past a tiny farming village. The onion-domed church spire soared in the clear air. Now Theo remembered. It was Sunday. *Is anyone in church this morning?* he wondered. *Or has everyone stayed home to pray in solitude for peace?*

Anna, breathless and beautiful on the platform, answered his question. Gathering husband and sons into her arms, she whispered through her tears, "Our Lord has not forgotten us. You are home! You are home!" And then she checked her watch and gasped that they must hurry or they would miss church this morning.

Stomachs rumbling with hunger, the three airmen followed meekly after her. Wilhelm and Dieter rolled their eyes. They had never enjoyed the services at the Anglican church Anna had chosen to attend. Week after week they had sat in the half-empty sanctuary and worked very hard to understand the English words. They read the Scripture in English. Sang hymns in English. Theo joked that they might as well get used to the language, but he still would pray in German.

The worshipers were usually diplomats or visiting politicians and businessmen. A handful of tourists sometimes joined the sparse crowd, but there had been fewer of them as the threat of Nazi invasion increased.

This morning, there was something different about the church. Men and women waited outside the huge bronze doors in a line that stretched clear out to the street. Heads nodded in greeting to Anna. She smiled back familiarly.

Had the fear of German bombs brought these newcomers to a sense of their own mortality? In searching the skies above Prague for bombers, had men caught a glimpse of the Almighty?

Theo took his place at the end of the queue.

"What is all this?" Wilhelm asked as the men in front of them removed their hats to enter the church. "I thought all the tourists had gone home."

Anna shrugged and a peculiar smile touched her lips. "Listen," she whispered, not willing to explain that these were the men and women who had come to the soup kitchen.

Theo, Wilhelm, and Dieter fell silent as the church bells chimed; a murmur of conversation caught their attention. All the words spoken by the strangers were in German. Theo recognized the soft accent of the Viennese.

"German?" asked Dieter.

"Austrian," explained Theo. He laughed a short laugh. "Family members from Austria, Anna? First you ask them to dinner, and then to church?"

Wilhelm's eyes widened as he scanned the line of worshipers. Not only were these strangers from Austria—they were Jews!

Snatches of Yiddish were heard here and there, but most of those who entered the Anglican church this morning spoke in the language of the cultured and educated. "*Guten Morgen*, Frau Anna!" Again and again the greeting echoed as they entered the building.

The pews were packed. Worshipers stood along the aisles and three deep against the back wall. The massive Church of England had been built to house eight hundred. This Sunday over one thousand crowded beneath the dark wood arches.

Anna, Theo, and the boys stood in the back and gazed in wonder at the sea of heads. Above them was a small choir loft where a dozen puzzled Englishmen filed into place. The rector, a small, gray-haired man, emerged onto the platform. He adjusted his spectacles as though he could not believe that he had at last been sent a congregation in this backwater outpost of the great Church of England.

He tugged the sleeves of his clerical robe, and in a flourish he directed the thousand to stand and sing. "Page 342 in the hymnal, please!"

The organ blared the opening chords of "A Mighty Fortress Is Our God." This was a Lutheran hymn, to be sure, but the congregation recognized the tune immediately—the melody found in Mendelssohn's Symphony No. 5, "The Reformation." Many had heard the symphony played at the Musikverein in Vienna over the years. With such a familiar melody, nearly everyone made an attempt to sing the words of Martin Luther's famous hymn. A mixture of accents rose up to echo the phrase:

> "A bulwark never failing;
> Our helper He, amid the flood
> Of mortal ills prevailing:
> For still our ancient foe
> Doth seek to work us woe;
> His craft and power are great,
> And, armed with cruel hate . . ."

With that sentiment, nods of understanding began to tip the heads of the congregation. They had not realized that the Fifth Symphony of the Jewish composer Mendelssohn actually had words! The song gained volume and momentum by the time the second verse began. Heads lifted, voices boomed the song! Here and there, the words were translated for those who did not speak English.

> "Did we in our own strength confide
> Our striving would be losing;
> Were not the right Man on our side;
> The Man of God's own choosing
> Dost ask Who that may be?
> Christ Jesus, it is He;
> Lord Sabaoth His Name,
> From age to age the same,
> And He must win the battle."

Had there ever been such a sermon preached? A Lutheran hymn in an Anglican church with a congregation of Jews!

> "And though this world, with devils filled,
> Should threaten to undo us;
> We will not fear, for God hath willed
> His truth to triumph through us."

When the last chord of the pipe organ faded into the rafters, the message was fresh and living in the hearts of the congregation. Tears streamed down many faces as the meek English priest preached a sermon on the Lord of the Sabbath and the Jewish rabbi from Galilee. *"'I am the way and the truth and the life,' says the Lord. 'No one comes to the Father except through Me.'"*

And when all was said, the English priest closed the Bible and looked out at the Chosen Ones who packed his pews. He cleared his throat and in a voice that seemed louder than the organ, he spoke again.

It was time to speak the truth. Perhaps there would not be another time. "I know why most of you have come here. You have come to request baptism."

The congregation sat in stunned silence as he continued. "Yes, I know that possessing an Anglican baptism certificate may help you gain entry into another country. We are all aware it will mean nothing if the Germans invade this country, since their determination is not against religion, but blood."

Anna grasped Theo's strong hand and prayed. He had been a Christian for years, but his faith had not helped him escape the terrors of the Nazi Reich. It would not save their sons. No. All that mattered to the Nazis was pure race. Pure blood, pure Aryan. What would become of them if the Czech government collapsed under their pressure?

The voice of the rector cracked with emotion. "Last week a girl of sixteen came to me to request baptism. I simply handed her a catechism and told her to come back when she knew it. Two days later she returned, after memorizing the entire catechism in a language with which she was only vaguely familiar!"

He paused. "I had not . . . expected . . ." He removed his glasses and began again. "I baptized that girl. She has her certificate now. And I wish to tell all of you who have come here for that reason, I will make no requirement that you memorize a book of doctrine! It matters not what your reasons are. I will baptize you, every one of you who asks."

A low, astonished murmur rippled through the crowd. Once again the rector drew a deep breath. "I ask only that you think on this: God will not turn you from the door of His kingdom if you call upon the name of His Son Jesus! Here, too, it is a matter of blood—the blood of Jesus, the Messiah of Israel, the Lamb of God, will cleanse you from all sin. The water of baptism is a symbol of His death for us and His resurrection. This is what you identify with when you partake of this sacrament." He raised his arms toward heaven. "And if the Nazis come, if the certificate of baptism is of no help to you at all, I pray that you will remember what the baptism itself meant, and that your heart will reach out to that Eternal Truth."

There was a solemn silence among those who had come for this sermon. Heads began to bow in thought, in prayer, questioning their own hearts and motives. The rector left the podium and stepped to the center of the platform. "No one will be refused. What happens in your hearts is God's business."

That day and far into the night, seven hundred and twenty-nine of the Chosen went forward to be baptized. And each cast a glance at Anna, who remained standing through it all.

42

The Munich Signature

Armed Czech soldiers were waiting on the steps of the church when Anna and Theo and their sons emerged near midnight. They held their weapons up and stepped forward to call the name of Theo Lindheim.

"You are on the list of criminals presented to President Beneš for extradition," explained a tall, serious colonel. "You will come with us. All of you."

Wilhelm looked as if he might fight. Anna placed a hand on his arm. *The rifles—would these men use them?*

"You will please get in the car." The officer bowed slightly and clicked his heels, waving his hand toward the open door of a black sedan.

"What has happened?" Theo asked, filled with foreboding.

There were tears in the eyes of the colonel. "Chamberlain and Daladier have signed us over to the Nazis. We must comply with their wishes or France and Britain will step back and let Hitler have even Prague."

"The Sudetenland has fallen?"

"Given away, without a shot." The colonel's shoulders sagged for a moment. "Now, please, Officer Lindheim. It is finished for us here. President Beneš has resigned. You are a part of the bargain. Please come with me."

In the German Embassy in Paris, Georg Wand raised a glass with his delicate hand in a toast to the end of Czechoslovakia. Hitler had been right. He had been right from the beginning. Cowards and fools had come to

Munich at his bidding, and there they had put their signatures to the death warrant of Czechoslovakia. Chamberlain called the document "Peace in Our Time." Such was the peace of a corpse.

For both Thomas and Ernst vom Rath the news was devastating. The military plot against Hitler had now been effectively demolished. Not only had Prime Minister Chamberlain taken the madman away from the Chancellery in Berlin, out of the grip of the military, he had also destroyed the very reason for the coup!

Accuse Hitler now of rushing Germany into a conflagration? Not a drop of Wehrmacht blood had been shed! The victory over the Czechs was complete, just as the Führer had told the people it would be! And now who in Germany could stand against him? The hordes of people cheered him as he rode proudly through the streets. The Wagnerian opera was being played out as he directed it. Anyone who opposed him now, any who dared to claim that he was mad and would destroy Germany, would himself be declared a traitor and shot.

Georg Wand stood at the center of the gathering, a self-satisfied smile on his ordinary face. "The tactics of terror, you see," he said to the attentive Nazi diplomats. "These are the elements of a modern war. Decent men cannot stand against such things because they have rules, ideas of what is honorable. The Führer shows us all a lesson; does he not? To have honor is to win or die." At this he paused and smiled strangely at Thomas. "What do you think of this, von Kleistmann?—you, with your ancient Prussian codes?"

"I suppose it all depends on your definition of winning; doesn't it, Wand?"

Georg Wand took a step forward. His smile was still in place but his eyes hardened. "And is your definition the same as that of the Führer, von Kleistmann? Or do you think yourself too far above our ways, as it is rumored some of the army officers believe?"

So here it was. The confrontation had come after the fact of the betrayal of the Czechs. It had come after it was too late for the Berlin plot to be carried out. Georg Wand and his kind had won an ultimate victory, and yet they still required something from those they had vanquished. Georg Wand would not be satisfied until Thomas had given him his soul in the form of frightened approval of his evil brutality.

Thomas raised his chin slightly in thought. The answer was firm in his mind. He towered over this dark and twisted creature in a thousand ways. He would not stoop to give him even a moment of victory over his soul.

"I cannot speak for the rest of the army officers, Georg," he said with a smile. Arrogant. Thomas could afford arrogance tonight.

"Then speak for yourself."

"Then I will tell you what I see in your way of winning."

"*Your* way, you say? Not *our* way?"

Now Thomas laughed. "Some months ago I saw the Franz von Stuck painting of our Führer. Demonic. The God of Creation and of Destruction. Now he creates, but he will also destroy those who follow him. He will destroy Germany." Someone gasped and dropped a champagne glass with a crash on the floor.

Thomas did not stop. It felt so good to say it. So good to come into the light after so many years of darkness. "He is the incarnation of all that is evil, and little beasts like you are his demons, crooked little gargoyles who have tumbled from the naves of the German church. You are the guardian of the gates of hell. And Adolf Hitler is the mouth of hell."

Thomas felt light and alive, although he knew this lone act of defiance condemned him. "But in the end you will not win. The end is far distant now. I cannot see it, except I know it will come; it must come. Rules and honor? The stuff that makes decent men stupid in your eyes. Someday you will see that against these things the gates of your hell will not prevail. And so that is my answer, Georg Wand. I do *not* agree with the Führer."

An absolute silence filled the room. Thomas had not touched a chord of conscience in the others of the embassy staff; he had simply aroused fury in most, fear in perhaps one other. Ernst vom Rath sat staring dully at the broken glass on the floor. He knew that Thomas had just committed suicide. Ernst could not look at him, could not watch as the snake eyes of Georg Wand opened with pleasure and he anticipated what must be done to finish off the handsome young Wehrmacht officer, this traitor to the Reich.

"Well—" Wand rose up on his toes—"there you have all heard it. He condemns himself from his own poisoned mouth! He is infected by the Jewish bitch he lies with. You see? The Führer is right even about such matters of race. A Jew can contaminate even the most worthy German blood. This woman—Elisa Lindheim is her name, her *Jewish* name—has contaminated you."

"And what sort of Untermensch must have crawled into the bed of your mother to beget Georg Wand?" Thomas smiled even as the fist of Wand struck his face.

The voice of the Gestapo agent became shrill. "He is under arrest! You are all witnesses to the way he has insulted our Reich and our Führer. We will determine just how deep his treason goes. Both he and the woman must stand trial in Berlin. We will have it all . . . *all*!" Wand spun on his heel, his face red with anger. "I will settle the entire matter within an hour. I know where to find this woman. Oh yes, there are rules and codes that such people follow, and these things make them easy for me to defeat. I know where she will be tonight, von Kleistmann. Do you hear me?"

Thomas smiled. "Who are you looking for exactly?" he asked, certain that by now Elisa was well on her way out of Paris. By now Suzanne had delivered the message to her at the bistro. Elisa would know what the events in Munich meant. She would know they had lost, and she would have left long ago.

He had no regrets except that he wished she had heard him speak tonight. And then he wished he had said such things years before in Berlin, when they might have made some difference.

❦

No one had counted the times lightning had struck the masts last night, but Tucker first raised his head to discover the reason the *Darien* was not receiving or transmitting radio signals. At the top of the first mast, the antenna had been blasted loose from the cable. The antenna was still attached at a cockeyed angle, but the cable to the radio dangled loosely below it.

The waves were still mountains, and the ship rolled violently on a quartering sea, but all the same Tucker donned one of six life jackets and pointed upward to the metal ladder that led to the top of the mast.

He had once told Shimon that he had taken his apprenticeship on a real sailing ship. He could climb the shrouds in a gale, he had boasted. Now he would prove it.

He crept from the wheelhouse and leaned into the wind. Feeling his way to the ladder, he grasped the lifelines and lowered himself down. Shimon held the wheel as Captain Burton moved forward to watch him. Shimon braced himself in the effort to hold the ship steady.

"We must get word! If we run her aground, we'll need help abandoning ship! If we can send word—" Burton yelled against the still-shrieking gale.

Shimon could see Tucker now, as bent and leathery as a hide in the sun. The first mate grasped the bottom rung of the ladder and pulled himself up until his arms hugged the mast. The force of the wind pushed his oilskin cap back off his head until it billowed from its chin strap like a kite behind him.

"Come on, Tuck!" Burton cheered, stepping back to share the strain of the wheel. "Come on, Tuck! We'll hold her steady for you!"

Indeed, for a few moments the *Darien* seemed to right herself and plow on a level sea. Then another wave crashed against her, engulfing the deck and flooding just below Tucker's boots. He crept upward, seeming not to notice the winds that sought to blow him away like the last leaf from a winter branch. Halfway up he stopped and took a better grip on the slick metal rungs, then began his climb again.

Up and up he climbed as the rain slashed sideways against him. Shimon thought of Leah now, and he wondered if Tucker had a family—wondered if the little man had any home besides this fickle, changing ocean.

Tucker reached up, grasping the cable to the radio. He carried it with him as he braced himself against the harsh gusts with each step.

Ten minutes of this precarious maneuvering finally placed him within reach of the severed antenna. He leaned in against the metal mast and carefully fastened his belt around a handhold, securing himself so that he could work with both hands without fear of being swept away. The *Darien* dipped first to one side and then the other, but First Mate Tucker remained in place.

Shimon watched the drama being played out so high above the decks where the motion must have been like the crack of a whip.

"Yes, Tucker!" Shimon shouted. "Just like you said."

Lightning flashed in the distance, and the roar of thunder reverberated against the ship. Then the flash came nearer, fracturing the sky a quarter of a mile to starboard. As if to answer, the light danced to the port, and then—

The light and ear-shattering roar knocked Shimon and Burton from their feet. The wheel spun crazily out of control like the blade of a saw.

The ship bowed to port and then to starboard until Shimon could see the surface of the trough from the side window. Burton thrust out his foot to stop the spinning wheel. He was shouting. Shimon could not understand his words. The whole thing had taken only a matter of seconds, but the *Darien* had been lifted up and spun around a full ninety degrees.

It was a moment before Shimon looked up at the top of the mast. Tucker was still there, dangling from his belt. Was that smoke that surrounded his body, or only spray from the waves?

Burton saw his friend at the same instant. The captain's face contorted again in rage and grief. "TUCK!" he shouted. Then he screamed something that Shimon could not understand.

The radioman remained on the floor, his eyes squeezed tight. It was hopeless. Hopeless without the antenna. He looked up at Captain Burton for help, then at Shimon. The radio. What were they to do without the radio?

᠗

The gray-haired proprietor of the bistro was sympathetic but firm. Elisa had sat alone for two and a half hours and Thomas had not come.

"Perhaps he has been delayed, mademoiselle?" The old woman placed a plate of tender veal before her. "You must eat, anyway. Whenever a man has stood me up I have said, 'Ah, well,' and I have eaten! And look at me now. A happy old woman, even alone."

Elisa did not touch the wine. She knew that tonight of all nights she must remain clearheaded. She listened to the sad French love songs played by a girl with an accordion. She drank her coffee and waited with a sense of dread.

It was finished. These weeks of intrigue and anger had come to nothing. By morning the Nazi takeover of the Czech fortifications would be complete. She felt personally betrayed by Chamberlain and his British government. Her father had been betrayed, her mother and brothers, President Beneš. And now what would become of them?

She did not need to think very far for the answer. What had come upon Austria was now to come upon the Czechs. There would be a little time before Hitler broke his promise and marched from the Sudetenland into Prague, but it would not be more than a matter of months. Perhaps it would be time enough for Anna and Theo and her brothers to leave Prague. At least they had their papers. These senseless weeks had been good for that much.

It was nearly eight o'clock. Elisa decided she would not wait more than five more minutes. The concert at L'Opera would begin, and she would be late if she delayed much longer.

Something terrible must have happened for Thomas not to come. She hoped not. She prayed not. She would wait one more minute and then she would leave this charade forever. She would contact Tedrick and tell him she had failed. What difference did it make now if her cover was blown? What possible use was she now that the British government had collapsed before the dragon breath of Hitler?

Elisa wanted only to find Leah, to embrace her friend and tell her that Shimon was alive! Alive on the *Darien*! This seemed to be the only bright thought in the absolute darkness she felt in her heart tonight. Chamberlain cried, "Peace, peace!" But there was no peace. The last stronghold had been given away by a single signature. She wanted to scream her frustration! How could they do this? Had everything she told them meant nothing? Hitler would have been in a Berlin jail tonight if only the British and the French had demanded that he fight for Czech soil! They were betrayed—not with a kiss, but with a signature in Munich. In her anger, Elisa could not find a fragment of fear for herself. She could only think that her part in all this was at an end.

For a moment she did not recognize the young woman who hailed her from the stone steps across the room. And then, as the girl made her way through tables of single men and eyed each one, Elisa remembered quite clearly the prostitute from le Panier Fleuri. She had once delivered a note to Thomas for Elisa. Now she had come at the request of Thomas for the same reason.

"Hello. You remember me, chéri? I took your note to Thomas. When you were first lovers, I think. Now he asks me to come meet you with this." The breathless young woman slipped a note onto the table. "The end of things, if you ask me. How many men ask a girl like me to deliver a note to a mistress? If I was you, I would be very angry with him. But if this is the end of things, then—"

Elisa read the note. She felt herself grow pale.

> *Leave Paris now! Gestapo is very close on our heels. It is finished, my love. No regrets, please. We have done what is honorable. I love you.*
> *Thomas*

"He told me you would pay me." Suzanne smiled brightly. "He gave me twenty francs. I need at least that much, even though I am a little late."

Elisa crammed the note into her handbag. She was suddenly afraid. Her hands trembled as she threw twenty francs on the table and rushed from the bistro.

Suzanne finished off the untouched veal.

43

"We Will Not Forget"

Shimon donned the oilskin coat, the cap, and the precious life preserver. Captain Burton did not look at him as he thrust open the door and emerged onto the bridge. He held tightly to the rail as the gale opposed him. His hands were strong. Those hands had made thunder a thousand times, and now their strength would help him up the mast.

The coarse hemp of the lifelines did not cut through the callouses of his palms. He could climb the mast! He could climb it as he had once climbed the ladder above the stage at the Musikverein straight up fifty feet.

Would God flip His wrist and send the fire of His tympani to scorch the life from me? Shimon wondered. He was afraid. He thought of Leah. He wondered where she was and what she would say when she heard about his death. Then he wondered if she would ever hear.

The wind wanted to flatten him, to pitch him off the back of the *Darien* like a horse throwing a rider. Shimon strained forward, looking up, past the limp body of Tucker. He would climb the mast that swayed above him like a giant cross. He lunged forward, grabbing the cold metal of the ladder. As slick as it was, how had Tucker kept from slipping? Water washed over him, and for a moment the *Darien* hung balancing on its side. Slowly, it yawed back upright, and Shimon strained closer to the lofty pole.

He shouted against the wind, unable to hear even his own voice. In the distance lightning flashed and flashed again. The rumble rolled over the waves. And Shimon prayed. He prayed to the God of his fathers; he asked for hands that would not slip, for the lightning to flash somewhere else.

Two hands on the rungs now, he reached upward and put his feet on the ladder. Tucker swung above him like a rag doll. Shimon looked up once. *So high!* He would not look again until he made it to the top. He would just climb this cross one rung at a time. He would take the wire and attach it as the meek little man in the wheelhouse had explained.

A fresh burst of saltwater exploded into his face, blinding him. He shook his head, trying to clear his vision. It did not matter. The water stung his face through his beard. The tempest whined with new fury as he moved up. Metal cables clanged like bells on the crosspiece. Tucker banged and spun above his head.

Halfway up, Shimon looked off the stern. He saw a flash of light. *Not lightning—a lighthouse!* "God!" he cried. "God, save us!"

Yes, over the tops of the mountainous waves, a lighthouse! "God, save us!" Shimon cried again, grasping the cable of the antenna. Then, "God, help me!" Tucker's boots banged against his head. Shimon would have to climb over the body of the dead man. "Help me!" he screamed, and the winds carried his voice away. He pushed the dead man to one side. He hung on with one hand as he groped for the buckle that held Tucker to the mast. He pulled. It held and the body swung, smashing against Shimon. His foot slipped and he cried out, "Please!" The wind seemed to have hands, pushing him back onto the rungs. He found the buckle once again and pulled harder, feeling the leather give. The body tumbled past him into the raging waters.

Shimon climbed higher, thrusting his hand toward the antenna. The lighthouse whirled around beyond the surf. *So close. So close. They had not known!* Shimon looped his arm through the topmost rung. He linked the two ends of the cables with trembling hands.

A moment of exultation—it was finished! He cried out with joy at the victory of it. *Yes! Send your message!* He laughed, and his mouth filled with salty water.

He looked toward the lighthouse, which Burton could not see for the height of the waves. And then he looked back out to sea. A hundred yards from where the *Darien* labored, a mountain of water roared toward them! Shimon screamed and clung to the mast. The wave boiled at the top where it crested.

There was nothing to do. Nothing. So close, and now it would end. The tidal wave rumbled deeper than the thunder as it struck, engulfing the ship.

Dwarfed by its force, the *Darien* was lifted up like a leaf in a whirlpool. Shimon was wrenched from the mast. He gasped for air as the water tumbled him over and sucked him down into its blackness. His lungs were scorched in their need for oxygen. He flailed his arms and legs. How long since his last breath? A minute? He reached up, his fingers clawing the water. Blood drummed in his ears, and then the hand of the deep thrust him upward out of the water—long enough for a breath, and then down again. Once more he flailed against death, fighting the water, uncertain if he swam up or down. How long? *How long?* The weight of his oilskins held him down, and he tumbled around and around like a pebble in the surf. *Oh, God,* there was light! He turned his face up and broke through the surface. His life vest buoyed him up, carrying him to the top of another swell.

He coughed and spit up water. Where was the *Darien?* They were not three miles from shore. Where was the ship?

Shimon sobbed. He reached up toward the dark and angry sky. He slid down the face of the wave, and at the bottom, bobbing like a little boat, was the coffin of Ada-Marie Holbein.

Shimon struggled to reach it. He tried to swim but found that he could not lift his right arm. It rested at a strange angle at his side. He kicked his feet and slapped his left arm against the water. The current spun the little coffin toward him, and he grasped the brass handle and clung to it while he sucked air into his tortured lungs. Another wave came, but Shimon held tightly to the handle as the water carried them up twenty feet until he once again caught a glimpse of the lighthouse. Kicking off his boots, he swung a leg up and over the little casket, lying across it. He laid his cheek against the little white jewel box. His own blood puddled beneath his face from a gash under his eye. "Where is the ship?" he cried. But there was no sign of the *Darien.*

∽

Prague was as still and silent as a tomb tonight. Theo held Anna's hand tightly in his own as the automobile wound through the streets.

"May we return for our clothing?" Theo asked.

"There is not time," came the chilling reply.

"Father," Wilhelm shouted, "why do we not fight them?"

"That will not be necessary," offered the colonel as they turned onto a dirt road leading to a small, private airfield.

A passenger plane sat on the grassy runway. The headlights of one army truck illuminated the strip with the eerie blue light that had bathed Prague through the nights of the past week.

Anna gasped as she recognized the figure of President Beneš leaning against the plane. His face looked years older. His eyes were red-rimmed.

He turned his head and walked wearily toward the car as it rolled to a stop. He opened the door and peered in, squinting his eyes to see.

"You are all here? Yes. Good." He stepped back. Anna could see his wife twenty paces behind him. Down the field a second plane was being loaded with luggage.

Theo climbed out of the car, then Wilhelm and Dieter after Anna. Theo towered over the diminutive Beneš. "Mr. President—," Theo began.

"Please," Beneš protested, "I am only a private citizen." He checked his watch. "In ten minutes I will be Doktor Beneš once again, and all this will be behind me." He frowned. "In ten minutes I will be unable to help you. But I have an obligation to repay. You are a pilot, yes?" He swept his hand toward the first of the two planes. "Tonight I must fly to London."

Theo and Anna exchanged looks. They were not being extradited— they were being rescued. Beneš' last act as president was to make sure the Lindheim family got out of Czechoslovakia safely.

"Your daughter and son-in-law saved my life," Beneš said simply. "Could I do otherwise?"

Theo closed his eyes in thanks. Beneš had not betrayed them as he himself had been betrayed. Theo nodded, unable to speak. What was left to say? One signature in Munich had said clearly what was in the hearts of men and governments. *Peace in our time*, no matter what the cost.

Beneš looked over at the black horizon where his beloved Prague crouched in terror of what the daylight would bring. "And so this is the end of all we had hoped for," Beneš whispered. It was finished.

C⊘⊘

Georg Wand hurried from the embassy. How appropriate it seemed to him that he would put an end to Elisa Murphy at a concert—just as she had effectively ended the life of Albert Sporer that night at the theatre in Prague.

He hailed a taxi, feeling exuberant that Himmler had been sensitive enough to leave this assignment to him. Yes. He had looked forward to this. The ending of the woman who had destroyed Sporer. Well, this was a night for happy endings. The Czechs were finished. The army marched through the Sudeten passes unopposed. Even Beneš was finished. It had not been as he and Sporer had planned it, but the little Czech president was finished all the same.

The lights of L'Opera were bright tonight. All of Paris was out, celebrating the fact that France would not have to go to war after all. It would be much the same in London. And Hitler would return to Berlin as conqueror and prophet. He had won against the opposition of the High Command. They would not dare to question him now.

In the backseat of the taxi, Wand checked his revolver once again. A nervous habit, double-checking his weapon—one he had picked up from Sporer. He smiled. A glint of gold. He somehow felt the presence of Sporer with him tonight. Watching him. Applauding the time. The place. The method.

The line of vehicles was backed up. "Let me out here," instructed Wand cheerfully. He paid the fare and tipped the man. He stepped out among the men and women in their evening clothes. He had not dressed for the occasion. Just street clothes. The clothing of an ordinary man.

He walked briskly toward the broad steps leading into L'Opera. He scanned the faces and the finery for some sign of his quarry. Elisa would meet him on the steps. She would meet John Murphy on the steps. He had seen the photograph of her at Hradcany Castle. A beautiful woman. He wondered if she would wear that same white dress. He imagined the red of her blood expanding on the fabric like a bright flower. A new ornament to adorn her.

So many people, so much noise. But she would be waiting for John Murphy. Or he would be waiting for her. Not eight thirty yet. He could not have missed them. He stopped on the edge of the steps and raised his pointed chin like a fox sniffing the air.

Yes. Framed in the center of the ornate entrance stood Elisa Linder. Lindheim. He must remember that this beautiful and treacherous creature was a Jewess. Should he wait for John Murphy? Yes, he would wait. He would finish them both at once.

She glittered in the dress. Her hair was polished gold. Strange that this was not an Aryan woman. She looked the part. He had a moment of regret that he could not have taken her somewhere private for the end, that he could not spend some time alone with her before, as he had done with Shelby Pence.

He put his foot on the bottom step and considered how easy it might be to press the gun into her side and quietly take her away from L'Opera. Yes. Perhaps that was the thing to do. The thought gave him pleasure. He took a step, and then—

He felt the press of a gun barrel in his back.

"Back up." The voice of Thomas von Kleistmann. Wand's eyes widened as the order was punctuated by yet one more jab with the gun. He stepped back. His fingers twitched, moving toward his pocket. Another painful jab. "I would not try it, Wand. Back up."

Wand took a few more steps back into the shadow of the alley. Away from the crowd. "How did you get out?" he asked. "You will not get away with this."

"I already have," said Thomas, pulling the trigger.

There was no sound. Remarkable, those German-made silencers. Georg Wand expelled his breath, and the blood came after. No one heard the strangled squeak that came from his throat. He crumpled onto the ground, his head slapping hard against the pavement.

Thomas was a dozen yards away from him before blood began to pool on the sidewalk. And no one noticed.

Thomas walked from the front of L'Opera and stood for a moment at the entrance. He looked back at Elisa standing on the top step. She waved and smiled. But not at him. A tall, lanky man inched through the crowd and raised his arm to take her hand and pull her to him. *John Murphy: He certainly looks American*, thought Thomas with a smile. Amusing, Elisa in love with an American.

The sounds of the train rumbled behind him. One last look. *Elisa . . . Murphy!* And Thomas hurried down the steps to catch the train. The train for somewhere . . .

Hundreds of Americans died in the hurricane. Thousands of boats and homes were smashed in what the newspapers said was "the worst storm to hit New England in 100 years". State by state, the list of damages ran into uncounted millions. Shipping was paralyzed in Boston Harbor. Train service was disrupted. Wind velocity on the Empire State Building was clocked at 120 miles an hour. Tidal waves ripped houses from their foundations and pushed them a quarter of a mile inland. Insurance companies called it an act of God.

There was so much destruction, so many suddenly homeless, that Americans barely noticed when Hitler marched into Czechoslovakia. And the sinking of the *Darien*? Ah well, a shame. But anyone could see that America had enough misery on its own without spending too much time considering the fate of those few hundred refugees.

A few small items appeared in newspapers describing the one man who had survived the carnage by clinging to a tiny casket. Some of the more literary of the journalists likened the survival of Shimon Feldstein to a scene from *Moby Dick*.

When he and his little coffin washed up on a littered beach, Shimon had wept and carried the casket himself on his broad shoulders. He had not let them take it away at the Red Cross station. He had ridden with it in the baggage compartment of the train up to New York, where, two weeks later, the State Department had reluctantly bowed to pressure, and agreed to give Ada-Marie Holbein her place on American soil.

⚭

It was a private ceremony. A homecoming. Shimon, his right arm in a cast, stood with his left arm around Leah. His forehead was creased in unyielding grief. Murphy and Elisa held hands as they stood behind the chairs where Bubbe Rosenfelt sat with Mr. Trump. Nieces and nephews were there, as well as Bubbe's sister. A big family. And yet, ramrod straight, Bubbe Rosenfelt seemed alone today.

Charles held the cello upright like a companion. Louis cradled Elisa's violin in his arms. At a signal from the rabbi, Elisa and Leah stepped forward and took their instruments.

Shimon bowed slightly toward Bubbe Rosenfelt and said through a half-choked voice, "Beethoven's Fifth. *Andante con moto*. We . . . will not . . . forget!" He raised his good arm and Elisa and Leah played together once more. Only two instruments when there had been so many. It was not nearly so fine as it had been the day the *Darien* Symphony Orchestra had played for the prince of Israel. "Blessed is he that cometh!"

"I WAS A STRANGER, AND YE TOOK ME NOT IN."

Digging Deeper into *Munich Signature*

1938 was a dark year for all of Europe, especially Germany, Austria, and Czechoslovakia. John Murphy described it well: "Wrong has become right, and the world is turned upside down!" (p. 71). All because one man had the tenacious ability to rally others around his vision. Others had considered this former transient and failed artist too weak and unimportant to bother with . . . and thus didn't take the steps they should have. Then, after Adolf Hitler's rise to power, it was, to every good person's horror, truly too late.

After a quick look at today's headlines, there is no doubt that Murphy's words could also be used to describe our contemporary culture. But is all lost? Certainly not! However, we must realize that apathy is the glove into which evil slips its hand (see p. 381). Apathy sees people in terms of categories, rather than seeing each one as "a person, a face, an individual with hopes and fears and a certain number of years to live on this earth, and then an eternity to face." Those on the coffin ship *Darien* "were not numbers or statistics—they were living, breathing, hurting, hoping souls" (p. 381).

Yet, in the midst of evil, good is still revealed. The picture of one dead child and her grieving mother and father transcends all considerations of race and religion and moves a nation to raise a public outcry on behalf of the refugees (see pp. 284-285). Those aboard the *Darien* sing a creative version of Beethoven's Symphony No. 5. Baby Israel is born. Anna Lindheim sets aside her own personal comfort to feed and house hungry refugees in Prague. The Wattenbargers risk the safety of their entire family when they choose to protect and aid those who are fleeing from the evil clutches of the Nazi regime. And because of people like Anna and the Wattenbargers, numerous children—like Louis and Charles Kronenberger—are saved.

What a ringing testimony these courageous souls are to the classic writer Edward Everett Hale's words:

> "I am only one,
> but I am one.
> I cannot do everything,
> but I can do something.
> And because I cannot do everything,
> I will not refuse
> to do the something
> that I can do."

And that takes us to you, dear reader. You are "only one," but you are noticed. We prayed for you as we wrote this book and continue to pray as we receive your letters and hear your soul cries. No doubt you have myriad life questions of your own. And you may wonder, at times, if anything you do is making a difference. Following are some questions designed to take you deeper into the answers to these questions. You may wish to delve into them on your own or share them with a friend or a discussion group.

We hope *Munich Signature* will encourage you in your search for answers to your daily dilemmas and life situations. But most of all, we pray that you will "discover the Truth through fiction." For we are convinced that if you seek diligently, you will find the One who holds all the answers to the universe (1 Chronicles 28:9).

Bodie & Brock Thoene

SEEK . . .

Prologue

1. When have you, like Tikki, longed for home and love (see pp. xii-xiii)?

_____

_____

2. Is there someone you wish you could measure up to? Who, and why?

_____

_____

3. How well do you know your parents? their stories? their hearts? Do you long to know a parent better—or to know him or her at all? Why or why not? How do your parents and their stories help form who you are?

_____

_____

Chapters 1–3

4. Imagine you are sitting in a church service. All of a sudden, you hear voices outside shout, "Get out!" Then the windows of the church shatter . . . and rain down in a million pieces. How would .you respond?

_____

_____

5. How can you tell if someone is who they say they are or a wolf in sheep's clothing (see p. 10)? What criteria do you use to judge someone's soul and actions?

_____

_____

6. Have you ever been rescued or shielded by a "gracious hand" (p. 14), as Shimon was? When? Recall the story and the hand that helped you.

_____

_____

7. "Months ago I told you to put away hope for your life. I did not mean that you should abandon all hope," Admiral Canaris tells Thomas von Kleistmann (p. 28). What is the difference between the two? For you, what cause would be worth dying for?

_____

_____

Chapters 4–5

8. "The problem is not in knowing the truth. It is in acting on it," a wounded colonel tells Murphy (p. 33). Would you agree? Why or why not?

_____

_____

9. Ephesians 6:11-13 says:

Put on the full armor of God so that you can take your stand against the devil's schemes. For our struggle is not against flesh and blood, but against the rulers, against the authorities, against the powers of this dark world and against the spiritual forces of evil in the heavenly realms. Therefore put on the full armor of God, so that when the day of evil comes, you may be able to stand your ground, and after you have done everything, to stand.

Have you ever felt like you were part of "a handful of mere men" (p. 39) fighting against evil? When? Explain the situation.

_____

_____

10. "America is well aware of what is happening here."
    "Aware, yes. The question is whether they care what happens in our faraway little democracy" (conversation between Murphy and President Beneš, president of Czechoslovakia, p. 48).
    How aware are you of events that happen in the U.S. today? events that happen around the world? Which do you consider to be more important, and why?

_____

_____

Chapters 6–7

11. "There is a hope that heals and also a hope that can destroy you if you hold too tightly to it," says Anna wisely (p. 58). When in your life have you experienced these two kinds of hope?

_____

_____

12. "We must be strong for the sake of the children. . . . We must teach them to live now, but also to see their lives through . . . hundred-year glasses. . . . Such a point of view somehow makes each moment, each action, each prayer seem much more important, I think. Especially in such dark times as these" (Anna, p. 60). If you adopted this point of view, how would your life change? Give some specifics. How can you help those younger than you to see the future through a long-range perspective?

_____

_____

13. When have you had to say good-bye (for a long time or forever) to a cherished friend or loved one? What thoughts ran through your head? What emotions pierced your heart? Were they similar in any way to Bubbe Rosenfelt's as she waved good-bye to the SS _Darien_ (p. 68-69)?

_____

_____

Chapters 8–9

14. If you were standing inside the American Embassy in Prague (see pp. 73-76), watching the crowds of refugees outside the gate, how would you respond, given the circumstances?

_____

_____

15. How were the Jews on the _Darien_ "God's message to the conscience of the world" (p. 81)?

_____

_____

16. *"To lose someone . . . that is to lose everything"* (p. 84). Would you agree? Why or why not?

_____

_____

17. "In the relative safety and comfort of the house on Mala Strana, a very quiet, personal battle was still taking place between Theo and the Nazis who had thrown him into Dachau" (p. 90). In what ways can you quietly and personally battle against evil?

_____

_____

Chapters 10–13

18. Have you ever kept going just for the sake of others (as Bubbe Rosenfelt does for Klaus, Maria, and the children; and later, as Maria does for her children on p. 298)? When?

_____

_____

19. "Our enemies rejoice at this moment," the doctor on the *Darien* says (p. 116). When have you felt this way? What was the outcome of the situation?

_____

_____

20. "One blade of grass is often lost to the big picture. Such are the affairs of politics and the lives of men. . . . And yet there are moments when the issues may well hinge on one another. The small story becomes the issue on which great matters are decided" (Winston Churchill, p. 131). What examples of these truths do you see in today's world? (For example, in 1938, the very life of Charles Kronenberger became a symbol of the church's resistance against forced sterilization and euthanasia.)

_____

_____

Chapters 14–17

21. It's easy to second-guess yourself after making a big decision. *Did I do the right thing?* you wonder. *If I had made a different choice, would my life be different now? Is God really guiding me, or am I on my own?* When Leah doubted, God provided Marta to encourage her (see p. 136). Who is your encourager? Whose encourager are you?

_____

_____

22. Anna could easily have sunk into despair when her sons and husband left to fight for Czechoslovakia. Instead, she was "moved with compassion" to organize meals for the hungry refugees (see p. 146). What is one compassionate thing you could do to help others this week?

_____

_____

23. "Only God knows who was rich and who was poor. And to Him it makes no difference," the rabbi of Nuremberg says (p. 147). Do you agree with this statement? Why or why not?

_____

_____

Chapters 18–19

24. Leah found peace and safety and spiritual encouragement at the Wattenbarger farm (see p. 173). Where or to whom do you go when you need those things?

_____

_____

25. Is there a person you long to be reconciled with, as Franz longed to reconcile with his brother, Otto (see p. 177)? What steps could you take in that direction?

_____

_____

26. If you were in charge of immigrant quotas in 1938, how would you have handled the situation (keeping in mind that for nine years American citizens had already suffered hunger and unemployment in the worst depression of their history). What would you have done the same? differently?

_____

_____

Chapters 20–22

27. In what ways did Charles Kronenberger and Bubbe Rosenfelt meet each other's needs (see pp. 191-192)?

_____

_____

28. Have you, like the Jews, ever been the object of someone else's hatred (whether toward you personally or the "category" in which that person placed you)? Why do you think that person hated you so much?

_____

_____

29. Step into Murphy's shoes. If you could swing the gates open for Jewish refugees in multiple countries just by "showing off" Charles Kronenberger and his severe cleft palate in the media, would you do it? embarrass one boy for the good of thousands? Why or why not? (See pp. 214-215.).

_____

_____

30. Do you believe that Christians should "pray with their hands and feet" (p. 215)? Why or why not?

_____

_____

Chapters 23–24

31. Have you ever been forced to "perform" when you didn't want to? (see p. 224). What was the result?

_____

_____

32. Is a democracy good or bad? List some pros and cons. Do you agree with the statement "America is a land of committees; most choices are so watered down that they become useless" (p. 231)? Explain.

_____

_____

33. If helping someone else would hurt or end your career, would you do it? What "determining factors" would help you decide (see p. 231)?

_____

_____

Chapters 25–28

34. *"Where are you, John Murphy? Have I not given you a voice and hands to hold a candle? What I tell you in darkness, speak in the light?"* (p. 239). Have you said, like Murphy, "Here I am, Lord. Use me"? Why or why not?

_____

_____

35. In the midst of such darkness on the *Darien*, the rabbi of Nuremberg says, "Who says God is still not in a business of miracles, *nu*? . . . Look here! Each one of us is here!" (p. 252). Are you able to say this in the midst of your own dark times? Or do you doubt, wondering if religion truly is the "crutch" and hope of the weak? Explain your response, using an example from your own life.

_____

_____

36. Put yourself in Klaus Holbein's place. If your daughter died so close to the "promised land" after such a long journey, how would you respond? How would it affect your view of or belief/disbelief in God? Would you be bitter, or would you be able to say, with Klaus, "We are safe at last" (p. 262)?

_____

_____

Chapters 29–34

37. "If we spend the present condemning the past, then we will lose the future. . . . There is much that can be done. It is not too late" (Elisa, p. 276). In what ways have your own personal regrets changed the way you live your live now? the way you encourage others to live their lives?

_____

_____

38. In the midst of her own grief about her great-grandchild, Bubbe Rosenfelt reached out to the terrified Charles (p. 285). Who could you reach out to, even if you're in the midst of a hard time? Who needs to know he or she is not alone?

_____

_____

39. Have you ever been at odds with a person you love because you could not—or were afraid to—tell the truth? How did the two of you work through that issue?

_____

_____

Chapters 35–39

40. How important do you think it is for a leader of a country to be moral and have integrity? Explain, using a specific example or two from history or contemporary culture.

_____

_____

41. "She felt suddenly as if a hand had seized her and shaken her. A warning flashed in her mind" (p. 344). Have you ever felt a warning nudge (as Elisa did) that kept you from harm? If so, when?

_____

_____

42. Why do you think that the Jews, of all nations of people, have been so persecuted throughout history? Why is it so difficult for them to find a "true home"?

_____

_____

Chapters 40–43

43. Have you run up against the thinking, *"One cannot save everyone . . . we cannot change our laws for a few"*? If so, when? How did you respond?

_____

_____

44. Each immigrant is an individual—a living, breathing, hurting, hoping soul (see p. 381). How could you offer a glimmer of hope to even one such individual? (Anna set up a soup kitchen and offered her home to refugees. But even "little things" can make a difference.)

_____

_____

45. How can you keep the lessons of history alive for yourself and for your family? How will you say, like Shimon, "We will not forget!" (p. 409)?

_____

_____

About the Authors

Bodie and Brock Thoene (pronounced *Tay-nee*) have written over 45 works of historical fiction. That these best sellers have sold more than 10 million copies and won eight ECPA Gold Medallion Awards affirms what millions of readers have already discovered—the Thoenes are not only master stylists but experts at capturing readers' minds and hearts.

In their timeless classic series about Israel (The Zion Chronicles, The Zion Covenant, and The Zion Legacy), the Thoenes' love for both story and research shines.

With The Shiloh Legacy series and *Shiloh Autumn*—poignant portrayals of the American depression—and The Galway Chronicles, which dramatically tell of the 1840s famine in Ireland, as well as the twelve Legends of the West, the Thoenes have made their mark in modern history.

In the A.D. Chronicles, their most recent series, they step seamlessly into the world of Yerushalyim and Rome, in the days when Yeshua walked the earth and transformed lives with His touch.

Bodie began her writing career as a teen journalist for her local newspaper. Eventually her byline appeared in prestigious periodicals such as *U.S. News and World Report*, *The American West*, and *The Saturday Evening Post*. She also worked for John Wayne's Batjac Productions (she's best known as author of *The Fall Guy*) and ABC Circle Films as a writer and researcher. John Wayne described her as "a writer with talent that captures the people and the times!" She has degrees in journalism and communications.

Brock has often been described by Bodie as "an essential half of this writing team." With degrees both in history and education, Brock has, in his role as researcher and story-line consultant, added the vital dimension of historical accuracy. Due to such careful research, The Zion Covenant and The Zion Chronicles series are recognized by the American Library Association, as well as Zionist libraries around the world, as classic historical novels and are used to teach history in college classrooms.

Bodie and Brock have four grown children—Rachel, Jake, Luke, and Ellie—and five grandchildren. Their sons, Jake and Luke, are carrying on the Thoene family talent as the next generation of writers, and Luke produces the Thoene audiobooks. Bodie and Brock divide their time between London and Nevada.

For more information visit:
www.thoenebooks.com
www.TheOneAudio.com

suspense with a mission

TITLES BY

Jake Thoene

"The Christian Tom Clancy"
Dale Hurd, *CBN Newswatch*

Shaiton's Fire

In this first book in the techno-thriller series by Jake Thoene, the bombing of a subway train is only the beginning of a master plan that Steve Alstead and Chapter 16 have to stop . . . before it's too late.
ISBN 0-8423-5361-5 SOFTCOVER
US $12.99

Firefly Blue

In this action-packed sequel to Shaiton's Fire, Chapter 16 is called in when barrels of cyanide are stolen during a truckjacking. Experience heart-stopping action as you read this gripping story that could have been ripped from today's headlines.
ISBN 0-8423-5362-3 SOFTCOVER
US $12.99

Fuel the Fire

In this third book in the series, Special Agent Steve Alstead and Chapter 16, the FBI's counterterrorism unit, must stop the scheme of an al Qaeda splinter cell . . . while America's future hangs in the balance.
ISBN 0-8423-5363-1 SOFTCOVER
US $12.99

for more information on other great Tyndale fiction,
visit www.tyndalefiction.com

THOENE FAMILY CLASSICS™

✪ ✪ ✪

THOENE FAMILY CLASSIC HISTORICALS
by Bodie and Brock Thoene
Gold Medallion Winners*

THE ZION COVENANT
Vienna Prelude*
Prague Counterpoint
Munich Signature
Jerusalem Interlude
Danzig Passage
Warsaw Requiem*
London Refrain
Paris Encore
Dunkirk Crescendo

THE ZION CHRONICLES
The Gates of Zion*
A Daughter of Zion
The Return to Zion
A Light in Zion
The Key to Zion*

THE SHILOH LEGACY
In My Father s House*
A Thousand Shall Fall
Say to This Mountain

SHILOH AUTUMN

THE GALWAY CHRONICLES
Only the River Runs Free*
Of Men and of Angels
Ashes of Remembrance*
All Rivers to the Sea

THE ZION LEGACY
Jerusalem Vigil
Thunder from Jerusalem
Jerusalem s Heart
Jerusalem Scrolls
Stones of Jerusalem
Jerusalem s Hope

A.D. CHRONICLES
First Light
Second Touch
Third Watch
Fourth Dawn
and more to come!

THOENE FAMILY CLASSICS™

✪ ✪ ✪

THOENE FAMILY CLASSIC AMERICAN LEGENDS

LEGENDS OF THE WEST
by Bodie and Brock Thoene

The Man from Shadow Ridge
Riders of the Silver Rim
Gold Rush Prodigal
Sequoia Scout
Cannons of the Comstock
Year of the Grizzly
Shooting Star
Legend of Storey County
Hope Valley War
Delta Passage
Hangtown Lawman
Cumberland Crossing

LEGENDS OF VALOR
by Luke Thoene

Sons of Valor
Brothers of Valor
Fathers of Valor

✪ ✪ ✪

THOENE CLASSIC NONFICTION
by Bodie and Brock Thoene

Writer-to-Writer

THOENE FAMILY CLASSIC SUSPENSE
by Jake Thoene

CHAPTER 16 SERIES

Shaiton s Fire
Firefly Blue
Fuel the Fire

✪ ✪ ✪

THOENE FAMILY CLASSICS FOR KIDS
by Jake and Luke Thoene

BAKER STREET DETECTIVES
The Mystery of the Yellow Hands
The Giant Rat of Sumatra
The Jeweled Peacock of Persia
The Thundering Underground

LAST CHANCE DETECTIVES
Mystery Lights of Navajo Mesa
Legend of the Desert Bigfoot

✪ ✪ ✪

THOENE FAMILY CLASSIC AUDIOBOOKS

Available from
www.thoenebooks.com or
www.TheOneAudio.com